Praise for The

A claustrophobic old mansion filled with secret rooms, a family of eccentric, somewhat dodgy characters, and a dark and moody plot packed with surprises. A bingeable, five-star read."
—Kimberly Belle, *USA TODAY* bestselling author of *The Paris Widow*

The Family Inside is a wild, suspenseful, and unpredictable thriller."
—Samantha Downing, *USA TODAY* bestselling author

A twist-a-minute thriller featuring one of the most suspicious and unsettling families you've ever read. Fans of Colleen Hoover and Geneva Rose will devour this one."
—Megan Collins, author of *The Family Plot*

An eerie, atmospheric mystery with twists around every dark corner."
—Allison Buccola, author of *Catch Her When She Falls* and *The Ascent*

This page-turning narrative builds relentlessly towards a climax filled with jaw-dropping twists!"
—Nishita Parekh, nationally bestselling author of *The Night of the Storm*

Katie Garner ropes you in with poignant characters and the simmering anxiety of family ties. Then she drops you into the creepiest gothic estate for an accelerating series of twists that will make you gasp." —Maia Chance, author of *The Body Next Door*

Brilliantly plotted and pulsing with suspense, *The Family Inside* kept me hooked until the last shocking twist. Atmospheric and eerie. Fans of Ruth Ware will devour this tilt-a-whirl of a novel."
—Lindsay Cameron, author of *No One Needs to Know*

Also by Katie Garner

The Night It Ended

THE
FAMILY INSIDE

KATIE GARNER

/||MIRA

/II MIRA

Recycling programs
for this product may
not exist in your area.

ISBN-13: 978-0-7783-3446-0

The Family Inside

Copyright © 2025 by Katie Garner

Mira
22 Adelaide St. West, 41st Floor
Toronto, Ontario M5H 4E3, Canada
MIRABooks.com

Printed in U.S.A.

For my husband—

don't worry, none of these characters were inspired by you.

Right down by the river
I took your life

I loved you once
I shot you twice

SEVEN MINUTES GONE

She deserved so much better, but you dug her a nice, deep grave.

It was the least you could do. She was, after all, the woman you'd hoped to be with forever. You didn't mean to kill her. Not like that. Not that fast. It was sad, actually, how quick it was. One second and all that was her had vanished. Gone.

You try to remember this spot in these woods so you can visit her again one day, but the trees are all identical in the dark, and the dirt is just like any dirt, and you hate how it feels now, pressing up beneath your fingernails, that chalky pressure, that filthiness you've been conditioned to despise.

And now she's gone. There's no going back to how things were before.

The air around you buzzes, a nebulous, ever-so-slight hum. You think maybe it's her soul escaping from the ground, seeping through the earth, floating in the air around you.

What would it tell you, her soul, which you've just severed from her body, cut off without warning? What would it say? Would it forgive you? Hate you?

Or would it feel indifferent because now she is free? Yes, that's it.

She's free now. Free to go where she wants, be who she wants, think what she wants.

You did that for her.

You.

You saved her like you always did, gave her another chance—another life—and for that, you wish you could dig her up, shake her awake, demand she show you gratitude. But you can't.

And they're calling your name now, forcing you to step away from this grave, this patch of land, nondescript, soon to be forgotten, no matter how much you wish you could remember it forever.

You won't, but you'll remember her forever. How you freed her.

How you gave birth to her new life.

SHOCK! RIVERSIDE MURDER HOUSE:
2 DEAD, REMAINS OF SEVERAL OTHERS FOUND

by: Vivian H. McNeal
Published: Jan 27, 2025 at 1:33 PM EDT

GREENWICH HILLS, NY (WLPL-TV)—At midnight on January 26, police dispatch received a 911 call traced to a historic manor on Starlight Path. According to the sheriff, police who first arrived at the scene discovered two victims whose identities are yet to be released, though authorities are still determining the causes of death.

Those weren't the only bodies police discovered. Upon further investigation, forensics teams, following an anonymous source, uncovered the buried remains of at least five other unidentified victims, police said.

"We're horrified," neighbor Evonne Erboss said. "The entire community is horrified. No one can believe what happened at that house. We're absolutely shocked."

State Attorney General Deborah Minnow provided the following statement: "We are working very closely with local police and forensic investigators to uncover what happened at this family estate. We are doing all we can to locate and identify all remains that may still be buried on the property. Our deepest sympathies are with the friends and families of the victims."

Anyone with information is asked to contact the Hollow Falls Police Department or the New York State Attorney General.

This is a developing story.

8 DAYS BEFORE

FRIDAY, JANUARY 17

1

Cold wind bites my cheeks as I look through the tiny window on my front door and peer inside my soulless house. It used to swell with sounds—my husband's laugh, my daughter singing along to *Frozen* while spinning around the living room in her Anna dress. The sounds of happiness, of life. Of family.

But I know, as soon as I push the door open, I'll be greeted by none of those sounds. Those memories are just that—memories. They can never be remade.

I lock the door behind me, glare at the foreclosure notice taped to the glass, dew-dropped and foggy with winter rain. Maybe if I lock the door tight enough, they'll never be able to evict us. Maybe, somehow, I can keep them away and keep our home.

That'd be impossible, especially now. I've just been fired from my job as a waitress at the local fine Italian restaurant. It wasn't much, but it's the best place in town for a nice dinner—birthdays, anniversaries—and a lot of tourists frequent it on the weekends, which is where I manage to make just enough to keep the heat and electricity on.

Just enough, yet never enough to pay the mortgage. I wonder who was the lucky one that bought our house at auction. A young couple, like we used to be? Maybe a bachelor or a pair of friends.

I blink my eyes clear as I shrug off my coat and slide off my boots, leave them near the staircase beside Ellory's dirty sneakers. I wish I could buy her another pair. But they'll have to last, at least until I can find another job. Maybe even after that.

I climb the stairs, admittedly a little slow, as I think of ways I can tell my daughter the news:

Ellory, the bank called today. The foreclosure auction was a success. The house was sold.

Ellory, also, I lost my job today. And we have to pack everything we own and move out.

Ellory, in three days, we're homeless and your mom has $98 in her checking account—but the good news is we get to live in my car.

The swell of disappointment fills me. It's a feeling I can no longer escape. Maybe I should keep this a secret, too.

I call out Ellory's name as I reach the top of the stairs. When she doesn't reply, I knock on her bedroom door, then nudge it open, peek inside.

There have been times when I open this door and don't find my daughter on the other side. She has a habit, sometimes, of disappearing. Of sneaking away with friends. A new boyfriend. Especially when she's angry with me, which lately has been often.

But today, for now, she's here, and I exhale in relief. Ellory sleeps on top of her blanket, a slip of golden light cascading in from her window, trailing across her bed, across the shoulder of her baggy gray sweatshirt.

She breathes lightly, sleeps deeply, dreams rarely. Unlike me, she's seldom plagued by insomnia or nightmares. If I didn't wake her, she wouldn't be up until dinner. Then she'd normally leave, stay out so late she's often getting back home just as my alarm goes off in the morning.

Hearing my footsteps, she groans, attempts to hide under her pillow. Wavy amber hair sticks to her cheeks.

"Ellory," I say softly. "Wake up, it's past two. You've slept all day." I scan her room. The clothes she left the house in last night are strewn across the dusty floor.

I should be sterner, angrier than I am. But I can't. I've never once yelled at her, not even when she was a toddler. Her favorite thing to do was paint the faces of her dolls with my most expensive lipstick. No matter how many times I washed them, the makeup never truly came off. Her father would shake his head, amused. *I know we're spoiling her,* he'd say, corkscrewing his lips shut to hide a laugh. *But I still won't tell her to stop, because one day, she will. And I'm not ready for my baby to grow up.*

Her father was right, of course. Ellory did stop. But even if she hadn't, I ran out of expensive makeup long ago.

"No..." Ellory groans, turns her head to look at me. "I'm still tired."

"How about I run you a hot shower." I look into her eyes. One is the color of a newborn fawn. The other, the color of the sky. Unique and unforgettable, like her. "Then after, I can make us some lunch."

Ellory looks queasy, covers her mouth with a hand. I reach to turn on her bedside lamp. Her skin is pale, clammy.

"Are you feeling okay? Let me get the thermometer—"

"I'm fine," Ellory says quickly, brushing away the hair stuck to her cheek. "Totally fine. I—I just ate something, that's all."

"What'd you do last night?" I ask, lean against a wall. "Anything fun?"

"No."

"You were with the boyfriend?"

"Yes."

"Are you ever going to tell me his name or is he doomed to forever be called *the boyfriend*?"

"Yeah," Ellory says, a punch too late. "Of course he has a name."

I shake my head. "You can't keep doing this."

"*You* can't keep doing this," she snaps. "You promised. It's like ever since Dad died, you put all your shit on me. I'm eighteen. I'm an adult now."

"You just turned eighteen. And you can't keep staying out all night like this. Coming home drunk, hanging out with— I don't even know who he is. I don't even know his name."

"Why does it matter who he is?" Ellory sits up in bed, pulls a blanket around her shoulders, shivers inside her oversize sweat-shirt. "You shouldn't be worrying about my boyfriend when you have your own to worry about. At least mine's normal."

"I'm not fighting with you about Hugh again. I can't have you doing this under my roof anymore, Ellory."

She laughs. "There's not going to be a roof soon, anyway, thanks to y—" She stops speaking the moment she catches my pained expression. The sentiment stings regardless. "I'm sorry. I didn't mean for it to sound like that. I'm just really upset. It's our *home*. First Dad, then our home."

"I know," I whisper. "I'm sorry."

I turn around, exit the room. She lets me leave. Right now, it's best I walk away. I can't have Ellory see me cry anymore. I'll tell her the news tomorrow. When my manager asked me to come into his office, he told me to close the door, sit down. I did, and he then explained how someone had called to complain about me.

"I've never had a complaint," I said, hoping he'd take my side. But he didn't, not this time.

"The woman who called claims you waited on her and that she saw you—" he paused, glanced down at the notepad on his desk "—drop her chicken Parmesan on the floor and blow off the dust caught in the cheese." He looked up at me, pointed down at the note. "Now, you tell me that's not a legitimate complaint."

Words escaped me as I imagined actually serving something like that to another human being. That would be horrible, terrible, something I'd never do, and so, that's what I told him. I told him the truth. "I'd *never* do that—I've never done anything like that," I said.

"I believe you." He looked at me, shook his head. "But I'm sorry. I still have to let you go, Iris."

That was it. That's all it took. I pleaded with him, of course. But it didn't matter. Nothing mattered. Only the reputation of the restaurant. I was asked to leave, right then and there.

I walked to my car in the parking lot, unlocked the door, fell inside. My phone rang. It was the bank, calling with more good news. The auction just ended. It was over. Our house was gone. It was then I allowed the tears to come.

Being independent, showing my daughter I can do it, that I can provide for her, for what's left of our family, matters greatly to me. I don't want her to end up like me. I want her to go to college, to be able to look back and be proud of where life has taken her. To not regret a single thing. It's something I wish *I* could say...

Sulking downstairs, I mull over ways to tell Ellory about my job. I also think about how to mention the alcohol I smelled, thick and heavy in her hair. Or what I saw—a condom wrapper on the floor, pink and orange, like candy.

She's bringing him home now, whoever he is. Sneaking him in while I'm asleep or at work. I wish she'd spend her valuable time working instead of on a boyfriend. But who am I to say that? Now I don't have a job anymore, either. Even if I did, even if we both worked eighty hours a week, it still wouldn't save us or our home. It's too late.

I unfold a cardboard box, finish packing the living room.

We still have a few days before we have to leave, but I don't want to delay the inevitable.

On a bookshelf, the first picture taken of me and Ellory rests in a wooden frame. I was young. Too young. I stare up at the camera, baby in my arms, a bone-weary girl bubbling over with dread after that night—the night everything changed.

My phone vibrates. It's a text from Sloane:

How's Ellory doing?

She's fine, I text back, and that's all I say for now. I'm going to go to the café soon where we can talk more, though I already know what Sloane's going to say: *Let Ellory hit rock bottom. Let her fall and learn to catch herself.*

But I can't. I've been at the bottom. I knew the bottom for years when I was young, younger than Ellory is now. I know what it can do to a person. I know how it can change a person into someone they hardly recognize.

Another text appears, this time from Hugh:

I can't wait to see you. I love you.

My stomach flips as I type back:

Love you too.

Later this afternoon, instead of laughing and getting to know each other better, I'm going to have to break the news to Hugh: not only am I jobless, but I'm now homeless, too.

And I'm terrified. I don't know what the future will bring, and I'm absolutely terrified.

After I tell Hugh these things, he'll most likely kindly disappear, fade away into the background, never to be seen again. I wouldn't blame him. Who'd want to deal with the hot mess that is my life? Especially when we've only been seeing each other for two months. He's handsome and brilliant—an architect with his own firm: H. Smoll & Associates.

Hugh gets his shirts starched and teeth whitened. His car is always clean. He buys me flowers and always smells good. He volunteers at his local soup kitchen and gives to charity. And Ellory may disagree, but Hugh is completely normal. In fact, he's amazing. Too good for me. Way out of my league...

Then there's me. *Me.*

I spray the kitchen counter with Windex, wipe it clean for the new owners. Then I pack up our collection of mugs, place them gently into a box so they don't break. I close my eyes when I wrap each one, afraid of the memories they'll conjure.

Maybe I'm bad luck incarnate. It doesn't seem to matter how positive I am. How kind I try to be. Being kind isn't cutting it. Clearly, I need to change. I'm sick of being pitied by people.

I need something big to happen. I need something *good* to happen. I want to be part owner of Sloane's café one day. I want to be able to pay for Ellory to go to college. Fearing the burden of school loans has pushed her away from even applying. But if I could help her, even a little, she could graduate and become someone better than me...

In order for my daughter to be proud of herself, to know she's accomplished something great, something has to change. And it needs to happen fast, because time has just run out.

Maybe I'm cursed. I only hope I don't somehow end up cursing my relationship with Hugh, too. It's beautiful, this new love affair we've fallen into. I don't want to ruin it. I'll do anything to keep it this way forever.

But I know something has to break eventually. I only hope if my relationship with Hugh ever ends, we both walk out alive. Because the only other man I was in love with ended up dead.

And his killer has never been found.

2

Hotté Latte is busier than usual for a Friday afternoon. Every table is taken by customers nestled into corners, laptops open, lattes drained. Crumbs sprinkle across the little white plates I helped Sloane pick out when she first opened the café. Every time I see them, it feels like a punch in the gut, a reminder of a missed chance.

Sloane's quick to catch sight of me. "Hey, Iris."

I unzip my coat, collapse onto a stool. "You guys are busy today." I inhale the delicious scents of caramel, espresso, and baked cookies. The smell is half the reason why I visit every day. That and to see Sloane.

She eyes me up and down. "Are you feeling okay?" Leaning over, she presses a hand to my forehead. I can tell she's searching her mental catalog for how she can make me feel better. Last time I had a headache, she suggested three drops of peppermint oil in willow bark tea. It actually helped.

"I'm fine. Just stressed."

I place my phone on the counter, check the time, click it off.

In the screen, my reflection stares back. My ink-black hair is straight and unstyled, and I'm getting the first whisper of fine lines, small and tapered, around my mouth. For the past few years, I've been forcing myself to smile more, to smile through the grief and pain. But there's a price for everything.

"If you or Ellory get sick, I bought some new herbs and oils that can help. Some things can really expand the lungs. Licorice, for example. Just opens everything right up." Sloane inhales a deep breath to demonstrate.

"I'll keep that in mind."

"So what has you stressed…more than normal?"

"I have news. Good news, bad news, and ugly, too," I admit and flip my phone over. I don't want to see my reflection anymore. "What do you want to hear first?"

Sloane leans on the counter, taps her chin as she thinks about the question. "Good news. I need some positivity."

"Okay. I'm meeting Hugh, right here, in this very spot, in ten minutes."

Sloane gasps, slaps my arm with the purple daisy dishrag she perpetually has slung over her shoulder. "He is so into you."

My cheeks go hot. Maybe I am sick. Or it could be because I know Sloane's right. I haven't had a man look twice at me in years. Even Jack grew to love me over time. We'd known each other since we were young and eventually realized we couldn't escape each other. Literally. When I first saw him, I thought he was cute, while he'd later admitted the opposite. But I didn't blame him. I first met Jack on the worst day of my life.

I try not to think about that day too much now. Generally, I try my best to be positive. To think about the good things. Happy things. It's the only way I'll make it. I think about how over the years, Jack and I never had a reason to break up, and so we stayed together, growing in love as we grew up together alongside our daughter.

"It's only been two months." I lean on the counter across from her. "I shouldn't even be dating anyone. It's too—"

"It's not too soon. You can't blame yourself forever. What happened to Jack wasn't your fault."

My body wilts. "I know."

"Besides, it's been three years. Eventually, you have to move on. Why can't it be with Hugh? Even if Ellory only tolerates him. Barely."

"I feel for him, I do. He tries so hard with her."

"It's the age. She'll come around."

I nod. "I hope you're right."

"I am. Everyone loves Hugh. He's good-looking *and* generous." Sloane glances at the tip jar. "And he does all that charity stuff, like you. He's a veritable Robin Hood—with good hair."

I can't help but laugh. This brings a smile to Sloane's face, too. "And who cares how long you've known him," she says. "Time will go by fast."

"You're right. You could know a person for years and never really know them."

She swallows hard as she examines me. "What did Hugh say about the foreclosure?"

"I haven't told him," I admit. "I'm not sure I can, especially not after I tell him what happened today."

"If you're embarrassed, don't be," Sloane says. "You've done nothing to be embarrassed about."

I shake my head. "It's not that… I'm ashamed. Ashamed my kid's going to have to live in a car. Ashamed I couldn't keep our house. Sometimes, I think Jack would be ashamed of me, too."

Another customer walks up to the counter. Sloane has to step away to take their order. When she comes back, I ask, "Where's Ainsley?" hoping to change the topic.

Sloane reads my expression, sensing I want to talk about something else. Kindly, she goes along with it. "Late, as usual.

And it's always her husband's fault, somehow. Even now, with their divorce almost finalized."

I think back to when we first met Ainsley, right here, in this very spot in the café, when Sloane was looking to hire someone new a couple of years ago. Ainsley was still somewhat happily married then, and matched her Loubs to her lipstick to interview as a barista. Sloane hired her immediately.

Looking back, maybe I should've applied. But I didn't yet know how dire my finances would soon become. Besides, it brought us Ainsley, so I can't be upset. I'd gladly surrender a job opportunity to gain an amazing friend.

"If only I took you up on your offer and became co-owner right in the beginning. Things would've been different," I admit. "I'm sorry I let you down."

"You didn't. And who knows? It's never too late. I have a feeling one day your stars will align," Sloane says, shaking me from my thoughts. "Even though you're a Virgo, no one can have bad luck all the time. And if Ainsley ever quits, I'll hire you in a heartbeat."

I clench my jaw. Replacing Ainsley as lead barista *would* solve many of my problems. But I know Ainsley needs this job, right now at least. Any other person would beg Sloane to let her go and hire me instead, but I'd never be able to live with myself. I'm still trying to atone for past mistakes—one of them being not working with Sloane right in the beginning. I blame it on the grief. I let it get the best of me, in more ways than one.

"I hope you're right. But even if you paid me a hundred an hour, it wouldn't be enough to buy back the house."

"Well, I can't do a hundred. But for now, I can do fifteen, plus tips." She shakes the empty tip jar. "Sorry, Hugh hasn't come in yet, so the jar's a little light."

The café goes quiet, the ambient background music suddenly pausing before a new melody begins.

"So what's the bad news and ugly news?" Sloane asks.

I begin to answer just as Hugh's sleek white Tesla effortlessly parallel parks in front of the café. He gets out, walks between his car and mine—an old beige CR-V, dented and duct-taped and ready to fall apart. A few customers sitting in the window watch him, eyes unblinking, as he walks to the door. Hugh tends to have that effect on people. Even I sometimes catch myself staring. He's magnetic—movie-star handsome in our small, cozy town.

Sloane tugs at my sleeve. I turn to see her leaning forward, face inches from mine.

"Quick—tell me the bad and ugly before he comes."

"I'll tell you later," I say as Hugh pulls open the door. Right now, I need to brace myself. I've lost nearly everything in the past twenty-four hours. The last thing I want is to lose Hugh, too.

3

The bell above the front door *tings*. Hugh steps inside. A whoosh of cold air flutters in, along with a burst of crisp brown leaves that tumble across the floor.

Subconsciously, I fiddle with my hair, try to perfect it. Hugh's a man made of only good parts—slice him in half and you'll find the best traits a person could ask for and then some—and he's beyond handsome, to boot. Clark Kent–like in appearance, his eyes are bright and molten blue. If I peered inside Hugh's closet, his ironed shirts would be sorted by shade and his shoes would glisten with mirror shine.

I've not once seen his hair grown too long or his stubble go unshaved. His shoes are always polished and his collars are always crisp. Even the soft lines emerging on his forehead are perfect: two faint lines centered splendidly above his perfectly dark eyebrows.

And today, as always, Hugh looks impeccable. We planned to only meet for coffee since he has an early day tomorrow, so jeans—even lounge pants—would be appropriate. But Hugh is…Hugh. He wears a navy blazer with a baby blue plaid pattern, white shirt, perfectly pressed navy pants, oh—I spotted it. He's not wearing a tie. This is casual Hugh.

He grins at me, heads over to where I sit at the counter. I look down at the wrinkled brown dress I pulled out from a cardboard moving box. Embarrassment flushes across my face. I'm not even sure it's still in style, but it's the only dress I have that isn't falling apart or a size too small.

"Hi, Iris," he says, pulling me in for a kiss. His lips are soft and full, and when he kisses me, he lingers close after, nudging the tip of his nose against mine.

Releasing me, he grins. "Hi, Sloane."

"How are you?" Her voice is effervescent. "How are things in the, uh, architecture business? Building stuff?"

Hugh's smile widens and I can tell Sloane is melting. "Yeah, you know, we're doing all right," he says. But I know he's being modest. "Not as well as coffee shops, though." He glances over his shoulder at the room full of people.

"Yeah, well," Sloane says, stretching out her back. "What can I say? The residents of this town have good taste." She laughs. But when I look at her, the dread written across my face from the news I have to confess makes her smile falter. "I'll leave you two alone and go get started on your favorites."

Hugh turns to face me, his knees knocking into mine. "Thanks, Sloane," he says, taking my hand. "So what's new? How's Ellory?"

I pinch my lips together. I can't hide the fact that I've been fired from him. That Ellory and I are losing our home. But once I tell him, will he finally see what a disappointment I am? Will he still want to be with me? We haven't been together long, but it doesn't matter. I love him enough that his rejection would unimaginably sting.

I try to speak, but I can't find the words. Hugh studies me intensely, cheeks reddened by the warmth of the café.

"Is everything okay?"

My shoulders deflate. It's now or never. "I have a confession to make. I was let go today. From my job."

Sloane gasps from the other end of the counter. I swear she's a professional eavesdropper.

Hugh's brows knit together as his fingers tighten around mine. "Oh, God, I'm so sorry, Iris. Why would they do that?"

"There's more," I say quickly. "I'm— We're—" I close my eyes, force out the words. "I've lost our home. By Monday, Ellory and I need to be out." Opening my eyes, I feel myself sway, unmoored, unsure if I did the right thing.

Hugh's lips part ever so slightly. I pause, wait for him to speak. He doesn't. For once, he has no perfect words. Silence fills the space between us. He leans back. His fingers loosen. I steel myself for rejection.

When he doesn't say anything, I add, "You didn't know this because every time you come over, I peel the eviction sign off the window. I have to somehow pay thousands in fees and back mortgage payments or move somewhere else with Ellory. In three days."

I pick up my latte, drink it all in one panicked gulp. *I just said that. I just said that. It's out, it's done, over, kaput.* This is it— this is when he'll break up with me. He has to. Anyone else would. They'd break up with me and walk away—*run* away— run from me and my problems and never look back.

But when I come up for air, Hugh smiles at me so wide and pure and perfect I nearly forget everything I just confessed.

"This is excellent timing."

"What?"

Taking my hand again, he whispers, "I wish you told me things were this bad. I could've helped."

"I don't want help. I want to fix this on my own."

"Iris, part of fixing something on your own is recognizing when you need to ask for help. Never be ashamed. You've done nothing wrong. Fuck, I can't even imagine how hard it is. You don't give yourself nearly enough credit. You horribly lost your husband, you raise your teenage daughter all by yourself, you try to do what's best for her by working six, sometimes seven days a week. I mean, I think you owe yourself a little grace."

"I do?"

"Hell yeah, you do. You're my hero. You're amazing." Hugh searches my eyes with his, bright blue and shining like gems beneath the overhead lights, and I swear, for a moment, I feel weightless.

Sloane approaches, slowly looking back and forth between us as if wondering if this is a good time to serve us the apple pie she's warmed for us.

"Thanks, Sloane," Hugh says, slipping a fifty-dollar bill into the tip jar. When Hugh isn't looking, she smiles at the jar, her expression radiant. "Iris, I have a confession of my own to make."

I look at him and wait.

Hugh sips his cappuccino. "We'd have to iron out the details, and I want you to know I love you. No matter what happens. But I also need to be sure Ellory's okay. She's a part of you. You're a package deal. Two for the price of one. As long as you and Ellory are safe, that's what matters. Your goal is my goal."

I relax, but only slightly. Suddenly, I feel hot. Too hot. What is he going to confess?

Hugh sips his cappuccino again, swirls it around the cup. "Do you ever wonder why we always meet at restaurants or the café or your place? Why you've never actually gone back to mine?"

He searches my face for a reaction. Oh, God, here it is. His secret. I control my breathing, try to stay cool. Supercool, cool as a cucumber.

"I've recently sold my house. It was too large for me, and my heart wasn't in it anymore," Hugh explains, gaze falling to the counter. "So for now, I've moved up to Greenwich Hills. It's only a thirty-minute drive from here and the house I'm stay-ing at has room to spare. The only thing is…it's my mother's."

I hold my breath. Each word he speaks feels monumental, somehow. A strange feeling swells inside me. A feeling like everything is about to change.

When I don't reply, Hugh continues. "I'm going to stay with her awhile to help with some repairs around the house. With her hip, she can't do much. And she refuses to let me bring in a crew." He scratches the back of his neck, looks at me nervously as I mull over his words.

My heart slows. I exhale, try to stay positive. "It's kind of you to help her."

He gives a beguiling smile, showing a mouth of white, per-fect teeth.

"I'm going to ask you something, and I hope you'll ac-cept." My heart creeps back into my throat. "If you and Ellory wanted—my mother and I would love to have you." Hugh sinks his teeth into his bottom lip, awaits my response.

I freeze. This is the last thing I expected.

My first reaction is to say *no* outright. I can't take my daugh-ter with me to move to a new town into a strange house with a woman we've never met. But I love Hugh. He's sweet and caring and kind. This man is not an axe murderer.

Plus, saying no would mean my daughter and I would be forced to live in my car. If I can avoid that completely, I'm willing to take a chance. No, not even that. I'm willing to do whatever it takes.

Hugh clenches his jaw, muscles working, eyes sharp as he awaits my answer.

I look down at our hands, intermingled on my knee, and I think about something Sloane told me years ago when Ellory was entering middle school: *If you don't find ways to keep her mind occupied, someone else will. And that someone may not have good in-tentions at heart.*

Her advice still rings true today: if I don't find a place for Ellory to live—*with me*—she'll most certainly find a place to live *without me*. And that place may not be safe.

I inhale a deep breath, hope I'm making the right choice.

"Yes." I pause to look at him, unsure if I said the word aloud.

Hugh hesitates. "Really? You're sure?"

I smile, bend forward, and kiss him, soft and sweet. "Yes, I'm sure. I mean, I have to talk to Ellory, but—yes."

His face ignites with a grin. "You won't regret it." He taps his mug with mine. "I promise."

6 DAYS BEFORE

SUNDAY, JANUARY 19

4

Outside my bedroom window, a cotton candy sunrise melts across the morning sky. Fog has gathered at the base of the mountains as I lace up an old pair of sneakers, tug on my last pair of jeans. I'm wearing my favorite sweater today, a soft gray cowl neck, hoping it'll bring me luck. All of my other clothes are stuffed into boxes or trash bags.

I pull on the hem of the sweater, try to stretch it out. No longer am I the sinewy teenage girl lurking in Jack's mom's basement. My clothes are tight. But it's my fault. I haven't bought myself anything new in years. Anything new is for Ellory.

She's downstairs packing, and on my way to help, I reach inside a bag of cookies Sloane brought over the other day, crunch into one as I step around towers of cardboard boxes.

"Oh, look who's finally decided to grace this kitchen with her presence." Ellory groans, glancing at the cat clock on the wall before she takes it off its nail. "Next time I sleep in late, I don't want to hear it."

I curl onto a wooden stool, pull down the sleeves of my

sweater, tuck them into my palms. "Mmm-hmm, well, last I checked, I was the mom around here. And Mom needs coffee."

Ellory stops packing, glances up at me. Her chest rises and falls, too heavy, too hard. Tears rim her eyes as she struggles to take a deep breath. I slide off the stool, collect her in my arms, smooth her dark amber hair down her back.

"Match my breaths." Sucking in an exaggerated breath, I hold it for a heartbeat, exhale long and deep. "In and out."

She tries to match my exhalation but it spins her into a coughing fit. I run to her purse, grab the plastic inhaler she's learned to always keep inside. She uncaps it, inhales a puff with a single, sharp breath.

Soon, she's back to breathing normally. Her tears have stopped. My heartbeat calms.

"I think it was… I was moving around a lot of boxes, and with the dust—I think I did too much," Ellory explains. "I pushed it."

Fresh tears begin to fall.

"Oh, honey, you're going to be okay. You're so brave, much braver than me…" I trail off.

Flashes of Ellory propped up in a hospital bed flicker in my mind. Clear tubes disappear up her nose. Bruises cover the tops of her hands from where they tried and failed to find veins to place the needles.

Ellory sniffles, dries her eyes. "No, I know. I'm not crying because of that. I know I have to live with this."

"Are you crying because of the boyfriend? Did he—"

"No." Ellory sniffles. "It's this whole move to some shitty place we've never been—it's going to mess *everything* up."

I bite my bottom lip, hold back my own flash flood of tears when she presses her cheek to my shoulder. "No, it won't mess everything up. Our plan will still work. I promise."

"You've only known Hugh for two months. Did you know it takes twenty-one days to form a habit?"

"What?"

"I read it online. Science says that's how long it takes people to form a habit. But it takes ninety days for that habit to become a permanent lifestyle change. So right now, you can still break up with him and be okay."

"You have to stop believing everything you read online."

Ellory shakes her head vehemently. I haven't seen her so intense about something in weeks. "If you don't break up with him now—before he becomes a bigger part of your life—you're going to forget Dad ever existed."

Ellory's words feel like a punch. I look into her eyes— *heterochromia*, the doctors said. One blue, the other, brown. "Honey, I can never forget your dad, ever. And no one can replace him as your dad. He raised you. He chose to be there with you, every day, ever since you were a baby."

Ellory's right. I don't know much about Hugh. I don't know what his first job was or what his favorite song is. Or anything about his past relationships and his family. But I'm looking forward to learning more, if he'll let me. And while I have no idea where I'm taking my daughter to live, what I do know is Hugh's mom is generous enough to invite two strangers to stay inside her home. That says a lot about who she is.

Ellory sighs. "I wish Dad was here."

I pull her in for a hug. Hugging my daughter always recharges me. I feel her energy, her love, and it melts into me, tethers us together. Her body wilts around mine. I hold her a little tighter.

If there's one thing I know about Ellory, it's that she'll never say anything she doesn't truly mean. I've come to appreciate her honesty, though I could sometimes do without her stubbornness. She and Sloane are the same in that way.

In the distance, the front door opens. Ellory detaches herself from me and we slip into the living room to see Sloane has entered the empty house.

"Hello, hello." Her heavy boots stomp across the wooden floor as she walks in, a paper bag in one hand, a tray of overflowing coffee cups in the other.

"I wasn't sure if you were still coming," I say and run to help, start to shut the door behind her.

"Hey, *wait*." Ainsley pokes her head in. "I'm here, *too*." She scoops her perfectly waved hair out of her face. "I come to offer my services, and I get a door to the face."

"I thought you wanted to wait in the car," Sloane says over her shoulder as she marches into the kitchen. "All right, I have coffee, muffins, cookies—no, don't eat that one," she says, as Ellory grabs a muffin. "I think that's the one I took a bite of in the car."

"Hey, what kind of business are you running here?" Ellory teases.

Ainsley and I enter the kitchen. It looks clean and open without clutter filling the countertops. The glass cabinet doors display nothing but empty shelves: no more mugs, bowls, glassware, nothing but old crumbs and dust. It's almost like we never lived here at all.

In a way, it reminds me of the house after Jack died. I was inconsolable. People preyed on me, sensing my weakness. Friends we shared for years "borrowed" things from the house, never to be seen or heard from again. It was Sloane who eventually realized what was happening. She moved in for two weeks, sleeping on the couch by the front door, keeping unwanted guests at bay so Ellory and I could attempt to heal.

It was during these weeks Sloane began dreaming up plans to open a coffee shop. I helped her design the napkins, logo, and menus. It helped bring me out of my fog, my grief. Sloane used our kitchen to practice baking muffins and bagels, and in between batches, she'd cook Ellory and me breakfast, lunch, and dinner. She made sure we were cared for.

"Vultures," she'd say, tapping her long black fingernails on the countertop. "Nothing like bad friends to kick you when you're down."

I'm not proud of how I handled things then. I didn't have it in me to fight people. And so I let myself be beaten down. I let myself be beaten. But I'm trying to rebuild myself, a little each day.

"Sorry we're late," Ainsley says, her pink coat flapping open, heels clacking across the linoleum floor. Her highlighted brown hair perfectly curls away from her smooth, pretty face. "Blame it on my *ex*-husband. Don't you two look pretty today." She scans her brown eyes, fanned with thick lashes, back and forth between me and Ellory.

"Thanks," I say as Ainsley tosses her coat and purse on a kitchen stool.

"And how, exactly, did he make you late?" Sloane asks, rotating around to face her.

"Ugh. He made me drive over to his house to pick up some paperwork I need for the lawyer tomorrow. He couldn't just, I don't know, email it to me? I swear that man lives only to piss me off. My tears fuel him."

Ellory holds back a laugh. Ainsley's nightmarish divorce began after something huge cleaved them apart. Ainsley still won't tell us what. All we know is she's fighting for half of his 401(k), pensions, homes—everything. He retaliated by closing their bank accounts and kicking her out. Their divorce has been Hollow Falls' hot gossip for months.

"We come bearing gifts," Sloane says, sliding the coffee and paper bag on the table.

"I love you, Sloane," Ellory says, slurping out of a paper cup.

Sloane grins, pinches Ellory's cheek. "Anything for my little family."

Ainsley touches up her lipstick in the reflection of the microwave. "Um, I'd totally help you pack your house if you asked, but it looks like you guys have done all the hard labor." She looks around at the empty house, the only contents cardboard boxes and trash bags bursting with what's left of our wardrobes.

"You would've? Aw, thanks, Ainsley—"

"No, no, I wouldn't. I was joking."

Sloane wraps her arm around Ainsley's tiny shoulders. "You're bad at it."

Ainsley pushes off her arm, turns toward Ellory. "Hey, I heard you have a new boyfriend. How'd you two meet? What's his *name*?"

Ellory freezes, coffee cup midair. She turns to me, and the look she gives me could freeze the entire town. "Oh, my God, why does everyone want to know?"

Ainsley bursts out laughing. "Your mom asked me to ask." Ellory rolls her eyes. Ainsley shrugs a shoulder at me. "*Tsk.* Sorry, I tried. But I mean, you set me up to fail—since I never even met *your* boyfriend, either, Iris."

"You've never met Hugh?" Ellory asks. "I'm surprised… Mom's always at the café with the guy. Wait till you *see* him. I don't know where she found him."

"Uh-oh," Ainsley says. "That bad, huh?"

Sloane laughs. "That *hot*, you mean." Ainsley raises a brow, intrigued. Ellory pretends to barf. I hide my face, embarrassed.

"So, Iris," Sloane begins, setting down her cup of coffee. "I've been studying something online and wanted to try it out on you. You up for it?"

"She's been studying this all week," Ainsley tells Ellory.

Before I can answer, Sloane takes me by the wrists, splays out my hands so my palms look at the ceiling.

"This line," Sloane says, tracing my palm with her pinky finger, "is your life line. The beginning is messy, meaning you had a difficult childhood or trauma. And this is your heart line. See how the line stops, then starts again? Do you know what that means?" she asks as if I know the answer. When I shake my head, she says, "You're about to embark on a romantic affair, *ooh lala,*" she coos. Her eyes still on my palm, her nose wrinkles. "But the line breaks into jagged lines at the end..."

"What does that mean?" I ask.

Sloane blinks. Her forehead creases. "Well, it's a sign your romantic affair will end terribly."

I pull my hands away. "Wow, thanks, Sloane."

Ainsley rolls up the sleeves of her white cashmere sweater, nails perfectly manicured in ballet pink. Her wrist is adorned with the latest Apple watch, and her fingers happily glitter with diamond rings stacked up to her knuckles. I look down at my own hands, decorated with the cracks and peels of dry skin.

"My turn," Ainsley says. "Come on. Show me what you got."

Sloane looks at her. "You know that the lines don't change when I read them twice, right?"

Ainsley smirks. "Yeah, yeah. I know. Just tell me if my bastard soon-to-be-ex will ever look at me and realize he's lost the *best* thing that's ever happened to him."

Ellory loudly tapes up a cardboard box behind us. "I don't think that's how this works."

Sloane spreads out Ainsley's delicate fingers, moves her face close like she's reading fine print. "Well, you definitely have *fire* hands. Iris has *earth* hands, which means while they may be short and stout, she's loyal and has integrity. But *you*..." Sloane grins, continues. "*Fire* hands are long and lean, but mean you're likely to be impulsive and charismatic."

Ainsley bites her bottom lip. "Maybe this is accurate after all."

Sloane stays silent as she examines Ainsley's palms. "And your head line breaks early, but that normally just means you'll have some kind of ailment having to do with the head."

"Can't wait," Ainsley says.

Sloane continues. "And...your life line is short." She stops, checks Ainsley's other hand. "Huh, that's weird. I didn't notice this the first time I read you. The life line on *both* of your hands is really short."

Ainsley tenses, remains silent.

"So, what does it mean?" I ask.

Ellory stops packing, moves closer.

Sloane glances up at Ainsley. "One hand with a short life line normally means a near-death experience. But two? I'll— I'll have to research more."

Ainsley pulls her hands out of Sloane's grasp. "You know how I invited you on that cruise after my divorce is finalized? Well, you're uninvited."

"Sloane, I think you should stick to tarot cards," Ellory says.

I narrow my eyes at Ainsley as she rolls down her sleeves. "What cruise?" I ask. Ainsley says nothing. I look at Sloane, repeat the question. "What cruise?"

Sloane sighs, glares at Ainsley. "We didn't want to bug you with it."

"It's nothing, really," Ainsley says. "We didn't think it was the right time for you, that's all."

The kitchen goes quiet, nothing but the hushed swish of a plastic bag as Ellory picks one up off the floor, carries it outside to start loading the car.

"I get it. I can't afford to buy lattes, let alone a cruise. It's fine. You guys should go. Have fun." A knot chokes my throat.

Sloane walks around the kitchen island, stands beside me. "I'm sorry."

I shrug her away. "I have to help Ellory. This is the last thing she wants to be doing, and her asthma is acting up again. I have to help her. Hugh will be here in an hour."

Ainsley grabs a blueberry muffin out of the bag, gives me a quick hug as Ellory returns to the room. Her musky perfume smells heavenly. "We should go."

Ellory and Ainsley say goodbye in the kitchen as Sloane walks with me to the door.

"You know I would've let you both move in with me—forever, if that's what you wanted. I just don't want Ellory to have an asthma attack."

"It's not your fault you have cats. Lots of people have allergies. It's not Ellory's fault and it's *not* yours."

"Still, I'm sorry," Sloane says. Then, leaning in, she whispers, "Are we still...?"

"Yes. No change."

She nods. "Good. Right, well, we'll leave you to it. Now, I know you're only moving thirty minutes north, but I'll still miss the hell out of you. Promise me we'll see each other as much as we can."

"I promise." I wrap my arms around her, pull her into a hug, hide my tears.

Bad luck has plagued me for years. But lately, I've been realizing my bad luck has been extending, spreading like a poisonous fog, afflicting those closest to me. Family. Friends. Husbands. No one is safe. Now that I'll be gone, hopefully Sloane and Ainsley will be outside the blast radius. When I'm gone, maybe they'll be safe.

"Sloane, you'll never hear me say this ever again," Ainsley calls, "but we need to get back to work."

Sloane grips my hand tight. "No change," she says. "Everything will work out, you'll see. Hugh better take care of my girls." She gives Ellory a long hug before getting in her car to drive away.

Ellory and I stand shoulder to shoulder as we watch them disappear into the morning fog. Silently, I cry and yell inside my head, my secret dark abyss where no one else can hear.

5

We drive on a narrow road that snakes through a dense forest on one side, the Hudson River at the bottom of a cliff on the other. Everything we need for the next few weeks is packed in trash bags and cardboard boxes and shoved in the backs of our cars. Everything else—furniture, mattresses, the coffee maker—will live in a storage unit until we move out of Hugh's mom's house.

I know only three things about where we're going:

1) The house is about a half hour north of Hollow Falls on the other side of the river in a hamlet called Greenwich Hills.

2) Hugh's mom doesn't have cats, so it's safe for Ellory's asthma and allergies.

3) A few other relatives are staying at the house for various reasons.

My palms sweat with anxiety. Here I am, a grown woman, bringing her teenage daughter to live inside a stranger's home. I hate to admit it, but I'm a little embarrassed this is happening to me at this stage in my life. I'm thirty-five. I should be years into a great career, a happy marriage, a thriving business—*something*. Instead, I'm jobless. Homeless. Penniless.

A widow.

Maybe Sloane was completely wrong this morning when she read my palms. Maybe I don't have integrity. *No.* I stop myself. I *do* have integrity. But I also have very bad luck. Maybe all that is about to change. The sudden feeling of hope fills me.

I never thought I'd be ready to date again after losing Jack. When I met Hugh, I didn't expect much, but he became someone who felt like home. I haven't felt that way since Jack. To me, that means something. Hugh is kind and sweet. He helps me through the hard days. He's always there for me and Ellory. Sometimes, I feel like Hugh understands my pain about losing Jack better than anyone, somehow. Even better than Sloane or Ainsley. While Ellory's feelings for him may still be mixed, I'm falling for him. I've fallen.

Moving in together is the next natural step. Granted, it's happening fast and the situation may not be ideal, but what is? Love is unpredictable.

"After you've settled in, I was thinking of taking Ellory out to shop for some new things for her bedroom. And anything you might need, too. Just let me know when," Hugh says. "Anything to make you more comfortable."

"You would do that?"

He nods. "Of course. The house can get a little cold, especially with the patchy roof. Drafts come in through the windows, too, so anywhere you'd like to shop for some extra blankets or anything at all, I'm happy to do that. For you *and* Ellory. Sky's the limit."

Through overgrown bushes, the hint of a mossy brick fence lines the road. An iron gate opens in the center. Hugh puts on his signal and slows down to turn into a shadowy driveway. Pointed straight toward the river, the long driveway is lined with mature pines, darkening the inside of the car.

Hugh slows down even further to drive across a tiny wooden bridge over a narrow ravine.

"Be extra careful driving over this bridge when it's below freezing," Hugh warns. "It ices up quickly and can be dangerous. The wood slats are old and may snap in the cold."

A small herd of deer dashes off at the sound of the car, jumping into the protective darkness of the woods. The hovering arms of evergreens break away, and we enter a sunny clearing. Hugh turns a curve, and it's then I see it.

The house is massive, towering, taller than it is wide, with twisted chimneys and leaded windows. It's made of stone the color of a dead mouse: dusty brown with a faint hue of decay. Wild ivy, moss, and gold lichen sprout from shadowy corners. Overgrown bushes and gnarled oak trees invade entire portions of the house. A spiked turret grows high over a mossy slate roof.

Burning orange sunlight reflects off arched windows, igniting the house like it's on fire from the inside out.

The more I stare, the more I can see how grand it used to be...before being neglected for years in the woods. It needs work. I can see why Hugh said he'd move in to help his mom. And from the look of things, it seems he'll need to stay longer than he thinks.

Hugh parks on the side of the house beside a short brick wall. On the other side, the river surges down below. "Welcome to Ravencliff." Hugh shuts off the engine. "At least, that's what it was called when it was completed in 1889, two years after its smaller Philadelphia counterpart, Ravenhill. I always admired the roof. It's part of why I want to help save it. See the intricacy of the cornices below the mansard roofline? That was rare during the time. It's stunning architecture."

I nod. Rooflines are the last thing I'm looking at. I was expecting a brick ranch house or townhome or split-level built in the '80s with beige carpet. Not...*this*. Hugh opens his door. I take his hand, tug him back in. He turns to me.

"Why didn't you ever say your mom lived *here*? You said you recently sold your house and moved in with your mom to help her with repairs. I was thinking along the lines of installing a new sink or cleaning the gutters."

"The projects at this house are a little more complicated than that." I nod for him to elaborate. "Well, the roof is a nightmare. It leaks buckets and that's damaging the stone foundation. Then there's the conservatory remodel, among other things."

"And you love the roof," I say.

"I do love the roof," he agrees. "And you know how I mentioned on the ride up how a few other relatives were staying here?"

I nod, feeling slightly relieved as I gaze at the house. I'd envisioned sharing a bathroom with strangers and sleeping on an air mattress. But *this*...this place can fit five families, let alone one.

"My brother's here," Hugh explains. "And his wife. And my sister's back, too, only until she finds a new apartment. That's part of why I wanted to move back in. We're all here, together, to help with the larger jobs that require more people."

"You never told me you had a brother," I say, surprised. "Or a sister. Don't you think that's something you should've told me?"

Hugh frowns. "I'm sorry, Iris. I—I haven't seen them in a long time and, well, we all moved away, really. My sister was living in Brooklyn and Gabe and Camille had bought a new townhome in New Jersey. I was busy with the business and then you happened and—" He stops himself.

I inch closer. "And what?"

"And...I didn't want you to be scared away."

I narrow my eyes. "Scared of what?"

Hugh bites his bottom lip. "The family."

"I'm sure they're nice people," I say with a laugh. But Hugh doesn't laugh back. "Why—should I be afraid?"

"Terrified." He looks at me, unblinking. The smile falls from my face.

He gets out of the car, closes the door behind him, peers back at me through the tinted glass. I wasn't expecting this. I wasn't expecting any of this. Our relationship has grown serious, and we've already talked about rings and *the next step*. So why didn't he mention his family?

I didn't even know they existed.

I close my eyes. This isn't a deal breaker. It may be a red flag, okay, but compared to Hugh, I'm a giant glowing red flag waving in the wind. Besides, there are many things Hugh doesn't know about me, either.

I never told him how when Jack died, all I was left with was $792 in our joint checking account and $200,000 in hospital loans from when Ellory had COVID—her asthma exacerbated by the virus, her lung had collapsed in what the doctors had called a pneumothorax.

On top of that, Jack's income had covered the mortgage, still with twenty-four years left to pay. Without his salary, the mortgage was late by the time I'd come home from his funeral.

We'd lived our normal lives, day in and day out, and never even realized that without health or life insurance, we were always just one accident or illness—or death—away from ruin.

Hugh opens my door, startling me. The thoughts evaporate. My eyes flip open.

"Ready to move in?" He holds out a hand to help me out of the car. I place my hand in his, and he smiles, though it doesn't reach his eyes.

Ellory takes off her sunglasses, stares up at the house. Without looking, she pulls her inhaler out of her pocket, inhales a deep puff before breathing out.

Hugh guides us toward the front of the house. There's nothing behind it, no mountains or land—nothing but air. Half the house clings onto the cliff side for dear life, the steep hill leading straight down to the river below.

I study the house as I approach it. It looms over me, disapproving. Everything about it seems unnecessarily large—the windows, doors, even the bushes that cling to the stone dwarf me, like I'm a child's new doll being brought back home.

For some reason, I feel like I should ask the house permission before stepping inside.

6

Barnacled to my side, Ellory looks up at the house and throws me a pointed look: *Seriously, Mom?*

Slowly, I detach from her side to step up the stairs to the front porch. It's barren and unkempt, with old forgotten Halloween decorations perched on little tables, sewn to the house by spiderwebs. Dead leaves scrape across the uneven fieldstones, and my toe gets caught, launching me forward into Hugh. He catches me thoughtfully, and I wave for Ellory to follow. She remains at the bottom of the stairs, still looking up at the house.

Hugh knocks on the door. It groans open. Standing in the shadows is a woman, still as stone.

"Hugh." She leans forward, delicately kisses him on his cheek before setting her eyes on me. "And you're Iris."

"Nice to meet you, Mrs. Smoll." I hold out a hand. Her pale face glows from the gloom of the house.

The woman, Hugh's mom, has a shock of white hair, perfectly waved away from her face, like she's been standing in front of an industrial-strength fan. She passes a carved black cane between arthritic hands, knuckles knotted like tree limbs. Though she's had cosmetic help, she looks stunning for a woman nearing seventy. If her hands didn't betray her, I would've guessed she was twenty years younger.

"Nice to meet you, too, Iris." She lifts an eyebrow as she examines me before looking over my shoulder. "And this must be Ellory."

Ellory finally stomps up the front steps and heaves a sigh. "Hi. Nice house." She tosses her long hair over a shoulder. "So are we staying in the room with the bats or the rats?"

Mrs. Smoll stares at Ellory's flushed face a heartbeat too long. "Bats or rats. Now you get the room with both."

"I'm sorry, Mrs. Smoll. She just turned eighteen." I nudge Ellory's arm. "You know that age."

Mrs. Smoll looks at me knowingly before turning back to stare at Ellory again. "I do. Too well. But please—call me Birdie. I haven't been a *Mrs.* in fifteen years, and I never want to be one again." She laughs, a low, gravelly laugh, cigarettes melded with grit.

Hugh rolls his eyes. "Can we go in the house now? My hands are going to snap off," he says, gripping our heavy bags tight in his fists.

"Of course." Birdie pushes open the door. "I'll get your brother to help you with the rest. Just leave it all in the foyer for now."

Hugh lets Ellory and me enter first. Birdie hovers close. The front door shuts behind us, the sound echoing across a wide foyer. I look around, curiosity mingling with trepidation. Ellory moves from my side, crosses the room. I stop myself from grabbing hold of her hand to pull her back, away from the stepping into the unknown.

It's dark inside, too dark, made darker by wood-paneled walls and a patchwork of exotic, threadbare rugs. A chandelier dangles from a high, vaulted ceiling, stretched up to an oval, stained-glass dome.

I scan the space for Ellory, but struggle to see much of anything in the shadows. The house is absurdly dark. Step away from a window and gloom descends.

A drop of water hits my face, and I flinch.

Hugh places the luggage at the bottom of a grand wooden staircase, looks up at the ceiling. "Sections of the glass dome are missing," he whispers. I unknot the look of surprise off my face, wipe the droplet away. "So be careful, there's a soft spot in the floorboards from the water damage."

"It's nothing my Hugh can't fix," Birdie purrs.

Ellory screams. I rush across the foyer to find her standing in a room with bookshelves bursting with porcelain dolls, sculptures, and miniature dollhouse furniture. A moth flutters in the dark air, lands in a cobweb.

"Is that a—raccoon?" she says, horrified.

Hugh hovers behind us. "Yeah, Father loved taxidermy. Don't worry, it won't bite. Hard." Ellory rolls her eyes and laughs, but still rushes from the room. I throw Hugh a chastising look as we follow her back to the foyer, but I have to admit even I'm a little afraid.

Footsteps behind us. "Nice to hear someone laughing in this place."

A man leans against the door frame. He's handsome, shorter than Hugh, with round tortoise glasses and combed, waving brown hair.

"Iris, this is my little brother, Gabe. Don't listen to anything he says."

"Iris, a pleasure." Gabe takes my hand, kisses the top. Ellory holds back another laugh. "And who's this?" He crosses his arms.

"My daughter, Ellory."

"Nice to meet you. Hey, Hugh, let's go grab the rest of their luggage and leave these two to wander the house on their own.

Just don't get lost," he says to Ellory with a grin. "We've lost quite a few guests over the years." She gasps in horror.

When they leave, Ellory looks at me incredulously, shakes her head. "I really hate you right now."

"It's better than sleeping in the car," I whisper, hooking her arm in mine. "Let's try to forget they have a taxidermy room."

"Oh, my God, come on, Mom. This place is weird."

"We should be grateful they opened their home to us. No judgment, promise me."

She huffs. "Fine."

We wander down the hallway where Hugh's mom has disappeared. The floorboards creak with each step. The air smells strange—meat and dead flowers, a stranger's home. Oil paintings cover the walls, and I let my fingertips travel down the lengths of a marble sculpture, the hard stone cool beneath my touch.

I get the feeling that this could've been a grand house back when it was built, and it seems all of the furniture and carpets hail from that time, never having been replaced. Every surface is crowded with dusty objects and trinkets and heirlooms.

This isn't a home. It's an exhibit.

The front door closes in the distance. Hugh's voice calls to us from down the hall. Ellory wraps her arms around herself as we head back.

"All right," Hugh says. "Everything's in. We'll give you a tour and show you the rooms before carrying everything up. Iris, you'll be in my room. Ellory, you can choose another bedroom in the same hall, whichever one you'd like."

To my surprise, Ellory gives a small smile.

Gabe hovers near the staircase, grips the carved banister. "This way."

We climb up a never-ending staircase. At the top is a gilded mirror. Ahead of me, Ellory, Hugh, and Gabe turn a corner. I glance at the mirror, lift a finger to trace a crack running side to side when something catches my eye behind me.

"Iris?" Hugh calls to me in the distance.

But I can't speak.

A girl stares back at me. No, not an actual girl. A photograph. In the image is a young woman, around Ellory's age, with red cheeks and freckles and rust-colored hair cascading down one shoulder. Her face is heart-shaped, with a tiny pointed chin and wide ear-to-ear smile. I feel like I know her. But it can't be real. It has to just be a girl who reminds me of someone else. It has to be—because the only other explanation is impossible.

Hugh calls for me again. "Iris, are you okay?"

I rush to catch up.

Ellory throws her head back in frustration. "Mom, these rooms all have weird vibes."

This entire place has a weird vibe, I want to say. I nod at her when Hugh's not looking. I don't want to make him feel bad about his childhood home. But when I turn back, Gabe is watching me.

After getting a tour of the second floor, we head back to the staircase to tour the third level. Passing the mirror again, I look at the wall. But when I search for the photograph of the girl, there's nothing but a ring of dust on the wallpaper.

7

Ellory chooses a bedroom facing the back of the house, looking down to the river. It's directly across from Hugh's bedroom, where we'll be staying. I love how my daughter doesn't want to be far from me, but I know her feelings for Hugh are lukewarm at best. I'm holding out hope things will change.

I unpack my clothes, stuffing them into the drawers of an old armoire. Hugh's childhood bedroom is a pleasant surprise. It doesn't have dark paneled walls like the rest of the house or peeling red wallpaper like Ellory's room. It's painted pale blue, with heavy drapes the color of the sea. The only art lining the walls are dusty seascapes of dunes and sailboats.

After I've unpacked a little, I go to help Ellory. I know my daughter. She won't stay here long if she doesn't feel comfortable. She'll leave again, move in with her boyfriend, have me wishing she'd come back home.

I nudge open her door. She's napping in her sleeping bag, which she's spread across the top of the four-post bed, so I return to my room to keep unpacking. The view from Hugh's room faces the front of the house, out toward the woods and driveway below.

A sporty red car breaks through the trees, circles in front. Two women exit, both brunettes, one in sneakers, the other in stilettos. The wind whips their long hair across their faces. One must be Hugh's sister—a sister I had no idea existed until today.

When Ellory wakes, we go downstairs to find Hugh and get introduced.

"This house creeps me out," Ellory says, as we follow voices through the halls.

I glance behind us to make sure nobody is nearby. "I'm starting to agree with you."

"The old lady creeps me out, too."

"You mean Hugh's mom, Birdie," I say.

"All she does is stare at me."

I tilt my head, curious.

"Watch her and see. She doesn't take her beady eyes off me. She's like one of those dolls with the glass eyes that follow you around the room. It's freaky."

I stop walking. We must be lost. Trying to figure out where things are feels impossible. It's a patchwork house, rooms leading into other rooms, sometimes connected by a hallway, other times a door. Endless rooms, like two mirrors pressed together.

Finally, we find the kitchen. My sneakers squeak on the terra-cotta floor. Voices quiet as we enter. Tiled white walls stretch high overhead, making it feel more spacious than the rest of the gloom-infested house. It must be a new addition added after the main home was built.

Behind a long black kitchen island, Hugh stands beside his mom washing dishes at a farmhouse sink. Flipping through a photography magazine, Gabe sits in a chair tucked in a corner, surrounded by shelves bursting with old cookbooks. The two women who'd exited the sporty red car stand on opposite sides of the island. They take turns staring at us with long, expectant gazes.

Escaping his mom's side, Hugh crosses the kitchen to introduce us.

"Guys," he begins, taking my hand, "this is Iris and her daughter, Ellory. Iris, this is my sister, Rebecca." He nods toward the slender girl with a long shock of shiny brown hair, dressed head to toe like she just came from CrossFit. "And Gabe's wife, Camille."

Camille, wrapped in a white faux-fur coat, toddles over in stiletto booties to shake my hand. "It's nice to meet you, Iris," she says with a soft Spanish accent. Pinching a strand of wavy highlighted hair, she guides it out of her lip gloss.

"Welcome to the house," Rebecca says, before looking to her mother. "What's for dinner?"

"Hugh's favorite," Birdie answers. "Baked macaroni and cheese."

Ellory stifles a laugh.

Gabe glances at Ellory and piles on, "Are we sure Hugh's an adult yet? Or is he only pretending?" He peers at Hugh over the top of his tortoise glasses and grins. His wife looks at him, rolls her eyes.

Hugh leans against the counter, turns to me. "I'm sorry you have to deal with this. It's not like this all the time."

"Yes, it is," Rebecca says. "All the time. And now with the renovation, it's like they're in constant competition."

"Good idea, Rebecca." Birdie stirs a large copper pot like a witch brewing a magic spell. "Show Iris what you've been working on."

I study Birdie as she moves around the kitchen. Ellory's right. Birdie can't seem to keep her eyes off my daughter, staring as if she were wearing the Hope diamond around her neck.

"Oh, the renovation?" I ask, shifting my gaze away. "What are you working on?"

"The conservatory," Gabe answers.

Hugh comes over, wraps an arm around my shoulders. "It has the best bones."

"And the biggest hole in the ceiling," Rebecca adds. "But Hugh has an amazing eye. His architecture firm is doing really well."

Hugh smiles at his sister and brings me in for a kiss. His lips are soft, and even in front of his family I can't help but linger.

"Gross," Ellory says. "I'm going upstairs. Please don't come and get me. Ever."

Camille turns toward Hugh. "You are a great architect, I'll give you that. And doing all this work pro bono when you could be making money is very generous of you."

"Thanks, Camille."

"I could never be an architect," she says. "I wanted to go to school for *drama*, but such is life."

"No, you didn't," Gabe says, turning to speak to me. "She went to college for law and dropped out. Let this be your lesson to never believe my wife—the actress."

"If I'm such an *actress*, did you ever stop to think maybe I would've been good at drama?" Camille shoots back.

"I never said you're a *good* actress."

I peek at Camille. She sits silent, gritting her teeth.

"Anyway," Gabe says. "Let's stop bickering in front of our guest. We don't want to be like Rebecca and her girlfriend, always fighting about some bullshit or another."

Rebecca scoffs. "Listen, just because we got into *one* fight—"

"Oh, so that's why you've moved back in again?" Gabe says. "I was wondering what happened. What'd you two fight about? Who forgot to wash the bras?"

Rebecca punches his arm.

I change the subject before the conversation heats up further. "I—I didn't see pictures anywhere. Do you have any from when Hugh was little?"

Birdie turns away from the stove, gives me a stern look of

caution. "Why would I? Cameras steal your soul." The blood drains from my face. "I'm joking, Iris, relax," she says. My shoulders wither with relief. "Gabe, did you take your heart medication today?"

He clears his throat. "Um, yes, Mother."

"Good. Because I don't want you to have an arrhythmia with what I'm about to say," Birdie begins, voice sharp. "Iris, my late husband burned all of our pictures. He didn't want to be reminded of things he destroyed." Birdie grips her cane tight.

"What?"

Hugh gulps, glances at me. "Iris just got here. Let's try not to scare her away."

A sly grin passes over Birdie's face. "She deserves to know your family history. After all, you're getting serious with this woman. She's going to be a member of the family soon, right?"

My eyes widen. Hugh wraps his arm around me, rubs my shoulder. "We have to wait and see. You never know what could happen."

Gabe loudly drops a metal baking tin onto the floor. The room jumps. Camille rolls her eyes at her husband. I can practically hear her hurling insults at him from inside her head.

I detach myself from Hugh's grip. "I wanted to thank you for letting us stay in your home. Hopefully, we won't be here too long."

"Why? Don't you like the house?" Birdie asks. Pulling a wooden spoon from a drawer, she holds it over her shoulder like a baseball bat.

"I— It's not that. I just don't want to impose."

Birdie narrows her eyes at me. Hugh cuts in before she can speak. "Mother, I'm sure Iris is eager to find her and her daughter a new home, somewhere closer to her friends."

"Right, exactly. It's nice for teens to have their support system nearby."

"Ellory is eighteen, correct?" Birdie puckers her lips. "Born what day? What month? December?" Her bony knuckles clench tighter around the wooden spoon.

Hugh clears his throat. Birdie loosens her fingers, arthritic knuckles popping. "I have a knack for birthdays, that's all." She lifts a shoulder. "Ellory is invited to stay as long as she wants. And you, too. Of course."

"Thanks. And I also wanted to thank you for not having any cats. It means Ellory can stay here asthma- and allergy-free."

"Can we thank each other later? We still have a ton of demolition to do," Gabe whines. "Plus, it's supposed to be cold tonight. That room has no heat."

"I'm coming, too." Rebecca pinches Gabe's arm on their way out of the kitchen.

"Camille can show you where the conservatory is when you're ready." Hugh kisses me again before following Rebecca and Gabe down the hall.

The kitchen quiets. Birdie digs the wooden spoon into shredded yellow cheese, scoops it up, lets it fall into the copper pot on the stove.

I turn to Camille. "What brings you and Gabe here?"

She inhales a deep breath, pivots her back toward Birdie. "It's a long story," she whispers. "I'll tell you later—not here." Her phone rings, a warbling ringtone of "Dance of the Sugar Plum Fairy." She answers the call, pausing to whisper to me on her way out, "It's nice to have another outsider here."

Alone with Hugh's mom, I walk around the kitchen, admire her collection of cookbooks. Next to the bookshelves is a corkboard bursting with old take-out menus and flyers. But still, there are no pictures, not even a small one, a school portrait, a family vacation. Nothing.

I flip open a take-out menu and a paper flutters to the floor. It's a flyer for a grief counseling group, dated over ten years ago. I pin it back to the board. The kitchen falls into silence. Awkwardly, I circle the room, try to think of something to talk about. She is Hugh's mother. She's letting my daughter and me stay in her house, leaks and taxidermy and dead moths aside. She's saving us, essentially, from destitution. The least I can do is try to be kind.

"I went to some of those groups, too," I begin, nodding at the corkboard. "After my husband died." Birdie purses her lips. "I guess it's not something Hugh would've mentioned."

She studies me behind her black cat-eye glasses. She seems so stylish and put together, like she's retired from working at a big fashion house. The white collar of her shirt pops up around a large necklace of polished green stones. Silver bracelets jingle up and down her thin, papery arms as she stirs the pot of pasta.

"I went to many grief sessions, years ago. When *my* husband died."

"I'm sorry."

"It's fine. He's better off where he is," Birdie says, steadying herself on her cane. "Why don't you go find Hugh and see what he's been working on? He may run his own architecture firm, but I refuse to let him bring a crew in here and muck everything up. No matter how good he claims they are, no one but family touches *my* house."

I open my mouth to speak, but she coldly waves me away.

Following the sounds of demolition, I wander through the house trying to find the conservatory. Only one window I pass is open, the drapes parted in the center. It's a beautiful stained-glass window of blooming vines encircling a well. Outside is the gravel driveway that cuts through the middle of a wide, windswept field. Behind the field, the forest grows, forming a perfect line of trees against the tall grass.

A coldness flickers through me. I turn away from the window. For some reason, I get the feeling that I've been here before.

5 DAYS BEFORE

MONDAY, JANUARY 20

8

Hugh wakes me at seven o'clock sharp, already shaved, showered, and dressed in a soft white sweater. As I hug him, I know it's made of cashmere, and I nuzzle his neck a moment longer, feel the softness brush across my cheek.

"Meet me downstairs in twenty minutes?" he asks. "Ellory, too." He bends over to kiss me, moves a hand behind my head to press us together. As he pulls away and leaves the room, I catch a smile on his face.

My stomach flips. Last night was amazing. We locked the door, put clean sheets on the bed, and *God*, I feel good. I get out of bed and instantly feel less achy—no headache, no joints popping. Being with Hugh has given me a surge of something I didn't know I'd been missing—freedom. Freedom from needing permission to feel alive again. Freedom to be happy and not regret it.

After feeling like I had a stamp on my forehead for three years—*widow*—it's nice to be with someone who doesn't look at me and see the stamp.

I tug on an old sweater, a pair of well-worn black jeans, and the sneakers I wore yesterday. Swiping on the last of my trusty foundation stick, I blend it with my fingertips. My mascara has long dried in the tube, but Ellory showed me that with a splash of warm water, I can reactivate it, and so I swipe it on, praying it doesn't weep under my eyes.

Once I'm ready, I run across the hall, check on Ellory to see if she's getting dressed. To my surprise, she's sitting on her bed texting, wearing yet another oversize sweatshirt and gray leggings.

"How'd you sleep?" I ask as we walk down the staircase together to meet Hugh.

She sighs, pulls her long hair out of the neck of her sweatshirt, swoops it down a shoulder. "Fine, I guess." Working hard to avoid eye contact, she picks up the end of her hair, examines it for split ends.

"Are you feeling better?"

She looks up, lets the hair fall from her hand. "I'm fine. Why? I mean, what are we doing, anyway? I'm tired. I want to go back to sleep."

"I know," I say. "You can go back to bed after we see what Hugh wants."

Ellory rubs her eyes awake as we turn a corner. To my surprise, instead of Hugh waiting for us, Rebecca stands in the foyer. Behind her, the hole in the stained-glass ceiling invites a faint waterfall of snow to drift down into the house. The snowflakes land on a Persian rug and quickly melt into the fibers. It's so beautiful, for a second I dislike the idea of Hugh repairing the ceiling.

"Good morning," we say, and already I feel underdressed. For what, I don't know. Just for the day. For life inside this house. Rebecca looks luminous—brown hair spun in a perfect twist resting at the nape of her slender neck. Her skin is sun-kissed, though it's the dead of winter, and the blue, high-necked dress she wears shows off her athletic figure.

I kick myself for wearing the sweater with the holes on the elbows. Already I wish I could glance in a mirror to check if my mascara has run. But Ellory always looks beautiful, so that's all that matters.

Rebecca weaves us through a maze of shadowy hallways toward the back of the house. Ellory's eyes are locked on her phone as we walk, and so I find this a good time to get to know Rebecca better.

"I—wanted to tell you," I begin, nervous for some reason. "I'm an only child, so I wouldn't know, but I think it's sweet that the three of you seem to get along—in your own way. It makes me wish I had a sibling."

Rebecca glances at me, questioning. "In our own way?"

"I mean, you seem to love and support each other. I wish my family had been like that. Maybe things would've been different for me growing up."

Rebecca smiles, satisfied with my answer. "Yeah, we do. Hugh is the responsible one. Helpful and kind, as you know. Gabe can be funny, but he's an instigator, and, well, Camille has her moods. Mother tries to be levelheaded and above the noise, but she has her feelings, too. Much more than what you see at first glance."

"And you?"

She laughs as we turn down another hallway. "Me? I like to have fun. Keep it simple, keep things easy. Work hard, play hard. But we all get along. Much more than a normal family, I think."

"Normal?"

She glances at me, looks away. "Yeah, you know, a family that doesn't have a weird old house and dead sister."

Dead sister?

I say nothing. She doesn't know I don't know.

I didn't even know about *her*, the living sister, let alone a dead one. Why is Hugh keeping his family a secret? What else is he hiding from me? *About as much as you're hiding from him*, a little voice inside me chirps. I squash it immediately.

Rebecca's words hang in the air, untouched, until I think of something to say.

"What happened to your sister?"

Rebecca sighs. "That's a story I can't share. Mother or Hugh would have to be the one to tell you," she says, opening a door. "I'm merely the middleman." The door leads into a small room with dark wood walls. All around, dusty coats and scarves hang from iron hooks.

"Here, Iris, for you." Rebecca shakes out a puffy white coat. A million dust motes erupt in the air.

I slip it on. It smells faintly of mothballs. "Mine's by the front door. I can go get—"

"Iris," Rebecca cuts me off, scrunches her pretty face. "That's on the other side of the house. Just wear this. It's cold outside. And it's white. You know, to match the snow."

Rebecca shrugs on a knee-length camel coat, buttons it closed from bottom to top. Ellory grabs a dusty black peacoat off a hook. It's surprisingly fitting with her outfit—she's recently been wearing nothing but oversize tees and tunics over sweats or leggings, all in morose colors of beige and gray and black.

Rebecca opens the door, leads us outside. A snow-tinged pathway curves ahead.

Ellory shivers, wraps her arm in mine. "Mom, why are we out here? We didn't even have coffee yet."

"I'm not sure," I say, "but I think we're about to find out."

My heart races as Rebecca leads us farther around the back of the house, which falls straight down a cliff's edge to the languid river below. She stops, pushes on a rusty gate. It creaks open and soon we're stepping into a winter garden.

Tucked away behind the house like a secret, it's so beautiful

I gasp. Instead of blossoms blooming in spring, paper lanterns glow dimly in the morning light. A carved stone fountain gurgles, the water quiet as it trickles through ice. The morning sun glows softly through topiaries and leafless willows. The trees are tall, with long, drooping arms, and the space feels whimsical, like stepping into a woodland fairy's lair.

Ellory's arm tenses around mine. I glance over to see Birdie, Gabe, and Camille standing across from us on the other side of a stone patio. Rebecca joins them as Hugh rises from a bench.

"No," Ellory whispers. "Please say this isn't happening."

Everyone's eyes are on me. Nervous, I start swaying back and forth. Ellory grips my arm, stops me. Hugh flashes a dazzling smile. We couldn't be more mismatched—me, dressed in faded black jeans and a torn sweater. And him—wearing a deep blue suit, tweed waistcoat, and crisp white shirt.

His smile spreads, blue eyes sparkling in the morning light. "Iris, you look beautiful." A white cloud puffs through his lips.

My teeth chatter. I shiver from the cold, but I'm also completely, utterly frozen. Is this really happening? I'm shocked, stunned. I've forgotten how to speak. Hugh walks over, takes my cold hand in his, clasps it tight.

He guides me closer to his family near the fountain. Ellory doesn't follow. Slowly, she backs away, disappearing into a line of tall trees. I motion for her to come be with me, to stand with me. But she doesn't move. Hugh clears his throat. A solitary crow caws.

"Iris Blodgett," Hugh begins, too loud, and I know it's a sign he's nervous, too.

My face breaks into a smile. I can feel my heart racing, warmth spreading through me, and for once, I'm no longer cold. I search his eyes as he kneels on the snow-dusted stones, peering up at me as excitement dances across his handsome face.

"Iris," he begins again. "We've only known each other a short time, but in that time, I've grown to love you. Every time I look at you, I can't help but want to call you my wife. You're such a caring person, and you're always there for me. You know my quirks and horrible eating habits and you love me anyway. And I know I can never replace Jack. But with time, hopefully—maybe—someday Ellory can accept me as a father figure, a stable presence. Someone who will *always* be there, to guide her and protect her. I love you, Iris. Would you do me the—" he pauses, voice catching, and he grips my hand tighter "—the honor of marrying me?"

I stare at him for a heartbeat, and in that heartbeat, a thousand thoughts collide. If I say yes, I'll get to wake up beside Hugh every day. We'd build a new life together, one filled with kindness and love and trust. I know Ellory feels we're moving too fast, but I have to admit, I think a lot about our little family—Ellory, me, and Jack. Having a family, having those few special people to share your life with, all the ups and downs, the good and the bad, makes our existence, our one tiny blip on earth, matter. And I want that chance again. I want a family again.

Ellory doesn't have to cut Jack from her heart to make a little room for Hugh. With time, hopefully they can both fit there together, as they fit for me.

But if I agree to marry him, Birdie will become my mother-in-law. I'll inherit an entire family along with a husband. A brother. A sister. I won't just be marrying Hugh. I'll be marrying them all.

But they can't be that bad.

Can they?

Suddenly, Jack's face appears inside my head. He's sitting at the kitchen table, like he always did, drinking coffee, reading the news on his phone. He glances up at me and smiles, almost imperceptibly, and whispers, *"Yes."*

I try to relax my smiling face and repeat the word through my lips. "Yes."

Hugh presses his lips together as he finds my finger, slips on an engagement ring. I glance down, see a flash of red. Shadows fall across the courtyard, the sun dipping behind a patch of clouds, just as Hugh stands and sweeps me in his arms for a kiss, then whispers "I love you" in my ear.

Fast as a bullet, we are engaged.

Hugh is my fiancé. And I am his.

I search for Ellory as Hugh spins me around. I keep looking, scanning over his shoulder, around the stone statues, behind the tall boxwoods. But I can't find her.

Rebecca erupts in cheers. Birdie claps, cane balanced in the crook of her elbow. Camille purses her lips, breaking out a bittersweet smile when our eyes connect. I turn to Gabe. A withering look passes over his somber face.

"I can't believe it," Hugh says. "We're going to get married!"

I nod absently, keep searching for Ellory.

Finally, I see her. She stands in the shadows, back nestled in a moss-covered corner. I run to her, open my arms for a hug. Instead, she goes rigid, glaring at me like I'm poison. I flinch, the shock of her anger stinging me.

"Ellory," I say, heartbroken. "Ellory—"

"Stop!" she screams as tears fall down her face.

"I love you—nothing is going to change that, not even being engaged. You have nothing to worry about. I'll never forget your father. I'll always love Jack. But I love Hugh, too. *Please, Ellory*," I say and stop myself when my voice breaks.

Jack's been gone three years. I'm too young to be alone and widowed forever. I've found someone. I've found someone *amazing*. Someone I trust. Someone whose kisses make me feel alive again. I can't be broken forever. Slowly, with Hugh, I hope to glue back the pieces.

But Ellory doesn't give me the chance. Instead, she says nothing. She doesn't even look at me as she spins around, fleeing the courtyard in a flurry of painful cries.

9

Rushing into the house after Ellory, I climb the stairs to her room, gently knock on her door. I call her name. I plead. I beg. She ignores me, choosing instead to make a call: *"Please get me out of here. I can't stay here anymore, I can't..."*

I knock one more time.

"I'm not coming out!" she cries.

Hugh's voice curls up to me from downstairs, asking if I'm okay. Reluctant, I abandon my spot outside her door, promising myself I'll return in an hour. She just needs time. Time to think, to call her friends, have the privacy and freedom to talk to her boyfriend. I owe her that much. It's the least I can do after I've flipped her entire world upside down.

I sulk downstairs. Following the sounds of banging mallets laced between radio commercials, I find Gabe and Rebecca hard at work in the conservatory, Hugh working alongside them. Already he's changed out of his tailored suit and into work clothes. Back to business as usual, as if his marriage proposal had never happened.

I step through crooked French doors. The room ahead is enormous, with high ceilings and puddles of dirty water hop-scotched across a wavy stone floor. The conservatory is over-grown with vines coming in through broken windows and glass shards litter the floor. Some windows have been boarded up with plywood to keep the elements out, but it's still freezing.

Gabe slams a sledgehammer into an old plaster wall. The house groans, voicing its displeasure.

Hugh sees me, his blue eyes igniting in the sunlight.

"Iris," he says, walking over to me. He wraps me in his arms and lifts me to where my feet dangle a little off the floor. Even though I'm a few—thirty—pounds overweight, he still man-ages to lift me as if I'm light as a feather.

"How's Ellory? Did you talk with her?" he asks, dark brows creasing with concern.

I look down at my dirty sneakers, dejected. He finds the an-swer in my sullen expression.

"I'm sorry," he says. "I know she'll come around. I can't imagine what she's going through."

When I don't reply, he takes my hand, squeezes it gently. "Don't get lost in your head," he says softly. "You can over-think things, drive yourself nuts. Don't mistake the forest for the trees."

A flash of a nightmare chills me. For a moment, I see them, staring. Three dark figures, backs against the woods. The sky dark. The moon overhead. A pearlized glow floats through the cold air. Suddenly, terror fills me.

I look up at him. "What?"

"I was just saying I bet it gets pretty lonely up there." Gently, Hugh swipes a fingertip down my temple, as if trying to sense what's inside my mind. "Are you okay? Talk to me. We can fix things together. Don't shut me out. I'm not going anywhere." He lifts my hand, marvels at my new engagement ring.

The terror and panic I felt moments ago dissipate when I realize I've hardly even glanced at the object now affixed to my finger. I look at my new ring. A large ruby rests in the center, sides flanked by oval-shaped diamonds. The clouds part, and I raise my hand to sunlight shining through a window. The light catches the stone, throwing rainbows of red and green and orange through the room.

It's stunning.

I turn back to see Hugh smiling.

I don't want my problems to be a burden. But I have to be open with him. I want to always be honest in this relationship. Well, almost always. Our relationship is still too new to share *every* secret. Some secrets can be so heavy, they tend to crush whoever you tell. My secrets are so heavy Hugh would be pulverized.

A *crash* as an entire wall falls to the ground, breaking apart into a million pieces.

"What's he doing?" I ask, pointing at Gabe.

"Demolition. We have to tear this whole thing down." Hugh waves a hand in the air. "All of this will be gone. I've drafted some blueprints adding a new addition instead. I can't wait to show you."

Rebecca raises the volume on an old radio, singing along with the music until her voice goes ragged. She wipes sweat from her forehead, though my teeth are chattering. Gabe reaches over to change the station, and Rebecca swats his hand away.

I can't help but grin when I catch a peek into what life could look like with siblings. Though they tease and joke, there's still an undercurrent of affection, a certain type of bond I'll never truly possess. "You're lucky to have a brother and sister who can help you," I tell Hugh. "It's something I never had."

The late-morning sun disappears behind a cloud, dropping the large, open room into shadows. Hugh clicks on a construction lamp, casting the space in a dance of shadows and light.

"I have a fiancée who can help, too." He grins down at me,

takes my hand in his, kisses the top. "Want to help? It relieves stress. Might get your mind off some things."

He drops my hand, stabs a crowbar into the wall, yanks it out. Bricks crumble at our feet. I step away, glance at the yawning gash in the wall. Hugh passes me the crowbar. I look at it, unsure what to punch it in.

Hugh shouts over the radio. "Hey, we should all go out tonight. Celebrate a little. What do you think?"

Rebecca lowers the volume, pushes safety goggles up her forehead. "Oh, hell yeah. Maybe Kara will come, too. I need to try to convince her to let me move back in. Plus, it'd be nice to get out."

"You were just out yesterday," Gabe laments. "While I've been trapped in here."

Rebecca laughs. "Yeah, but you seemed pretty happy when I took Camille out with me." Gabe barks a laugh, slams a sledgehammer into the floor.

I lift a hand, draw a heart in a foggy glass window. The windowpane shudders beneath my fingertip. For some reason, I get the feeling the house is annoyed by my touch.

"Okay, I know the perfect place," Hugh suggests. "Let's work until four, then stop to shower and get ready." We all agree.

I step away from the noise to give Sloane a call. She answers, out of breath. "Hotté Latte, where we make your mocha dreams come true."

"Please say you're answering every call like that."

Sloane laughs. "No, I saw it was you. What's up?"

"Do you have any plans tonight after closing? Want to come out for dinner?"

She laughs again. "Actually, I have a big date planned with Philip."

My mouth falls open. Sloane always tells me when she's found a new guy on one of her infamous dating apps. She was shocked when I met Hugh organically in the café and joked I'd traveled back in time before the internet to meet him.

"Philip? Who's he?"

"My new cat. So yeah, I guess you can say I'm free tonight. What's the occasion?"

"No occasion…" I lie, not wanting to break the news of our engagement over the phone. I want to see the surprise on her face when I tell her the good news in person. Sloane knows I'm a sucker for love stories. After Jack died, we never could've guessed I'd have my own again one day.

In the background, the espresso machine churns.

"How's it going over there? You know…with *the family*." I imagine her eyebrow rising.

"It's a lot of change," I admit. "Hey, why don't you ask Ainsley if she wants to come? She seems to be going through a hard time."

"True, she can use a night out."

Sloane waves Ainsley over, invites her to come.

"Girls' night?" Ainsley asks in the background.

"Something like that," Sloane says. "Hey, Iris, I'm back. Ainsley's in. We'll see you later."

I tell Sloane I'll text her the details and hang up, about to go upstairs to knock on Ellory's door again, when an agonizing scream rips through the house. I rush back into the conservatory. Hugh kneels on the ground, Rebecca and Gabe standing over him. Blood drips from his hand, down his forearm, soaking through his sweater.

Gabe lifts him off the floor, steers him through hallways, into the nearest bathroom. I turn on the hot water as Rebecca runs to get bandages.

"You're going to be fine." I hold his torn-open finger under the water.

"Goddamn saws," he cries, wincing with pain.

Rebecca slingshots into the bathroom with a box of cotton wrap and an old tube of antibiotic ointment.

"I—I don't know how it happened," Hugh says as we cluster around him. "I was careful."

"It happens," Gabe says. "Be glad you didn't lose a finger."

Hugh steadies his breath, leans against the wall. "It's okay. The pain is fading."

"We should stay in tonight," Gabe says. "You should take it easy."

"No—" Hugh breathes out. "I'll be fine. We're going out. I want to celebrate with my fiancée." He looks up at me. Sweat gathers on his forehead and blood is smeared across his cheek, but his lips still bend into a smile.

For the rest of the day, I continue to unpack, sporadically stopping to knock on Ellory's locked bedroom door. Hugh rests in the living room, bandaged finger on ice, while Camille sits across from him, reading something on her phone.

Birdie drifts around the kitchen, as Gabe and Rebecca continue the demolition. When the grandfather clock chimes four times, we get ready to leave, as Hugh suggested.

A whoosh of strong scents hits my nose. I peer into the hall-way, see where the smell is coming from. Ellory has cracked open her bedroom door. I whisper her name, and she emerges from the shadows. The room has a perpetual musty odor, and she's tried in vain to cover it with floral perfume. Now it's just a toxic mix of fungus and peonies.

"Can I come in?" I pinch the door open. She roots her foot behind it.

Ellory looks at me, bottom lip quivering. "You can't get married," she chokes out. "You're still married to Dad. You'll *always* be married to Dad."

I clench my teeth. Ellory's words sting like a thousand bees. Maybe she's right. Maybe three years isn't long enough. Maybe I'm betraying Jack—betraying *her*. No…no, I'm not. I can't be. How can falling in love be a betrayal?

"Ellory, no one can replace your dad. But please, try to understand—"

"I can't. I won't." She crosses her arms.

I study her face in the dim hallway light: her translucent ivory skin. A nose that comes to a fine, little point. Dark amber hair so multifaceted it changes color, like a mood ring. I don't know what I'll do when the time comes that I can't see her beautiful face every day.

"Please. I can't leave you like this." Tears fill my eyes. I blink them away.

"Bye, Mom. Congratulations," she says, closing the door.

"Bye, Ellory," I whisper, though I know she can't hear. A sick feeling fills my stomach. Sometimes, I can't help but think that I deserve all the bad things that have happened to me. It's payback. A balancing of scales.

An eye for an eye.

We pile into Hugh's SUV. Birdie says she'll stay home, promising to watch Ellory—if she ever escapes her bedroom. Gabe, Camille, and Rebecca squish into the back seat. Camille insists Rebecca sit in the middle between her and Gabe. Gabe rolls his eyes as Hugh circles the driveway, passing through the dark, misty woods.

In the side mirror, I watch the house as it fades away, the arched windows glowing white in the moonlight like a monster with curling fangs.

10

The restaurant is crowded and dark and swelling with energy. Sitting at our corner table, I feel my mouth begin to water as I inhale the scents drifting in the air—smoked hickory wood, grilled steaks, and something sweet, like honey.

I'd been hoping Sloane would already be here when we arrive, but she comes fashionably late, ordering her usual dry martini. Hugh sits next to me, taking my hand beneath the table as he leans in to whisper, "You look beautiful."

I can't help but grin, and though he compliments me often, his words make my stomach flip. He catches me smiling and slowly lets his eyes trail down my neck and shoulders, before pulling them back up, and in the warm light of the restaurant, his bright blue eyes appear dark, shiny and black like volcanic glass.

"So, how'd you guys meet?" Rebecca singsongs down the long table, a huge smile spread across her face. She looks luminous, her dark hair shining in a low ponytail, gray pearl earrings dangling from silver wires.

Hugh and I exchange a glance and he, to my relief, tells the table the story: how we met at Sloane's café after he bumped into me, spilled coffee all over us. After asking if I had a spare napkin, he suggested taking me out to dinner as an apology. I accepted, and before we knew it, two months had zoomed by.

Rebecca laughs, jabs an elbow into Gabe's arm. He looks unamused, his legs crossed and rested up against the rim of the table. Camille sits beside him, dressed all in black, shiny bronze hair glowing in the golden light of the chandelier overhead.

I glance around the table. The tension between Camille and Gabe feels ripe. Gabe shifts uncomfortably in his seat next to her. Camille can't even look him in the eye. I wonder what has turned their marriage sour.

Sloane orders another martini. "Look who's finally here." She nods her head toward the front door.

Ainsley struts in, weaving around the tables, wearing a bright red dress. Gabe turns and stares. Camille smacks him on the back of his head.

"Hi, Ainsley." I stand, pull her into a hug. "Thanks for coming."

"Thanks for inviting me." Ainsley detaches from me, pulls out the chair on the other side of Sloane. "Hello, hello, every-one. I'm Ainsley—and I am *so* happy."

"What happened to you?" Sloane asks, eyeing her up and down. "You're too cheery. What's wrong?"

Ainsley laughs. "My divorce is finalized. I'm officially sin-gle." She shimmies her shoulders in excitement.

Hugh glances at Gabe and their eyes harden. Tension in-stantly floods Hugh's face. He grinds his teeth, the muscles in his jaw flexing. They both fall silent. The mood shifts.

"Well, congratulations. Divorce sounds *amazing*," Camille leans over to loudly say before sitting back in her chair and emptying her glass of rosé.

Sloane turns to me. "You look nice tonight." I glance down,

forgetting what I even put on. I chose a pale pink shirt, cut loose and open at the top, showing my shoulders, and combed my short hair into a perfect part down the center.

"So how's Ellory?" Concern blooms across Sloane's face.

"Ellory...is fine. Not doing so well after the news." Under the table, I spin my ring around my finger, count the stones.

Sloane freezes, martini hovering midair. "Oh, God, you're pregnant."

"What? No." I laugh and my stomach flutters, knowing what I have to do. It's now or never.

Nervous, I turn toward the rest of the table and steal a deep breath. Public speaking, even in front of friends and family, is something I've never been good at. Warmth spreads through me, and I know my cheeks are probably glowing hot pink with apprehension.

"Can I please have everyone's attention?" Faces flip toward me. "Thank you all for coming out tonight to celebrate our engagement."

I can feel Sloane's stare on me, but she claps along with everyone else, except Ainsley. Freshly divorced and thrilled about it, Ainsley only raises a brow, no doubt confused as to why two people would do such a thing.

Next to me, Hugh raises his glass. The table quiets. "I'd like to propose a toast to my beautiful fiancée and thank everyone for being here. I'm also looking forward to seeing you all at our wedding, because, big surprise, you're all invited."

Everyone toasts and offers congratulations. I sip my glass of wine as Hugh gently swipes a finger over my blood-flushed cheeks before he leans in, kisses my neck.

Sloane nudges me, shocked. "You're engaged? Oh, my God, Iris—congratulations." She pulls me into a tight hug. "This is amazing. I'm so happy for you. You deserve only good, positive things. It's all I ever wanted for you, all these years."

"Thanks, Sloane. I'm excited. I'm still really surprised this is all happening."

"How'd Ellory take the news?"

Her name floats in the air for a moment. "Well—it was a surprise. I didn't have a chance to talk to her before or after… so she kind of shut me out. But Hugh's a great guy. She just has to get to know him better, and I think it'll all be fine." I laugh nervously.

"I hope so," Sloane whispers darkly. I look at her worried face. "If Ellory doesn't like him—if she rejects him—who knows what she'll do. She could do what she did the last time you fought."

I drain my white wine, slide the glass on the table, say nothing.

She won't. Ellory won't. She's older now, more mature. I trust her.

The food comes. Hugh ordered pasta, as always, with chicken and broccoli. His palate is plain and he likes things simple, while I'm a little more daring. I ordered bacon-wrapped filet mignon, rare, and it sits on a bed of mashed potatoes reddened by beet juice.

Rebecca leans forward, nods my way. "Iris, we ordered the same thing," she says and tilts her dinner plate at me. "Looks like a murder scene, though, right?" She laughs.

Sloane sits back in her chair, looks at me knowingly. "It's about Jack, isn't it? Ellory probably thinks it's too soon. She probably thinks by marrying Hugh, you've already forgotten him."

Of course Sloane's right. But I don't want to cry forever, even though I know I could. I want to feel light again, not be filled with guilt or dread or sadness. Wouldn't Jack want that? I would've wanted that for him. I would've wanted him to be happy.

Sloane watches my expression shift. I can't think about this anymore. I don't want to be upset, not in front of all these people, people I just met. I inhale a deep breath, offer Sloane a smile.

All that matters is I love Hugh, no matter what else festers in my heart.

"Jack?" Camille asks. She's been eavesdropping, but I don't mind. I want her to feel included, especially since her husband has built an invisible blockade between them. "Who's Jack?"

"Iris's late husband," Sloane answers.

I sigh, sip my wine. The last thing I wanted during my engagement party was discussion of my husband.

"*Late* husband?" Rebecca asks. "Hugh never mentioned that."

"No, I wouldn't." Hugh looks at his sister. "It's not for me to do so."

"What happened to him?" Gabe asks. Suddenly interested, he leans forward, crosses his arms on the table.

I look at Sloane. Immediately, she picks up on my discomfort. "He passed away a few years ago," she answers simply, taking my hand beneath the table. "But we're not here to talk about that—"

"Oh, I'm so sorry," Camille says, twirling a forkful of linguine. "That's sad."

Gabe snorts. "You have such a way with words, darling."

"Oh, shut up, *darling*," Camille snarls.

A waiter suddenly manifests behind me. "Can I get anyone anything else?"

Everyone lifts an empty glass.

The waiter points at Rebecca. "Can I see your ID, please?"

"Oh, I showed the other waiter my ID."

He looks unamused. "I have to ask everyone who looks under the age of forty."

Ainsley looks down, dejected. Sloane catches her expression, barks out a laugh.

Rebecca huffs, passes me her ID across the table to hand to

the waiter. He takes it, but it slips from his hand. I bend to grab it off the floor and steal a quick peek, not surprised at all to see Rebecca managing to look amazing even in a tiny square photo.

While I look like a mottled potato in my picture, Rebecca's skin is smooth and glowing, her hair dyed a bright burning red, the color of a thumb held up to the sun. As I hand the ID back, I catch the name on her driver's license.

Rebecca Haplehorn.

Haplehorn—not Smoll, Hugh's surname. Maybe she's been married before. If she wasn't, wouldn't her name still be Smoll? But she's so young, many years younger than Hugh, closer to twenty when Hugh and Gabe are nearing forty.

Passing Rebecca's ID back to her, I chide myself. I married Jack when I was barely eighteen… *Ellory's age*, I realize with a jolt. Of course Rebecca could've been married before. She could've been married and divorced twice over, for all I know. I just met her yesterday. God, I only learned of her existence yesterday.

"So, Iris…" I look over, see Gabe staring at me intensely from down the table. "Now that you're part of the family, I think there's something you should know."

Hugh elbows him in the arm to try to get him to stop, but Gabe waves him off. The bustling restaurant reaches a lull of silence.

Gabe's deep voice booms in the small space. "Did Hugh tell you about the family curse?"

Sloane chokes on her martini.

I pat her on the back and my fingers tingle with the rush of too much wine. I'm already starting on my third glass, more than I've had to drink in years. I'm not used to it.

"It's true," Rebecca says. "Our family's cursed."

"You can't be serious," I say.

"As a heart attack," Gabe says, eyes trained on me.

Camille bats him on the shoulder. "What are you doing?"

"What?"

"Are you forgetting this is your brother's engagement dinner? Why would you bring that up? What's the matter with you?"

Gabe's face goes red. He turns toward Camille, obviously disliking being lectured in front of people. "Maybe, for once, you—"

"Hey, assholes," Rebecca shouts. The table quiets. "We're here to celebrate, so can you try to not air out all your marital difficulties?"

Gabe and Camille stop arguing. Hugh pats his lips with a napkin. Sloane applies plum-colored lipstick using the back of a knife as a mirror. I sit back in my chair, mortified.

"Well," Ainsley says sharply, standing from the table. "As of today, I am officially a very rich divorcée. Rich divorcées don't do curses."

She pulls a bright red wallet out of her purse, matched perfectly to her clingy scarlet dress. Hugh whips his gaze away as if looking at her will cast a spell on him. But Gabe keeps his eyes locked on her, jaw clenched. Camille watches her husband, sure to memorize every second he spends looking at another woman.

"Allow me." Ainsley drops a silver credit card on the table. "Sloane, take it, use it, give it back to me tomorrow at work, okay?"

Sloane nods. Hugh's protests to pay go unheard.

Ainsley walks around the table gifting everyone quick, sideways hugs. When she gets to Hugh, his spine stiffens. Ainsley steps away from him, and I watch them, as the table hums with conversation and laughter all around me, and for a moment it's the three of us—me, Hugh, and Ainsley—frozen in slow motion amid the chaos of the room.

Their eyes meet for the briefest of seconds before Ainsley twists herself away. Hugh's jaw unclenches. The moment passes.

"I—I'm going to check out The Velvet Lion. It's the new nightclub across town," Ainsley announces. "Anyone want to join me?" Everyone shakes their heads. "Okay, congrats again, Iris…I think." She walks off.

"Family curse?" Sloane whispers, twirling her spiky auburn hair. "Hopefully, Gabe is the funny sibling?"

I laugh, shake my head. Across the room is a window. I make the mistake of glancing outside.

One.

Two.

Three.

They're in the parking lot, standing shoulder to shoulder. The three dark figures are nothing but faceless shadows beneath the tall lantern lights, but still, I know it's them. They're here. They've found me.

Nightmares have a habit of doing that. They chase you, strangle you, make it so you can't breathe, can't think. Suffocate you. They turn into your reality, and no matter how many times you dream of them, still, you can't escape.

I blink, shake my head clear, look back. The three dark figures have disappeared.

"Are you okay, Iris?" Sloane asks. She places her hand on my knee beneath the table, shakes me out of my trance. "Iris?"

"Yeah, yeah, I'm fine."

She looks worried but still turns back to Rebecca.

I glance at Hugh. He seems to be deep in thought, too. I wonder if he has his own nightmares. So far I've managed to keep mine a secret. Has Hugh done the same? I only hope his aren't as dark as mine. As brutal. As unnerving. We can't both be hiding something.

Can we?

I glance around the table, let my eyes fall back to the window, to the crowded parking lot. Even if Gabe wasn't joking about the family being cursed, it doesn't matter. I've already been cursed, long before I met them.

11

Everyone's a little drunk by the time we get home. Hugh, Gabe, and Rebecca scatter through the house like centipedes. I attempt to find the long path to the kitchen to get a glass of water when movement catches my eye.

In the courtyard, a brown dog wanders in the cold. I unlatch the doors and step outside. In the dim moonlight, the dead ground sparkles with dew frost. Without the decorations and white paper lanterns paired with the shock of Hugh proposing, I realize the courtyard isn't a courtyard at all, but a garden swelling with the bones of dead plants and bushes that have long grown out of their cut decorative shapes.

I call for the dog, hold out my palm for it to sniff. It stops, looks up at me, drops something out of its mouth. I move closer. The dog wavers, steps back, but doesn't run. I look at the ground, see it's dropped a small, curved bone.

"Come here, it's okay," I say in a soft voice. "I'm not going to hurt you."

The dog has an adorable little face, with soft pink gums that droop below its teeth. It wears a collar around its neck, and I'm trying to read it when the door opens behind me. Startled, the dog cowers and runs away, disappearing behind a stone wall.

Camille closes the door, tiptoes into the garden. Seeing the dirty bone by my feet, she grimaces.

"Do you know whose dog that was?"

"No," Camille says, her body swaying. "The only dog I know was Birdie's. She used to have a little white one."

"Oh, must've been a neighbor's dog." I look around to see if there are any lights from neighbors living nearby, but only darkness surrounds us.

"It's funny…" Camille begins. She lets out a breathy laugh. "They used to call this the bone garden." I raise an eyebrow. Camille laughs again. "I think this is where all the family pets are buried. I guess the little white dog is here, somewhere." Her dark eyes scan the ground.

"I don't see headstones or anything," I say.

She doesn't reply. Instead, worry pains her expression. She looks as if she's about to admit something horrible.

"Are you okay, Camille?"

She exhales. "Listen, I know I don't know you very well—but can I talk to you? It's about Gabe."

"Of course you can."

Camille shivers inside her white fur coat, knots her arms together. "Y-you know," she begins, words slurring together, "in the spring, about six years ago, Gabe proposed to me. Right here, actually. Right where Hugh proposed to you."

I try to imagine how the garden might look in spring: dollops of cool water dribbling from the marble fountain, bulging English roses swaying in tumbling river winds, ivy growing in rings around a stone archway.

I glance up to see her sobbing. "It's okay. I'm here."

"I'm sorry." She dries her eyes with the back of a hand. "It's just, being here, in this house. It brings back memories, you know?"

I rub her arm. "I understand."

"I—I don't know what happened between us," Camille says. "Things were going okay but—he has a temper. You'd never guess from looking at him."

I picture Gabe in my head: collared shirt layered under a sweater, coiffed brown hair, round tortoise glasses. He has the air of a bookish transplant from London. I can imagine him wearing a bow tie and writing in leather-bound journals. Between his mannerisms and smaller stature, he seems completely harmless—not a man with anger issues.

"No, I had no idea," I admit, then remind myself, how could I? I only just learned of his existence yesterday.

Camille sniffs. "I have to go to bed soon before I get hungover, but I wanted—*needed*—to tell someone. In case something happened to me. I wanted someone else to know."

"Know what?" A chill comes over me. The wine I had at dinner no longer warms my blood.

She gulps. "I'm afraid of him. He can't control the—*outbursts*. I can't keep doing this. I can't let him take it out on me anymore. I deserve better."

"I know you do."

"I want a career—I want to *act*." She looks up at the stars. "How can I do that with him? I can't."

As she sobs, I gently squeeze her shoulder. She flinches.

"Ah," Camille cries out.

I pull my hand away. "I'm sorry. Did I hurt you?"

She sniffles. "No—not you. It's my fault. I provoke him…" She trails off, knits her hands together.

"No one should be hurt in a relationship," I say and mean it. I've been lucky so far in my life to never have been in an abusive relationship. But then, I'd only ever been with Jack until I met Hugh.

"Why don't we go inside?" Hesitant, I place a hand on her arm, try to lead her back to the house. "We can go to sleep. You don't have to tell me this tonight. We can talk tomorrow. We can figure out what to do." I edge closer to the door, to a warm bed, to Hugh.

"No." Camille roots herself to the ground. "I'm used to it. It's nothing new. I've called the police countless times. They've only arrested him once."

"Gabe's been arrested?"

Camille nods. "I'm asking him for a divorce. Tonight. What do you think?" Her dark eyes widen with hope, awaiting my answer.

"I—uh," I stammer, not knowing what to say. "Tonight?" Camille nods fervently. "I think if he's hurting you, you should of course get away from him...but maybe you should wait until the morning, when—"

"Thank you." Camille exhales in relief. "Thank you for listening." She leans in to kiss my cheek, her breath heavy with alcohol. We turn to walk back inside.

"Iris..." she calls out to me. "Has Hugh told you about Paige?"

I turn around, almost trip. "Who's Paige?" A million questions bolt into my head. Strong gusts of wind blow in from the river, bringing the bitter January cold. I shiver.

Camille looks down at the ground. "You need to ask him. And *please* don't tell anyone what I tol—told you," she slurs. "If Gabe finds out, he'll kill me."

12

I stand in the doorway, watch Hugh as he sleeps. He's left the light on next to him, so I can see his bare chest rise and fall. A jagged scar runs along his rib cage from a surgery he had as a teenager, he once told me. Quietly, I unzip my jeans, pull off my shirt, slip on my pajamas. When I turn, his eyes are open.

Wine always loosens my inhibitions, so I peel off the pajama top I just put on, watch as his eyes widen. I approach him from the side of the bed, lay myself directly on top of him, and he sighs, feeling my skin on his, our bodies exchanging heat.

He begins to kiss my shoulder when the words tumble out. "Who's Paige?"

I stay silent, awaiting an answer.

Hugh's body tenses beneath me, and he guides me off. I fall onto the mattress beside him, tug the blankets up to cover myself. Suddenly, I feel exposed.

He sits up in bed, shakes his head. "I'm sorry. I should've told you. I should've told you a lot of things before you came here." Leaning over, he curls a short strand of hair behind my ear. "But I was afraid of scaring you away," he confesses with an anxious laugh. "I mean, would you still have come here, knowing what you know now?"

"What do you mean?"

"I mean, between meeting my family—I know Gabe can be an asshole sometimes—and Ellory upset over our engagement." Hugh lifts his head, blue eyes dark in the soft light. "I never wanted to hurt her. But maybe you would've had a different answer if you knew how she'd react…"

My head pounds. He's avoiding my question. But why? "Hugh, is there something you want to tell me? Something about Paige?"

A bitter expression passes over his face. "Okay, why don't you ask, and I'll answer. Anything." He turns to look at me. "Anything at all. I want this to work—want *us* to work. I promise I'll do my best to answer."

I nod. "Okay. Tell me who Paige is."

Hugh lets out a heavy sigh, falls back onto his pillow. "You mean…who Paige *was*."

My back goes straight. I curl the blanket up to my chin.

He clears his throat. "It was…about twenty years ago. Her name was Paige. She was my little sister and she died."

So this was the *dead sister* Rebecca had mentioned while leading me and Ellory out to the garden before Hugh proposed. Her name was Paige.

Pausing, I wait for him to continue. He doesn't.

I knit my eyebrows together, stand from the bed. "That's it? That's all you have to say about her?" I throw my pajamas back on.

He massages his forehead. "I was young. I was away at college. The whole thing was strange. There was never a funeral."

"Never?"

"No. But we had one for Father. He died a few years later."

I study him, feeling slightly guilty for resurrecting all these ancient family memories. Especially since he hardly knows anything about me. It's a fact I try not to bring attention to. Other than that I was born in Ohio and came to Hollow Falls when I was sixteen, Hugh doesn't know much about my past.

"Okay," I say, wanting to start over. I climb back into bed. "Tell me about Gabe and Camille. Why are they here? All I know is they're having issues with their marriage."

Hugh inhales. "Well, they've fallen on hard times." Taking my hand, he gently traces the lines with a fingertip. "He has a bad heart condition he's recently learned about and had surgery for it last year. Gabe was a freelance photographer. He didn't have insurance."

"Oh, Hugh."

"Every penny they had went to hospital bills. He and Camille were saving to move out of their townhome and buy a house. I'm pretty sure all of it is gone."

I bite my lip, think about what Camille said in the garden. She doesn't want to divorce Gabe because he's ill. She wants to divorce him because he's an abusive asshole. I wish I'd asked Camille to come sleep in our bedroom tonight. We could've slept on the floor. Anything to keep her away from him.

"Can I ask you about Jack?" Hugh says.

The sudden mention of his name sounds like a thunderclap. "What about him?"

"Do the police have any idea who killed him? Any leads? Anything at all?"

I say nothing. After a moment, I force a smile, attempting to lighten the conversation. With a jolt, I realize this is our first night together as fiancés, and I want to enjoy the slight buzz I still have from dinner.

"Hey, I thought I was the one who was asking the questions here," I tease.

Hugh doesn't smile back. Instead, he holds my hand tight, eyes intense as he studies me.

"What would you do if you found the man who killed your husband?"

"What?"

"Would you kill him yourself?"

"Hugh—no, of course not." His grip around my hand loosens. "I'd want him arrested," I say. "I'd want him to go to prison—for life."

For a heartbeat, a flash of darkness passes in Hugh's eyes, but he catches it, offers a faint smile instead.

"And what if, after he's arrested, the man who murdered your husband is brought to trial?"

"That'd be great news," I say, buoyant with the proposition. It's a dream I've had for years. That one day, I'd be able to watch on TV as they marched him up the courthouse steps.

"And what if during the trial, something happens and it's declared a mistrial?"

"What?"

"About ten percent of all cases that end up in court result in a mistrial. What if the case is thrown out of court and Jack's killer walks away free? Or what if he's acquitted, say, if there's not enough evidence to convict? What then?"

My face flatlines. I exhale a deep breath. "You're such a buzzkill." I flop back onto my pillow, stare up at the ceiling. "Since we're talking about our families, tell me more about Rebecca. Why's she here?"

Hugh doesn't hesitate to answer my question, allowing the sudden change in topic. His eyes grow soft as he begins talking about his sister. "She just moved back in last week. She's a singer trying to make it in the city. Her girlfriend kicked her out after a fight, and Rebecca can't afford a place to rent without a roommate. Not in this economy."

"She's much younger than you," I note. "Maybe fifteen years?"

He smiles. "Yeah, fourteen."

I smile back. "So, there's you, the oldest, wisest son." He lets out a short laugh. "Then Gabe, the middle child. Rebecca, and...Paige."

"You got it," he confirms. "The four Smoll children."

My heart glows thinking of what it might've been like—having family. Having others around you who love you. People there to celebrate holidays and birthdays. Siblings who have shared memories of growing up together. It's something I never had. Something I always felt I'd missed out on.

"It's wonderful you got the chance to grow up in a big family," I say into my pillowcase. "I envy you."

I reach to click on my phone. Past two in the morning. I yawn. Hugh stretches to turn off the lamp, then coils his arm around my waist. The room falls into darkness.

Soon, the sounds of sleep encroach: Hugh's heavy breathing, the creaking of the old roof, the icy winds rattling drafty window frames.

And then, in a heartbeat, the sounds stop, as if the house demanded silence.

Hugh falls asleep fast and hard, like Ellory. Meanwhile, I toss and turn and try to force my eyelids shut. Just as I click on my phone to check the time, a loud thud sounds overhead.

I snap up.

The thud sounds again, louder, stronger, just above our bed. Sounds swish across the ceiling. Another thud.

I click on a lamp. There's something in the attic.

The sound disappears. I climb out of bed, step into the hallway, listen for noises. Maybe an animal is trapped up there, alone and starving. Maybe a bird.

And then nothing.

I turn back to bed. Voices echo from down the hall. The floor creaks under my feet as I pad closer. The voices magnify as I near the door at the end. Camille and Gabe's room.

"No."

Gabe's voice. Loud and guttural.

Camille screams. A bang travels down the hall.

They fall silent.

Shadows flicker along the floor. Someone's coming.

I rush back to our room, lock the door behind me. Hugh has turned off the light. I feel my way to the bed in the dark. My eyelids grow heavy. I accept sleep when it comes. Unfortunately, the nightmares come with it.

Jack's phone vibrated in his pocket. He looked at me before answering.

"Finally, someone could be calling about the truck," he said, his smile radiant. He'd been trying to sell it for months with no interested buyers.

When he hung up, Jack looked at me again, said, "I have to go. I love you."

Ten minutes passed. Ten more. He should've been home, should've been back. But he never came. I called his phone, hoping he'd answer, just answer, even for a second, and tell me he was okay.

He did.

"Jack…where are you?"

Muted silence. Then the call disconnected. I called back. Again and again. The calls went straight to voicemail. I used the GPS on his phone. It pointed me to his location—a spot on a rural back road.

I feared what I'd find when I got to where the GPS was leading me. But nothing could've prepared me.

His truck was gone. But still, the GPS was adamant his phone was pinned in that exact location. I pulled onto the shoulder, got out, walked along the side of the road in the dirty snow.

And—

With a jolt, I wake. Gasping, I wipe sweat off my forehead. A sob escapes me, and I turn to see if I've woken Hugh.

But I'm alone.

A noise echoes around me. Too close. Eerily close. Something crawls inside the walls. But this time it's not coming from the attic. It's coming from outside.

I get out of bed, open the drapes, peer out to the woods.

The forest ends in a straight line against the overgrown grass, faintly dusted with midnight snow.

Camille's sporty red car is parked next to Hugh's white Tesla in the driveway. The front porch lights are on, glowing the driveway gold.

I close my eyes, listen for the sound again. It's fainter now, distant, steady. Moving to another window, I look down to the ground. Someone's out there.

Though it's dark, I can make out a small figure in the distance near the trees. A flashlight flickers in the night. I listen close, crack open the window.

Then I realize what the sound is.

Digging.

A man is digging, shovel flinging over his shoulder as he rushes to burrow deeper into the earth.

Dread coils inside my chest. The man slams the shovel into the ground, drops the flashlight into the snow-dusted dirt.

I glance to our empty bed.

Looking back out the window, I study the man's movements. He's shorter than Hugh, slighter. The man moves quickly, catlike, lithe. Dark glasses rest on his face.

It's not Hugh.

It's Gabe.

He picks up the shovel again, jumps into the hole, scoops up the earth, flings it over the edge. The hole becomes so deep he vanishes into the ground.

I clamp my hands over my mouth to stop myself from screaming. I was wrong. I was terribly, terribly wrong. It's not a hole.

It's a grave.

4 DAYS BEFORE

TUESDAY, JANUARY 21

13

I stay up the rest of the night waiting for Hugh to return to bed.

Somehow, somewhere in the night, I must've fallen back asleep. A side effect of the wine. Hugh must've come into the bedroom while I was sleeping, as he's here in the morning when I wake, a new bandage wrapped around his saw-cut finger.

Before I get the chance to ask where he's been, the dream about Gabe flickers inside my head. But it wasn't a dream.

Was it?

I toss on an old pink cardigan and leggings and run downstairs, unlock the front door, and step into the biting cold. Tilting my head back, I locate our bedroom window on the third floor on the side of the house facing the woods. Where had I seen Gabe digging? I circle the entire house, find nothing.

I know what I saw. He was there, in the black of night, digging a human-size hole in the earth. It wasn't a dream.

It was real.

Do I tell Hugh what I saw? Especially now, after I circled

the house and found no fresh dirt, no hole, not even a single footprint on the snow-dusted ground?

I walk farther, expand my search. Soon I'm at the edge of the property line, the house looming at the top of the hill, the river roaring down below.

Nothing. No hole, no dirt. Only a misshapen mound of snow from where it has slid off the roof, fallen to the ground. No other sign of activity, let alone a fresh grave.

How…?

And how do I go inside, knowing what I saw, and face Gabe?

I have no choice. I go back inside, determined to avoid him. It's all I can do. Hugh rushes into the foyer, hearing the sound of the door thudding closed behind me.

He takes me in his arms. "You're like ice. Where'd you go?"

I tilt my head back, gaze up at him. "For a walk. Where did *you* go?" His face is a question mark. "Last night, I woke up and you weren't there."

"Last night?" he asks, confused. "Oh…last night. Yeah, my hand was killing me, so I got up to try to find some aspirin or something. Cleaned my bandage, too. It's healing fine, by the way."

"Oh, Hugh…"

"It's fine, really." He backs away. "I mean, where'd you think I went? We were all drinking last night—"

"*You* weren't," I note, feeling oddly betrayed. "All you had was club soda."

"Well, yeah, *I* wasn't. I had to drive, remember? I *never* drink and drive. Iris—is this about the engagement? Do you regret saying yes?" he asks, dejection swelling in his eyes.

"No, of course not."

"You can plan the wedding—anything you want." His face brightens with the glow of anticipation. "And don't worry about money. There's no limit."

Footsteps echo down the hall. Gabe walks into the foyer holding a coffee mug. He glances at us. "Morning."

I look down, avert my eyes. I can't look at him. I can't even bring myself to speak.

"Good morning," Hugh says. "Where's Mother?"

"Kitchen," Gabe says before going upstairs.

We walk down the hall toward the scent of bacon and coffee. Birdie stands behind the island scooping scrambled eggs onto a plate. Rebecca leans over, knife in hand.

Gabe enters the kitchen behind me. He lifts his mug. "Forgot cream," he says and opens the refrigerator.

"Where's Camille?" The words pour out of me before I can stop them. "Has anyone seen her?"

Birdie slides the pan back onto the stove. "Most likely she's still upstairs asleep." She raises her arched brows, and her forehead would crinkle if it could.

I look at Gabe. He tugs his eyes away, pours too much creamer into his coffee.

Birdie notices, slaps his hand away. "That's too much. Your *heart*, Gabe. You have to be more careful. Did you take your medication?"

"Yes, Mother," he groans and walks away.

"Is Camille sleeping?" I ask as he passes.

He shrugs. "Probably. She drank too much. Always does."

"I heard you last night." Everyone stops, turns to face me. I didn't mean to say the thought aloud. Fumbling, I try to explain. "I heard you with her...in your bedroom."

"*I-ris,*" Rebecca singsongs. An embarrassed flush climbs up her throat. "Naughty, naughty."

"I—I mean, I heard you both arguing about something. Is everything okay?"

Gabe freezes. "Um, yes, we had a fight, thank you, Iris. Because Camille and I are...getting a divorce." He throws me a murderous glare.

Birdie covers her mouth in shock.

"Oh, *no*," Rebecca says, heartbroken.

Hugh looks down, shakes his head. "I'm sorry, Gabe. Is there anything I can do to help?"

They ignore Hugh's question and turn to stare at me. Birdie's eyes scream, *How could you?* Rebecca tosses me a look of embarrassment. I feel like a fool.

"Thanks, Iris," Gabe mutters. "I was going to break the news to everyone at dinner tonight, but I guess if *you* want the news now, everyone else is forced to hear it, too. Camille left me last night. Got in her car, probably still half-drunk, and drove off. She could be dead in a car crash right now, and I wouldn't know because she hates me, so, thanks a lot." Gabe slams his mug of coffee on the counter and leaves.

I stare at my feet.

"*Fuck,*" Rebecca whispers. "Mother, are you okay?"

Birdie leans against her cane, looking like she's about to tip over. Rebecca guides her to rest on a stool.

Mother.

Ellory.

"Has anyone seen Ellory?" I ask, kicking myself. I've been so wrapped up in Gabe and Camille and the grave I swore I saw him digging that I forgot to check on Ellory.

I glance at the cuckoo clock on a wall. Almost ten. How could I have slept so late? I run upstairs, knock on Ellory's door. It groans open.

"Ellory?" I call out. "Ellory?"

She doesn't reply. Her bedroom is empty.

My daughter is gone.

192 HOURS LEFT

She didn't think what she'd done was bad. It was necessary. Reckless, maybe. But she had to leave. She had to get out of that house.

He waited for her until late at night, parked at the end of the long drive, curling and waving up the edge of the river cliff like a snake. Something about him seemed off, tense, his lips pressing together to stop himself from speaking. He leaned over, opened the door, let her inside.

She sat down, shoved her too-full bag behind the car seat.

"Ready?"

She nodded. It was all she could do. She closed her eyes as they pulled away, hoping and wishing she'd soon be forgotten about, that this choice and its effects would cease to exist by morning.

They neared the Pennsylvania state line, entering into already unfamiliar territory. She didn't want the car to stop. She wanted to keep driving, to watch the road, to count other cars, to talk to him, however little they felt like talking. Driving meant less of a chance for her mind to wander to thinking about what she'd done.

She'd made a choice. She'd had no option but to make this decision. Everything in her life had been spiraling and twisting, leading her nowhere else *but* this choice.

He sighed deeply next to her. "We'll have to stop soon for gas. Can you keep a lookout for gas stations?"

"Mmm-hmm," she said, her eyes straight toward the black road. There were no streetlamps here, not much of anything, really. She didn't even know what town they were passing through, or what highway they were driving on. Maybe it was better that way.

She wondered when her mother would realize she was gone. Maybe she already had. Maybe it wouldn't be until the morning or the next night or the next. She had a habit, sometimes, of disappearing. Weekends often bled into the weekdays—Monday, Tuesday—before she realized she'd never returned home.

It was his idea, really. Maybe it was both their ideas. Either way, she'd agreed. She just couldn't admit it. She couldn't admit the pain and worry her decision may be inflicting on her mother. She didn't want to admit she was that important to someone, that her actions could cause another person pain. She didn't want to admit to anything.

They pulled off a highway exit, following signs leading to a gas station and diner. He got out and filled up while she stayed in the car, counted the cash they had left. He'd stolen a little from his parents before he left to get her, and she'd saved some over time, a little each birthday and holiday she had before she'd met him, before she'd allowed him to own all her time.

Another bad choice. Or was it? She couldn't decide, couldn't think. It was great at the time, of course. But looking back, what did they really do? She loved her boyfriend. But why couldn't she have worked? Gone to school?

She had so many options, her mother would say. So many

chances. Why did she choose to take none of them? She wouldn't allow herself to blame him for that, too. Being with him was her choice. His choice. Theirs. It was worth it, being with him. Day in, day out, hanging out, staying in.

Wasn't it?

The back-seat door opened behind her, startling her. She turned to see a black backpack drop inside. Someone sat down in the back seat, their weight lowering the car. She stared at this new person, this intruder, this stranger, her mouth set frozen in shock, too shocked to even speak.

The person lowered their heavy hood and shook out their hair, like a dog. In the fluorescent gas-station lights, she could see tangled bleached blond hair, ratty and thick with ink-black roots. A girl. A girl her age, maybe even younger.

She stared at the girl and the girl stared back.

The driver's door opened. He got in, started the car. "Hundred bucks if we take her to Cincinnati."

Did this happen? Did people really do this? Why would a girl, so young, be alone out here?

She could never do it. She knew she couldn't. But then, twenty-four hours ago, she didn't think she'd run away with her boyfriend, either, with no plan other than to drive as far west from everything as they could.

"Hi," the girl said.

"Hey," her boyfriend said. "Like I said before, I'm Shaw. This is—"

"Ellory," she said. "Like the singer."

"Hi, Ellory. I'm Jade."

Shaw let out a deep laugh, started the car. "Oh, this life. So full of surprises."

They pulled back onto the highway, the car feeling heavy with the weight of a full gas tank and a new addition to the previously empty back seat. Ellory was somehow relieved they'd met Jade. It was as if her existence gave them a new purpose. A goal.

Cincinnati.

She said the word in her head, over and over, wondering if this would be the place they'd stay forever, put down roots.

Cincinnati. Cincinnati.

"Are you from there?" Ellory asked Jade. "Cincinnati?" It sounded better inside her head.

"Um," Jade mumbled. "Well, I was born there. But no, not really. I have an aunt there. She said I could stay with her."

"You have nowhere to go? No parents?" Shaw asked.

"You seem a little young to be out there alone," Ellory said, feeling a surge of concern for Jade, though she knew they were around the same age. She'd heard horror stories of what happened to young girls when they'd dared do things on their own. The world couldn't handle their existence without sparking a war against them.

"I'm not *that* young," Jade said. "There are a lot of people out there younger than me."

Shaw laughed. Ellory laughed, too. And for the first time since she'd left her mother, her life, her home, Ellory felt things might somehow be okay.

14

Hugh, Rebecca, and Gabe search the house while I stay in the kitchen with Birdie and call Ellory's phone, over and over. It's not until I've called twenty times that I stop. Raising the volume on my phone as high as it goes in case she calls back, I lean my shoulder against a window frame and stare out at the sprawling fields.

Ellory is gone. She's gone and it's my fault. I pushed her away. I knew she'd leave eventually, but not so soon. What did I expect her to do? What could I expect after her home was taken from her and she was forced to live in a crumbling mansion with a family she didn't know? Will she ever forgive me? Can I ever forgive myself?

Birdie leans against the kitchen island, thin silver bracelets clattering down her arm. Her bobbed hair is sleek and smooth this morning, and she wears her usual white shirt, buttons open near the neck, the oversize sleeves pushed to her elbows. Silver cat-eye glasses rest at the tip of her long nose as she appraises me.

"Has your daughter done this before?" she asks as she straightens a tea towel resting on the countertop.

I nod. "I can't blame her," I whisper and clear the frog in my throat. "It's genetic."

Birdie lifts her chin, questioning, and I imagine what she'd look like if she could furrow her eyebrows.

I answer her curious expression. "I ran away from home," I confess. "When I was around her age. My mom was...hard to live with. I was an only child and didn't turn out how she'd planned. I was a disappointment to her. I've always disappointed people." Tears push against my eyes as I speak. "I've never told Hugh this, but years later, around when Ellory turned three, I realized my mom was human, just like me. She loved me, in her own way, as hard and forever as I love Ellory. And I stole that from her. I left her without warning. Essentially, I disappeared."

Hope fills Birdie's eyes. "Did you ever go back home? Back to your mother?"

"I tried once. I returned to our home, and she was gone. The neighbors said she'd left about a year after I did. I didn't know until years later, but Jack found her. He found her and never told me."

"Jack was your first husband, correct?" Birdie asks, and I nod. "And he never told you?"

I shake my head. "By the time he'd located her, she had already died. He didn't have the heart to tell me. I never even looked for her. I always assumed she never tried looking for me, either."

"She did," Birdie whispers. She reaches across the countertop and, to my surprise, takes my hand. "Mothers always look for their children. Even if the child had good reason for leaving and they both know maybe it was for the best. It's in our blood. So I'll help you find your daughter. I want to find her as much as you do."

"Thanks, Birdie," I say, and I know she's right. But Birdie doesn't know I fear I've been slowly losing Ellory ever since

Jack died. Week by week, she's been drifting further away, and one day, she'll be gone.

When Jack died, I had to work more. Take a second job, nights, weekends. Ellory was alone. She fell into the wrong group of friends, got into trouble. But I didn't have a choice. I had to feed my daughter. I had to take care of her, and to do so, I had to work.

What I realize now is when Jack died, Ellory really lost both of her parents. She only had one left, and I was hardly around. I tried to make money to keep her home life as stable as I could after her dad died, but in the end, I failed her anyway. And now I've lost my husband, our home, and my daughter.

Somehow, I need to make things right.

Birdie taps her cane against the side of the counter, forcing my thoughts away. "Camille is gone, too." She fidgets with her armful of bracelets. I admit I've not known Birdie long, but her nervousness for Ellory seems genuine, as if it's her child who's missing. "Chances are they're together. Let's not worry too much before we can contact one of them."

I nod absently. "Please don't take this the wrong way, but I thought you were keeping an eye on her last night. Did you see anything strange?"

Birdie steps away, heads over toward the kitchen sink. "Don't blame this on me," she chokes out, and for a moment, her voice warbles, thick with emotion. "I didn't do anything wrong."

Hugh enters the kitchen, Rebecca and Gabe behind him. "We looked in every room, closet, bathroom, everywhere," Hugh says, out of breath. "Camille's car is gone. I bet Ellory left with her."

"She won't call me until she's cooled off. She's still upset," I admit.

"About what?" Rebecca asks.

Birdie lifts her chin knowingly. "The engagement."

I glance down at the giant ruby affixed to my finger, a faceted stone of blood.

"She'd leave without telling you?" Hugh asks.

"Yes. She's done this in the past. She always comes back," I say, more for myself than for anyone else. But deep in my heart, I'm terrified. This time, I'm unsure if things will be okay in the end. I have a feeling this time is different. Different, like we're about to cross into something we have no business being in. Different…like we're about to shift the dynamics of our lives, forever.

Gabe gives me a sharp look, uncrosses his arms. "You mean this isn't anything new? You have us running through the house—"

"*Gabe,*" Hugh warns.

"No, Hugh, someone has to say it," Gabe barks. "My wife left me. Camille is leaving me and you all just sit here acting like everything is okay. Well, it's *not*."

"How are we acting like everything's okay?" Rebecca asks. "Camille's car's gone—you said you tried calling her, right?" Rebecca looks at Gabe. He nods. "So she's not answering. And, Iris, you called Ellory, right?" I nod.

Hugh clears his throat. "Camille took her phone and purse with her. Did Ellory do the same?"

I nod again. "Yeah, Ellory's bag isn't in her room."

"Okay," Hugh says, trying to sort everything out. "Let's not panic. We can figure this out logically. They have their phones and purses—clearly, they're together. Ellory and Camille are both upset for different reasons. Gabe." He looks toward his brother. Gabe slowly turns to him. "Give Iris Camille's number. Let her try calling it."

Rebecca cackles. "Good idea. She probably wants to avoid answering any of *your* calls."

"Don't act like this is *my* fault," Gabe snaps. "I didn't want her to leave."

"You shouldn't have let her. She was drunk."

The room falls silent.

"Listen, everyone," I begin after a moment. "Ellory *has* done this before. She's done it to be with friends, but now she has this boyfriend—"

"Boyfriend?" Hugh asks. "I didn't know she had a boyfriend. Do you have his number? We can call him."

"I have no idea."

Birdie tuts, expressing her disapproval.

"I'm sorry," I say and feel the tears sting all over again. "I should know, but I don't. I've yelled at her and punished her, and I've tried everything I can think of, and still, she keeps doing this. Let's just give her time, okay? She'll come back."

"She will." Hugh squeezes my hand. "I know she will. We have to think positive thoughts. Ellory is smart. She has boundaries and limits and common sense. You taught her well, Iris." He kisses the top of my head, pulls me close to his chest. "You're an amazing mom. Please don't blame yourself. We'll find her."

His arms tighten around me as the doorbell sounds in the distance.

15

"God, am I glad to see you."

Sloane brings me into a hug, and when she pulls away, a troubled look passes over her face, as if she can somehow sense the mood of the house. "I come bearing gifts," she says softly, handing Hugh her long black coat. He hangs it on a hook in the taxidermy room, closes the door behind him. Sloane hands me a small paper bag, the handles tied thoughtfully with red ribbon. "For you."

I take the bag, offer a smile. "Thanks, Sloane. I'm glad you're here. I can't believe Ellory's gone."

"I know. I'm sorry," she says and squeezes my hand.

I've been texting Sloane and Ainsley the news of the house, keeping them up-to-date about me and Ellory, Hugh and his family, Gabe and Camille, and everything in between. I may not have siblings I can confide in, as Hugh does, but I have some amazing friends.

Hugh takes my hand, rubs the top with his thumb to soothe me. "If you ladies would like privacy to catch up, no one will bother you in the great room." He leads us through a maze of hallways until we step through an archway into a wide room with ceilings twice as tall as the rest of the house.

Sloane spins in astonishment. By the time she finally sits in front of the fireplace Hugh lights for us, every object has her fingerprints on it.

I'm grateful Sloane made the drive up to visit. If anyone can find out where Ellory is, it's Sloane, and I tell Hugh as much. She knows everyone, hears everything, and currently reigns as Hollow Falls' queen of gossip.

Hugh kisses my cheek as he leaves. "If you need anything, let me know."

"Thanks, Hugh," Sloane calls after him before turning back to me.

I take her hand. She moves to sit beside me on a green velvet couch. "I only wish Ellory told me goodbye before leaving," I say. "I know she didn't want to stay here."

"Getting engaged probably didn't help, either."

"Thanks," I mumble. "I know that now. But there's no going back."

"And you shouldn't wish to. After overcoming so much, you found love after loss," Sloane says with a half smile. "See? That's a bit of luck for you. Even Virgos can't have bad luck all the time."

For the first time today, I feel like smiling. But I can't. Not with my daughter elsewhere, away from me.

"How's your tea?" she asks, nodding toward my untouched mug. "You know it's made by monks."

"Delicious," I lie. She tilts her head, seeking honesty. "It's maybe a little bitter," I confess. "You didn't have to."

"It's a gift. From me to you. Everyone can use a little calming tea, especially you, especially now. Drink it and manifest only positive thoughts." Sloane loosens the scarf around her neck. "Don't you find it a little odd?"

"You mean all this?" I wave a hand through the air—at the life-size silver knight standing in a far corner. At the towering, half-dead palm trees flanking the sides of a cavernous fireplace. At the creepy porcelain dolls nestled on a filigree shelf.

"Good point," Sloane says, letting a cackle escape. "I mean Camille—the wife. Don't you find it odd she's gone, too?"

I lean in to whisper, "Gabe won't even tell anyone places she'd go so we could call and check to see if she's okay. He's acting like he already knows where she is. What if he's keeping her trapped somewhere?" I shudder at the thought.

Sloane exhales. "We have an angry wife fed up with the man she married—a man who you claim has a short temper. There's something else going on here."

"Camille told me, Sloane."

"What'd she tell you?"

I think back to last night in the garden. Camille's drunken sobs. Her words: *if Gabe finds out, he'll kill me.* "Camille knew he'd hurt her. He *was* hurting her."

Sloane's face goes blank. "Shit."

"I had a dream about them," I say quietly. "Gabe was digging a grave in the backyard."

She presses her lips together. "Are you sure it was a dream?"

"It had to have been, right? I mean, I walked all around the house and I never found a hole or anything at all."

"Maybe Gabe's an axe murderer." Sloane lifts a hand to her throat and pretends to choke herself. She smiles glumly, saddened by my failure to laugh. "Either that or it was a vision. An omen," she says, sipping her tea. "I believe in *all* that stuff. Premonitions, prophecies—"

"Curses?"

"The family curse, *oooh*, I'm scared." She laughs, remembering what Gabe said at the restaurant. Lifting her head, she glances around the room. "All jokes aside, after what you've been through, you can live through anything."

"Still, I wonder."

"What?"

I shift on the sofa, suddenly uncomfortable. "I've been see-ing things. Hearing things. It's just stress, right? I mean, ever since Jack died, I've been a little on edge. Sometimes, I think I see them—those three dark figures I told you about. I've seen them for years, but I know no one's there. That's normal, right?"

"Oh, Iris." Sloane's expression wilts. "You have to forgive yourself. What happened…it wasn't your fault."

I say nothing.

She casts a furtive glance at me. "One day, you'll have to forgive yourself. And you'll feel free. Until then, I'm here. As your best friend, you can officially tell me anything. So if you say you're hearing things and seeing things, I believe you. I mean, if I lived here, I'd see and hear things, too."

"You might."

Noticing my expression, undoubtedly knotted with worry, Sloane quietly asks, "What did you hear?"

I gulp. "Noises in the attic. Once, in a reflection, I thought I saw the portrait of a girl I used to know, but it was gone min-utes later."

"Do you believe in ghosts?"

"Me? No, not ghosts. But I believe in visions, I guess."

Sloane nods sagely. "Visions, ghosts—either way, they come to you for a reason. They come when you need them to, when you need to be reminded of something."

I stare into the fireplace. "I don't want to remember any-thing, let alone be reminded." I shake my head, turn back to her. "I mean, I'm having a hard time sleeping. I keep hearing things. I dreamed I saw Gabe digging a grave, and now his wife is missing, along with my daughter. I should talk to Hugh, try to convince him to move us out. I don't want him to know about the dream, but maybe we can move someplace nearby so he can still come here to work on the house and—"

I stop the thoughts as quickly as they come. I can't leave. I can't go anywhere. Not without Ellory.

Sloane's coloring pales. "Iris, you know I love you. You, Ainsley, and Ellory are my world. So I'm going to be honest. Ever since Jack died, I've witnessed your uphill climb, and I think by being here, you're— *Hi, Hugh.*" Sloane stares over my shoulder. "We were just talking about you."

"All good things, I hope." He sits on an armrest beside me. "Sorry, I was walking by and thought I heard my name. But I can leave—"

"No, wait," Sloane calls him back. "Any news on the missing Camille?"

He shakes his head. "Nothing yet. Any news on Ellory?"

I shake my head.

"You seem calm, considering what's happened," Hugh says to me. "Good for you. You're taking everything in stride."

"Either that or it's the tea I brought for her to calm her nerves. It's made from reishi mushrooms and ashwagandha."

"You gave me mushrooms?"

Sloane laughs. "Not that kind. But I have those, too." Sloane slides her mug onto the coffee table. "Nice to see you, Hugh, but I gotta go. I'll let myself out. Iris, please call if you need anything." She stands, leans over to kiss me on the forehead. "You'll see Ellory soon. Don't worry."

"Thanks for the tea."

We stay silent until the door closes in the distance.

The firelight dulls.

Hugh sits on the sofa and holds his arms up, an invitation to curl into his lap. "That was nice of her to visit," Hugh says as I lean my head on his shoulder. "You seemed to be locked in conversation. I think I heard Jack's name mentioned."

I wonder how much of our conversation he heard. "That's who we were talking about."

"You never really shared with me what happened."

I shake my head, glance up at him. "You know what happened."

He exhales. "I know generally what happened to him. But you never told me what happened to *you*."

"It was hell," I whisper. A sudden tear falls down my cheek, landing with the faintest tap on Hugh's pale blue shirt. "They still haven't caught his killer."

"You mean the man Jack was selling his truck to on the test-drive?"

I nod against his chest, letting my body rise and fall with his breathing. The room has grown cold from the dying fireplace, but I don't mind sharing our warmth.

"I guess we'll never really know what happened," Hugh says, kissing the top of my head. "It's pretty scary, if you think about it. A murderer is running loose out there. But sometimes justice doesn't come right away. Sometimes, it takes years. Decades, even."

"God, I hope it doesn't take that long," I say, desperate to end the topic. It might be Sloane's strong herbal tea, but I'm feeling relaxed, like I'm floating over the sofa. When my lips move, I hardly notice. "I'm worried about Ellory." When I say her name, his brow furrows in concern. I sit up, and he reaches for a fire poker, jabs at the embers and ash. "I'm trying to stay positive, but Jack's death took every ounce of strength I had. And now I have to just trust Ellory, trust that she's eighteen and an adult and will be okay. She has to be. Because if she's not—I can't allow myself to think about it. If I do, I'll never come back."

"You're doing amazing. Not everyone would be able to keep their head on straight."

I nod. "I've had practice," I admit. "After Jack died, Ellory left. She was gone for five days."

Hugh replaces the poker as the fire brightens like a bonfire. "I can't imagine what you went through."

"I've disappointed her. Between losing the house and my job and the move. I mean, how can I blame her for leaving?"

Hugh stays with me, listening quietly as the thoughts unravel from me like falling rain, thoughts I didn't even know I had inside, tumbling out, faster and faster. It's a terrible comfort, being listened to. It means someone else now knows the deepest parts of you, the parts you didn't even want to know. Parts you didn't even know existed are now exposed, held up to the light, spilled out like water poured from a glass. It can never go back in again. Your darkest parts are forever unleashed.

That's what love is, I suppose. Allowing those dark parts to see the daylight and knowing someone else will inspect them, in their own way, in their own mind, with their own past and history and experiences. They will take your words and dissect them in a way you never could, see things you never would, and it may change what they think of you, how they look at you. But that's what love is—seeing someone at a billion different angles, seeing their soft white underbelly, their raw and rotten truth. And loving them anyway.

We talk for so long we only stop when our stomachs start rumbling. In the kitchen with Birdie, we make Hugh's favorite—mac and cheese—before he starts working on the conservatory roof with Rebecca and Gabe.

I go upstairs and, after calling Ellory's phone again, curl into her bed. The room falls into darkness, stars blinking in the window beside me. I stare out at them, wishing my daughter good-night.

3 DAYS BEFORE

WEDNESDAY, JANUARY 22

16

A woman cries in the attic.

I snap awake. Once more, Hugh isn't beside me. I sharpen my hearing, rub my eyes clear. Looking up at the ceiling, I listen to the stillness of the house. Soon, the cries dissipate. The house settles back to sleep.

Something about this house claws at me, makes me feel uneasy. A thought hits me. What if it's Camille? What if she's trapped in the attic? I'd have to find her, help her.

Sunlight bleeds through a crack in the drapes. The air is cold. Chills wash over me as I fling on the same clothes I wore yesterday—an old pink sweater and leggings—comb my fingers through my hair, tie it back in a nubby ponytail.

Silently, I creep down the hall. Our bedroom is on the third floor, the highest level of the house, so the entrance to the attic has to be somewhere on this floor. I creak open a door to peek inside when a phone rings from down the hallway.

It's not a ring—it's music, warbling notes from the song

"Dance of the Sugar Plum Fairy." I follow the music until the hallway ends. There's only one door nearby.

Gabe's bedroom.

I push the door open. The room is dingy gray, with peeling striped wallpaper and heavy black furniture. I listen to where the sound comes from, isolating it to his armoire. Pulling open the doors, I scan inside: folded pants and sweaters, watches stored in small boxes, and a set of keys dangling on a hook.

There are also three drawers, so I grip a handle, slide one open. The music grows louder before stopping. On a stack of folded shirts is a phone. The screen lights up, displaying a message that an alarm clock has ended.

Unless Gabe prefers his phones to have hot-pink metallic cases, I have to assume it belongs to Camille.

Footsteps in the hall.

I drop her phone back in the drawer and cross the room to the closet. Someone is coming, and I need a place to quickly hide, so I rush inside and pull the door shut. Metal hangers poke my spine. Gabe's closet reeks of old socks. I hold my breath, hand clenching the doorknob, afraid to let go.

Why is Gabe hiding Camille's phone?

I clamp my eyes shut as footsteps enter the room. Not just one person, but two.

They close the door behind them. Gabe speaks. I press my ear to the door.

"You need to relax."

Silence. Then the second voice.

"How could you do this to me?"

Hugh.

"You know what she did," Gabe whispers.

"Of *course* I do." Hugh sounds infuriated. I picture him pacing around the room, arms crossed, a stern look etched across his smooth face, the look he gets when he's frustrated. "Like I could ever forget."

"Well," Gabe says with a heavy sigh. "There's nothing we can do about it now. There was a party outside, a ton of people. There was no way. It wasn't safe. This way it's over."

Hugh chokes out a strangled laugh. "Yeah. It's over. Good, fine. But you really fucked us on this one."

"Your emotions always got in the way," Gabe argues. "So this time things ended a little differently. So what?"

Hugh scoffs. "So what? So *what*? This is my life you're fucking with. My life and Iris's. And yours and Camille's and— Fuck, Gabe. Just…fix this."

Angry footsteps cross the room. The door slams shut. One person left. I tense my shoulders, wait for the second person to leave. If the person still in the room is Hugh, I can open the closet door. But if it's Gabe…

The person walks toward the closet. I hold my breath as he hovers close, inches away from where I hide. Then he turns away, exits the room, footsteps receding into the distance.

I release my breath, pinch open the door.

I'm alone. Glancing at the armoire, I mull over taking Camille's phone out of the drawer. But what would I prove? I could use it as evidence to the family that Gabe is a liar. But I already know they'd take his side. One day, I'm going to be part of this family. Until then, I'm an outsider.

Deciding to leave the phone where I found it, I quietly escape Gabe's bedroom and rush back down the hall.

17

After calling the police to file a missing person's report for Ellory, I'm not sure they're taking it seriously. She's eighteen, they said, an adult who can decide to leave home at any time. I need someone who can find her on their own, separate from the police. Scouring the internet, I finally find him—the perfect person for the job.

PI Duplain. A private investigator, he's worked with his local police department for the past thirteen years. His cases are primarily more serious crimes, such as cold cases, murder, and kidnappings.

From my search, he seems most famous for solving a cold case where a girl had been missing for eleven months. She'd been hidden in her estranged father's basement. Hands down, PI Duplain appears to be the best in the area. Problem is, Duplain only takes on special cases—cases he finds *intense interest* in.

Somehow, I need him to find *intense interest* in Ellory. But how do I hook him, make him want to drop everything to find my daughter?

I locate Duplain's number from his simple one-page website,

dial it on my phone. I leave a brief, urgent message for him, asking him to please call me back regarding my missing daughter, Ellory, ending the call as I enter the kitchen.

Instantly, I know Hugh helped with breakfast—when he wasn't upstairs conspiring with Gabe. He makes fantastic pancakes but douses his eggs with ketchup, so much you can practically smell it over the bacon grease.

Hugh sits next to Gabe on one end of the island, Birdie and Rebecca on the other. I sit somewhere in the middle, unable to look at Gabe, and strangely unable to look at Hugh, either. What did I overhear while hiding in Gabe's closet?

You know what she did.

Who were they talking about? My only guess is Camille. Maybe Gabe was discussing how she'd left and their impending divorce. But it's what Hugh said that bothers me most.

This is my life you're fucking with. My life and Iris's.

"Iris—Iris?"

I snap out of my trance, look up. Rebecca stares at me.

"What?"

"I said, have you heard from Ellory?"

"Oh, no. I haven't," I say, disappointed. "But I did file a missing person's report with the police this morning, and I have a call in with a private investigator."

Gabe snorts. "Is that necessary?"

"Yes." I stare down at the table, unable to look at him.

He laughs. "Unbelievable."

"Enough, Gabe," Hugh scolds.

"Oh, come on," he says. "She's a teenage girl. She'll return whenever she wants. You were that age once. Although it was a very long time ago."

"Yes, I was," Hugh snaps. "And I'd never do anything like that to my mom, *ever.*"

Gabe glares at Hugh for a moment, almost in warning, before tossing his hands up in mock surprise. "Oh, I'm sorry. I forgot—you're the perfect son."

"Gabe," Birdie scolds. "Stop it. Take your medicine." She points her chin toward the orange bottles of heart medication next to his empty plate.

I bite my bottom lip, try to hold back what I want to say. Rebecca can obviously sense it. She taps on the countertop to get my attention. "I know you'll find her soon," she whispers, scowling at Gabe.

"Gabe," I begin, finally able to bring myself to look him in the eyes. "I heard a phone ringing in your bedroom this morning. It had a very specific ringtone. 'Dance of the Sugar Plum Fairy.'"

"I love that song," Rebecca says.

"Do you know whose phone it is?" I ask, wait to see his reaction.

Gabe tears off a piece of toast, slips it into his mouth. "No idea. Mine, maybe."

"Not Camille's?"

He lifts his eyes to look at me, dark and menacing behind his glasses. "Camille's?"

Rebecca tosses her long hair over a shoulder. "Oh, that would make sense. She told me she used to dance ballet."

"Where'd you say you found it?" Birdie asks me.

"In Gabe's bedroom."

Gabe freezes. Realizing he's caught, he rolls his shoulders and grins. "Oh, I forgot. I found it outside on the driveway. She must've dropped it while she was leaving me. She won't be back to get it, though, I promise."

"Why not?" Birdie asks. "Didn't you say you called her? Spoke with her?"

Gabe laughs awkwardly. "I never said that. I said I *tried* to call her. She never answered."

"And now we know why," I say. "Because you had her phone the entire time."

He drops his toast, looks at me in earnest. "Look, Iris, I only found it when we were outside searching for Ellory, okay? I know Camille will never come back for it because she said she never wants to see me again."

I shrug. "Okay. But you lied."

"*I did not lie.*" Gabe bares his teeth, a wild, threatened animal. "How do we even know who *you* are, anyway? You could be making up Ellory's entire disappearance, for all we know. You could be making all of this up—just like how you made up seeing me bury Camille in the backyard."

Rebecca chokes on her coffee. "Excuse me?"

"You were listening to my conversation?" Heat crawls up my throat, into my cheeks. I feel ashamed, seen, naked, though I know I did nothing wrong.

Gabe lifts a shoulder. "I heard some of it, found it boring, and left."

"I've had enough." I stand to leave.

"I know you think I'm a liar, Iris," Gabe says as I escape the kitchen, "but it's you who's hiding something, and I'm not going to let my brother marry you before I find out what it is."

"Gabe—enough," Hugh says, holding up a hand.

I stop. Turn around. Words curl behind my teeth. I try to swallow them, but fail, spit them out instead: "Where is your wife?"

Gabe smirks. "I don't owe an insane person a sane answer."

"Gabe, stop..."

Hugh's words fall away in the distance as I run outside to the garden, sit near the spot where Hugh proposed. I need to be alone. Icy air freezes tears of anger and frustration on my cheeks. I listen to the sound of the river roaring below the rocky cliffs, to the sound of doves cooing nearby in a crooked willow tree.

The door to the garden opens behind me. A heavy blanket

weighs down my shoulders. Hugh sits next to me on the bench, silent and shivering.

I say nothing, just stare straight ahead to where the garden ends and the cliff begins, falling off in rocky slabs toward the waves of the icy river below.

"If there are any secrets between us," Hugh begins, "let's share them now. No judgment. And no leaving. We have to listen to the end, no matter what."

I bite my lip, look down. Hugh's hand is extended out to me, and I take it. His touch is warm, his skin rough from working on the house. I never want to compare Hugh with Jack, ever, and I've made a very conscious decision not to, but for the slightest of moments, his hand reminds me of Jack's. Maybe this is a sign, his way of showing it'll all be okay.

"I never told you," Hugh says, his words dulled in the strangling cold, "but I've been married once before."

His words feel like a slap. Glancing down to my engagement ring, I can't help but wonder if this was ever really mine to begin with.

I remain silent, stare straight ahead. Hugh continues. "Gabe always protected me after that," he says, voice cracking. "It was beyond painful."

"How long ago?" I ask numbly.

He sighs. "About five years now. She— I was in pretty bad shape." He laughs lightly. "I guess Gabe's right about our family curse. It's like all our lives rotate around grief therapy. It helped. But then, so did Gabe."

I think about his words. I've been hiding something, too. Though I'll never admit it. Not ever. How I think about Jack. How I think about him often, maybe more often than I should. I think about his smile, how I used to smooth my hands through his soft brown hair. The stubble on his cheeks, and the way he made me laugh, like no one else before and no one else after.

I wonder if whenever Hugh looks at me, he sees his wife.

"Why have you never told me?" I ask, wiping a tear away. "What else aren't you telling me?"

"Nothing," he rushes to say, squeezing my hand. His skin is warm. I don't pull away, though I know I should. "That's it. That's all there is to me. You *know* me, Iris. Now you know it all."

I pause, mull things over in my head. "Fine, I believe you," I whisper. "So when I ask you this, you'll be honest with me."

"Of course." His blue eyes trace the lines of my face. "You can ask me anything."

I steal a deep breath. "Why can't Gabe leave?" Hugh sighs, releases my hand. "Seriously. Camille's gone—why can't he go, too? She left her phone behind and she's not coming back, not even for that. So why can't he move out?"

"Iris."

"You said yourself how you have all this extra money from the sale of your house. Why can't you give him some so he can move out?"

Hugh sighs. "It's not that easy. Gabe would never take it. And…Camille has done things like this—" he begins, stumbling over his words "—before. In the past. She does it to mess with Gabe. She likes to play head games."

"Did you know Gabe hurts Camille?"

Hugh's expression twists. "What?"

"Did you know he's been arrested? Tell me you didn't know."

Hugh pauses, sighs. "Yeah. I knew."

"So why can't *we* leave?"

"I told you why, Iris," he says, searching my eyes with his. "I need to help Mother. Have you taken a look at this place?" he asks, turning to stare at the towering structure looming around us. "She needs help. She needs *me*. This roof is so water-damaged it's about to collapse. There are so many patches in the slate— that's why the house is an icebox. Just let me fix her roof, at least, okay? That's it. I promise."

My phone rings in my pocket. Hugh lets out a long sigh. I glance at the screen.

"I have to answer. It's about Ellory."

Hugh nods. I answer the phone. "Hello?"

"Hi, is this Iris Blodgett?"

"Yes."

"This is Private Investigator Duplain calling you back. I got your voicemail." I put the phone on speaker so Hugh can hear, too. But he stands, motions he's going inside to work on the house.

"Thanks for calling back."

"Anytime. Now—I have to ask, uh, verify. You said your daughter is missing?"

"Yes. Ellory. She just turned eighteen."

A pause. "Wow…that's an interesting name. I've never heard anyone go by that. Is it a family name?"

"In a way. Why?"

Duplain clears his throat. "Let me just say I only take on cases where I hold genuine interest. Now, Mrs. Blodgett, I'm unfortunately contacted regarding missing person's cases quite frequently. So I won't waste your time or mine. Let me ask you some questions, then, uh, Mrs. Blodgett."

"Are you interested in Ellory's case?" I ask, my heart leaping into my throat. My entire body clenches until I hear his reply.

"Well…" He breathes into the phone as if debating. "Well, uh, yeah. Yes, I am."

My muscles relax. A smile crawls onto my face.

PI Duplain asks dozens of questions—some questions the police already asked, others they didn't. If I'd seen Ellory leave with anyone. Where I was when I realized she was missing. Whether Ellory has ever done anything like this in the past. If she said anything to anyone before disappearing, left a note, text, or voicemail.

"No, nothing," I say quickly. "I'm scared something happened."

"I understand, Mrs. Blodgett. Let's set up a day and time to meet. I can come straight to your house. That sound good?"

"Sounds great." A flood of relief spills from me. "Thank you so much."

The call ends. As I glance up to the white winter sky, the sound of crunching leaves echoes across the garden. The same dog has returned, something in its mouth. It approaches me, unafraid, dropping it at my feet.

The blackbird twitches, still alive. I recoil away in disgust. The dog looks at me, saddened at my reaction to its gift. The bird flutters its wings before flipping upright, flying away toward the rocky cliff.

It disappears over the river, its little black body stark against the white winter sky. A single snowflake flutters down, melting on my cheek.

A storm is coming.

181 HOURS LEFT

It was supposed to only be the two of them, road-weary, in it together. It was their escape, their only chance.

But then there were three.

And then there were five.

It wasn't just her and Shaw anymore. In a single day, it had become them and three others, three other kids they'd somehow picked up along the way, like souvenirs. Stop, pick up someone. Stop again, get two more.

The air inside the tiny car hummed with energy, everyone's thoughts brewing in their heads, desperate to break out.

Ellory knew there wasn't enough food. Not for five of them.

Shaw said he knew the last two from his old school, the one he'd gone to before he'd moved. They were his friends, he said. Old friends from an old school. And he wanted to do them this favor. That way, they'd owe *him*. Owe him what, exactly, Ellory wanted to know.

Now the car was bursting, with no room for anything anymore. Ellory wondered if it could even support so much weight.

The trunk was filled with Shaw's clothes and shoes, with no room for much else. Ellory's too-full bag was now shoved between her knees, and in her lap, the quiet boy's heavy backpack sat, making her thighs go numb.

There was Jade, the first person they'd picked up. She'd been hiking, she'd said, alone, in the woods. Ellory doubted her story. She could tell by the girl's bleached hair, ink-black roots thick with oil. There were no leaves caught in her tangled strands. No dirt from the forest floor swiped across her ghost-white cheeks. Jade wore a heavy, oversize army-green coat, something Ellory imagined she'd find in a thrift store. Something her father would've worn.

Ellory liked Jade, even though she knew Jade was using a phony name. Strangely, Ellory wanted her here, like their adventure wasn't complete without Jade being there with them.

But the other two, Shaw's old friends, Ellory wasn't sure about. Davey and Mars. Two brothers. One tall, one short. One fat, one thin. Like an old silent film, yin and yang, opposites showing diametric diversity from the same family tree.

Davey was the youngest, younger than Ellory, even younger than Jade, maybe fifteen. He was the quiet one. He was also the taller one, the one who had a deeper voice and always spoke in one-word answers.

Shaw acted strange around him. But Shaw acted even stranger around Mars, the older brother. He was shorter, thicker, with meaty fingers and a chubby face. Ellory could tell he bossed his little brother around, ordering him to put their bags in the car, demanding he get in first.

She watched them now, all three lined up in the back seat. Flipping down the visor, she pretended to pick eyelashes off her cheeks. She didn't have any, not now. But she wanted to study them in this silence, wanted to see what kind of people they could be.

She still didn't know.

Davey and Mars weren't hiking alone in the woods, like Jade. They had a better story, though still fake. They said their parents were getting a divorce and kicked them out, allowing them to take nothing but whatever they could shove in the bags they had in their bedrooms. She wondered if their names, like their story, were invented.

Ellory didn't know what to believe anymore. Not as the sun began to rise as Shaw drove farther and farther away from her life. Not as the highway thinned and the pink sky of sunrise turned dish-soap blue. The stars no longer sparkled over their heads, and Ellory knew they were so far away she'd never be able to find her way back home.

Shaw yawned. Ellory watched him carefully as he drove, his eyelids falling heavy with exhaustion. They'd been driving all night in darkness. Ellory suggested they pull over at the next exit, park the car somewhere safe, lock the doors, and take a nap until the sun went back to sleep.

No one else agreed.

They kept driving, stopping occasionally throughout the day for food breaks and bathroom breaks, breaks to stretch their legs, to give the old car a rest. And soon, the moon had swallowed the sun again, and the stars sparkled above.

Shaw exited the highway, but he didn't park the car somewhere safe. He pulled into the dusty lot of a shabby motel, fluorescent lights buzzing. The scent of stale cigarettes singed Ellory's nose as she waited for Shaw to rent two rooms for the night.

Ellory insisted she and Jade share their own room. The three boys would share another. While Ellory wanted to be alone with Shaw, she also didn't feel right about abandoning Jade, forcing her to sleep in a strange room with two strange boys. It was her first real night away from home, the first night she'd spend in another bed, far away in a new state, in a city she didn't know the name of. If she was afraid, she imagined Jade could be, too.

Shaw paid for the two rooms in cash. Davey and Mars thanked him, promised they'd buy them all breakfast. Ellory didn't know why Shaw had done that. They had a plan. They were going to be careful. They were going to save their money, save it and never spend it, not unless it was an emergency.

Everything seemed to be an emergency now. Cigarettes, new cell phone chargers, expensive energy drinks. These motel rooms, when they'd promised each other they'd sleep together in the back seat of the car. But now the two of them had multiplied into five, and Ellory knew five people couldn't sleep in a car—not comfortably, at least.

She was able to do math in her head. Well, some. If they kept spending nights in fancy motel rooms, their money would only last another two nights. That wasn't counting gas, food, and water. Then, maybe, they could eke out one more night in fancy rooms. Ellory had some bags of beef jerky and cheesy puffs hidden in her duffel bag, but that couldn't feed them, not all five of them, not for long.

Ellory opened the door to the motel room and told the three boys good-night. They'd be down the hall, so it would just be her and Jade, her and a stranger. Ellory locked the door and used the chain, then tossed her overstuffed bag onto one of the twin beds. Jade shrugged off her army coat and began stripping her clothes to take a shower.

Ellory had learned new things that day. She knew Jade was a loner, yes, but she was kind. Motherly, almost, with a way of always trying to soothe and care for others. It reminded her of her mother when she was still the mother she always knew.

But the past few years had changed her, turned her into a different person, swapped out the mother she knew with a mother she didn't. She didn't even want to think about all that had happened with her father...

She'd also learned Shaw wanted to be the leader. She hadn't known that about him. He had a protective instinct, too. But it wasn't the same as Jade's. Jade wanted to protect others, to make sure they were safe. Shaw wanted to be in charge. Ellory wondered how long he could keep pretending to be in control.

The shower turned off sooner than she'd expected, and Jade asked her for a towel. Ellory tossed a tiny white towel over the top of the shower stall.

"I saved you half of the soap and shampoo," Jade said, towel-drying her parched platinum hair. Once wet, the tangles had grown into a thick mesh of impossible knots.

Feeling sorry for her, Ellory hoped she had packed a comb to offer Jade. But she had a feeling Jade would sooner offer her one instead. The girl was always doing things like that. It seemed she had little self-preservation.

Jade was always offering others anything and everything she had, like an odd reflex: *Here, take mine. Please, eat it, I'm full. No, really, I don't want it.*

Ellory didn't like always taking from her. She made a promise to herself she would stop taking and start giving—if she ever had anything decent to give anyone ever again.

They lay in their separate beds, bellies empty and faces clean. It was the first night Ellory had stayed in a motel since she was a little girl. She knew it had to be the last night, too, because they really couldn't afford this luxury anymore.

She played a game on her phone to distract herself. But she couldn't help it. She wondered what Shaw, Davey, and Mars were doing in their room down the hall and silently wished they wouldn't come knocking on the door. To prevent that, Ellory turned off the lamps, and the room fell into peaceful darkness.

Jade sat at the edge of the bed, fluffing her thin motel pillow. Ellory watched the black outline of her body against the glowing white drapes until Jade fell back on the bed and sighed. Ellory wanted to ask Jade a million questions, but she was tired. Too tired.

She reached over to the chair beside the bed where she'd tossed her coat and felt the pockets. Her inhaler was still there, just where she'd left it, just in case.

Relaxing, she rolled back over and looked at the glowing green numbers on the motel clock. The sun would soon be rising.

Ellory stayed awake in the darkness listening to Jade's breathing until she knew Jade had fallen asleep. And soon, she fell asleep, too, her hands on her growing belly and her head buzzing with a million screaming fears.

18

Snow turns to freezing rain. Warm inside the house, I glance through the window into the garden. The dog is still there, shivering in the cold. I can't leave it outside alone, but I'm not sure I should bring a stray wet dog into Birdie's house, either.

I toss on my coat, grab an umbrella from the mudroom, go out to the garden to check the dog's collar. It comes right over to smell my hand. I check the tag, a tiny silver one, with just enough space for a name and phone number.

"Douglas?" I ask the dog. He glances at me in recognition, trots off to dig up a dead flower bed.

I dial the number. A woman answers. She introduces herself as Evonne, explains she lives next door—if you can call it next door. With a brick wall separating the properties, Evonne's house can only be accessed via her front driveway gate.

I don't want to be inside this house, not with Gabe and not with Hugh—especially after he has only now told me he's been married before—so I ask Birdie if she has a leash from when she had a dog, the little white one Camille mentioned.

Being a woman who never throws anything away—making her sprawling mansion somehow feel claustrophobic—she hands me a leash, and I begin the long walk down the never-ending drive to Evonne's house, the leather smooth in my hand.

Douglas happily walks with me in the rain. I let my mind go numb until we reach the next driveway on the quiet road just as the rain calms. A sign with painted white letters hanging on a wrought-iron gate—*Erboss 112*—signals I've found the right house.

We walk up the looping driveway toward an ornate Victorian mansion. If Hugh were here, he'd call it *voluptuous*, with its curving rooflines and rounded windows. I like the colors: sunny yellow, eggplant, and pastel pink.

A woman stands on an enclosed front porch. "Oh, Dougie," she shouts, giggling, her marionette lines going sharp. "You're Iris, I assume?" I nod. "Thanks for bringing him home. He always sneaks outside. Can I tempt you to come in?"

"No, thanks. I have to get back." Evonne's gray hair is tinged purple, hovering like cotton candy over a shiny scalp. She smells like sugar cookies and cigarettes. "I've never met a dog named Douglas before. He's a sweet little guy."

"Oh, thank you. He's my second love named Dougie." Questioning, I tilt my head. "The first was my late husband, Douglas," Evonne clarifies. "Some people said they look alike." She lets out another giggle.

I glance down at the big, wrinkly dog. He stares back with bulbous brown eyes.

"Evonne," I begin, tugging out my phone. She raises thin eyebrows. "Can I ask you—have you seen my daughter, Ellory?" I hold up my phone. She narrows her eyes, grabs my hand to pull the phone closer.

"No..." she says, deep in thought. "She looks familiar, though. Something about her. Why?"

"She's missing. She disappeared the night before last." I angle my head in the direction of Hugh's family house.

Evonne stares at me in concentration. "Next door?" she asks. "You're living there?" I nod. The confused look on her face unsettles me. "I'm sorry. When you called earlier about Dougie, I assumed you lived down the other way. I never would've guessed you lived *there*."

"Why not?"

"Well, I—I didn't know Birdie had moved out. Oh, my gosh, but how are you able to live in that house—after what happened?"

"No, Birdie's still there. I'm her future daughter-in-law." I fight the urge to hold up my left hand, show my new ring.

"You are?"

"Yeah, why—what happened?"

Evonne unhooks Dougie's leash, ushers him inside. "If you don't already know, I wouldn't want to be the one to spook you." She laughs. "You seem like a nice girl."

"No, really," I press. "Tell me."

"Well, I'll spare you the gory details…" Evonne looks in the direction of Birdie's house, her expression pained. "But your daughter isn't the first girl to go missing from that house."

19

Paige.

Hugh's younger sister. Evonne confessed the missing girl was Birdie's daughter. She couldn't remember her name. But I did— Paige. No one seems to ever want to talk about her. Would her family go on forever pretending she never existed? The thought saddens me.

The storm clouds have cleared and the rain has ended. The woods are quiet around me as I walk up the long driveway. I tug my phone from my coat pocket and search her name to see if anything comes up in the news.

Paige Smoll.

Why didn't Hugh say Paige went missing? When I pressed him, he only told me she'd died many years ago. She could still be out there, alive, somewhere. Was Hugh trying to avoid me worrying about another missing girl, especially with Ellory gone? That has to be it. He's worried about me. Or is there more to the story?

I hold my breath, scan the search results.

The house comes into view. I slow my pace, look up, catch a flicker in a window. Gabe peers down at me from his bedroom window, a camera obscuring his face. He moves it away, drops it down, yet still continues to stare. Was he taking photos of me?

I shudder, look away from the window. When I turn back, he's already disappeared.

Sitting on the front porch, I open the top link on my phone. It's an ad for reverse lookup, asking for my credit card. I go back, click on every link for the first five pages of the search, but they're all either a college sports article or a LinkedIn account.

It's as if *Paige Smoll* never existed.

Wanting a second opinion, I call Sloane. When she answers, immediately I can tell she's agitated.

"Hello," she says sharply.

"Is this Hotté Latte? Best coffee in Hollow Falls?"

She sighs. "Hi, Iris, listen, I can't talk now. We're super busy and Ainsley didn't show up today."

"You sure she's not just late again?"

"Ugh, I don't know. She's been acting weird ever since her divorce settlement went through," Sloane says. "She got a shit ton of money from that sleazy lawyer ex of hers. I'm worried she'll quit."

"She'd quit without telling you?"

"God, I hope not."

A knot catches in my throat. "Sloane, I have to tell you something."

"Oh, no. What happened?"

"Nothing bad, I think. I just found out Hugh has a sister who went missing years ago—Paige. I searched for her online, but can't find anything."

"Missing? How long ago?"

I didn't think about that. I force myself to remember what Hugh said, but so much has happened since that night. It feels like a lifetime ago.

"I don't remember, exactly. Maybe ten, twenty years?"

Sloane grumbles into the phone. "Might be too long. But I don't know. We had the internet then."

"Tell me I should let this coincidence go. Tell me I don't want to go down this road."

"You don't want to go down this road." A long pause before Sloane says, "I know what you're thinking. And I'm going to be the little angel on your shoulder that tells you *not* to think what you're thinking, okay?"

"You thought it, too, then," I whisper. "Maybe Gabe is involved in Camille's disappearance—*and* his younger sister's. Oh, what am I doing? My daughter is missing. I can't search for Paige, too."

"You're not wrong about that." I imagine Sloane shrugging a shoulder, her favorite gemstone earrings swaying near her face. I only saw her yesterday, and already I miss her. "Listen to me. Drink the tea I gave you and go take a nap. If you're not passed out in five minutes, I have something stronger that might work."

"Yes, ma'am."

Sloane sighs deeply into the phone. "Can I be honest?"

"Of course."

"Maybe we shouldn't ignore this whole Paige thing," she begins, voice somber. "Not yet. Not until we know more."

"You're probably right. Thanks, Sloane. I miss you."

"I miss you, too. Now, go nap. Call me when you're up."

I hang up, turn to go inside.

"How did the leash work out for you?"

Birdie stares at me from within the shadows of the house, through the crack of the open front door. I clutch my heart, startled. "How long have you been standing there?" Suddenly, I'm nervous. How much of our conversation did she overhear?

Birdie backs away, her cane tangling in the hem of her long skirt. Saying nothing, she disappears like a ghost down a hall.

I push on the door. It creaks open.

"I'm making dinner soon. Maybe you can join us…" Her voice disappears inside the house as if it swallowed her whole.

I rush upstairs, turn on our bathroom faucet as hot as it will go, dunk two of Sloane's calming tea bags into a glass I keep near the sink. I tilt my head back, drink the entire thing, and collapse into bed.

A soft thud in the attic. I stare at the ceiling, head swirling. A thought sifts through, floats to the top.

What if Paige never disappeared?

What if she's alive—and still inside the house?

I exhale, let go of my thoughts of Paige. Shutting my eyes, I clutch my phone, just in case Ellory might need me.

A deep voice speaks above me. "Your phone is buzzing."

My eyes snap open. Hugh hovers over me. He's covered in dust from the renovation, sweat beading across his forehead. The white bandage wrapped around his finger is stained with blood.

I must've fallen asleep. Checking my phone that's still in my hand, I see Sloane texted me an article. Hugh leans over, turns on the lamp beside me.

"I wanted to apologize to you." He sits on the bed. "It's not that I purposely kept my first wife a secret from you, it's just— I know you understand, more than anyone, how hard it can be to talk about people from the past."

"You mean Jack," I clarify, searching Hugh's eyes. "My husband was murdered. Of course I know how hard it is. And I would never keep him—or my past—a secret from you." I want to retract the lie as soon as it leaves my mouth.

"I know you wouldn't," he says after a moment. "When my wife and I parted…I got depressed. I don't like talking about it."

"I wish you'd told me."

"I know. There was just never a right time," he says, and I can see the hurt in his eyes. I hate seeing Hugh or Ellory or anyone I love feeling like this. I wish I could take all their pain away.

"It's completely normal to feel that way after a tragic life event," I say softly. "If it's that hurtful for you, I won't bring it up again, okay?"

He gulps, leans in to kiss me. "Thank you." He looks down at his bandage. "I should clean this." He stands, heads toward the bathroom.

Waiting until he turns on the faucet, I open the article Sloane texted me.

The headline reads:

LOCAL RUNAWAY BELIEVED DEAD

Chills wash up my spine.

My phone buzzes again. A new text from Sloane:

So what do you think?

Then another text:

The article is 20 yrs old. No picture included—she was under 18.

And another:

The family was interviewed. Her body was never found. Sorry, this is all I could find online.

I text her back:

Thanks, I'll check it out.

Hugh walks into the bedroom, wrapping a fresh bandage around his finger. "Everything okay?"

"Yeah." I drop my phone on the bed. "Just Sloane asking how I like that tea she gave me. You know, it's made by monks."

He laughs absently, steps back into the bathroom.

"Hey, Hugh?" He pokes his head out. "Can I ask you something? About Paige…"

"I thought we already talked about this."

"We did. But I wanted to ask you—how did she die?"

Hugh sighs, leans a shoulder against the door frame. "It was a long time ago. If the police couldn't figure it out, I doubt you could." He disappears back inside the bathroom. "I'm going to shower."

He turns the water on and shuts the door, effectively ending the conversation.

170 HOURS LEFT

They'd packed their motel rooms and trudged back out into the cold parking lot. For once, Ellory knew exactly what she was doing today. Drive. Drive until the sun set on the blurry horizon. Drive farther than she'd ever been before. Only Jade had a destination. No one else had anywhere to be. Davey and Mars said they wanted to make it to the West Coast. But that was it. First Cincinnati, then the West Coast.

Ellory imagined what was on the West Coast. California. Palm trees, deserts, the sea. It was a place so broad and general, Ellory suspected they could go anywhere and find a place to be happy. She said it over and over in her head. *Cincinnati, West Coast. Cincinnati, West Coast.* She liked it. It sounded good. Felt good.

Until the gas tank went dry, they'd forage the highways on their way to Cincinnati. No one said a word for their first hour back on the road, bellies empty, nervousness creeping into the car like a poisonous fog.

They knew they had no place to go except Shaw's car. They

hardly had any belongings. No food, no water, little money left. They could sell their phones, but what good would that do? It wouldn't be enough to buy shelter. It was winter, freezing, the sky twisting and low, ready to snow.

And so, they sat in cold, icy silence, waiting for someone to speak.

Finally, it was Jade who punctured the quiet.

"I'm starving," she said, rubbing her belly next to Ellory in the back seat.

They pulled over at the first stop they saw after passing over the border into Ohio. It was the third state they'd been in after leaving New York. First was Pennsylvania. Then, for just a few minutes, West Virginia. Now Ohio.

Soon, they'd drop off Jade. Then only several more square states to go and they'd be on the West Coast. A fuzzy feeling flooded over her, of success, of boldness, that she could do anything.

After buying two bags of fried food from a place called Karla's Hot Spot, Ellory fell into the back seat next to Jade and Davey. She didn't want to sit in the front anymore, and so when Mars asked if he could ride shotgun next to Shaw, Ellory said yes.

Shaw started the car and roared out of the dusty parking lot, onto a no-name road in rolling hills, the casts of gray mountains ever present in the distance around them. They didn't know where they were going. They were following the road, trusting Shaw to follow the sun and the signs to take them west of wherever they were. It stayed that way until the sun fell again, replaced by darkness.

Mars lowered the volume of the song playing on the radio, tilted his head toward his little brother Davey in the back seat. "Hey, what do you say we stop and get ourselves a little well-deserved bubbly? Some hitch and stitch Jimmy Crockett."

"What the hell are you talking about, man?" Shaw asked, turning the radio off.

"Some whiskey, beer. You know, it will make the drive go by faster."

Davey grinned, leaned up between the two front seats. "I second this."

"Sit back, Davey," Mars scolded. "Jesus. Shaw, pull over at the next liquor store you see. I have something I wanna try out."

Davey rolled his eyes in the darkness. Jade looked at Ellory, gripped her arm tight. Ellory wasn't sure if it was because she was scared or because she sensed Ellory was. After everything she'd learned in the short time she'd known Jade, Ellory guessed it was the latter.

Before Ellory could think of something to say to convince Shaw to stay on the road and not make another stop, the brakes screeched in front of a small stucco liquor store. No other cars were in the parking lot. Beer signs flickered in the windows. Shaw cut the engine.

Mars got out of the car, walked to the back, and dug around for a minute until he slammed the trunk closed, making Ellory jump. She followed the sound of his footsteps crunching in the gravel. He stopped in front of Shaw's window and leaned close, elbows on the ledge.

Shaw rolled his window down, cold air flooding the car.

"Hey, man—what the fuck," Shaw said nervously.

Ellory had known Shaw for almost a year, and she'd never heard his voice sound so clipped and frightened, not even after she'd once forgotten to call him when she got home, and he'd feared she'd gotten into a car accident.

Davey leaned forward, pushing Jade aside to get closer. "I thought you said you sold that. Why'd you bring it? What if we got pulled over?"

"You brought a fucking gun in my car?" Shaw said, opening his door. Mars tucked it into the back of his jeans. "Are you serious?"

Mars shrugged. "I thought you'd be cool with it."

"Cool? Really, man?"

"It's not like I'm gonna do anything with it. I'm going to play it cool. Just sit in the car if you don't want to come," Mars said. "God, you fucking pussy."

Shaw's eyes flickered toward Ellory in the back seat. "What'd you call me?"

"Nothing," Mars said, holding his arms out, innocent. "Just stop acting like my brother. I can't be around *two* fucking pussies."

Davey shook his head, slumped deeper into the back seat.

"You're not robbing this place," Shaw insisted.

Mars laughed. Jade gripped Ellory's arm tighter. Ellory's lungs constricted.

"No, man. There's always a back door. I'm just going to walk around and see what I can grab off the shelves. Watch. Maybe you'll learn something."

The gravel crunched as Mars disappeared behind the stucco building. Jade released her grip on Ellory's arm. Ellory reached into her coat pocket and clasped her inhaler. Knowing it was there, just in case, loosened her lungs.

Shaw leaned against the side of his car. The wait was agonizing, but soon Mars returned holding bottles of vodka in each of his hands.

"Start the car," he said quietly, then louder, *"Start the car."*

Shaw got in, turned the key. Mars fell into the front seat, dropped the bottles on the floor by his feet.

"Fucking drive, Shaw, *go.*"

Shaw reversed out of the parking lot and sped back onto the road. Ellory remained silent, gripping her cell phone in her coat pocket. She could call her mother. Ask her to please come and get her, wherever she was. She could call the police, too, if she really wanted.

But she didn't. She was afraid.

"Hey, wait," Jade said. "Wait!"

Mars lowered the radio. Jade never raised her voice. It squeaked a little after being quiet for so long.

Ellory looked over at her. The streetlights ignited her face every few seconds. She pointed out the window.

"Why did we just pass a sign that said Columbus? That's on the other side of the state," Jade said. "We should be in Cincinnati by now. We've been driving all day."

No one said a word until Mars exploded with laughter. Davey followed, then Shaw.

Gasping for air, Mars said, "We—we're not in Ohio anymore, little lady." And he laughed even harder.

Ellory felt faint. She didn't know why. She wanted to throw up. She held it back. Sensing it, Jade took her hand, squeezed it tight. Ellory turned to look at her. Tears streaked Jade's cheeks in the streetlights.

"Where are we, then?" Ellory asked shakily. "Are we going home?"

Shaw cleared his throat, spoke loud above their laughter. "We're never going home. We're in Columbus, *Indiana*, now. Some sign back there said."

Jade gulped. Ellory knew she was fighting back tears.

"But you said we were going to drop Jade off in Cincinnati," Ellory said. "Remember? Cincinnati, then the West Coast?" She repeated the mantra in her head, knowing it wasn't a lie: *Cincinnati, West Coast. Cincinnati, West Coast.*

Mars spun around in the passenger seat, passed a bottle of stolen vodka back to Davey. "We're taking a detour— Oh," he said, seeing Jade's tears. "Come on, Jade. No one wants to go to Cincinnati. Where you really wanna go is Vegas."

"Vegas!" Davey cheered, holding up the bottle. He uncapped it. A little sloshed out, tapped onto Ellory's thigh.

She leaned back. Still holding Jade's hand, Ellory turned to stare out the rear window into the night, knowing everything between them had just irrevocably shifted.

20

Another night I can't sleep. Hugh snores gently beside me in the dark. I envy him. I envy his seemingly dreamless sleep. He's just like Ellory in that way. They both sleep peacefully, barely shifting and moving throughout the night. Me? I'm a hurricane.

I get out of bed, deciding to leave a quick voicemail for Duplain. Maybe he's an early bird and will see my message before he gets too busy with other work. Maybe seeing how serious I am will make him take Ellory's case more seriously, too.

In the hallway, so I don't wake Hugh, I dial his number.

"Hello?"

I look at the screen. It's nearly three in the morning.

"Hello—hi, God, I'm sorry for calling so late. I just assumed I'd get your voicemail. I hope I didn't wake you. This is Iris. Iris Blodgett, Ellory's mom."

Music cuts out in the background. A bang. "Yeah, yes, uh, it is late, but I'm a night owl. I don't mind. Actually, I'm glad you called, in a way. I was going to reach out to you later today to ask further questions."

"Oh, sure." I hear a noise, walk down the hall. "I'm an open book."

He sighs. "Great. So, uh, has Ellory contacted you in any way?" I listen as he types quickly on a keyboard, the keys clacking.

"No."

Another sound echoes, a scraping sound, but it's not coming from this floor of the house. It's coming from downstairs.

"I need to know what else I can do. If there's anything I can do—"

"No, not necessary." The typing stops. "I'm doing all I can on my end. All you have to do is, uh, stay calm and trust me. You called *me* for a reason, right?"

I pause, pick at my nails. "Yes. I certainly did."

"Okay, listen. Sit tight. Contact me if the police get in touch with you."

"I will."

I follow the sound down the staircase to the second floor, an area of the house I've yet to explore.

"Great," Duplain says. "Try to limit your contact with others—Ellory's friends and any messages she's received on social media, for example. Don't write back. Leave all interviewing and prodding to me, okay? I know it can be difficult. I'll call you tomorrow, and we can set up a time to meet at your place, okay?"

"Okay. Thanks for answering."

"Anytime." He hangs up.

I follow the sound to a door, cracked open, golden light seeping into the dark hallway. When I press my shoulder against it, it whines open. Rebecca stands inside, her back to me. She's changed out of her demolition clothes into a silky white nightgown, thin strap fallen off one shoulder.

Startled, she spins around.

Her long brown hair is scooped up in a bun. A bandage

wraps around her forearm, a violent red line slashing through the gauze.

My eyes go wide. "My God, Rebecca, are you okay?" I ask, staring at her arm. "That looks serious."

She glances down at the blood-soaked bandage as if she's forgotten it's there. She scoffs. "Oh, this old thing? Yeah. Got it from working on the conservatory today. Nice, huh? It's my return favor for fixing this shitty old house." Rebecca gestures around the room in one sweeping motion.

I follow her gaze. The room glows with crystallized light from a chandelier in the recessed ceiling. An open space, it's divided into sections using furniture: sofas curled near a fireplace; opposing chairs by a wall of bookshelves; a desk facing outward in a corner, nestled between stained-glass windows. On the desk is an old computer, cobwebs connecting the monitor to the wood like sinew.

I drag my eyes back to Rebecca's arm. "What happened? Please don't say it was the same saw that cut Hugh's finger."

She breathes out, fills a shot glass from a label-less bottle. "No, not that. I cut it too close when I tried to squeeze into a small space. My sweater got caught on a nail. It was sticking out and was really sharp, apparently. I'll probably have to go get stitches in the morning. But I've already had my tetanus shot, so, silver linings."

"I'm sorry."

"It's okay." She shrugs. "Not your fault. Accidents happen, I guess. I wish they'd happen to someone else, though." She raises the shot glass to her mouth, laughs between sips.

"What are you doing in here?" I ask.

"Can't sleep. Plus, I'm kind of hoping Mother gets pissed at me for being in here."

"Why?"

"This room belonged to that asshole husband of hers."

My eyes go wide. "You mean…your father?"

"Yeah. You're right. My father." She falls back onto a leather sofa, the plump cushions groaning as she sits. Tipping the glass back, she glances around the room as she swallows with a wince. "This was his study. I think Hugh wanted to rip down that wallpaper." She nods toward the desk. I look over at the wallpaper peeling at the corners.

Rebecca slides the glass onto a table, walks over to the desk. Grabbing a second shot glass from inside a cabinet, she fills it to the brim, passing it to me before refilling hers again.

"Should we be in here?" I take a sip. It burns my throat. I hold back a gag. It smells of corn, raw and earthen. "What is this?" I ask, slightly terrified.

Rebecca studies me, her brown eyes bloodshot. "It's homemade." She lifts a hand, pinches a peeling slice of wallpaper. "Did Hugh ever tell you what happened in this room?" The wallpaper flays off the wall easily, like dead skin.

"No." I step closer. "Why? What would he have said?"

Rebecca throws her head back and cackles. For a moment, I'm terrified.

"Father did it right here," she whispers, nodding at the spot where I'm standing.

I inch away. "Did what?"

"Killed himself, of course."

She places her glass on the desk, reaches up, and tears the paper again. It falls in a curling ribbon near her feet. I look up at the wall. A jolt of panic shoots through me.

On the wall, hidden beneath the wallpaper—*blood*, in a butterfly-shaped splatter, the color of old meat. Blood, smeared in long swipes from where someone had attempted to clean it.

I sip my drink, feel it burn on the way down, but soon it doesn't burn anymore at all. Rebecca watches, grinning like a cat, peering at me over the top of her rim. Soon, my body feels heavy from my head to my thighs, like gravity has amplified and is trying to swallow me into the earth.

"I don't understand," I breathe out. "Why would you do this?"

She shrugs, crosses the room, pours herself another glass, refills mine, too. "Do you know how bad my arm hurts?" she asks. "It throbs. All the time. I'm going to have a scar. When my singing career takes off, I'm going to be the singer with the giant scar."

I blink. "You did this knowing Birdie would see it?" She looks at me coyly, answers my question with her eyes. "You *want* her to see it. But why?"

"Because," she seethes, "I'm just trying to help Hugh and Gabe with these repairs. And now look at me." She holds out her arm as if I somehow missed the white gauze with the giant bloodstain oozing through it. "It's her fault. All these years she never once attempted to try to fix this giant old house. And now look at it. It's literally falling apart—from *her* neglect." Rebecca's already flushed cheeks turn a sharp cherry red.

I inch to leave. She steps closer.

"Don't you want to know what else happened in here?"

I step back. "Not really."

"After Paige died, the entire family went to shit." I narrow my eyes, hover in the doorway. I'm battling whether to stay or go. Listen or leave. I choose to listen. I want to know about Paige. But as my head begins to swirl, I doubt my decision.

"Mother grew distant and Father grew angry. He shot her..." Rebecca points to her hip. "It's why she walks with a cane. Bastard tried to kill her. Then turned the gun on himself. Right here."

I force myself not to look at the blood-soaked wall behind the desk.

Rebecca reaches for the bottle again. My mind spins. I've only had one glass—no, two?—and I feel this way. How much has Rebecca had? How is she still standing when I feel like I'm about to collapse?

Rebecca barks out a laugh, pokes her tongue between her teeth.

"You're fun, Iris," she whispers. "I like you. Even if Gabe doesn't."

"Thanks?"

"You should talk to him. I think he has something to tell you about Camille."

"Camille?"

"We keep asking him where she went, but he'll never say." Rebecca's hair has come loose from her bun, falling down the side of her head like a melted candle. "I'm worried you were right. What if he *did* do something?"

My concentration breaks. I turn to stare at the blood-soaked wall.

"What?"

She ushers me out of the room, shuts the door behind us. In the light from the staircase, her pupils look like tiny fires.

Rebecca drains what's left of her glass. "What if what you said is right? What if Gabe *did* kill Camille?"

21

As I rush back down the hall to my bedroom, a tingling feeling crawls across my skin, like someone is watching me. Careful not to wake Hugh, I cross the room, trying to avoid the squeaky spots. My legs move like jelly but feel heavy as stone as I step into the bathroom and shut the door.

What did Rebecca put in that drink? I didn't think I'd had that much, but the world spins, a carousel inside my pounding head. As I splash cold water on my face, someone calls my name, faint at first, then louder.

Screaming.

"Iris…*Iris. IRIS!*"

I turn off the water, listen closely.

The voice comes from outside.

It's Jack.

I look out the window to the woods. The sky is pale purple and glowing, bulging with the weight of winter. Jack's voice disappears, but there's movement in the distance. I step closer to see; my nose taps the glass. Dark figures hover at the edge of the tree line.

One.

Two.

Three.

Standing in a line. Motionless, staring.

My heart pounds like a drum.

I turn to see if Hugh hears it, too. But he's still dead asleep. I look back out the window. The three figures have disappeared, but something else has replaced them. Through the trees, two lights glow bright. Headlights.

A car idles at the end of the driveway.

Grabbing my phone, I rush downstairs. The house is dark. The walls groan from the wind. Shadows flutter outside in the courtyard. I turn on the flashlight on my phone. A doorknob rattles. Someone's here—someone's trying to get in the house.

It's them. I know it is. I'd seen them, a row of shadowy figures, backs lined up against the trees. They must've parked at the end of the driveway and walked through the woods. It has to be them. They always knew where to find me.

I unlock my phone, dial 911.

The front door creaks open. Footsteps swish across the floor.

A woman answers. "911, what's your emergency?"

I whisper *"There's someone in our house"* and give her the address as I creep along the perimeter of each room.

Hanging up, I look outside to see if I see anything. But no one is there. Moonlight spills in through an open window, igniting a corner of the room. Something silver glows on a bookshelf, and I reach for the object, feel the sharp edge, the metal cold in my palm. A knife.

I grip the handle tight in my fist, inch into the kitchen, hold it out in front of me. A copper pot falls to the floor, the sound rupturing the silence. I scream, jump backward. The knife tumbles out of my hand, skitters across the floor.

Shadows grow from the darkness.

I trip, fall forward, catch myself on the kitchen island, stomach slamming on the granite edge. Air plunges out of me. My stomach heaves. Light rockets through the air, singeing my eyes. I wince away, slam my eyelids shut.

"*Iris.*"

Rebecca stands behind me, hand covering her mouth in shock. Another woman is here, someone I don't recognize. Her black hair is long and straight, with bangs cut sharp at her eyebrows. The woman stares at me, terrified, back pressed against a wall.

"What are you doing? Why do you have a knife?" Rebecca screams, then turns to the other woman. "My God, are you okay?"

I blink my eyes, try to clear them. My vision blurs. "I don't feel good." Vomit stirs at the base of my throat. I hunch over, clutch my stomach. *What was in that drink?*

"I didn't think she had that much," Rebecca says softly to the woman near the wall. "I had more than she did, and I'm fine."

Rebecca moves closer to the woman, takes her in her arms, tells her she's sorry, asks again if she's all right. Her girlfriend, I realize, after reading their body language.

"Iris?" Hugh's voice carries from down the hall.

He enters the kitchen. Rebecca goes silent.

"What's going on?" He steals a look at me, and whatever he sees must shock him. He runs to me, takes me in his arms.

Rebecca shakes her head, still frozen with panic. "Kara came over to talk. We were outside smoking and came in for something to eat when Iris fucking *attacked* us."

"I thought someone broke in," I struggle to explain. My vision doubles. "I saw a car outside and people—"

"People?" Hugh asks. "What people?"

"Outside. Three of them. They were standing there watching the house and— No, wait." I stop. Pause. "You put something in my drink." I point at Rebecca.

"What? No, I didn't."

"You did. You poisoned me."

Rebecca laughs. Kara laughs, too, and for a moment I want to melt into the floor.

"I didn't *poison* you," Rebecca says, her pretty face carved into a look of sympathy. "You drank moonshine. And a little too much of it, I think."

"Moon—what?"

Hugh shakes his head. "Iris hardly drinks, Rebecca," he tells his sister. "She's drunk off two glasses of wine. Our engagement dinner should've told you that much. She has no tolerance."

With the mention of our engagement, I glance down at my left hand, see the ring affixed on my finger, diamonds and rubies gleaming in the fluorescent light. For a moment, it looks like I'm wearing someone else's hand.

Rebecca's lips flatline. Kara looks at me apologetically in understanding. *I've been there*, her eyes say.

"Is everyone okay? I heard screaming." Gabe explodes into the kitchen. The room shrinks. "Hey, Kara." He nods to Rebecca's girlfriend. "What's going on?"

"Nothing," Rebecca says. "Go back to bed."

"Not until someone tells me what's going on."

The doorbell rings in the distance.

"Crap," I swear under my breath.

Hugh looks at me. "Who's that?" But I can't find the words to answer him.

He glances at the phone clenched in my hand, then scrapes his gaze across my face. I shut my eyes, press my lips together as if, somehow, I can hide.

"Iris," Hugh begins. "Did you call the police?"

Kara's mouth falls open.

"Dammit, Iris." Rebecca's voice is thick with disappointment. "Why'd you have to do that?"

Hugh releases me to go answer the door. I collapse onto a nearby stool.

"I can't fucking believe this," Gabe grumbles.

I gulp, clench my teeth together, try to keep myself composed when two cops walk into the kitchen, Hugh right behind them.

"What seems to be the problem?" the taller of the two says. All heads snap to me. Hugh walks out from behind them, stands next to me.

When no one answers, Hugh tries to calm the situation. "It's a misunderstanding. My fiancée believed there was an intruder, and she called 911 as a precaution."

Gabe rolls his eyes. Kara nudges him in his ribs.

The cop writes in a notepad. "Mmm-hmm," he says to himself. "And what's that knife there, some kind of weapon?" He points his pen to the unsheathed dagger resting on the kitchen island. "That blood on it?"

"What? No," I rush to say.

Gabe laughs. "That's an antique dagger used in the Civil War," he explains. "The blood on it is older than this house."

"Mmm-hmm," the cop mumbles. "And no one's hurt?" We all look at each other, shake our heads. "And...you." He glances at me. "You're the one who made the call to Dispatch?" I nod. "Can you tell me what prompted you to call?"

I tell him about the idling car, the headlights at the end of the driveway, the three dark figures I saw when I looked out the window. He nods as I speak, jots down a few notes.

When I'm done speaking, he asks Rebecca, "What happened to your arm? Looks like a pretty nasty wound."

Rebecca removes her arm from around Kara's shoulders. The blood seeping through the bandage has dried to a dark cherry stain. "I hurt it in a construction accident."

The shorter of the two cops grunts as he eyes Rebecca up

and down: her long legs and shiny chocolate-brown hair. The flowery pastel sweater she wears over a silky white nightgown.

"It's *true*," Kara says, giving the cop a sharp glare. "It happened today on a shitty old nail."

"And who are you?" the taller cop asks.

"Her girlfriend," Kara says. Tilting her chin up, she squares her shoulders, unafraid.

The cop steps closer to Rebecca and Kara, drops his gaze. "And do you have any drugs in your possession?" He sniffs the air around them like a dog. "I smell marijuana."

"Legal," Kara says.

"No," the cop retorts, taking another sniff. "I'm thinking there's a little something *extra* mixed in."

The other cop asks, "Angel dust? Acid? Now, *that* would be illegal."

"What? *No...*" Rebecca trails off. Her lips tremble, eyes burgeoning with tears.

"You fucking bitch." I turn to see Gabe searing a hole through me.

The cop angles himself toward Gabe. "Sir, don't use that language."

"Look what you're doing to Rebecca. You called the police because you imagine things," he seethes.

"Gabe," Hugh barks.

"Shut up," Gabe shouts back.

"Sir—"

"She's a liar, Officer." Gabe shoves his finger in my face.

When I look up, he's towering over me, so close I can see my reflection in his smudged glasses.

Hugh presses a hand on Gabe's chest, shoves him away. "Back off."

"Hey," the cop warns Hugh. "That's *enough*."

Words pour from me, so fast I can't stop. "He's calling me a liar because I know he *killed his wife*."

"Come on, Iris," Hugh says in my ear. "You're not helping here."

"What did you say?" the short cop asks.

"What's going on in here?" We spin around. Birdie stands in the doorway wearing a velvet robe and matching slippers. "Oh, dear God," she gasps.

"Are you the homeowner?" the tall cop asks.

"Yes," she says. "Someone tell me what's happened."

The short cop turns back to Gabe. "Sir, where's your wife?"

Gabe's eyes fill with seething hatred, and he lunges at me, arms extended, fingers curling like claws. His grip fastens tight around my neck. My bones pop. I wriggle away. His grip tightens. Air bubbles through my lips.

In a heartbeat, Hugh jumps forward, grabs Gabe's hands, rips him off me so forcefully I don't know how he doesn't shatter Gabe's wrists. The cops grab Gabe by his arms, pull him away.

I stumble backward, terrified, instinctively reach for the knife. Rebecca sees what I'm after, runs to snatch it away.

"What are you doing?" Gabe screams, trying to escape their grip on him. They push him against a wall, handcuff him.

"Oh, dear God," Birdie cries, tears streaming down her cheeks. "Gabe—*no*, you can't take him, he needs his medication. Please take his medication. His heart, his heart, *his heart!*"

"Sir, we're placing you under arrest for assault and resisting arrest…"

"Iris!" Gabe screams, his face flash-boiling with rage. "You did this, Iris. You *bitch*."

Kara steps forward, yells at the cops, "You can't do this!" Her eyes fill with frustration as she speaks. "*We* called *you*—you can't do this. You can't just come in here and do this!"

The cops pull Gabe down the hall. Rebecca and Kara run after them. Hugh holds me tight, his arms wrapped around me, and I know I'd crumple without him.

Birdie wipes her eyes dry. "I don't understand—why did he

do that? He needs his medication. Hugh, Hugh." She waves her hand to get his attention. "Please, he needs his heart medication."

Rebecca and Kara return. "They said we can call the station in the morning, that Gabe will probably make bail tomorrow, and we can pick him up then," Rebecca explains.

"He should be okay for one night without his prescription," Kara says softly, glancing at Birdie.

"I'm sorry," I whisper. But no one says another word.

Hugh helps Birdie back to bed. Rebecca and Kara follow behind, turning off the kitchen lights before they leave. No one bothers with me, and I know it's for the best. I sit alone in the darkness, the room spinning until the sun rises through the trees.

158 HOURS LEFT

"Truth or dare," Shaw asked Mars.

Shaw had driven until the sky grew darker and the air grew colder, pulling into a little dirt lane with the headlights off. The tires crunched through the gravel, leading them deep into a forgotten cemetery, granite tombstones sprouting from the frostbitten earth like fingernails.

They'd parked between a looming statue of an angel and one of the few twisted bare trees in the wide-open field. It gave Ellory chills. She hated cemeteries. She vowed, after watching her grandfather be buried, that she never wanted to be buried. She wanted to be placed in a mausoleum, or a pyramid, like an ancient Egyptian queen, a stone-carved coffin left alone in a dark room to grow a century's worth of spiderwebs. Not having worms and beetles eat her from the inside out.

Ellory glanced at the nearby tombstone Mars sat on. Between his legs, she could read a name: *Grace*, and a year: *1991*. She hoped that was the year Grace had died, not the year she was born.

Mars wiped his mouth dry with the back of his sleeve. "Truth."

Shaw took the bottle of stolen vodka, held it in two hands, raised it to his lips. It sloshed in the plastic jug as he passed it to Ellory, who was next in the circle. She looked into the mouth, stared down at the clear liquid in the darkness.

Ellory leaned her back against the side of the car, knowing if she drank, she'd be, in a way, condoning Mars's choice to rob the liquor store. What would that make her? An accomplice? That wasn't like her. That wasn't like Shaw, either. Or was it?

Ever since they'd picked up his old friends, things had changed. Shifted. Ellory feared it wasn't for the better. She wondered for the hundredth time why Shaw ever befriended someone like Mars.

They were locked in a constant battle with each other, Shaw and Mars, each fighting to take control of the pack, like wolves. Ellory felt Mars's gaze on her. If she wanted to remain a member of the pack, she'd have to drink.

The bottle felt heavy as she raised it to her lips, pretending to swallow. Mars leaned forward, tipped the bottom of the jug up, forced the liquid deeper into her throat. It slid down her chin and she reflexively gulped down a mouthful to clear her airway. She pulled the bottle away, gasping, and passed the jug to Jade before any of them could see her wince.

Shaw draped his heavy arm over her shoulders. It felt like it weighed a hundred pounds. "All right," he drawled, as if the vodka had already hit. "Truth... Why don't you tell us all why you and your brother really left home?"

Mars peered at Shaw, folded his arms. Ellory felt this was all a game to him, just to see who could make it out alive. She guessed this wasn't his first time away from home. He and his brother always seemed to hover over their food, like a vulture was about to swoop down and steal it. They always seemed to be on the lookout, dark eyes flitting back and forth, like any second someone would walk up behind them and take a baseball bat to the backs of their skulls.

Shaw didn't act that way. He'd always been kind, laid-back, honest. She liked Shaw. She thought she loved him. She did love him, in a way. She had to now.

Mars spit into the frost-slicked grass, stood from Grace's grave. Ellory could read the entire tombstone now. Grace Ann Poole: 1902–1991. She breathed a sigh of relief.

"Our dad beat us," Davey said when Mars failed to answer the question.

Shaw's eyebrows knit together. Jade shifted uncomfortably. Ellory studied Davey and Mars but was careful not to let it show.

"It's true," Mars said when Shaw threw a doubtful look. "He beat us bad, liked to use hammerheads. Left us with welts the size of baseballs."

Shaw gulped. "Her—um—Ellory's dad used to beat her, too."

Ellory's eyes expanded. *"Shaw,"* she scolded, pushing his arm off her shoulder. "What the fuck?"

He gave her a wry smile and looked back at Mars.

Mars sat back on Grace, crossed his arms.

"That so?"

"Yeah, it's so," Shaw rebuffed, as if telling Mars how his girlfriend's father used to beat her would mold him into a tougher man.

"It's not so," Ellory said, stunned she had the gumption to speak up. Her father was a lot of things, did a lot of things, but he'd never beaten her. He was more creative than that.

Shaw snatched the vodka bottle out of Davey's hands. "Oh, yeah?" Shaw said. "You told me he did. Were you lying?"

Ellory's body went cold. She looked at Grace's tombstone. In the moonlight, the granite had a hint of pink. Jade curled her arm in Ellory's, subtly tugged her away.

"N–no, I wasn't," Ellory said. "He didn't beat me. He locked me in the attic."

She mumbled it under her breath on purpose, hoping they heard, hoping they didn't. More than anything, she hoped they'd all just drop it and move on to something else.

Davey laughed. "Didn't your mom do something?"

Ellory sighed wearily. "My mom doesn't have good taste in men."

"Unlike you," Shaw joked.

The boys laughed and soon disbanded, leaving Ellory and Jade alone.

"Is that true?" Jade asked Ellory. "What you said about your dad? And the attic?"

Ellory looked down, kicked at a stone with her toe. She looked up at Grace, then back at Jade. Jade curled her brittle blond hair behind an ear, looking like she was about to cry. If Ellory had a mean streak in her, she could tease Jade now, like other girls would do, but she wouldn't.

Instead, Ellory smiled at her so she didn't begin to cry, too. Jade smiled back.

"Yeah, it's true," Ellory whispered.

Jade's eyes filled with tears. "I'm sorry," she said. "My dad was an asshole, but he left, so he doesn't sound like your dad. My mom's worse, though. She comes home drunk with guys and they beat me, too. Gang up on me. I figured my mom's life would be better if I wasn't there. So I left. But you didn't deserve that. I would hate being locked in the attic. I'd hate being trapped anywhere I didn't wanna be."

"Thanks. But in a way, I think it worked out for the best. My dad would lock me up there when I misbehaved, and my mother assumed I had just run away. The first few times," Ellory said, "my mother would call the police to report me as missing because my dad wouldn't tell her where I was. But now that I've really run away this time, I know the police won't do anything."

"Why?" Jade asked, wiping a tear from her eye, and Ellory knew Jade's empathy could be the death of her.

Ellory shrugged and scanned the tombstones, black dots against the lipstick-red sunrise. "Because she called so much, they got sick of her. Said I was just a girl who liked to disappear. She didn't know all those times I was never missing. I was still always inside the house."

"*Fuck.*"

Ellory looked over to find Shaw sitting in the driver's seat, nervously grinding the key in the ignition. The engine heaved mechanical cries, but no matter how many times Shaw tried, the car failed to start.

"Fucking *shit.*" Shaw banged his fists against the steering wheel. Mars began arguing with Shaw. Davey started cursing.

Ellory turned away. The red sunrise danced off the polished tombstones like gems. Jade followed Ellory as she walked deeper into the cemetery, wishing for the first time in her life she could crawl down into the earth and disappear.

2 DAYS BEFORE

THURSDAY, JANUARY 23

22

I'm standing in a world of white...

The woods behind our house were thick with mature trees. Each time you left, you had no choice but to travel down a narrow lane before connecting with the busier main road. No matter what time of year, I always loved those few minutes of driving down that lane.

In the summer, the papery trunks of birch trees would peel away, flutter into the road. In the spring, the sugary scent of blossoms would linger in the air from the honeysuckle hedges. And in the fall, golden leaves would trail across the pavement, pushed by the wind, and each time Ellory thought they were a mouse, and she'd shout, Don't run it over!

No one knew this winding, narrow road that looped through the woods. No one, unless you were local. It was a beautiful area of town, especially in the winter when it snowed, when the smoothly paved road turned black, as if shined up with grease like an old boot, and the dark river of road snaked through the world of white.

This is where I found his body.

I wake. It was only a dream, one I've been having often, one I fear will haunt me forever.

It's a new day, and I stretch awake, slide out of bed. The shower is running, so I hurry to get dressed before Hugh comes out. I can't face him today. I just need one day to let things settle, to get the family's anger off me and let things calm.

I tug on a pair of jeans, pull on a cream-colored sweater with little yellow flecks of yarn, lace up a pair of chunky leather boots. Checking in the mirror, I see my skin looks blotchy and my black hair somehow seems even darker against my lifeless complexion.

But I can't help that now, not when the shower shuts off. A moment later Hugh emerges into the bedroom, towel slung low around his hips. The scar along his rib cage has deepened to a dark pink hue from the hot water.

I smile politely at him, cross the room to get my coat.

"Iris…" he mumbles, sighing when I don't reply. "Iris, please."

"I'm just going to take a drive, that's all. And when I come back, can we please start looking for somewhere else to go? I don't care where. We'll have to make it work."

Hugh places a hand on his heart. "You're that desperate to get away from me? To leave me? Please, don't go."

"Of course I don't want to leave you. But you have to understand why I'd want to leave this house." I grab my purse off the chair near the door, place my hand on the knob.

The muscles in his jaw flex as he examines me. "I don't want you to leave. I want you to stay." He comes at me, arms open for a hug. "Stay. Help me with the renovation. I promise…I'll only work on it for two more weeks." His hands find me, pull me close, water cooling me as my sweater soaks it off his bare chest. "That's it. Two weeks. There are holes in the roof. I can't leave it the way it is, not in the middle of winter. We can do it together. Why don't you give me some design tips? Let me know how you'd like the house to look if it were ours."

"I'd want everything gone. I'd want it to look like a different house."

Hugh shifts uncomfortably. "Okay..." He trails off, dejected. "Or we can talk about the wedding. We can start to plan. We can plan the *biggest* reception you want, anywhere in the world."

"Why can't Birdie just hire someone to come and fix the roof, anyway? Why are you the only one who can do it?"

He inches back toward the bathroom door, clamps the towel closed around his waist. "She doesn't want any outsiders on the property."

I narrow my eyes at him. "I'm an outsider. I'm on the property."

He laughs, nervous. "You're different. But anyway, none of that matters. Let's think of where we want to get married. We can go to Hawaii." He grins with the prospect. "Italy. Maybe Paris."

I know he's trying to get me to stay, but I'm hanging on by a thread and the last thing I want to talk about when I'm upset is our wedding. *As if I'd ever think of planning anything without Ellory, anyway,* I think but don't say.

"Look," he begins, adjusting the towel around his waist. Water drips down his chest. "It's fine. I understand your mind is preoccupied with Ellory. Mine is, too, and for a moment, I thought I could help you think about something else, something good and positive. All I worry about is her and having her home and—" He stops himself, exhales a deep breath. "I'm sorry. Listen to me, blubbering. I only want her safe. I worry. Teens drive recklessly. Teens, generally, are reckless." He laughs, trying to lighten the mood. I can't help but smile back, only a little. "I just want to know she's okay. Don't you want to know she's okay?"

"Of *course* I do."

"Then see?" He steps forward, places a hand on my shoulder, the other holding the towel closed. "You understand, then, why I like to dream about our wedding or plan our honeymoon or play around with color schemes for our future bedroom. It helps keep my mind calm, if only for a second."

"Hugh," I say sharply. "I need to leave this house."

He looks at me, eyes widening with fury. Pivoting away, he goes back into the bathroom, slamming the door shut so hard a painting rattles off its nail and falls to the floor. The house groans with displeasure.

I stand frozen, shocked by his reaction. He's never acted like this before, ever. And he wants me to stay in this house—*live* in this house with his family for two more weeks, after everything that's happened.

No matter how much I love Hugh, even in his moment of anger, I can't subject myself to his family much longer. I can't. I won't. Before he opens the door again, I run from the bedroom and through the house, only stopping when I reach my car, locking the doors before I speed away.

I drive straight to see Sloane. She's working today, like every day, and I walk in, needing strong coffee and someone to tell me I'm doing the right thing by leaving.

Sloane is busy with a customer, so I sit on a stool, hold my head in a hand. Soon, she slides over a latte and leans forward, elbows on the counter.

"I've never seen you like this, Iris."

"I know." I take a sip. It's too hot and burns my tongue. I keep drinking anyway.

"What happened?"

I raise my eyebrows, unfurl the knit scarf around my neck. "Where to begin? Should I tell you how Hugh just exploded at me? Or how his entire family is pissed at me because I'm the reason why Gabe was arrested last night?"

"What?" she gasps. "Hugh's brother?"

"Yes, the giant asshole with a missing wife and domestic abuse record who tried to strangle me."

"Wait..." Sloane begins. "What the hell's happening over there? You move away for five minutes and you're getting fucking strangled? Where is this guy? I'll—"

"In jail."

"Jail?"

I nod, glance down at my engagement ring. In the shadows beneath the counter, the ruby looks like a black diamond. My eyes space out. It feels like I'm staring into an abyss. I blink, look up.

"How do you think Ellory is?"

Sloane pushes herself off the counter. "I know she's doing fine. But what I'm worried about right now is *you*. Did that investigator of yours turn anything up?"

"You mean Duplain?" I say, glancing at Sloane, and for some reason, I get the impression she refuses to use his name. "Not yet, but I should call him today. He wants to meet at the house. I know this is what I need to do for Ellory, but I don't want to go back there."

Sloane raises an eyebrow.

I bite my nails, resigned. "Don't worry, I'm going back there to meet with him. That's the plan. I have to, right? I have no choice."

She sighs. "Tell me what happened." She grabs a brownie from the glass display case, slides it over on a plate.

It melts in my mouth as I tell Sloane everything, from last night with Rebecca in her father's study: the blood on the wall, the drink that made me sick. How I swore I saw three dark figures in the woods and heard someone in the house. How I called the police and everything after.

What I don't tell her is how I've never felt like more of an outsider.

"I hope they keep him locked up forever. He lunged at you? Choked you? What was he going to do? Murder you right there in front of the police? In front of Hugh and his mom?"

"The worst part is Camille still hasn't shown up. Even Rebecca said she agreed with me."

"She did?"

I nod. "Yeah. She was questioning if Gabe had something to do with Camille's disappearance. Something's seriously wrong. But I don't know what."

Sloane steals a bite of the brownie. "You know what I think?" she says, mouth full. "I think after you go back to the house to meet with Duplain, you need to try and stay away from Hugh's family for a while. At least until Hugh shows he has your back and supports you over his family. You want me to talk to him?"

"No, don't. I'll figure it out."

Sloane wipes the counter clean, wrings out the towel in her hands. "Okay. I trust your judgment. Always have."

I exhale. "Somehow, I have to make things right."

"If you can't, Ainsley's new place is nice. You've been there. I'll ask her if you can crash there awhile—if I ever see her again."

"What's going on with her?"

Sloane gives a worried glance. "She never came to work. The night of your engagement dinner is the last time I saw her. I've texted, called, left messages. When I get a chance, I'm going to go knock on her door, see if she's home."

"Well, she just won her divorce battle and got a huge settlement, right?"

Sloane nods.

"So maybe she just took off on a fancy vacation somewhere and doesn't need the job anymore. Maybe she took that cruise you guys talked about."

"She would've told me." Sloane taps her shiny red nails on the counter.

"Now you have me worried." I unlock my phone, text Ainsley:

Hey, where are you? We miss you. Are you ok?

I press Send, look up. Sloane gives me a grim smile. "Maybe she'll text you back."

"I hope so."

Sloane looks at me. Her brown eyes dim and her shoulders slump, and for a heartbeat, I see what she'll look like in twenty years.

She reaches over, places a hand on my arm, and sighs. "The past few weeks, I've noticed Ainsley seemed...preoccupied. I chalked it up as her dealing with that lousy husband and their lawyers with the divorce, but it felt like, I don't know, like it had become more than that. She dodged my questions."

"What kind of questions?"

Her mouth lifts at the corner as she thinks. "Anytime I'd asked her how the divorce was going, if she needed any help. I'd ask *why* she was getting divorced—did he cheat? Did she cheat? Was it something else? I mean, look at me, I've been through two. I know the reason most marriages end is money."

I nod in agreement. Steadily, the line of customers is building, and I pick up on Sloane's nervous energy that she needs to rush over soon to help her employees.

"But considering their house, money wasn't their problem," Sloane says. *"House."* She rolls her eyes, gives a short laugh. "If you could call it that. Place was so big they had two ovens. Who has two ovens?"

An employee, a pretty girl with flame-red hair, calls Sloane's name.

She calls back, "Be right there, Lani," turns to me, grabs my hand, squeezes. "Don't tell Ainsley what I'm about to tell you. Promise me."

"You know I won't," I say.

Sloane glances over a shoulder to be sure the customers at a nearby table don't hear. She leans over the counter, whispers, "I know something about Ainsley. Something awful. Something I think you should know."

My phone buzzes violently on the counter. We both jump. I glance at the screen. "It's the police. I need to get this," I say and answer the call, my blood humming with nerves. Sloane inches closer to listen in above the low roar of the café.

"Hello," a woman's husky voice sounds on the other end, "is this Iris Blodgett?"

"Yes."

"Are you available to come by the station today? It pertains to your daughter, Ellory Blodgett."

"I'll be right there." The call ends.

"What happened?" Sloane rushes to ask. "Is everything okay?"

"They need me to come by. It's about Ellory."

Sloane fidgets nervously with her beaded bracelets. Giving a worried look, she asks, "What if someone saw Ellory?"

I pull out my car keys. "If someone did, we need to know."

23

I sprint to the front counter of the police station, my heart in my throat.

"Hi, someone just called and said they had to speak with me about my missing daughter?"

"Name?" asks a woman sitting behind a glass partition.

"Ellory Blodgett."

"*Ellory...*" She types in Ellory's information, says, "Okay, looks like we still need a recent photo to update our file." Under the glass partition, she slides a piece of paper. "Also fill that out. Height, weight, clothes last seen in."

I glance at the paper. "This is all you needed me to come in for?"

The woman looks up at me for the first time, says nothing.

I try to stay calm when all I want to do is cry. "I already told them all of this over the phone when I called to make the missing person's report."

"Yeah," the woman says, rolling her chair over to grab something off a printer. "I guess they need it again. Fill that out.

You can email us a recent picture to the address on the top of that page."

"That's it?"

The woman stares at me from behind her thick glasses. "That's it. We'll call you if we learn anything new."

My hand shakes as I grab the paper off the counter. "My daughter is missing. Why isn't more being done to find her?"

An officer approaches the woman from behind, places a hand on the back of her chair.

"What's the problem?"

The woman glances up at the officer behind her, turns back to me. "Please stay calm, ma'am. Keep in mind it isn't a crime to go missing as an adult. And..." She trails off, adjusts her glasses to read the computer screen. "Ms. Blodgett is eighteen. Individuals over eighteen who are mentally competent can choose to disappear."

The officer, picking up on the situation, adds, "Things like this always put us in a difficult spot. We're limited in our response with cases where there isn't any clear evidence of involuntary disappearance."

I look back and forth between them. "You mean if there was evidence my daughter was *kidnapped*, you'd do something."

Another officer emerges from around a corner, drops a stack of files on the desk. "Filing, Jessa, today if you can. Sir, please walk around. Jessa will process you out."

"Ma'am, step aside," Jessa orders.

Before I can move, a man rounds the corner and comes toward me.

Not just any man. Gabe.

He stares at me, shuffles over to the counter.

"Sign here." Jessa slides him a piece of paper and a pen.

"You made bail?" I don't attempt to mask my shock. "How could they have let you out so fast? You assaulted me. You have domestic abuse on your record. I know what you did to Camille in the past and—"

Gabe talks over me. "You know, you have some nerve being here. What are you doing? Waiting for me to be released? You want to see me at my lowest?" Gritting his teeth, he picks up the pen, signs his name, throws it down. "You're a piece of work."

"I'm here because my daughter is missing, in case you forgot."

"Oh, I kind of did. Sorry."

"Sign here, too, sir," Jessa says, sliding the paper back to him under the glass partition.

"So you don't care about Ellory. Don't you care about your wife?" He glances at me, flips the paper, signs his name again. "Where is she?"

"My wife?" he snarls. "My *wife*? Why don't you mind your own goddamn business?"

"I can't. I care about Camille, even if you don't." I cross my arms. "Rebecca knows you did something. *I* know you did something. I saw you that night. I saw you outside digging. You did something to your wife. Why don't you just admit it?"

Gabe lets out a grim laugh. "And Mother is always asking why I never get along with anyone. It's because I know how people really are."

"Where is she, Gabe?"

The officers have vanished, leaving only Jessa. Soon, she disappears, too. And then it's only the two of us.

Gabe steps closer, licks his dry lips. If he touches me, if he—

"Are you ready?"

I turn toward the voice.

Camille walks down the hall, two coats folded over her arm.

"Oh. Iris," she says when she sees me, laughing nervously. "What are you doing here?"

"Camille?"

Gabe sighs, oozing satisfaction. "I didn't do anything to her," he says, gleeful. "In fact, she drove back from her mom's house in Connecticut to pay my bail."

I look at her standing there, confused, glancing back and forth between us.

Gabe leans close to whisper in my ear. "Things will be better than ever. Camille decided to stay with me. After she goes back to her mom's house to pack, she's going to move into the house with me—permanently. So if you want to keep blaming me for hurting my wife, go ahead. Do it. Make yourself look even crazier than we already *know* you are. My brother deserves better."

The blood drains from my face. I gulp down the knot in my throat, grip the strap of my bag so tight my knuckles burn.

I look at Camille, concern filling me. "Are you sure you're okay? I was so worried about you."

Camille says nothing. She looks down at the floor.

Gabe laughs at me cruelly, shakes his head. I can almost read his thoughts: *Oh, Iris. You sick, sad bitch.*

Tears prick my eyes. I rush out of the building, yank open my car door. I stare through the windows of the police station, watch as he grabs Camille's wrist, tugs her to the door.

All my life, people pitied me. They used my kindness against me and took advantage. They looked at me and saw weakness. *Teen mom. Widow. Single mother. Unemployed. Homeless.*

Now, thanks to Gabe, I've finally decided to prove them all wrong.

For once, I want to be the person who gets to make the decisions. Who people turn to in a crisis. I can't be, not yet. But I can try. From now on, I have to try. I may not have anything to offer anyone, but I can offer my help, my time, and I can always offer kindness—while still keeping boundaries.

One day, I want to be the port in the storm, to not need anything from anyone. I want to stand on my own two feet, self-supporting, independent, brave, fierce. Right now, I'm none of those things, no matter how much I want to be. I'm not there yet. But I can try. Every day, I can try. If not for myself, then for Ellory. I won't allow Gabe or anyone else to ever hurt me again.

It starts today.

24

After leaving the police station, I'd climbed into the car and sped away, still in shock from seeing Camille—alive, *happy*—though I'd sworn I'd witnessed Gabe digging her grave.

It wasn't a dream. And it wasn't reality. Maybe I'd been thinking of something else. A memory. A memory I've been trying to suppress for far too long.

A memory I'm dying to forget.

Since I was out of the house anyway, I'd decided to stop at the local food pantry I always used to volunteer for before I needed every spare moment to put in hours working at the restaurant to earn extra tips.

I'd been trying to atone for past mistakes. When Jack was alive and food wasn't something we worried about, I emptied our cabinets to donate to the Hollow Falls food bank. On weekends, I volunteered for them to sort and pack boxes.

Though I hadn't volunteered in a while, working there always made me feel better. And this time had been no different—I'd almost forgotten my troubles while I pitched in for a few hours.

Now the sky deepens to ink-pot blue as my car warms up

in the parking lot. My phone vibrates on my dashboard. I'd placed it on silent when I was working and didn't hear it ring. Swiping in my passcode unlocks my phone, displaying three new texts from Hugh:

I don't know where you are but if you ever come back, I won't be there.

Fear floods over me. I rush to read the rest of his texts.

Gabe had a heart attack at the police station. We're going to the hospital now.

At the police station? It must've happened hours ago, right after I left. Then I think the unimaginable. Did he have a heart attack because of *me*? Did he get so angry he had a heart attack moments after I sped away?

Birdie was right—last night, when Gabe lunged at me, the police pulled him out of the house immediately. He didn't take his heart medications with him. Would just a handful of hours without them cause such a sudden downfall? Or was it me?

My hands start to shake as I read the last of his texts:

I'm sorry how I acted earlier. You deserve better from me. How can I make it up to you?

You can move us out of that house, I type but delete it.

His brother just had a heart attack. First I should see how he is…if he's even alive.

How's Gabe? I text.

But Hugh doesn't reply.

The thought of Gabe being out of the picture overwhelms me, and I push the dark thought away, shocked at myself. I drop my phone in my lap, rub my eyes.

Someone's calling, a number I don't know.

I answer, put it on speakerphone.

"Hello?"

Music in the background.

"Are you Ellory Blodgett's mom?"

Oh, God. No conversation ever ends well when it begins like that.

"Yes—who's this?"

"Leah," a girl says. "Is Ellory okay?"

"She's missing. Do you know where she is? Have you seen her?"

Silence.

"Please," I say when she doesn't respond. "I need to find her."

A deep sigh into the phone. "Last time I saw her was Monday night."

Monday—the night we went out to dinner for our engagement. When I woke up the next morning, Ellory was gone.

Leah continues. "My mom had your number. I keep calling Ellory but she won't answer. She's never like that."

"You're a good friend. Can you tell me what happened Monday night? Please," I say, sensing her uneasiness. "You're not in trouble. I need to find her."

Leah sighs. "She told me where to pick her up. Some big creepy house on the river."

"And where'd you take her?"

"A nightclub—a local place that opened in town. The Velvet Lion."

"So after you picked her up, you went to the nightclub. Did she leave with you?"

Leah lets out a breath. "No."

"Where'd she go?"

"Um," Leah says, hesitant. "I—I saw her get into a car with someone."

My heart flips. "Who? What kind of car? Was it her boyfriend?"

Leah scoffs. "No, it wasn't him. It was a black car. I was outside smoking when it pulled up," she explains. "When I asked Ellory who it was, she didn't really want to tell me."

"Who was it?" I ask, my heart in my throat.

"Well, I thought I saw a woman driving. But Ellory told me it was her father."

Her father.

Impossible. Ellory's father is dead. Jack is dead. I saw it—saw *him*—his eyes open, yet unseeing. I saw him in the snow. At the morgue. At his funeral… And with each memory, my mind flips to the different images of my husband, images I see every night before I go to sleep.

I stop the gloom-filled thoughts.

No.

I don't want to admit it, not even to myself.

Jack, the man who'd raised Ellory, who'd raised her as his own daughter since she was a newborn, is dead.

Ellory's father—Ellory's *biological* father—is very much alive.

"Thanks, Leah," I say. "When I find her I'll have her call you."

I lean back, shut my eyes. Ellory's friend Leah witnessed her getting into a black car and driving away. Then I remember. Ainsley mentioned going to the same nightclub on Monday night. As she was leaving the restaurant, she asked if anyone wanted to go. No one did. And so, she left. Alone.

Did Ainsley see Ellory there? Did she see who Ellory was with? The simplest way to find answers is to ask Ainsley. I shake my head clear, pick up my phone, text Sloane:

Have you heard from Ainsley yet?

Little dots flicker at the bottom of the screen. Sloane is typing.

Weird you ask that. I was going to ask if you're free, can you stop by her place? She never entered her hours for the week and I need to submit payroll tonight. I can't submit without her, but she's still not answering. I'd go but we're slammed. Can't leave.

I've been thinking about Ainsley almost as much as I've been thinking about Ellory, so the decision is an easy one. I text Sloane back with my answer:

Sure—what's Ainsley's new address?

Almost instantly, I receive a reply.

350 Edgemont Ave #238, Ferryville IOU thank you!

I tap on the address. My phone links to a map. Ainsley's new place is south of Hollow Falls in a town called Ferryville, about twenty minutes from where I am now, parked outside the food pantry. I've only been to Ainsley's apartment once before. She hasn't invited us over since.

I drive out of the parking lot and head to the address. It's a development of attached housing complexes, all with the same brown exterior siding and matching brown garage doors. Dim lamplights dot the circular parking lot nestled in the center of the structures. Only a few people have left their front lights on, and I squint in the darkness trying to read the numbers nailed next to each brown identical door.

When Ainsley downsized, Sloane and I were in shock. We never imagined Ainsley living anywhere that wasn't the chic white mansion we'd grown accustomed to seeing her in.

But after filing for divorce, she had no choice but to trade her custom-built home for an apartment. We helped her move in, squishing her expensive furniture into a space ten times smaller than the home she'd once inhabited.

Ainsley seemed happy. And so, as her friends, Sloane and I were happy. Now she's blowing off Sloane at work and won't answer our calls. I hope I was right when I told Sloane she probably went on the cruise without her. At this point, Sloane wouldn't even care that she was ditched, as long as Ainsley's okay.

Circling the development looking for #238, I finally find it and park my car along the curb next to a dumpster. My phone buzzes inside my purse. I swipe open the screen, see I have a new text from Hugh:

Where are you?

I get out of the car, run up to her door, text Hugh back a quick:

Be home soon.

Ainsley has a cranberry-encrusted wreath hanging on her front door, partially blocking the number. I move it aside, knock on the door, ring the bell. The door has a thin vertical window beside it, and through the pebbled glass, no lights glow from inside. I try the doorknob. Locked.

I text Sloane:

Door's locked, lights are out. What now?

Right away, she replies:

I think Ainsley keeps a spare key on the left side of her doormat.

Bending down, I lift the welcome mat, grab the silver key beneath. Kneeling close, I click on my phone's flashlight, aim the light at the ground. The hair on the back of my neck rises.

Next to the door are four drops of blood.

My heart hammers. I stand, slip the key into the lock. The door opens. Slowly, I step inside. I repeat her name in the darkness, feel the walls for light switches, flicking them on as I go.

"Ainsley? Ainsley? It's Iris."

No answer.

I don't expect her to be home, but I still call out her name as I circle her apartment. Entering the kitchen, I turn on the ceiling light. Everything is pristine, untouched. No dishes in the sink, no dirt or dust, let alone any blood.

So whose blood is outside?

I comb the kitchen and living room, then do it again before I head down the tiny hall. As I walk, I open each door I pass. One is a linen closet, another a tiny powder room. I pause. Something foul seeps through the air. I look in the trash can to see if Ainsley left food to rot. But it's empty.

My eyes begin to water. Backing out of the bathroom, I turn, rush into the hallway. There's one more closed door at the end of the hall. Each step feels heavier and heavier. I place my hand on the doorknob, twist it open.

The smell amplifies, thick and rancid. I gag, spin around. A whoosh of the sour smell slaps my lungs. Acid crawls up my throat. I swallow it down, claw the wall for a light switch. The room swells with light.

Ainsley is home. She's in her bed, hair splayed all around her. I step closer, knees tapping the side of the mattress.

"Ainsley?"

Hair covers her face. Gently, I move it aside. Her eyes are open. Blood has dried on her pillow, the shape of a butterfly's wings. I nudge her arm. It's not until I realize her skin is cold that I scream.

142 HOURS LEFT

Ellory's feet ached. They'd been walking for hours through some town in a state she didn't know. Most license plates around read Indiana, and she couldn't remember where that was on the map. All she knew was it was the farthest she'd ever been from home.

Every so often, she twirled her phone in her fingers and thought about calling home. She almost did, once, but then she thought about it. Really thought about it. And decided against it. There was nothing her mom could do or say that could lure her home. She was too far away. No going back.

The road they walked on was lit by tall streetlamps, lighting up expensive houses with long driveways that sat perched on little hills. Trees and shrubs clustered around them, and Ellory could tell everything was exactly as it should be for the families nestled inside.

Most houses had darkened, the ghostly glow of TVs the only lights on inside. *What are you watching?* What did these happy little families watch late at night, snug and safe in their flawless pretty homes?

Ellory didn't know, but she knew she needed to sit. Her feet ached and were swelling inside her sneakers. She wanted to nap or at least get something warm to eat. It was freezing, and while the snow had been plowed, her socks were soggy with icy water.

Shaw walked ahead, between Mars and Davey. Occasionally, he'd look over a shoulder, make sure she was still there. Ellory glanced at the sullen girl to her left. Jade had barely said a word since the sun had fallen. She guessed it was because Jade was exhausted, too.

"Where are we going, Shaw?" Ellory called out.

Shaw turned and opened his mouth to speak, but before he could get a word out, Mars said, "To find a car."

Ellory furrowed her eyebrows. Her shoulder ached from carrying her backpack and her purse. With Shaw's car gone, now whatever they had, they carried in their arms.

"Where are we going to get a car?" Ellory asked.

Mars stopped walking. Davey stopped, too, turning toward his brother. She couldn't see their faces in the dark space between streetlamps. All she could see was a vague smudge of features, some semblance of a nose, two eyes, shapes and shadows like someone had smudged petroleum jelly on their skin.

"Truth or dare," Shaw said when Mars ignored Ellory.

Ellory dropped her bag on the street. A car whizzed by, honked its horn at them. Jade jumped sideways, tripping over the bag. Davey caught her just before she slammed into a mound of snow. His arms remained wrapped around her a pulse too long.

Mars lunged forward, ripped Davey's hands off her. "Hey, don't touch her."

Jade looked stunned, hobbling back to stand beside Ellory. Davey said nothing. Shaw said nothing, either. Ellory wondered why he cared if Davey touched Jade. If it had to do with Mars trying to assert himself over her, over them all, the alpha wolf. But Ellory never agreed to belong to a pack.

She looked at Shaw. "Truth."

"Quit it with these stupid games," Mars said.

Ellory kept looking at Shaw, anger and frustration bubbling inside her so violently she swore she was going to explode.

"Why the fuck are all of you so damn upset?" Mars yelled. "I'm gonna find us a car, okay?"

"If you just let me try to fix my car—"

"No, fuck your car," Mars said. "We're getting a better car."

Shaw rolled his eyes, bent down to pick up Ellory's heavy bag. He slung it over her shoulder, then clasped her hand in his. "Whatever. Let's just keep walking."

Jade hovered behind them and, when the boys' backs were turned, hooked her arm in Ellory's.

"When are you going to tell him?" Jade whispered so Shaw couldn't hear.

Shock washed over Ellory, but she couldn't let it show, not with Shaw standing so close, not with Mars and Davey walking two steps in front of them. But the more Ellory thought, the more she wasn't so surprised Jade had guessed her secret. Jade had been watching her, protective, but not in a curious way. Protective in a caring and kind way, a way her mother rarely looked at her, but should've done more often.

Ellory glimpsed at Jade and, in the golden light of a streetlamp, saw her black eyeliner was smudged from old tears. "I'll tell you later," Ellory whispered, looked away.

"What?" Shaw asked.

"Nothing."

"Hey, you said truth, right?"

Ellory nodded.

"Okay. Truth. Are you happy we decided to leave?"

Shaw's smooth face fell into shadows as they reached a stretch without streetlamps, leaving nothing to light their path.

Ellory tried not to hesitate, but she couldn't think of the right thing to say.

"I knew it," Shaw breathed out. "You regret it. You regret *me*—"

"No—" Ellory tried to say. Pain ricocheted through her stomach. She gritted her teeth. She couldn't walk much longer. Somehow, she'd have to get them to stop.

She began again, hoping no one noticed her pained expression in the looming darkness. But one person saw how her hands shook, how her teeth made a hollow tapping sound as they chattered together from the cold.

"We should stop," Jade said, tugging on Mars's hoodie. *"Stop."*

Mars and Davey spun around, adjusted their heavy canvas bags over their shoulders.

"Why are we stopping?" Davey asked.

Jade's eyes flashed to Ellory. "I—I need a break," Jade said. "I'm tired. We should find somewhere for the night."

Mars laughed and circled the empty street as snowflakes began to fall from the night sky. "Okay, Jade," he said. "I'll give you your wish."

"Where are we gonna go?" Shaw asked.

Mars marched past him down the street until he reached the nearest residence.

They followed, stopping outside a closed driveway gate. "It's not even locked," Mars said, tugging it open. "It's only for show." Shaw and Davey followed behind Mars as he headed up the driveway.

Ellory and Jade hesitated.

Shaw turned back. "Come on," he whispered. "Let's go."

Ellory looked at Jade and shivered. The snow fell harder. The sky began to mutate into pale purple, lighting up a black driveway, leading up to a dark house.

Jade took Ellory's bag off her shoulder, slung it across her chest beside her own. "Come on," Jade said, sensing Ellory's unease. "Don't worry. Shaw won't let Mars do anything stupid."

Ellory climbed the hill, feeling like she was carrying the

weight of five men on her back, even though Jade carried her bag for her. Her knees ached. Her throat was dry. She uncapped the inhaler rattling in her coat pocket, sucked a blast of medicine down her lungs.

Her head pounded as she thought about her answer to Shaw's question. He already knew what she'd say. With every step she took to the house, Ellory felt something. Pain, mostly.

But above all, she felt the enormity of her regret.

25

A car idles in the middle of Hugh's driveway, brake lights glowing like two red eyes in the dark. The door slams shut and Sloane emerges, tears glistening down her face as she stands wearily in the light from my headlights.

I didn't expect to see her tonight. Through blurry eyes, I watch as she approaches my car, stepping through a cloud of exhaust like a ghost. Maybe I shouldn't expect anything less. While I was driving, I called to tell her the basics: I went to Ainsley's as she'd asked. I'd found Ainsley—dead—and called the police.

Sometimes, friends need to hear more than the basics.

I put my car in Park. Sloane runs to me, reaching her arms into the car to hug me the moment I open the door.

"Iris…" Her tears wet my neck. "Please say this isn't happening."

"I know."

"I'm sorry," she starts, curling her hair behind an ear. "I didn't know what to do, but I had to see you. I didn't want to wake anyone, so I stayed at the bottom of the driveway." She waves a hand over her shoulder toward her car. In her hands are clumps of used tissues. She blots at her reddened nose.

Wiping my eyes dry, I say, "I'm glad you're here. I need a friend."

Sloane leans against the side of the car. "You went inside her apartment?" she asks, rubbing her hands together to keep warm. "What did you see?"

The last memory of Ainsley I'll ever have fills my mind. There was so much blood. Too much. Too much for her to have survived. Dried to a deep red stain, it saturated the top of her floral bedsheets. Her head tilted to one side, hair and blood spilling across her pillow.

I slam my eyelids shut, push the image away.

"I saw blood outside her door," I begin, wrapping my arms tight around myself. "I used the spare key to get inside. I opened the door, and then I found her. I ran outside. Called the police. When they came, they questioned me. I told them what I knew, how she just got divorced." Nausea burns in the back of my throat. My stomach has been empty for hours, and mixed with the stress, my insides are volcanic.

"Oh, honey." Sloane takes me in her arms. "I'm so sorry. I'm here. It's okay. You did nothing wrong. You did the right thing." She smooths my hair, rocks me as we cry.

Tonight we lost a friend. The only other friend we have. For the past year, it's always been the four of us—me, Ellory, Sloane, and Ainsley. Over the past few days, our little family has shrunk considerably.

"Come sit inside. The heat's on." She releases me, shivers in her oversize puffy coat. The passenger door opens, and she falls into the car, shuts the door.

I read the time on my dashboard: 3:32 in the morning. No wonder Hugh's been blowing up my phone. But I just don't have it in me to speak with him yet. He never replied to my text. I don't even know if his brother survived the heart attack. I wish he'd told me. Then again, how do you convey news like that over a text? Even I didn't tell him about Ainsley yet. Some news is too big to be written on a phone in tiny letters.

Sloane shakes her head. "I promised to keep this a secret, but I need to tell you."

"What?"

"It's about Ainsley," she says. "It feels so wrong to talk about her now, but I meant to tell you this when I saw you earlier in the café. But then you got that call from the police and you had to leave so…"

"I'm sorry. I'm here now. You can tell me anything."

Sloane breathes out, massages her temples. "Ainsley was arrested. Years ago, before we ever met her, before I hired her to work at the café. Before she and her husband moved to Hollow Falls."

I think of Ainsley. It's hard imagining her being arrested. She's always so polished. Put together. Everything she wears— wore—is styled, from heels to hair. I've never seen her without false lashes. She gifts us makeup and curling irons for birthdays. And she buys gifts for Ellory, too.

There's nothing Ainsley isn't generous with. Her time, money, even her thoughts—she's always thinking of others. Wondering which colors look best on Sloane when buying her something for a first date she's going on. Gifting Ellory and me the dresses we wore to Ellory's graduation.

Without Ainsley, Ellory wouldn't have much at all. I can't afford it. A few times, Ainsley even took Ellory shopping for new clothes and shoes for school. Just another example of how I'd failed at being a good mom.

A pang of heartbreak intrudes. I force the thoughts—and guilt—away.

Ainsley was always late, but that was part of her charm. She was decent. She was *good*. Knowing that kindness is gone from the world shatters my heart.

"Please…go on," I say, a tear slipping down my cheek.

Sloane nods. "Ainsley had two DWIs. One was many years ago. The other was more recent, four or five years ago. She went to AA after the first one."

"That makes sense. I never saw her drink. Even at the engagement party, she and Hugh were the only ones who didn't," I say. "But I don't know, Sloane…" I give her an uneasy look in the darkness of the car. "I don't know if we should talk about this anymore. Whatever happened, we shouldn't be talking about anything bad. We should be focusing on the good."

Sloane shakes her head. "No, just listen. This might make something click for you. As a formality, I ran a background check when I hired her. It didn't come back totally clean, but I knew she needed the job and couldn't turn her away." She pauses, glances out her side window as if someone is standing outside in the dark listening. The thought gives me chills. Sloane takes my hand, swallows hard. "Iris, I think I know who killed her."

I raise my eyebrows. "Who?"

She licks her lips. "Her ex-husband." The moment she says it, I understand. Sloane sees the recognition in my eyes. "See, I knew it would click something in your mind."

"It's not that. It's… I mentioned that to the cops when they questioned me."

"You did?"

I nod. "Yeah, I said Ainsley just went through a tough divorce, that they were estranged. They didn't seem to care. They said she did it to herself." Sloane eyes me knowingly. "Why? What did you find? You think he'd kill her *after* she already got all that money from their divorce settlement?"

Sloane shakes her head. "Something happened that I think would make her ex want her dead."

"What?"

"Years ago, when Ainsley was arrested for those two DWIs," Sloane begins, "the first one was a warning. But the second... the second one killed someone, Iris."

My mouth pops open like a window. I nod for Sloane to continue.

"One night a few months ago, we were the only two closing up the café. All I did was ask her about the DWI that'd popped up when I ran the background check. It wasn't a big deal. I was just curious. But she was so scared, Iris. The way she looked at me..." She trails off in thought, gazes out the windshield. "She didn't want to say a word. But I pressed her. I pressed and pressed, and finally, she made me promise."

"Promise what?"

"Promise I wouldn't tell another soul."

I shake my head. "If you don't want to tell me—"

"*Iris,*" Sloane says. "It's been eating me up inside. It's throwing me out of balance." She stops, swipes away fresh tears caught in her long lashes. "Ainsley...she said legally she had to keep it secret. After what happened, her ex-husband forced her to sign an NDA. She said she didn't want to lose me as a friend, and so she told me everything. I'm so sorry I didn't tell you."

"It's okay. I understand. You thought you were protecting a friend."

She nods. "I did. I do."

"Why did Ainsley's ex make her sign a nondisclosure agreement?" I ask.

"That DWI I just mentioned? The accident that killed someone?" Sloane says, turning to look at me in the dark. "It wasn't just one person. The accident killed an entire family."

My breathing stops.

She gives me a minute to wrap my mind around this before she continues. "The husband. The wife. And their baby."

"*No,*" I cry. "No—Ainsley wouldn't have done this. She couldn't have…"

Sloane takes my hand again, squeezes tight. "*She* didn't." She gulps, turns down the heat, unknots her long knit scarf from around her neck.

"Who, then?" I ask. "Her ex?"

She nods. "*He* was the one who was driving. But he didn't want to take the fall for it. It would've ruined his career. Besides, Ainsley already had one DWI before."

"He should've been ruined," I say. "He should pay for what he did."

"He did, in a way. After the accident, since they were both in the car that night, he convinced Ainsley to take the fall. He promised he'd get her out of going to prison, and somehow, he *did* keep that promise to her. She told me she still loved him then, so she agreed."

"But it wasn't enough," I whisper.

"No, it wasn't," she agrees. "Ainsley said after a while, she couldn't even look at him anymore."

"So she filed for divorce," I say.

Sloane exhales a deep breath. "And she ended up with everything—she demanded it."

"Demanded?"

"He's a lawyer, Iris. A brilliant but sleazy one. Do you really think he didn't try to swindle her out of everything? Ainsley knew he'd try to fuck her. So she told him she'd tell everyone the truth of what really happened that night."

"Oh, God." I lean back on the headrest. My mind whirls. "I always assumed he'd cheated on her or something, but Ainsley never wanted to talk about him or the divorce. She would only say how they were estranged and that she hated him. She never wanted to discuss specifics, so I didn't know what to think. Something else, maybe. Anything but *this.*"

"I know," Sloane says softly. "I keep thinking there's something we could've done. Maybe we could've helped in some way. But she kept all of this a secret. How could we have ever known?"

"None of this is your fault, Sloane."

She exhales, sniffles. "I mean, if her ex wanted her dead, why wouldn't he kill her *before* giving her all that money?"

"He might still be the beneficiary," I say. "Or maybe she had life insurance. I don't think we'll ever know."

I look at Sloane. We're both exhausted. My eyelids begin to feel heavy even though my heart is racing.

"Sloane," I begin. She turns and for a moment I picture her turning to look at Ainsley instead of me. "He did it. He murdered our friend. Ainsley's ex-husband killed her." The tears fall faster now, harder, until I can hardly see the numbers glowing bright red on my dashboard, and all I see is fuzzy, fiery light.

She nods, leans over the armrest, takes me in her arms. "That bastard's going to get what's coming to him, Iris, because after all the shit I've seen, there's one thing I trust. And that's karma. Do you know why?" I shake my head, my tears soaking into her coat. "Because karma is always there, a part of you that you never asked for. Its existence depends on you, like your shadow. But unlike your shadow, karma doesn't disappear in the darkness. It blooms."

141 HOURS LEFT

Ellory broke away from Jade and followed Shaw around the side of the house. In the dark, the white house looked gray, with little capped windows that sprouted from the roof. Skeletons of lavish landscaping were painted white with snow.

"No one's home," Davey said from behind her.

Jade asked, "How do you know?"

"No lights are on."

"No...but someone's home," Shaw said.

Ellory followed his voice to find him gazing through a window into an attached garage.

"Two cars inside."

Ellory stepped beside Shaw. Though dark, the glowing purple sky lit the inside of the garage, just barely, just enough to see the polished, waxy shine of two vehicles.

The snow fell heavier as they crouched beside the edge of the house.

"Well," Mars began. "Let's go."

"Wait," Davey whispered, grabbing his brother's arm. "You can't do this."

Mars grinned, snowflakes gathering in his black hair. He shifted his heavy canvas bag on his shoulder, opened it to show a gun hidden inside. "Watch me."

Davey sighed, shook his head. "Mars, *no*. This is more fucked up than anything you've done before."

Mars shrugged off his brother's hand. "I know."

Shaw stepped in. "Hey, man, there's someone home. They could have cameras. They could be watching us right now—"

"You want to get outta here? You want a car? Then you either help me or piss off, Shaw, got it?"

Shaw was seething as he turned to look back at Ellory, the muscles in his jaw flexing.

She didn't know what to do, how to make Mars stop. But she also didn't know how else they were going to get out of here. They needed a car. Especially now. Especially when the snow fell harder, landing all around her, dripping icy water down the back of her neck.

She shivered, but she didn't remember a time when she wasn't shivering anymore.

Mars knelt beside the door of the garage. He began to fiddle with the lock, first with his driver's license, then with a pocketknife.

"Shit."

Mars shoved his knife into his pocket and stood, gazed through the window. After a heartbeat of silence, he shrugged off his bag and let it fall to the ground.

"Mars—stop," Davey said, voice low. His expression twisted with anxiety as he glanced up, scanned the side of the house to see if any lights had been turned on.

Ellory followed his logic and walked to the front of the house. She peeked around a corner, saw the house was still completely dark. When she walked back, Mars had removed his coat and was wrapping it around his fist.

"Mars—*stop*."

Davey's words exploded from his throat the moment Mars's hand met with the pane of glass, shattering it instantly with a crash so loud someone must've heard it. If not the people inside, then a neighbor nearby.

Glass clattered onto the stone walkway, onto the concrete floor inside. Mars lifted an arm, twisted his elbow, and soon, the door popped open. For a moment, he waited for the sound of an alarm. But none came.

"No sirens," Mars said.

Shaw shifted uncomfortably beside Ellory. "Could be silent alarms. My dad has those."

Mars pulled out his gun, stepped into the stranger's garage. "Truth or dare, motherfuckers."

Davey rolled his eyes but followed. Shaw walked in behind them. Ellory grabbed his arm to spin him around.

"Shaw—don't. What if the police come?"

"Then they come," he whispered, kissing her on the cheek. "We can just run."

"I can't," Ellory said, gripping her belly under her coat. Sharp cramps had begun pounding over her the moment Mars had broken the glass. She winced, clenched her teeth. "I can't run, Shaw," she said, voice cracking, as brittle as the broken glass. "And I—I *can't* walk anymore."

Shaw kissed her again. "Then we better get you a car."

He followed Davey into the darkness, leaving Ellory and Jade outside in the snow. Ellory's skin was on fire, but after a moment she realized she wasn't hot at all. She was frigid. The snow had melted into her clothes, burning her skin, numbing her, making her entire body convulse with shivers. Her stomach cramped again.

Jade wrapped an arm around her back and pushed her into the garage, out of the snow.

The garage was warm. A wave of euphoria flooded over Ellory as forced heat from a vent over her head showered her with warmth. Slowly, she relaxed, watched as Shaw and Davey and Mars circled the two SUVs parked side by side. One was white, sleek, like a shark. The other was big, blocky, and bright blue, with huge tires and silver handles that sparkled even in darkness.

Mars and Davey searched for keys inside the SUVs while Shaw used his phone as a makeshift flashlight to illuminate inside toolbox drawers, anywhere a key could be stored.

Ellory felt her body tense as Mars stepped out of the bright blue one, a set of keys dangling from his fingertip. "Jackpot, ladies," he said and laughed, tossing the keys up in the air before catching them. "Guys, come on. Let's get the hell outta here."

Ellory's stomach cramped, so hard she thought her spine would snap in two. A flooding feeling unleashed through her, loose and liquid, like she'd wet herself. Something fell from her, down the legs of her jeans, and slopped onto the concrete floor.

The air sucked from her lungs, and she screamed, panicked, terrified of what was happening to her.

"Shut the fuck up," Mars snapped at her.

But she couldn't stop. She kept crying as Jade held her tight, making sure Ellory didn't crumple to the ground, break her kneecaps on the concrete.

"I said shut the fuck up." Mars lunged at Ellory, slamming her back into the wall.

Tears streamed down her frozen cheeks as she stared back at him, so close, she could feel his hot breath sinking into her pores, warming her. Swallowing a scream, Ellory turned to see Shaw staring at her: her back against the wall, Mars's arm tightening around her throat.

She tried to scream, tried to speak his name, but she couldn't.

And yet Shaw did nothing. Nothing but stare at her as Mars slowly suffocated her.

Out of nowhere, Jade barreled her shoulder straight into Mars, knocking him away. He fell back into the side of an SUV.

"Let her go," Jade cried out.

Mars held up his hands, innocent, as the garage door lifted with a loud, mechanical whir. The door to the house flung open. Lights exploded on, igniting the dark air like fireworks. Ellory's eyes burned, and she looked away just as she caught the outline of a man standing in the doorway, a shotgun clenched in his hands.

"Get out of my house. *Get out. Get out. Get out!*"

Jade ran to open the car door, slipping in the clear puddle of whatever had just come out of Ellory. Ellory stared at it as Jade shoved her headfirst into the back seat of the blue SUV.

The man screamed, though clearly afraid to step into the garage knowing he was outnumbered. His voice was so loud and booming it shook the inside of the car. He lifted the shotgun, aimed it at Shaw.

Ellory watched as Shaw froze, stopped breathing altogether.

"I've called the police. I saw all your goddamn faces. Yours, and yours," the man said, aiming the shotgun at Davey and Mars. "And yours." He aimed it back at Shaw.

The garage door began to close. Mars noticed, ran to open the driver-side door of the SUV, and climbed inside. Slamming it shut, he started the car, the sound of the engine muted by the loudest sound system Ellory had ever heard. Heavy metal guitars split her head in two.

Davey rushed to the passenger seat, slammed the door shut in Shaw's face. Terrified to be left behind, Shaw snapped out of his trance, fumbled to get inside, throwing himself in the back seat, knocking into Jade just as Mars tore out of the garage.

Mars hit the gas so hard it launched Shaw sideways, smashing Ellory's head into the headrest. Shaw cursed under his breath as he fought to close the open rear door, slamming it shut, turning the car into a vacuum filled with Ellory's amplified screams of pain.

"I can't—I can't breathe," Ellory yelled. "I can't breathe! Help me, Jade…"

Jade soothed her, held her hand, told her to pinch her pinky finger as hard as she could to ease away the pain.

"I'm here," Jade said. "I'm with you. I'll always stay with you."

"I can't—breathe," Ellory cried, and then, as clear as she saw Jade's face, she heard her mother's voice.

Don't ever lose this. Always keep it with you. It's your lifeline.

Ellory plunged her hand into her coat pocket, fumbled to find her inhaler. She shook the canister, held it to her lips, inhaled two pumps of the soothing aerosol spray. Instantly, she felt her lungs expand and fill with air. Her shoulders relaxed. But the pain gripped her again, rolling over her in huge, crushing waves.

She screamed.

"Shut the fuck up, Ellory," Mars snapped.

"My God, what's wrong with her?" Shaw asked in a panic as he glanced at Ellory. As he watched her, shock seized his expression.

"I think she was having an asthma attack," Davey said.

"Oh, my God…" Shaw trailed off. Ellory looked over to see his face had gone bone white.

"What?" Mars said as he peeled the SUV around a corner, tires screeching. "What is it? Someone tell me what's going on."

From the front seat, Davey stared back at Ellory, his expression fluttering with sudden understanding. "Oh, shit. Is she—"

Jade smoothed Ellory's wet hair down her cheek. "It's going to be okay," she whispered. "You're going to be fine. Everything is going to be fine. *Mars*," Jade said, and for the first time, Ellory heard a tinge of fear in her sweet voice. "You have to find a hospital. Now. Ellory's in labor."

26

The house is dark as I creep into the kitchen, pour a glass of wine. Normally, I never do this—I'm not much of a drinker—but I desperately need to sleep, and tonight isn't going to be a night where that happens easily. I don't need Sloane's tarot cards to tell me that.

Stepping into our bedroom, I place the wine on a table and quietly begin to undress. The drapes are open. Dim moonlight fills the room, bright enough for me to see Hugh's phone on his nightstand, though I'm alone.

Taking a sip, I stare out the window. The view stretches across the field to the woods. I examine the spot where I swore I'd seen Gabe digging a grave. But I was wrong. It never happened. I imagined it.

I wish I imagined this entire day.

Something moves outside. I press my forehead against the icy glass, squint into the darkness. I imagined Gabe digging a grave, but am I imagining this?

I saw them here before. I *wasn't* dreaming.

Three figures loom in the distance.

One.

Two.

Three.

They stand still, perched at the edge of the tree line, staring straight at the house. I close my eyes, squeeze them tight. No, I'm not imagining this, not this time. They're real. They're here.

I open my eyes, look out the window again. My heart stops. Fear lunges through me.

The glass of wine slips from my hand and shatters on the floor. In the reflection, a dark figure hovers behind me.

"Iris, where have you been?"

Hugh crosses the room, takes me in his arms. My lungs shrink. I gasp for air, adrenaline still coursing through me. *It's only Hugh. They're not real.*

I don't know how to respond, what to say, where to start. Gently, he moves me to sit on the bed. I jump up, pull the drapes closed so fast the rods pop off the wall. Fabric crumbles to my feet, the metal rods clanging across the wooden floorboards.

Hugh is unbothered. He clicks on a lamp. The room blooms with soft light. "Iris, are you okay? You're shaking. What's wrong?"

I look at him, then down at the shattered glass of wine. At the fallen drapes and broken rods. And I'm frozen, unable to move. Hugh wears nothing but pajama bottoms, chest bare. He kneels at my feet, begins to pick up the broken shards. Standing, he drops the glass shards into a trash can in the corner.

"I'm sorry. I didn't mean to scare you," he says. "I didn't know you'd be here. I should've knocked."

"How's Gabe?" I ask.

Hugh exhales. "He's in the hospital."

I nod. Good. He's alive. He survived. I'm glad. The last thing I want is more bad karma, as Sloane would say.

"Where were you?" Hugh asks. "God, Iris. You had me worried."

"Ainsley's dead."

The words spill out. Some things are too big to be kept inside.

Hugh's eye twitches. "What? How? How do you know? What did you see?"

"I...found her," I say and can't help but cry. "I went in and found her." Hugh remains silent as I speak, his expression twisting. "She was in bed. I called the police and they asked me a bunch of questions. I—I told them I think her ex-husband was involved and—"

"Why would you think that?"

I remember what Sloane said: *It's been eating me up inside. It's throwing me out of balance.*

I know I should share everything that's happened with Hugh. But I can't. At least, not tonight. I shrug, give a tight smile. "Just a feeling," I whisper numbly. "But I'm really tired, so I'm not thinking clearly."

Hugh gently rubs my hand. "Oh, my poor Iris. I'm *so* sorry you had to see your friend like that. Come here." He pulls me to his chest again, smooths my hair out of my face. "Do you know how much I love you?" I bend my neck to look at him. "I love you so much. You're so strong. So much stronger than me."

I sniffle. "I have to apologize." I twirl my engagement ring around my finger, tuck the ruby into my palm.

"For what?"

"For thinking Gabe was involved in Camille's disappearance. I was wrong, and I'm sorry."

"I'd probably think the same thing if I were in your shoes."

"You would?"

He nods. "Yeah, sure. I mean, I know how Gabe can seem. But he'd never hurt anyone unless they deserved it." He stops to laugh. I can tell he's trying to lighten my mood, but I'm not sure if anything ever could. "You have to let this go—this anger toward him—toward any member of my family."

Unsure what to say, I attempt to change the topic. "He's in the hospital?"

Hugh inhales a deep breath. "They want to keep him there a little longer. Gabe's a tough bastard, and he's been through a lot, but his heart needs time to heal."

"What has he been through?"

Hugh shifts away, suddenly uncomfortable. "You know, his sister's death was really hard on him. A lot of things have stemmed from that in his life. How he sees the world. How he views other people."

I tilt my head. "Don't you mean *our* sister's death?"

"Well, yeah. Of course. But I was talking about Gabe. I took her death differently than he did. We all did."

Ainsley's face appears in my mind. Her open eyes and pale skin, turned the color of a rain cloud. I drop my head in a hand.

Hugh angles his head down, nudges his forehead against mine. "We've been through hardships. You, most of all. I'm sorry you had to live through another one tonight."

"Thank you," I say, knowing he's right, knowing he's survived his fair share of hardships in his life, too. From the loss of his sister all those years ago, to losing his father, to divorcing his first wife.

"What was the hardest thing you've had to live through?" I ask, wondering how he deals with so many heartaches and somehow manages to do so much with his life: run his own architecture firm, help repair his mom's house, volunteer for charities.

He gulps, inhales a deep breath. "The hardest thing of all was the death of my wife."

What? I think and want to blurt—scream—out. What? Instead, I freeze, think about my next words carefully. I can't overreact, show Hugh how much I want to punch a hole through his head right now.

I look down, look away. "I—I thought you said you got a divorce."

"I never said that," he says flatly, with absolute certainty. "I *never* would've said that."

I run through everything I know of his first wife. He told me in the garden he'd lost his first wife— *No.* Not lost. He said they'd *parted.* But he never said that she'd died. I guess my mind filled in the blanks and assumed they'd divorced.

I want to kick myself. Why didn't I ever ask him what had really happened?

I stop myself.

None of this is my fault. I'm going to marry this man. He should've told me his first wife died before proposing. He should've told me, right in the beginning.

So why didn't he?

"What happened to her?" I ask, glancing again at the engagement ring on my finger. It's rotated sideways, fallen under its own weight. I adjust it, make it sit upright in the center. The facets shimmer in the lamplight, deep red and bloody.

Hugh exhales a ragged breath. "You know how I told you after things fell apart I was depressed?"

I nod. "You said you went to therapy."

His shoulders relax. He falls back on the bed, looks up at the ceiling. "It was more than that," he whispers, almost as if speaking to himself. "I went to grief therapy. I wanted to die. I didn't know how to live my life without her."

Taking his hand in mine, I rest them together on his bare chest, our fingers intertwined, rising and falling with each of his breaths. I know exactly the feeling he's describing. I felt it before—with Jack's death. I was his wife for nearly half my life. It's all I knew how to be. Over the past three years, I've had to reinvent myself, find myself—find who I really am—without him.

And I thought I did. I was Ellory's mom. I was her mom, and she was my daughter and we would be together, always. We both learned how to mow the lawn, fix the dishwasher, change the air filters. We both absorbed what Jack had unknowingly taught us. We both became strong.

It's only been more recently that my mind has wandered to darker things. Since Ellory's been missing, a hole has grown inside me. It's just waiting for her to come home to be filled, and until then, I'll remain only partly whole. Until then, I fear I'll disintegrate.

Without Ellory, I feel less like *me*. Not only as a person but as a mom. *Her* mom. But am I, still? If I never saw my daughter again, if she never came back, would I still be her mom?

Yes, I tell myself. Of course. It's a title that's nonrefundable. Throughout the rest of time, nothing can dissolve that fact. Nothing.

There is no *till death do we part* for our children.

Jack was mine until his death. And Hugh was *hers* until…

"It's as if she took a piece of me when she died," he says, blinking through tears. "I've been trying to get that piece back for a long time. And I've finally found it again—with you." My heart twists. "After it happened," he says, "a friend suggested I go to a group to talk to others living through the same grief. They helped me. They saved my life."

"I know—too well—what you've been through," I confess. "With Jack."

He sighs. "I know you have. I think it's one of the reasons I've fallen in love with you. You understand. You know what it's like to have been at the lowest point in your life and still find the courage to survive."

"If that's true, why not tell me about her? It could've brought us closer. I'd *never* keep Jack a secret from you."

His face softens. "You're right. I'm sorry."

I lie down beside him, place a hand on his chest. "What happened to her?" I ask again.

Hugh sighs, stares back up at the ceiling. "I'm sorry… I just can't talk about it. Not tonight."

Though I'm a little disappointed, I nod in understanding. If there's one thing I know, it's not to push stories of grief out of people when they're not ready to relive it. I want Hugh to tell me his story with his heart open, not under pressure. And so I let it go.

"Tell me," he begins, turning to me. "Are there any updates on Ellory?"

I begin to speak, begin to tell him how I went to the station to fill out paperwork and ran into Gabe, just before he had a heart attack, but stop myself. How much should I confess to him? He shared something important with me. Maybe I should reciprocate. I like this open, threadbare honesty forging between us. I want nothing else.

And so, I confess. But instead of confessing how I saw Gabe, I confess to something much more difficult. I decide I can keep what happened with Gabe a secret a little while longer, but there's one other secret that's been aching to come out.

A secret that's been festering in my heart for eighteen years.

"No updates yet, but…"

Hugh inches closer, takes my hand. "Whatever you need to tell me, I'm here. I'm listening."

I exhale. "Sometimes, I wonder if Ellory found out."

"Found what out?"

"The truth." I offer a grim smile. "I never told anyone this, but Jack isn't Ellory's biological father."

Hugh thinks a moment before speaking. "Do you think she found out? Maybe that's what made her run away?"

"Maybe…" I trail off. Between that and our engagement and the move, Ellory had every reason to leave.

"I'm sorry you're going through this. I know she'll be back soon. She loves you." He kisses the top of my head. "So do I. Neither of us would ever do anything to hurt you. Not on purpose."

I nestle into his chest and close my eyes.

"One day, will you tell me who her biological father is? When you're ready?"

A chilly tear streams down my face. "Maybe one day," I say. "When it's the right time."

I close my eyes, think about if there ever would be a right time. Honestly, I'm not sure if I can tell Hugh about him, or the truth about how Ellory came to be. Because anytime I imagine the face of her real father, every thought inside my head is snuffed out, and all I hear is the sound of a woman screaming in fear.

1 DAY BEFORE

FRIDAY, JANUARY 24

27

Hugh gets dressed in the bathroom, the door shut. We'd only been asleep a few hours when a light knock sounded at the door. It was Rebecca, asking Hugh to get ready to visit Gabe at the hospital. Neither one asked if I'd like to visit, too.

The day has just begun and already I need to find strength to make it through today. I shut my eyes, take a deep breath, and meditate, just for a moment, to center myself. Sloane taught me this. She taught me a lot after Jack died.

She instilled in Ellory—and me—that having strength as a woman does not mean being stubborn, living inside a shell, or putting others down. Strength—real strength—is different. It means having the courage to make your own decisions. Pursuing what you want to accomplish in your one life. Voicing your opinions without fear.

Ellory learned this lesson quickly. I always admired her. And Sloane. And Ainsley. I've been lucky to be surrounded by strong women.

Sometimes, on a good day, I can almost see myself in them. But I don't know how to get there.

I reach over to the nightstand to grab my phone and text Sloane, see how she's doing after I told her about Ainsley. But it's disappeared. I look beneath the table and bed, flip my purse inside out, search the blankets.

Thinking maybe Hugh found it and put it somewhere, I check the nightstands but find nothing. I was wearing a cardigan last night, and I scan the bedroom floor to find it, look in the laundry bin, the closet. Maybe I stuffed my phone inside the pocket.

But I can't find it.

When I open the armoire, the strong scent of mildewy wood fills my nose. I check between Hugh's perfectly folded sweaters, thinking maybe he mistook mine for his and tucked it on a shelf. But there's nothing inside save for a tasteful collection of cashmere and wool in various shades of blue. I pause, spotting something else. Something I never noticed.

A black box rests in a little cubbyhole at the bottom. I yank it out. On the box is a pin-pad, the buttons black metal, a small digital screen above.

"What are you doing?"

Hugh stands in the doorway, dark hair slick with water. Steam lilts out of the bathroom like a wraith.

"Is this a gun?" I hold the heavy box in both hands.

He nods, steps out of the bathroom. I glare at him. "It's for protection," he says, answering my cold stare. "I told you about it."

I gulp down the knot in my throat. Hugh picks up on my uneasiness, comes closer. Snatching the gun box from my hands, he shoves it back into the armoire, closes the doors.

"You know I hate guns. It's how Jack died."

"Iris," Hugh begins softly, taking my hands. "I'm sorry if I've upset you. The last thing I want is for you to ever feel unsafe here. I've owned this gun since I was twenty-five. I've never used it." Wrapping his arms around me, he holds me tight. "I'll sell it soon. I promise."

Rebecca's voice curls into the bedroom.

"Hugh, hurry up—we're waiting outside."

I wriggle out of his grip.

He sighs. "Why were you looking in the armoire? Did you lose something? I can try and help you find it before I leave."

"I can't find my phone."

"I bet I know where it is. Mother probably found it and put it in the desk in the study. She puts all electronics in there. Wires, chargers, headphones, whatever."

I gulp, stare down at my feet. "Okay, thanks," I say, wishing I didn't have to go back into that room, not after what I know resides beneath the wallpaper. In the past twenty-four hours, I've seen enough blood for a lifetime.

"I have to go before Rebecca kills me." He buttons his dark blue shirt. "Just relax today, okay? You don't have to do anything if you don't want to." Hugh kisses me on the cheek. "I love you."

I walk to the window, gaze down to the driveway. After a few moments, Hugh opens the car door, climbs inside. When the car disappears into the trees, I turn away from the window, throw on whatever clothes I can find—an old white T-shirt, black sweatpants, and one of Hugh's cashmere cardigans. I slide on a second pair of socks, my feet freezing from the inescapable chill of the house, and head downstairs to the study to find my phone.

The room is quiet and still. In the daylight, black blood seeps out of the walls like wounded skin. Dust motes float through the air, dance in sunlight slicing through the window blinds. Standing behind Hugh's father's old desk, I avert my eyes, angle my back to the blood-splattered wall.

The desk is ancient carved wood with four drawers down each side. I sit on the leather chair, tug each drawer open. Inside there's nothing but outdated bills, a lifetime supply of water-stained birthday cards, empty bottles of bourbon, and a long letter opener.

Another drawer bursts with old newspaper clippings, mostly obituaries, but one sits on top, the paper white while the rest are sepia-toned. I glance at it before closing the drawer: *Doug Erboss*. The name feels familiar, but I can't remember why.

I shift to the other side of the desk. The top drawer contains orphaned chargers, grungy earbuds, and a tangled snake of wires knotted beyond hope. Resting on top is my phone.

Relieved, I shove it in my back pocket, vowing to never return to this room again.

I step into the hallway, close the door behind me. Upstairs, the layout of the top floor is shaped like an elongated letter *E*, if the center served as the main stairwell and the two ends leading down each wing. I wander the never-ending hallways on my way to Ellory's room. I want to be near things that she used, that still carry her scent. Just to be near her, somehow.

After opening the curtains, I fall on her bed, pull the blankets around me. I want Ellory to come home, yes, *of course*. But first I want—before anything—a home Ellory wants to come back *to*. I want us to be in a place where she doesn't feel the need to leave again. Where she doesn't want to get away from me, but instead to be with me. All I want is to provide a better life for her in the wake of losing her father and her home.

I've failed her miserably, given her every reason to leave—first with all the secrets I kept. Then with Jack's death, when I drowned in my grief instead of taking care of *her* first. And losing our home. On top of it all, I moved us in with Hugh, a man Ellory doesn't yet feel comfortable around, and then got engaged to him. I'm trying to do what I think is best for my daughter, but in reality, it only seems to be pushing her further away.

After everything I've lived through, I fear three things:

1) Losing Ellory forever—like how my mom lost me.

2) Ellory's life mimicking her mother's.

3) Those three dark figures lurking in the trees.

My eyes snap open. I must've fallen asleep. Above me, in the ceiling, a noise. A creak. *Bang.* It sounds like a small child playing with toys...two footsteps. A clatter. A gentle *tap tap tap.*

Throwing the blankets off me, I get out of bed, step into the hallway. The family is gone, for now. I need to use this time wisely.

I need to find the attic.

I've already searched the main corridor, where our bedrooms are, but there's a separate wing no one seems to use. On my way, I peek behind every door. Most open into empty rooms. Some doors open to small closets, most likely used in the past by maids tucking away cleaning supplies on each level so they didn't need to carry them floor to floor.

There's one door left until the end. I nudge it open.

The room is dark and reeks of old wooden furniture. When I flip on a light switch, a chandelier flickers in the center of the ceiling. Only one bulb works, buzzing on and off like in a creepy cellar in a horror movie.

This room feels different from the rest. There's no bed, no sense of what the room should be. It has no identity. The only furniture inside is clustered along a wall—cabinets, dressers, chairs—and then on the opposite end is a door.

My phone rings in my back pocket. A headache erupts at the base of my skull. I answer.

"Hello?"

A deep voice sounds on the other end. "It's Private Investigator Duplain calling. We haven't spoken in a while, and I wanted to reconnect." I breathe out in relief.

"Thanks for calling. Have you—"

"Not a problem. So I'm assuming you're interested in hearing if I have any updates on your daughter, Ellory." He pauses. In the background, I hear paper fluttering.

"Have you found her?"

"Um, no, I'm sorry to say. But…hang on. Uh, Mrs. Blodgett? I'm sorry—I'll have to call you back. I'll call you in five, all right?"

"Okay, sure."

He hangs up. I turn around, walk toward the door, try the handle.

Locked.

Why would someone keep this door locked? It doesn't look like anyone ever accesses this room, let alone this random door, so what could be hiding in there? Another room? A closet? Or is it the door to the attic?

Chills travel down my spine. What's up there that's been making the noises I hear every night? It sounds like a person. But that can't be. It's January. Freezing—especially at night. I shake my head. I'm hearing something. Or someone. But who?

Who could be inside the attic?

140 HOURS LEFT

"Shaw, did you know?"

Ellory caught their conversation in bits and pieces as she struggled to breathe in the back seat of the stolen SUV.

"I—I had a feeling. But she never said anything, not really," Shaw said to Davey.

Ellory glanced at Shaw as she shifted her body down, putting her legs up on each of the car seats in front of her. Jade held her hand tight, tried to get Ellory to calm down. But it was too late for that.

Ellory knew she was having a panic attack. Chest heaving, heart pounding, head dizzy—she couldn't get a deep breath. The world spun.

A sharp pain zipped up her spine. She cried out. This wasn't supposed to happen now. She wasn't sure when, exactly, it was supposed to happen, but not now. Not this soon. Not here. Not like this. Not before she and Shaw had made it to the West Coast, like they'd planned, put down roots, found a place to settle.

Not without her mother…

Ellory knew this was early. Too early. Something was wrong. She was hardly showing—though she chose to wear baggy sweaters, and she'd begun to roll down her stretchy leggings at the top. No maternity clothes—she didn't want her mother to find out. The rapid onslaught of thoughts made her feel more nauseous as she struggled to get a full breath.

"You're going to be okay," Jade repeated, over and over. "You're going to be fine. Deep breaths. You can do it. Here—" she took Ellory's hand "—try to pinch your pinky finger. It will take the pain away."

Ellory pinched her finger, but she still felt like she was dying.

Shaw studied them, his back pressed against the side window, trying to give them as much space as possible. Luckily, the car Mars had chosen to steal was roomy enough for Ellory to spread out. It was a small mercy.

Mars jerked the car through the dark, unfamiliar streets. The motion sent Ellory's stomach reeling.

"Where's the hospital?" Mars asked, frantic.

"How should I know?" Davey answered. "I don't even know where we are."

Mars shook his head. "Use the navigation system—*fuck*."

Davey groaned but started pressing buttons on the SUV's built-in GPS. As he read directions to Mars, Ellory felt like she was fighting for her life. She couldn't breathe. The pain was excruciating. This wasn't normal, couldn't be normal. Cold sweat broke out all over her body. Jade rubbed her belly and tried to relax her the only way she knew how.

"You're going to be fine. Everything will be okay. Shaw," Jade said, turning her attention away from Ellory to the panicked boy sitting beside her. "How could you *not* know?"

Shaw shook his head in the darkness. "I don't— I mean, why the fuck wouldn't you tell me?" he asked Ellory.

Ellory didn't answer. She couldn't. Another cramp shot through her and she screamed. Screaming helped and so she kept doing it. It helped with her breathing. *Scream. Inhale. Scream. Inhale.*

"We're almost there," Davey said, the light from the screen glowing his face white.

"Did you hear that?" Jade asked her. "We're almost there. You're going to be okay."

Ellory nodded, tried to inhale a breath.

"What the fuck— How am I— What are we going to do?" Shaw spit-fired at himself. "How am I going to pay for a baby? How am I going to be a dad? I have no money—shit—what are we going to do?"

"You're going to deal with it," Jade said calmly, holding Ellory's hand tight. "You have no other choice."

"We're here," Mars said.

The tires screeched to a stop. Shaw exploded out of the car. Mars got out, ripped Ellory's door open. She fell out, saved only by Jade, who grabbed her arms to hold her upright. Jade held Ellory under her armpits as they scrambled inside.

"My girlfriend is…having a baby," Shaw said to the woman at the ER counter, his face empty as the shock of everything collided.

Ellory screamed and clutched her stomach. The woman called over two nurses who sat her in a wheelchair, pushed her down a narrow white-walled hallway.

"Are you family?" a nurse asked Jade when she refused to release Ellory's hand.

"I'm her sister," she lied, and the nurse swept her eyes back and forth between them, knowing it wasn't the truth. Ellory screamed again.

"Fine. Sister, follow me."

Ellory dropped her head. The bright white hospital lights stung her eyes. Jade stayed by her side while the nurses wheeled her away from Shaw.

"See?" Jade said, looking down at her. "Everything's going

to be fine." Jade smiled at her, but for some reason, Ellory couldn't believe her. This was wrong. This was all wrong. Nothing was ever going to be *fine* again. Ellory knew this deep inside her bones.

She lifted her head, tilted it back toward the ceiling, and widened her eyes to welcome in the stinging white lights. And as they wheeled her into a labor room, Ellory made a wish. She wished she could erase the past few years of her life and start over, as if they'd never happened at all.

28

The last remaining light bulb in the chandelier explodes in a flash of white light. Holding my hands out, I cross the dark room, stop when my fingertips tap the wall. Feeling for the blinds, I draw them open. Decades of dust erupt into the air as sunlight floods the room.

Part of me wants to give up, to crawl back into bed until Hugh comes home. I could take a hot shower, have some of Sloane's calming tea, relax, read one of the old books from the library. But I can't. I have to see what's behind this door.

I know I saw keys somewhere. But where? I can picture them in my head, but I can't remember where I saw them. Iron keys? Maybe a skeleton key? I know I saw it, somewhere, inside this giant old house. But where?

I leave the room, walk back to my bedroom, stop.

I remember.

My phone rings, and I answer. "Hello?"

"Sorry about that." *Duplain.* "Back to Ellory." I listen closely, rush down the hall as he speaks. "I wanted to run over some of the details with you, if you have time."

"Of course." I push open Gabe's bedroom door. "I'm free right now."

Duplain exhales. I hear him lick his lips, wet, moist, into the phone. "Wonderful." Papers shuffle in the background, the sound mingling with the burbling voices of a TV show. "The night you last saw your, uh, daughter, did you happen to know of any plans she may have mentioned? Going out with friends, maybe? Or a boyfriend?"

"No, she never mentioned anything like that. I would've remembered."

"Okay," Duplain says. "And when you first realized she was missing—what made you first suspect something was wrong? Were there any signs of a struggle? Did she maybe leave something important behind? Money, a note—" Something makes a loud thud on the other end. "Damn, um, sorry, dropped something. Give me a moment, Mrs. Blodgett."

I cross Gabe's bedroom, stare at the black armoire. I haven't been in here since the day I found Camille's phone, since the day I hid inside his closet.

I reach out, place my fingertips on the handle, push the door open. A white moth flutters out. I recoil, the bitter scent of mildew clouding the air. I'd seen a set of keys on a tiny hook nailed inside the armoire, right before I found Camille's phone. But they didn't matter at the time. They were just there.

I stretch on my toes, peer into the cavernous insides. The keys are there, just as I remember. But something else is there, too, something I know wasn't there before.

Hello? His voice explodes into the silence. I jump back, my heart skipping a beat. "Are you there?" he asks, and I can tell he's in a different area, someplace quiet with no background noise.

"I'm here."

"Sorry about that. You know, maybe this would be better if

I came to your house. I'm free anytime tomorrow. How about eleven? I have my lunch at one, so that would work great."

"That's perfect." I give him the address. He repeats it back.

"Okay, see you Saturday." I end the call.

Reaching into Gabe's armoire, I pick up the red leather wallet hidden inside. It doesn't fit in with its surroundings: gray slacks, dark-wash jeans. Gray sweats, white crewnecks.

Red woman's designer wallet.

My hands shake as I slowly, dreadfully, unzip the top.

29

Ainsley looks back at me, eyes empty.

In the tiny photo on the ID card, her usual sun-kissed skin is blanched by the camera flash. Unsmiling with a clean face, she looks like a different person.

Why would Gabe have Ainsley's wallet in his bedroom? *How* would he have it? Did she forget it the night we went to the restaurant? She did offer to pay for the entire table. Did she leave it behind somehow?

Closing my eyes, I think of that night. The restaurant glowed with warm light. I remember Hugh grinning at me all night— except for when Ainsley was around. His expression stiffened. I remember the food. Sloane. Her shock. The heaviness of my ring, the proposal celebration, his family. I remember the wine.

And I remember this red wallet—bright, stinging scarlet— matched perfectly to Ainsley's handbag and dress. I could never forget. I watched her unzip this wallet, pull out her credit card, pay for the entire table, drinks and all. I never even got a chance to properly thank her. And now I never will.

If Gabe is hiding this, what else could he be hiding? I grab the keys off the hook, shove them in my pocket. Also inside his armoire is a manila folder, wedged into the corner beside some sweaters. I take that, too.

I march back to my bedroom, lock the door behind me. Dropping the keys on the bed, I toss the manila folder aside, peer into Ainsley's wallet.

Inside are her license, credit cards, and $600 in cash. I slip the cash back into the little flap, zip the wallet shut. Picking up the manila folder, I pinch it open. The first page shows balances for Gabe's bank accounts with his address, most likely where he and Camille had lived before moving in with Birdie.

I do a double take.

If I thought *Ainsley* had a lot of cash, I was severely mistaken.

Gabe has enough money saved to pay off my old mortgage. I flip the pages, searching for where the money came from. But it's only a monthly statement, and so it must've been deposited before then.

I try to remember what exactly Hugh had said…

Rebecca moved back because her girlfriend, Kara, kicked her out of their apartment after they got into a fight. I haven't seen Kara since the night Gabe attacked me in the kitchen, but I hope she and Rebecca have made amends.

Hugh moved back because he sold his house and wanted to fix Birdie's roof before it collapsed.

And Gabe—Hugh claimed Gabe moved back because he and Camille had fallen on hard times.

Then I remember. Gabe discovered he had a heart condition. Hugh told me he had surgery for it last year, that every penny they'd saved had gone to hospital bills.

I narrow my eyes. Maybe every penny did go toward hospital bills. At least, every penny Camille knew about. I glance at the name on the bank statement again. The accounts are only in his name—not hers.

But not his name, exactly.

A different surname is printed on top.

"Gabriel...*Vieira*," I read aloud.

Why does he have a different surname than Hugh? His name should be Gabe Smoll, not Vieira. I read the bank statement again. Behind it is another folded letter. I open it. A slip of paper flutters to the floor.

It's a small bank receipt, the kind printed by an ATM. On top, it lists the bank name, date, and transaction type. I shut my eyes, try to focus, do the timeline in my head. The receipt is dated one day after we went out to dinner. The day I woke up and found Ellory gone.

Gabe deposited a check for $107,000 the day after Hugh proposed. I look out the window, imagine how it would feel to possess such a sum.

How did Gabe get so much money the last day Sloane and I saw Ainsley? At our engagement dinner, Ainsley made it known to the entire table that she'd recently come into a lot of money from her divorce. Did Gabe somehow get some of that money? Did they know each other? Is it only a coincidence?

What if that night at the restaurant was the last time Ainsley was alive, the last time she ever saw her friends, ate a meal, drove a car...?

I force myself to refocus. The medical examiner would know her exact time of death. She'd been missing for days before I found her.

But what if she died *that* night?

What if, after Ainsley got home, Gabe was already inside waiting for her? He'd have her wallet. Her address.

No.

He couldn't.

Besides, if Gabe stole from Ainsley, why leave all that cash in her wallet? I push the thoughts away. I once believed Gabe killed Camille, too. And I was wrong. Horribly wrong. Even more horrible is how I can't trust my gut instincts anymore. Every time I do, I'm led down the wrong path.

From now on, maybe I should think the opposite of what my gut is telling me:

1) Gabe is innocent.

2) I'll never see Ellory again.

3) I won't escape this house alive.

"You're being ridiculous, Iris," I tell myself and stand from the floor.

I grab the manila folder with the bank receipts and Ainsley's red wallet to hide them back in Gabe's room. A piece of paper detaches from the back of the folder, slips to the floor. I unfold it, eyes skimming the small printed handwriting. It's a list of names. None are familiar, except the last one.

Doug Erboss.

It's still fresh in my mind from earlier when I rummaged through the desk in the study looking for my phone.

I read the list of names, stop when I reach a small statement at the bottom.

I, Gabe P. Vieira, swear that I, and I alone, have committed crimes, including homicide, against the above-named people...

Below the statement is a signature.

Gabriel Paul Vieira

I read it again. The list of names. The short statement, reading like legal sworn testimony. No, not testimony.

A signed confession.

My vision blurs. I hold in my hands a confession, signed by Hugh's brother.

I alone have committed crimes...

Including homicide...

My mind races. Before I realize it, I'm running downstairs to the study, a room I vowed to never enter again. I burst through the door, yank open the desk drawer, grab the newspaper clipping, angle it toward the light from the window.

LOCAL LONG-LOST HUSBAND, ENTREPRENEUR, MISSING 15 YEARS, DECLARED DEAD

GREENWICH HILLS, NY (NEWS12)—Officials have issued a declaration of death for Douglas Erboss following a 15-year search for the Greenwich Hills man who went missing in 2009.

.The 45-year-old father of three was last seen leaving his home on the morning of June 8, 2009. Erboss's whereabouts have been unknown ever since. A lengthy investigation into the disappearance yielded few clues and left law-enforcement investigators with little hope of solving the case after over a decade of searching for evidence.

In an official press conference, Douglas Erboss's wife, Evonne, gave a public statement following the declaration. "It's been fifteen years," Mrs. Erboss said. "It's time to legally put him to rest, whether or not we ever find his remains."

Mrs. Erboss states she wishes to know the location of his body, but does not hold out hope. "One day, maybe, someone will find him. I just want people to know how much we miss him. We think of him every day."

Evonne—the neighbor next door. The neighbor whose dog I've seen so often in the garden. I brought her dog back to her, saw their name, *Erboss*, on the front gate. That's why the name felt familiar. I'd seen it before.

I remember Evonne saying she was a widow, too, like me. But her husband had never been found. He'd disappeared, never to be seen again.

I lean against the wall, try to catch my breath. Glancing back and forth between the newspaper article, the signed confession, and Ainsley's wallet, I realize maybe there are no coincidences. There's only one thing I can do. I pull my phone from my pocket and call the police.

"Officer Sawicki. How may I direct your call?"

"Hi, I have information about a crime. I think I…" I pause, unsure what to say. I think I just learned my future brother-in-law may be a serial killer? That I found a murder confession? That a man who went missing fifteen years ago might've been killed by the same man who has the wallet of a woman I found dead in her apartment last night?

My mind races. I can't make the thoughts stop. *Focus*, I tell myself. *What would Ellory do? What would Sloane do?*

"Hello? This is Officer Sawicki—did you say you needed to call in a tip? *Hello?*"

I gulp, throat suddenly parched. "My name is Iris Blodgett, and I've found something serious. I think I found a confession to murder."

"Hang on. Did you say you've found a murder confession? Miss?"

"I'm sorry—what was your name?"

"Officer Sawicki. What's *your* name?"

"Iris Blodgett," I repeat.

A sound echoes behind me. I turn, glance out the window. Hugh's SUV breaks through the trees.

"*Crap—*"

"Excuse me?"

"I—I'm sorry—"

"You said your name was Iris Blodgett?"

"Uh, yes."

Sweat beads across my forehead as Rebecca, Birdie, and Hugh step out of the car.

"What exactly did you find, ma'am?"

"I have a signed confession. I have a murder victim's wallet, and I know who killed her." Tears of frustration well in my eyes.

The front door slams shut.

Officer Sawicki clears his throat into the phone. "Let me redirect you to our tip line—"

"Iris? Iris, are you up there?" Hugh's voice echoes from the stairwell.

"*No—no,*" I whisper into the phone. *"I don't have a tip. I have the killer. I know who killed her and other people. You have to believe me. I have a confession. I found it."*

"I'm transferring you to the tip line. Have a nice day."

I wait to be transferred. But the call ends. I've been disconnected.

Hugh's heavy footsteps sound from down the hall.

In my hand, I hold Ainsley's wallet, Gabe's signed confession folded around it. If Hugh finds me here, if he sees me—

"Iris?" He steps into the study, blue eyes locking with mine. "My God, are you okay?"

My entire body goes rigid. He steps toward me, hands outstretched. I flinch away like a startled stray cat.

"What are you doing in here?"

I hold out my arm, open my shaking hand. Gabe's confession unfurls like a flower, Ainsley's wallet tucked inside.

"What's that?"

I ignore him. "What are you doing here?"

He tilts his head, questioning. "Gabe wasn't feeling well today, so we left the hospital early."

"Why does Gabe have her wallet?"

"What?"

"Why does Gabe have Ainsley's wallet?" Each word is harsh, biting.

"I don't know what you're talking—"

"Why does he have her wallet?" My bottom lip starts to tremble. I clench my teeth together, hold it all inside.

"*Ains*—ley." Hugh says her name slowly like it's a disease. "I think she left it at the restaurant. Gabe never got a chance to return it."

"Because I put him in the hospital."

"What? No—*you* did not put him in the hospital. Iris, look

at me. *Look at me.*" Hugh steps forward, grabs hold of my shoulders. "What's wrong with you?"

"Why is there a signed confession? And to murder? Hugh, we have to go to the police."

Hugh's eyes widen. He releases me, stumbles back. "What did you say?"

"Your brother," I say through gritted teeth, "killed my friend. He's killed other people." I unfold the confession note, hold it up to his face.

He takes it from my hand. Softly, he asks, "Where did you find this?"

"That shouldn't matter."

"Listen to me. You're not thinking clearly. Look at you— you're shaking. You have to stop this."

"No. I'm going to the police. Give it back." I reach for the paper in his hand. He steps back, snaps it out of my grasp. "Give it back, Hugh."

"No," he barks, shoving the note in his pocket. "Think about what you're saying."

"I'm going to the police…" Tears break loose, flood down my cheeks. My entire body shakes with sobs.

"No," he repeats. "You're not. We have to talk about this. We have to learn to communicate. You're going to be my wife."

I push past him toward the doorway. Soon, I'm flying down the staircase to the front door, Ainsley's wallet clenched in my hand.

"Iris." Hugh's voice booms behind me. I run outside, feel the cold bite my skin, feel the tears harden into ice on my cheeks. "Iris, stop. Please." Still, he chases me. Why won't he stop? Why won't he stop chasing me? *"Iris."*

Outside, the world is crystallized, bare branches and field grass glistening with hoarfrost. I run across the field, and soon, I reach the tree line. Still, Hugh's deep voice booms, his footsteps heavy as he runs through the forest behind me.

"Iris!"

I want to stop running, but I can't. Something overtakes me, something raw and real and terrifying. My lungs burn as I fling myself over fallen trees, spin between saplings, careful not to trip. I can't trip. I can't fall. *They're here. They're chasing me. Close, so close. I can't let them catch me. They'll catch me, kill me…*

The cold air slices through me, freezing the sweat on my face.

"Iris. Stop!"

I run through the cold, dark woods, the trees growing thicker, and still, I keep going. And then I trip, toe catching on a stone. My body hurls through the air. I'm light, flightless, falling. I land hard, the air compressing out of me.

The crystallized world collapses to black.

136 HOURS LEFT

Bleary-eyed with exhaustion, Ellory peered down for the first time at her baby girl.

She was a cute, little thing, much smaller than Ellory had imagined, with the same dark amber hair as hers. She wondered if her little girl's eyes would be sky blue or brown: the color of a newborn fawn. Maybe she would have full lips with a Cupid's bow in the middle, like Shaw, but Ellory couldn't tell yet.

After all the pain she'd gone through to bring this little baby into the world, she thought she'd hate her newborn daughter or, at the very least, hold a slight grudge. But all of the pain had evaporated the moment the infant opened her mouth and Ellory saw her little pink tongue.

The moment she saw how infinitesimal, how delicate, her baby's fingers were.

A nurse leaned over, plucked her baby from her arms.

"Where are you taking her?"

"The neonatal physician," the nurse said, placing the baby on a flat pillow in a silver cart. "We believe your baby was born a little premature. She's on the small side, but everything so far looks great. She was just ready to meet you early. It's perfectly normal. We only need to monitor her for a short time to be sure she's healthy," the nurse explained. "The doctor will be back soon, after you've rested."

Ellory shook her head. "I want to see her father—can he come in? Can I see him?"

The nurse nodded, kind, polite. "Of course."

Ellory exhaled a deep breath, closed her eyes. Before she knew it, Jade and Shaw were standing beside her bed. In the doorway, she caught the hovering shadows of Mars and Davey.

"I saw her," Shaw whispered, smoothed Ellory's hair. "I saw our daughter."

"She's beautiful," Jade said. "What are you going to name her?"

Ellory struggled to swallow. Jade passed her a plastic cup of ice water.

"I don't know," Ellory confessed and looked at Shaw. "What were you thinking?"

"Me?" he said, surprised. "I—I didn't even think about that yet."

Jade asked, "When can you leave? Did they say?"

Ellory shook her head. She was tired, with fuzzy eyes and a sore, pounding head. Her back hurt, her insides hurt, even her hair hurt as Shaw petted it down her clammy cheeks.

"We have to get out of here soon," Shaw said, glancing over a shoulder toward the doorway. Mars stood with his arms crossed, popped his head in to see what was going on.

"Jade," Ellory began, "can you tell Mars to wait in the waiting room? He's making me nervous."

"Sure," she said and left, closing the door behind her.

Shaw remained, stared down at her, examined her head to toe. "You look tired."

"I am tired."

"Listen," Shaw began, "I don't know what information you're going to give them, but I don't think you should use your real name. Or address."

Ellory gulped. "I know."

"Maybe, I don't know, make one up or something," he suggested. "They probably won't let us leave without having an address to send the bill to, anyway."

"Okay," Ellory said and fixed her eyes on the doorway, wondering how much longer it would be before the nurse wheeled back in her baby's little cart. "Yeah, you're right."

Shaw nodded, satisfied with her compliance. "Okay. I'll be back to check on you later."

He leaned over, kissed her forehead.

Ellory wouldn't see him again for three days.

30

I'm lying in our bedroom when I wake.

Hugh's beside me holding my hand. I was outside, running. It was cold. I was being chased. Rationally, I know it was Hugh behind me, but somewhere deep inside my head I can't help but see *them*.

Then I was in a hospital bed. A doctor used words like *concussion, avulsion fracture, torn tendons*.

"Iris, you're awake." Hugh squeezes my hand. "How are you feeling?" he asks and turns on the lamp on the nightstand, hands me a glass of water. "You fell and hit your head. I carried you and drove you to the hospital."

The moment he mentions my head, a dull pressure aches at the back of my skull.

"You hurt your ankle," he says quietly. "They took X-rays. They said a piece of bone and tendon had ruptured. They gave you a cast to wear for the next six weeks." I lift the covers, see nothing but my bare feet, a bandage wrapped around the one that hurts.

"I took it off for you to sleep," he says, answering my confused expression. "The doctor said if you don't wear it every minute you're not sleeping or bathing, you risk more damage."

"It hurts really bad."

Hugh nods. "I'm sure it does. But I still don't know why you would run from me. It makes me feel horrible that you would." He pouts, pride wounded, but I can't think about that now.

I know why I ran into the woods. Hearing my name, hearing those footsteps crunching in the cold field grass…instinctively, my mind brought me back to that night. The night everything changed. They were there with me, all over again—*one, two, three*.

As I ran, Ainsley's wallet was clenched in my hand. I'm sure of it. I'd stake my life on it. Hugh had taken Gabe's signed confession from me, but Ainsley's wallet was mine. So where is it? I vaguely remember asking Hugh on the drive to the hospital. He said he didn't know. But he must have it. Either that or her wallet is lost in the woods, slipped from my grasp as I fell.

Hugh closes the drapes, darkening the room.

"I'm going to change, then work with Rebecca in the conservatory. I'll be back later with dinner." Reaching into his coat pocket, he unrolls a paper bag from the pharmacy, pulls out the bottle of painkillers the doctor prescribed. Placing it on the nightstand, he hands me a bottle of water.

"Do you have to go?" I ask, taking a sip.

Hugh looks at me appraisingly. His dark brown hair has grown longer since we've moved into the house. For the first time, he's not kept up with his meticulous weekly hair trim. His cheeks are rough, darkened by stubble. A pearl button on his wrinkled blue shirt has a loose string. He's faltering. The slight imperfections are showing. The cracks in the plaster.

"Tomorrow, if you have to go anywhere, I'll drive you."

Crap. I didn't think of that. I can't drive, not now, not with a cast strapped around my right foot. I could move to press the brake pedal and instead step on the gas. The last thing I want is to cause an accident or hurt someone.

I can't walk. I can't drive. I'm officially trapped inside this house. And my fiancé is covering for someone who may be a killer.

Hugh leans over the side of the bed, kisses me on the forehead. I grab the bottom of his shirt, tug him close.

"I'm sorry I ran from you. I know you'd never hurt me," I whisper. "But you have to understand that what I found terrified me."

I stop speaking, astonished when relief is the emotion that creeps into his blue eyes. Out of everything he could be feeling, it's relief that finds a home on his handsome face.

He squeezes my hand tight, painfully pressing the prongs of my ring into the sides of my fingers. "There's nothing to forgive." Hugh stands to leave, and I take his hand. He turns around. Fine lines sprout in the corners of his eyes as he smiles down at me. "Did I forget something?"

"When we were in the woods," I breathe out, try to find a way to say it without scaring him away. Though he's purposely avoiding talking about the confession I found, I deserve to know why. "When we were running, I was holding something. Do you know where it went?"

"Oh, I almost forgot." Opening his coat, he reaches into the inner pocket, pulls out my phone. "The screen broke." He passes it to me. I frown down at it. The glass has shattered.

"It might still accept calls. You won't be able to make them, but it looks like it still works. I'll go out tomorrow and get you a new one. Promise."

"I'd be really grateful. It's important. I have to know if anything happens to Ellory." I click it on. A rainbow of colored lines streaks down the center, blocking most of the screen. I try to swipe in my passcode, but the glass is so cracked it doesn't recognize my touch. "How did this happen?"

Hugh shrugs. "When you fell in the woods."

I examine it closer. It looks like someone has busted the screen with a hammer.

"Did you find anything *else* I was holding?"

His expression twists when he understands what I'm asking. "Iris, stop."

I grip his hand tight. "Please. Where's Ainsley's wallet? It's bright red. You can't miss it."

"When I carried you home, you had nothing in your hands. Just the phone in your pocket."

"Then her wallet must still be out in the woods."

I turn toward the window facing the forest, the view blocked by the drapes. How would I ever get out there? Even if I could, I don't know what direction I was running. The wallet could be anywhere. I'm not sure I'd ever be able to find it, even if my ankle *wasn't* broken.

Hugh sits on the bed, watches me until his eyes go grainy. He blinks hard, looks away. "If our marriage is to be a success," he begins softly, gaze shifting down to my engagement ring, "we need to trust one another. Especially with something like this. I want you—I *need* you—to get along with my family. You don't have to love them. I'm not asking you to. But at least try. For me. Please—like your life depended on it—please try to get them to like you."

I flinch from his words, too surprised to speak. Why does it matter so much if they like me or not?

Before I can ask, he adds, "Especially now, with Gabe coming home." My eyes widen with horror. "When you were in the hospital, I went to visit him. The doctor said he'll be discharged soon. Mother is preparing his room."

"When?"

"Tomorrow morning."

Under the blanket, my hands clench into fists. "Tomorrow," I repeat, cursing my broken ankle. "Gabe will be here *tomorrow*."

"I need you both to at least *try* to get along. I know things have been—strained, but you have to promise me you'll try."

I look at Hugh. "I don't want to see him."

He drops his head in his hand. "I understand you're overwhelmed—"

"Hugh—"

"You're overwhelmed with losing your home. With losing Ellory. Those two things alone are enough for most people to act in ways that aren't normal."

"I didn't *lose* Ell—"

"And on top of it, you moved into a new house, with new people you don't know. And your ankle, and the engagement, and—" He stops himself. "Ainsley's death. Finding her the way that you did."

"I'm fine."

"There's no way you can be fine," he says fervently. "*No one* would be fine. You're focusing on this Gabe-confession bullshit just to take your mind off the myriad of other things you really should be thinking about."

"Nothing's more important than this. This is all *anyone* would think about—"

"What about our wedding? Do you even want to marry me?" Hugh asks before turning away. "You know, I don't—" He stops himself.

I wait for him to continue. He doesn't.

"You don't what, Hugh?" The room settles into silence. When he doesn't reply, I press on. "This has nothing to do with our wedding, and I don't know how you can call what I found *bullshit*. Are you upset I found it? I know you have your brother's back, but come on. This is serious. I'm scared. Can't you see I'm frustrated with how you're ignoring my concerns here?"

"I have to leave tomorrow," he says, changing the subject. "After Gabe comes home, I have to go to the office. I know I'm supposed to be off for the next two weeks to be with you and work on the house, but the crew needs approval for a new project and it's something that has to begin now."

I sniffle, and soon, I'm holding back sudden tears. "I can't believe this. Now you're leaving me. You're leaving me with *him*. After everything I just told you. After I told you how *scared* I am."

"Sometimes you need to be alone with a person before you really get to know them."

"Please don't—"

Footsteps shuffle outside the door. Hugh pulls his hand away. I glance up. Birdie stands in the doorway, holding a teacup, her old wooden cane nestled into the crook of her elbow. Her white hair waves away from her face, showcasing ruby earrings and a matching necklace, stones big enough to rival my ring. As I take a second look, I realize they must all belong to the same matching set.

Her eyes fall to my hand as if reading my thoughts. I hide it under the blanket.

"Can I have a moment alone with Iris?"

Hugh obeys, stands from the bed, leans to kiss me on the forehead. "I'll be back after dinner."

The door closes behind him. Birdie moves to the foot of the bed. "Brought you something useful," she says, stepping forward to pass me the teacup she holds. I reach out a hand to take it. Then she stops, slowly lifts the teacup to her lips, and takes a sip. "I know what you're trying to do. You're trying to blame Gabe for things *you* have done."

"What?"

"Cut the act," she snaps. "Hugh has told me everything." Birdie shrugs, as if there was never any doubt Hugh shared every minute detail about me with her. "He's concerned for you. I am concerned for you."

My lip trembles. I try not to cry. Birdie takes another sip of tea. In the air, the sweet scent of orange blossoms mixes with cloves. I know this tea. It's *my* tea—the calming tea Sloane gave me when I first moved into the house.

"You're not concerned for me," I say and feel my shoulders stiffen. "You're concerned about Gabe. I get it. But your son is a monster, if what I found is true."

"Maybe." She raises an arched brow. "But who are they going to believe? You? A woman who hallucinates seeing shadows in the woods? A woman lying to her own daughter about who her real father is?"

The blood drains from my face. "Hugh—he *told* you that?" The sting of betrayal burns through me.

Birdie releases a wry smile. "And now you're on heavy doses of pain medications." Her pale eyes flicker to the nightstand, to the little paper bag Hugh picked up at the pharmacy. "So I ask you—who will they believe? You? Or me? A figurehead in this community. A rational, wealthy widow." She laughs coldly. "We both know who they'll believe." Birdie steps around the bed, comes closer. I turn toward the door, wishing Hugh would come back. "Stop accusing my son. He is innocent. *You* are the guilty one."

I gulp, tilt my chin up. *What would Ellory do? What would Sloane?* They'd be polite and kind and cutthroat. They'd be sweet and ruthless. God, I want to be like them. I want to be strong and merciless and tough.

My heart races. I wish for strength. I wish for my daughter to be by my side.

"Birdie, if I'm so guilty, I wonder why you seem hell-bent on threatening me. You wouldn't try so hard to protect him if you didn't think I was telling the truth."

Birdie smiles and nods. She's proud. *Proud.* "It's not too late for us to like each other, Iris." She walks to the door, sways in the doorway before steadying herself on her cane. "I think, even after all this, there is still a chance for us to get along.

Yes…" she mutters to herself, studying me as I lie helpless. "I think we still might."

"Please get Hugh. Or just ask if he can get me a new phone today so—"

I stop speaking, realizing how desperate and vulnerable I sound. But I am. On the inside, I'm panicking at the thought of being trapped in this room with nothing to do and no one to talk to. And tomorrow, I'll still be trapped—but Gabe will be here with me. The thought feels raw and painful, an open sore.

Birdie lets out a laugh. "Why would *you* need a phone?" she asks, eyes filled with venom. "Your friend is dead. Your daughter has abandoned you. Your husband was murdered. Oh, Iris, you poor thing. There is no one left for you to call."

I don't reply. Twisting my ring around my finger, I close my eyes, listen to the winter owls hooting outside the window, how they fall in sync with the faint roar of river waves. A tear slips down my cheek. *I'll be fine. It's all going to be okay.*

I don't open my eyes again until I hear the sound of the door closing. Birdie is gone. I'm alone—in this room, in this house—and tomorrow morning, when the owls go to sleep and the river waves calm, I'll still be alone.

But I'll be trapped inside with a killer. And nobody knows but me.

52 HOURS LEFT

Ellory stood under the canopy of the hospital, holding her newborn baby girl in her arms. The snow had returned, bringing an influx of wind with it. She held her baby tight, fearing the wrong gust would take the little one right out of her arms, carry her away into the sky. She was so small, so light, she could've been stuffed with feathers.

The nurse had helped Ellory in more ways than one. She showed her how to bathe her baby for the first time. How to get the newborn to latch on to feed for the first time. How to hold her baby's head. And even explained what Ellory would experience as she recovered: bleeding, pain, emotional whiplash—all normal. All a part of motherhood.

The nurse told Ellory her baby weighed an even six pounds— *That's good luck*, she'd said. And she'd noted that Ellory carried small, which she claimed was lucky, because many women didn't, though it often happened with taller women. Ellory said she was only five foot seven inches and never really thought of herself as tall. But the nurse insisted she was and should be grateful.

The nurse also said she was impressed by Ellory, though Ellory couldn't understand why. Maybe it was because she was keeping the baby. Maybe it was something else. Maybe it was nothing. She glanced down at her baby, at this tiny, helpless thing that needed her to survive, and tears fell down her cold cheeks for no reason at all.

She reminded herself about the hormones and emotions and shivered as she patiently waited outside the entrance of the hospital. Even if Shaw forgot what time to pick her up, Jade would never forget. But as the minutes ticked by, Ellory grew nervous. She imagined the nurses running the information she'd given through their computers. She imagined them seeing how there was no one out there with that name, with that address, if the address she gave even existed.

A bright blue SUV peeled around a corner, music blaring. The same SUV they'd stolen from that man's garage. Ellory stepped into the road before they came to a stop. The hospital's sliding doors opened behind her.

"Ellory?" her favorite nurse called.

Ellory froze. She kept her back to the woman, waited for Shaw to open the door.

"Ellory? You forgot this."

Slowly, Ellory turned. The nurse approached her.

"You forgot your hat, sweetie." The nurse's black hair whipped wildly around her face as she stepped forward, placed Ellory's hat askew on her head.

"Thank you," Ellory said quietly. "For everything."

The car door popped open.

"Hey. Come on—get in."

The nurse eyed the inside of the car as if it led deep into an evil underground lair. She stared at Ellory, their eyes locking

just long enough for Ellory to know what the nurse was probably thinking: *Poor baby. Doesn't stand a chance.*

"Thank you," Ellory said, bending her body to fit in the
back seat of the car, careful not to rattle the baby.

"Do you have a car seat?" the nurse asked. Shaw slammed
the door shut. He rolled down the rear window, just a crack.

"We sure do."

"We do?" Ellory asked as Mars slammed his foot on the gas
pedal, tearing out of the parking lot.

Shaw rolled his eyes. "Of course not. Just hold her."

Ellory looked at her baby, leaned down to kiss her soft head.

Jade smiled. "Did you think of a name yet?"

Ellory shook her head. "Not yet."

"I think you should name her Venom, like the comic book
character," Davey said from the passenger seat.

"No—Venom's a dude. You'd have to name her Black Widow,"
Mars said and laughed. "Whatever, who cares. Listen, Ellory.
You've been in that shithole for days and some things have
changed that we have to tell you about. Shaw's gonna tell you."

Shaw sighed next to Ellory. Ellory held her daughter just a
little tighter, braced herself.

"Yeah, uh, we decided some things. Past few days we've
been staying in some abandoned apartment complex. And we
all did some thinking," Shaw said.

"Come on, Shaw. Tell her," Davey said.

Mars turned a sharp corner, merged onto a highway.

"I *am* telling her," Shaw said. "We compromised. Mars and
Davey…they want you to leave the baby somewhere, like an
adoption—"

"No, asshole, you're getting it wrong," Mars said. "All I said
was that she leave the baby at the hospital or some shit, you
know, like with the nuns."

"Not an option," Ellory said fiercely.

Shaw leaned close to Ellory to whisper in her ear. "I told

them that was out of the question. I mean, it was your choice, so if you wanted to—"

"*I don't,*" Ellory snapped. Next to her, she felt Jade's shoulders relax.

"Oh, okay, good, yeah, that's what I said, too. So, the other option is you keep the baby, obviously," Shaw said, rubbing his neck. "But babies are expensive."

"Real expensive," Mars cut in.

"And we'd need to find a place to live."

"Which takes money."

"So, I was telling the guys how your mom is loaded—"

"My mother isn't loaded. She's broke. Just because we live in a big house—"

"I tried to tell them," Shaw interrupted. "But they wouldn't believe me."

Ellory's heart crept to her throat. She knew exactly what Shaw was going to say before he even said it. Looking away, she tilted her head down, keeping her eyes on her beautiful baby girl as he spoke.

Every one of his words felt like a slap. Every one took her further and further from her dreams, her hopes, everything she'd ever wanted. It was there, right there, so close she could reach out and touch it.

And then it was gone, fast as a bullet.

"We're driving back," Shaw said. "Back home to New York. Back to your house."

THE DAY OF

SATURDAY, JANUARY 25

31

The day I've been dreading has arrived. Gabe is coming home.

Hugh stands in the corner of the bedroom in a cloud of white as he steams a blue suit jacket. Turning it off, he slips the jacket on as the fog dissipates. Most of the men in Hollow Falls wear flannel and boots and jeans. But Hugh...Hugh is different, entirely. Everything about Hugh is thought-out, perfected, purposeful.

Planned.

He turns to face me. Wearing a crisp white shirt beneath the jacket, he tightens a watch around his wrist and laces up a shiny pair of cognac brogues. He looks styled for a network news show. Instead, he's only going to the hospital.

Wanting to get up and get ready, I stretch my legs out under the blankets. Bad idea. I gasp in pain. Hugh rushes over, helps me sit up. Burning pain shoots up and down my leg. My foot feels like I've stepped in lava.

"You have to take it easy. For your bone to heal, the doctor said you can't move it, remember? Not even slow movements.

Here." He kneels onto the floor, slides over the padded black cast, gently lifts my leg. He guides my foot, tightens the Velcro. "Are you sure you'll be okay while I'm gone?"

I nod absently, but he doesn't see.

"Is this too much?" he asks, looking down at his polished shoes. He looks back at me, dressed in an oversize Henley and Ellory's old black leggings.

"You look great," I say. "Can you help me downstairs before you leave?"

"Of course. Come on." He helps me stand.

He stays in front of me as we descend the stairs, in case I fall. I take each step one at a time. Balancing myself on my left foot, I move the crutch Birdie found for me down to the next step. When we finally reach the foyer, I feel monumentally proud.

Hugh leans over to speak softly in my ear. "Now I know you trust me. You know I would've caught you if you slipped."

I toss him a grin. "Good thing I didn't."

He throws his head back and laughs. In a completely different mood today than yesterday, he's all smiles. Walking with a bounce in his step, he leads me toward the kitchen. Today, it seems, is the day all his dreams are coming true. His brother is coming home. And his fiancée appears to have forgiven him for what happened in the woods.

I think of yesterday—the woods, the list of names, the wallet. Ainsley's bedroom, the blood, her face…

"Coffee, Iris?"

I blink. Look up. Rebecca's smiling face blossoms in front of me, first hazy, then fine-tuning until she's sharp. Hugh's voice whispers inside my head: *There's no way you can be fine. No one would be fine.*

"Sure. Thanks."

Birdie mills around the kitchen, wearing a billowy black skirt, a crisp white shirt tucked into the waist. Her glasses are different: green plastic and cat-eye. She sizzles a new batch of bacon on the stove, and the scent fills the entire room.

Rebecca wears shiny black joggers, almost patent, with a pale purple T-shirt, one side tucked into the elastic band. She grabs me a clean mug, hums a song as the espresso machine beeps.

The house is alive with anticipation. The heavy drapes are open, allowing sunlight to pour in. For the first time, the antique brass statues seem to sparkle, and the gilded face of the grandfather clock appears to grin. The dusty colors of the Persian rugs look vivid and somehow even the walls seem higher, as if the house has inhaled a deep breath, holds it in as it awaits Gabe's grand entrance.

"You sure you'll be okay while we're gone?" Hugh asks as he washes his hands in the sink.

I nod, maybe a little too enthusiastically.

They chat about Gabe and Camille and how Hugh has generously offered to help them move into a new house he has put a down payment on for them. But I hear none of the details. My mind is on other things. One thing, actually.

Ellory.

Left unoccupied, my mind always drifts to her. I wonder where she is. If she's safe. When I'll see her next. Then my mind travels to other thoughts. Darker thoughts. Will Duplain find anything? Will the police?

I didn't want to mention this to Hugh, but Gabe's homecoming isn't the only reason I've been dreading this day. Today is the third anniversary of Jack's death. For three years I've been a widow. For three years Ellory hasn't had her father. If I could name this passage of time, I'd call it a tiny eternity.

Ellory and I always visit Jack's grave today. It's always cold, snowy, and we always bring him a number-one-dad mug, filling it with hot chocolate from his favorite thermos, and adding marshmallows while we wade in the snow. We watch as the steam rises, until the chocolate cools. And we hold on to each other, just for one day. No matter what's happening in our lives, no matter how busy we are, we come together.

Afterward, we visit Sloane at the café, where she leaves out a plate of croissants, just for Jack. They were his favorite, and were the last breakfast he'd eaten the morning before he died. But this year, I'm alone. And so is Jack. I don't have Ellory, and I don't have him. With no way of driving to the cemetery, I make a promise to him that I'll visit the second I can.

I feel Hugh kiss my cheek. I must've gone through the proper motions of saying goodbye, because soon the sound of the front door echoes from the other side of the house, and I'm standing alone in the kitchen.

Grabbing my crutch, I hobble down the hall to watch TV in the great room when I hear a dog whimper outside. The sound is soft but unmistakable. Turning back to the kitchen, I grab the last of Birdie's bacon and return down the hall.

Through the patio door, I spot Evonne's dog, Dougie, digging up a dead flower bed, dirt flying behind him, crashing into the side of a moss-eaten fence. I slide the door open, step outside. It's freezing, the morning sky restless and gray.

Sitting on a crooked bench, I hold out the bacon. Dougie approaches, licks my hand, inhales the bacon in a single bite. I'd always wanted a dog. My mom had one when I was young, before I left home. It was white with little pink pads on its feet, like jelly beans. My mom would kiss them, one by one, and I'd watch her close, wishing she'd show me that same kindness.

I wanted my own dog, too. I wanted to hug it, brush it, let it sleep next to me at night, curled up underneath my arm. But my mom wouldn't let me. And if she caught me playing with *her* dog, feeding treats to *her* dog, petting *her* dog, I'd be punished. No one else was supposed to touch her dog. She didn't want her dog to like anyone else but her.

That was around the time when I pledged to myself if I ever had a baby, I'd treat them how I'd always wanted to be treated—the opposite of how my mom had treated me. With love. Kindness. Comfort. I couldn't wait for my own baby. I couldn't wait for Ellory.

With the thought, my worry for Ellory skyrockets again. God, I wish I could be with her, hug her—especially today.

A voice carries on the wind. For a heartbeat, I think it's her. "Doo-gie," the voice calls. "Doo-gie!"

Dougie's ears perk up. He runs out of the garden.

It's not Ellory, but someone else I'm still comforted to see.

Evonne appears behind the stone wall. Her eyes dart side to side, checking to see if I'm alone before she nudges open the gate and steps closer. Seeing the crutch, she says, "Oh, no. What did you do to yourself?" Sitting next to me, she pulls me into a tight little hug.

"I'll be fine. I fell," I say, answering her intense stare on my cast. Dougie runs over, resumes his digging.

Evonne scolds him, but he doesn't stop. "I'm sorry. I hope it's better soon."

"Thanks."

"You know," she begins. In the wind, her thin hair flies up on her scalp, and she lifts a hand, smooths it back in place. "I'm glad I ran into you. I wanted to come over and talk to you, but…I don't like coming here." She shivers.

I study her as she looks up, heavily mascaraed green eyes scanning the giant, looming house around us. A haunted mansion filled with ghosts.

"Why not?"

Evonne ignores the question, asks, "Have you found your daughter yet?"

"Not yet."

"She'll come home—you'll see. In the meantime, if you need anything at all—"

"Actually, there's something I wanted to ask you." She tilts her head. "Gabe, Hugh's brother, is coming home today from the hospital. He had a heart attack," I add when I notice her thin eyebrows furrow. "Do you know much about him?"

Evonne lets out a long sigh. "Well, not much. I only know his wife's a piece of work. I used to hear them fighting out here in the garden when I'd take my long walks. But I haven't heard them in a while. I guess things are better now," she says with a cackle. "But before that, before her, I never saw him. The mother—Birdie—what a *saint* she is. What she did for her daughter, she should be given an award."

"What did she do?" I ask, easily believing Birdie would do anything for her kids. But I find it hard imagining her as a saint.

"Oh, well, this was years ago. Poor Rebecca. Her entire family had been killed in a fire. I'd heard Birdie adopted her. Otherwise, I imagine she would've been an orphan, hopping around, foster home to foster home. Things like that never turn out well."

"Rebecca was adopted?" My mouth falls open in surprise. "No one ever said anything about it."

Evonne shrugs. "No, they wouldn't, would they?"

That explains the different name I saw on Rebecca's ID the night we went to the restaurant. At the time I thought it strange, but ignored it, assuming she'd been married and divorced in the past.

That explains things with Rebecca, but what about Gabe? Was Gabe's last name *Smoll*, like Hugh's surname—or *Vieira*, as written on his bank statements?

There was only one way to find out. "Evonne, what about Gabe? Was he adopted, too? Or Hugh?"

"Oh, no. Not that I know. Just Rebecca. Honestly, and I'm sad to say it," Evonne begins, "I think Birdie was looking to fill a hole. Her daughter, Paige, had disappeared. I think she wanted another daughter to try and— I shouldn't even say it. It's too cruel."

"To replace Paige?"

Evonne shrugs again. "You can say that. That's just what it seemed like to me, from the outside looking in. Well, you'll freeze to death if I keep you out here any longer. Dougie, come. We're going home." She lets out a whistle. Hesitating, Evonne stops, turns around. "You know, now that I think of it, I don't remember seeing any of them when they were little, except Paige. Not even Rebecca, even though I'd heard she was only a child when Birdie adopted her."

"What do you mean?"

Evonne's thin eyebrows come together in thought. "It's like all three of them just popped up one day, out of nowhere, fully grown. Like they were forced to live inside the house all their lives, never allowed to go outside. Who knows? Maybe they were prisoners."

Chills flutter through me. I look over a shoulder, up toward the attic window. When I turn back around, Evonne and Dougie have gone, and I'm outside alone.

49 HOURS LEFT

"I *can't* go home," Ellory said.

The baby started crying, long, thick cries, cries that made her eardrums rattle. Mars turned up the music, opened his window, which only made the baby cry harder until she was shaking with sobs in Ellory's arms.

"Close the fucking window!" Jade screamed. "Close it, Mars."

He closed it, lowered the music. "Make that baby shut up."

Tears streamed down Ellory's cheeks. Her daughter's face was turning red. She didn't know what to do. She didn't know how to calm her, how to make her stop. All she did know was what the nurses had taught her. Ellory tugged down her shirt. Knowing what Ellory was doing, Jade helped her take off her heavy winter coat.

Ellory pressed her baby's lips to her skin and let her feed. Davey turned around, gave a look like he wanted to puke. Mars adjusted the rearview mirror down.

"Is it weird I find that strangely erotic?"

Shaw punched the back of his headrest. "Shut the fuck up. I have to tell her the plan."

Mars laughed but still kept the rearview mirror tilted down. Jade took off her army coat, held it up like a curtain.

"Why are we going back to New York?" Ellory asked, wiping tears on her sweater sleeve.

"We're going back to your house," Shaw said, staring out the window, unable to look her in the eyes. "They have money there. Either that or they can get it for us. We need money. Money's at your place. It's a simple plan. I won't bore you with details."

Ellory's lips began to tremble. She turned to Jade, who sat silent next to her. From what Ellory could tell, this wasn't Jade's idea. But she needed a chance to be alone with her, to talk to her without Shaw or Mars or Davey there to hear. They needed to speak in private—they needed to find a way to escape.

She looked down at her baby girl. Ellory feared maybe the nurse was right. Maybe her baby didn't stand a chance at all.

"So tell us, Ellory," Mars began. "How do we break into your house without getting caught?"

Ellory gulped. She felt carsick. Her stomach flipped. She moved her daughter away, shrugged on her coat. "Can we pull over?"

At the next exit, Mars pulled into a gas station, filled the tank with Shaw's last remaining twenty-dollar bill.

Ellory circled the parking lot. The snow had stopped. Jade walked up behind her. Ellory thought Jade looked worse than the last time she'd seen her at the hospital. Where had she been sleeping? On the dirty floor of an abandoned apartment? Had she eaten anything?

At least Ellory was fed hospital food. But Jade's face seemed to have sunken since she'd last seen her. Her face had grown pale and thin, yet swollen at the same time.

"Ellory," Jade began. Tears bubbled along her thick eyelashes, fell down her face, eyeliner staining translucent gray streaks. "I'm so sorry I didn't come see you. Mars wouldn't take me. I—I didn't have a way—"

"It's fine," Ellory said. Holding the baby with one hand, she placed the other on Jade's bony shoulder. Jade hugged her tight, tighter than anyone had ever hugged her before. The baby cooed.

"You know I'd never let them force you to abandon your baby," Jade whispered, choking back a sob.

"I know," Ellory said softly, looking down at her daughter's chubby cheeks. "I know you wouldn't."

"And I don't want them to break into your house, either. But without you, it's me against them, you know? Shaw, Davey, Mars."

"I know."

Jade wiped her tears away, leaving gray smudges across her cheeks like diluted ink. "We have to leave them," Jade said quietly so they couldn't hear. "We can't get back in that car. If we get back in, we have no choice. They're going to drive us to your house, and they're going to break in. We can't—"

"We have to. Besides, it's too late," Ellory said, eyes staring ahead as Shaw marched straight toward them. Ellory held her baby tighter.

"It's never too late," Jade whispered to her. "Never."

"Come on. We have to go," Shaw said, keeping his eyes on the ground. Ellory wondered when he would ever look at his baby—his daughter. He put his hands on their backs, corralled them back into the car like escaped livestock.

Mars merged back on the highway.

With every mile marker they passed, Ellory's heart sank.

"Okay, now, Ellory," Mars said, cutting in and out of traffic. "We waited three days for you. Three days in some shit apartment. Now you have to tell us how to get into your house without getting caught."

Ellory bit her bottom lip, swallowed hard.

Shaw nudged her arm. "Come on. Just tell them," he whispered. "They'll do it with or without you. Tell them a way they can do it so no one gets hurt."

Ellory wanted to sob. But she couldn't, not again. She feared she'd dehydrate herself or make the baby cry. All she could do was hold it in. Hold it back. Keep her daughter warm. Keep her daughter safe.

Ellory gulped down her sadness. "You have to park—"

"What?" Mars said, turning off the music. "Speak up. We can't hear you."

Ellory gulped again. Streetlights flickered on and off, bright and dark, faster and faster as Mars sped up. Her head swam. Jade put a hand on her knee, gave a little squeeze. She turned just in time to see Jade shaking her head: *Don't tell them.*

I have to, Ellory mouthed.

Ellory turned away from Jade, cleared her throat, spoke louder. "You have to park down the hill and walk through the woods," she said. "Do it at night. Turn off the headlights. No one will see the car."

Jade's face flashed under the flickering streetlights. In the orange glow, Ellory could see her expression shift as they fell back into shadows.

"And where's the money?" Mars asked.

"Anything we can sell? Is there a safe?" Davey asked when Ellory failed to reply.

"Please," Shaw said. Ellory watched him. Finally, he was looking at his daughter. His face fell into peaceful serenity, and Ellory knew she was seeing his heart grow.

"Come on. Tell us!" Mars yelled.

Shaw blinked out of his trance, turned away. "There has to be something in there," he said, trying to get her to talk. "Just tell us. We have the entire car ride. You have to tell us."

"She will," Mars said.

"Of course she will," Davey chimed in. "She's got that baby to think of now."

Ellory couldn't think of anything valuable inside the house. Nothing at all. To her, everything there was as worthless as dirt. But she needed to keep them quiet. She wanted her baby to sleep. She told them about the paintings and antiques and relics that littered every room of the house.

They meant nothing to her, so she told them about it all.

And while she'd never imagined going home again, a part of her wanted nothing more than to see her mother. To make peace with her. To introduce her to her new granddaughter. After everything she'd been through, Ellory would do anything to have the chance to stay inside that house with her mother forever.

As each passenger fell asleep, the car grew silent. Ellory watched the streetlights flicker across her sleeping daughter's beautiful little face. And she made a promise.

She promised when she saw her mom again, she'd never let her go.

32

Standing in the doorway of the study, I stare at the old computer and think. Rebecca was adopted. That's nothing to be ashamed of. Quite the opposite. It says a lot about Birdie that she brought a girl into her home, a girl who'd lost her entire family. And now Rebecca's part of Birdie's family. Blood relation or not.

So why didn't Hugh tell me?

Peeking through a window, I check the driveway. I'm still alone. For now. While they're gone, there's something I need to do. I know I could be wrong, but I have to at least ease my doubts. Maybe I can find something. Maybe there's something that will shatter my assumption about Gabe. Or confirm it.

With the screen on my phone broken, I have no other choice but to turn on the ancient computer. The screen wheezes awake. I click open the internet and type:

Gabe Vieira New York

My finger hovers over the search button. If he's using a fake name, then nothing true would come up about him. I imagine seeing a picture of the real Gabe Vieira, a man who looks completely different from him. Or his picture would come up, crushing my theory. I'm not sure which one I'd more like to be true.

Either I'm obsessing over nothing and have scorned a man whose actions are misunderstood or, at the very least, misguided. Or I'm about to be in a house with a man with a fake identity. A thief. A killer.

Something moves above my head in the ceiling. In the attic. It sounded like someone dropped something. A thud.

Then silence.

I inhale, click Search.

Slowly, the results load. I hold my breath. At the top is a Facebook account. I click on it, see a man from California. The name could be common, so I go back to the search results, click open every link, not exactly sure what I'm hoping to find.

The first few results are links to Facebook and other social media. I open each of them, see they're men sprinkled across the country. None of them are Gabe.

Most are random websites or LinkedIn profiles. But still, I keep searching, clicking on page two, where a news article populates. I open the link.

LOCAL WOMAN FOUND RAPED, MURDERED DAY BEFORE 21ST BIRTHDAY

The article is dated nearly a decade ago. I hover close to the dusty screen but the article fails to load. I click the refresh button, wait for it to load again. But the contents are gone. Only the headline shows.

I go back, search the headline only:

local woman raped murdered day before 21st birthday

The only exact result is the same link to the news article. Without the woman's name, I can't find more. I try clicking the link again. Still, nothing but the headline loads. The web page fails.

My mind falls down an endless rabbit hole of possibilities: *What if Gabe killed this woman, too?* I saw the confession. I read it, held it in my hands. It was a list of names, a list of *victims'* names. And at the bottom was Gabe's signature.

If he killed this woman, could he have also killed his little sister, Paige?

I inhale a deep breath. I have to push forward and find more solid evidence. It can only help bring Gabe to justice. And it could help make the cops take me more seriously—about Ainsley *and* Ellory.

I search for another name:

Rebecca

I stop myself. I've forgotten the last name I saw that night on Rebecca's ID. Evonne said Rebecca was adopted, that her entire family had been killed in a fire. For some reason, my mind, now hell-bent on blaming every terrible thing on Gabe, thinks maybe he was involved in that, too.

I shake my head to clear it. *Think. Focus.* You were sitting in the restaurant. The lights were dim. Rebecca passed her ID to you so you could hand it to the waiter. He had to check her age so she could order a drink. I remember the picture: small and square. Bright red hair, long and straight, framed her oval, unsmiling face.

But I can't remember the name.

Resigned, I type in:

Rebecca family fire New York

Assuming the fire even happened in the state of New York, I click Search.

Eight million results populate.

I open the first link, an article on a prominent news site. If this is about Rebecca and her family, it made national news.

The top of the page gives a disclaimer, stating the article is archival content over ten years old. I look at the date: June 14, 2004.

The headline reads:

NO SUSPECTS IN HOUSE FIRE THAT KILLED FAMILY, 1 SURVIVOR

I scan the article, knowing immediately Evonne has been telling the truth. This is Rebecca and her biological family. I know when I read their surname:

Haplehorn.

I keep reading the article. It details a horrible night when suspected arsonists burned down Rebecca's home while they all slept. Her mother, father, older brother, and one-year-old sister all died from smoke inhalation.

Only Rebecca was able to be rescued by firefighters. She'd been sleeping in a room farthest away from the fire, closest to the front door.

I lean back in the leather chair. My ankle throbs. My head aches. A heavy, crushing feeling of sorrow washes over me—for her family and for what Rebecca had lived through. She was so young. Only six years old.

After clearing the internet history, I push myself out of the chair.

The thud happens again, louder, above my head in the attic.

I clench my jaw. Now is the time; it has to be. They're gone, away for at least a little while. I have to use this time efficiently. Every second counts.

I stand from the desk, slowly climb up the stairs to our bedroom. Inside a secret compartment of my luggage, I'd hidden the set of keys. I unzip the side, and clothes tumble out. I search through the fabric, loop the ring around my finger, hobble down the hall.

Someone doesn't want me to find what's behind this door.

But now I have the keys. A way in. Leaning on my crutch, I insert the first key into the keyhole.

I turn it, twist the porcelain knob.

It doesn't open.

I try again, this time with a key with a filigree crown at the top. Still, the door doesn't open. There's one key left. I hold my breath, slide it into the keyhole. It glides in smooth, unlocks with a click. I turn the doorknob.

The door creaks open.

50 MINUTES LEFT

It felt like it had taken a lifetime to leave her old world behind, but it only took two days to get it back.

They'd timed it perfectly. It was just past midnight when their stolen car glided up the back road leading to the house. Ten minutes later, they were walking through the cold, dark woods. Ellory carried her newborn baby in her arms, staying close to Shaw and the flashlight he held in his hand.

The ground shook with each step, pounding her head into a perpetual ache. Shaw's flashlight bobbed up and down, making her dizzy as she struggled to keep her footing on the uneven forest ground.

Jade walked beside her, an empty backpack slung over her shoulder. Soon, if everything went to plan, the backpack would be bursting with stolen goods from the house, maybe even cash, which was what Shaw was hoping for. They'd split it five ways, though Ellory was doubtful that, in the end, Mars would let anything be even.

Mars walked in front of the pack, stepping into the light of

Shaw's flashlight. He didn't carry anything with him. Only his gun. Davey walked next to him in silence. Every minute that passed on the drive up to the house, Davey was the one who'd expressed fear of getting caught, while Jade tried to snuff out the plans altogether. Shaw went along with it, pushed Mars into action.

At first, Ellory didn't believe they'd go through with it. But she was wrong.

As they reached the outskirts of the woods, they stopped. The house was a giant black blip in the distance, in the dark, blotting out all the stars behind it. If Ellory listened close enough, she could hear the beating sound of the nearby river waves, a liquid heartbeat.

Mars stepped out of the woods, hovering at the edge of the tree line. Shaw followed. Then Davey. Jade stayed behind with Ellory in the dark safety net of the woods.

While no lights were on inside the house, Ellory still didn't want to be seen. She knew if she emerged from the forest this close, someone would spot her, even if she only looked like a shadowy figure smudged in the distance.

Mars turned, walked back into the woods. Leaning his back against a tree, he said, "Okay, let's run through this again."

Shaw and Davey followed and together they stood in a circle. Ellory's teeth began to chatter. White puffs of air blew from her mouth with each exhalation. At least she had her baby's warmth. She only hoped her warmth was enough to keep the baby from freezing.

"So, we're going to go in through the kitchen window," Shaw began. "That's where you said the lowest window is? Where we'd be able to get inside?"

Jade nudged Ellory's arm. She looked up from her baby to see them all staring at her.

"What?"

"The kitchen window," Davey said. "Where is it?"

"Oh," Ellory said, shaking her head clear. "On the left," she said, pointing toward the house. "The window is low and no one ever locks it. You can just climb in there—"

"What do you mean *you*—aren't you coming with us?" Davey asked.

"You have to show us where the safe is," Shaw said.

"I don't even know if there *is* a safe—"

Mars slammed his fist against the tree. "What do you mean you don't know if there's a safe?" He moved close to her, hovering inches from her face. Her baby began to fuss. Ellory held her closer to her chest, tucked her scarf around her tiny head.

"Just leave me alone, Mars," Ellory said.

Jade stepped forward, shoved her arm between them. "Enough, Mars. Leave her alone."

Mars laughed. Ellory turned to Shaw, who looked away. Tears filled her eyes.

"I—I can't do this," Ellory began.

"What? You can't do what?" Mars yelled in her face.

"Shut up. Someone will hear you," Davey said, grabbing his brother's arm.

"What can't you do, huh?" Mars said again.

Ellory's lips trembled. She was tired. Tired of running. Tired of Mars and Davey. Of Shaw never standing up for her. She didn't want to be on the road with them anymore. Now that she was home, all she wanted to do was run out of the woods, across the field, and bang on the door. All she wanted was her mother.

Ellory lifted her head in defiance. "Fuck you, Mars. I'm not helping you. My mother is asleep in that house right now, and I'm not going to let you—"

A sharp pain bloomed across her cheek.

"What the fuck, Mars?" Shaw screamed. The light from his flashlight flickered frantically across the forest floor.

Ellory lifted a hand to her face. Her skin was pulsing, burning. He'd *slapped* her. He'd slapped her while she held her newborn baby. A little patter of blood dribbled onto her dingy white coat.

Jade wrapped her arms around Ellory, helped her hold the baby up. Ellory's arms were shaking. Her entire body was shaking.

"Give her to me," Jade said. Ellory passed the baby to her.

Ellory shook out her tingling arms, set her eyes on Mars.

"You fucking coward!" Ellory yelled. "All of you." She kept her eyes locked on Shaw as she spoke. "You want to break into my house? Fine. Go ahead. But I'm not helping you do it. Come on, Jade."

Ellory turned to walk back to the car.

"Hey," Shaw called after her. "We have to do this. We have no choice. Think of our baby. How are we going to take care of her? Your mom would do anything for you. You're her only child. We have to go through with this."

"*No.*"

In the darkness, Shaw's eyes burned with hatred. At that moment, she knew he despised her. He despised their baby. He despised that she'd gotten pregnant. Most of all, Ellory knew he despised that he couldn't stand up to Mars. He was weak. Weak, and he knew it. And he knew *she* knew it, too.

"Ellory," Jade said softly. "Come on. Let's go."

"No—you're *not* leaving." Shaw grabbed Ellory's head with one quick jerk, every root of hair feeling like it would pop out from her scalp.

"Shaw—let go—you're hurting me."

Obeying, he released her hair, moved his hand around her neck, thumb pressed hard against her voice box.

"Shaw," Jade called. "Let her go."

"Come on, Shaw," Davey said, grabbing Shaw's arm. "Drop her. Let her go."

Ellory gulped for air as Shaw held his hand tight around her throat. She couldn't breathe. She couldn't move.

"Let her go!" Jade's screams echoed through the cold, dark woods.

Ellory's heartbeat pounded in her ears like thunder.

Shaw released her. Ellory fell to her knees, gasped for air.

"You—you *fucking bastard*."

Thick, choking sobs overtook her. Shaw was no longer strangling her, but still, she couldn't breathe. She clawed herself off the forest floor, tears streaking down her face, so thick she couldn't see anything but darkness.

Reaching into her coat pocket, she fumbled for her inhaler. Grabbing hold of it, she shook it hard, held it to her lips, inhaled a deep breath, then another, until her lungs calmed and her wheezing quieted.

Wiping her eyes clear, she capped her inhaler, looked up at Shaw. She couldn't help it. All she felt was rage. She saw him and ran at him, shoving him as hard as she could. She had to defend herself if only this once.

They were over now anyway. It would just be her and her beautiful baby girl. She was home now. She'd live with her mother and daughter. The three of them, a little family. She'd convince her mother to leave that man—they didn't need him. Ellory held on to the thought as her palms connected with Shaw's chest, pushing him hard against a tree.

In one quick jerk, Shaw grabbed her by her wrists and flung her away, as easily as if she were a piece of paper. Ellory tripped over the root of a tree, ankle twisting. She felt herself plummet. Her inhaler catapulted out of her grip, disappeared into the darkness of the woods.

She stretched her hands out to brace the fall. But it happened too fast. She couldn't stop it. She slammed to the ground, head exploding with fire. The air punched out of her so hard she saw stars.

And then she saw nothing at all.

33

The darkness is choking.

New smells fill my nose: mold, bitter fruit, sawdust. Leaning on the crutch, I tug my phone out of my back pocket. I can't access any of the apps or the flashlight, but I can hold it up, use whatever light emits from the screen to light the way.

I squint in the dark, run my hand along the walls to find a light switch. Finding one, I click it on. Soft light fills the space. A long, narrow staircase looms ahead of me, stretching up into the darkness of the attic.

I take a deep breath, ready myself to make the climb. Tucking the keys into my cast, I lift the crutch, grab the banister, pull myself up, step by step. I can do it. I have to.

At the top, I use the light from my phone to brighten the walls, find another light switch, flick it on. Old lights whir with a low hum of electricity. I heave myself up the final step, glare into the depths of the attic.

Something up here has been making noise—enough to wake me in the middle of the night. But what? Slowly, I make my way down the length of the room, little windows sitting in dormers giving some extra light, though the sky outside has fallen into stormy darkness.

The damaged roof above lets out a low, angry moan. Was that the sound I'd been hearing? I freeze, hold my breath. Wind lashes against the roof. The old wooden beams howl. Unknotting clenched fists, I exhale a deep breath.

The attic is longer than it is wide, with the high, tilted angle of a mansard roof. The floorboards are uneven, lifting in spots as I wobble on one foot, making me lose my already precarious balance. I scan the open space, search for something responsible for the noise.

But there's nothing. Nothing but wooden crates and furniture and dust.

Still, I push myself down the length of the room, the scent of sawdust and mold filling my lungs. It's overpowering. I don't have a spare hand to cover my nose, so I reach for a window to see if it unlatches. The window frame unhooks. I shove it open, gulp down fresh air. In the distance, I hear gravel crunching.

Crap.

A white car curls up the driveway. *No, no, no*, it's too soon, much too soon. I imagine the family pulling in front of the house, seeing me hanging out of the attic window. Stepping back, I shut it tight, watch as the car breaks through the trees.

It comes closer, stops too far from the house—something a stranger would do. I don't know this car. It's not Hugh's Tesla, which they took to the hospital. It's not Camille's sporty red car.

The engine stops. A man slams the door behind him. He gazes up, stares at the house. The house stares back. The man reaches the front porch, removes his hat, presses the doorbell. He peers through the stained-glass windows that flank the front door.

In the porch light, I can vaguely make out his face. I squint to better see, but I already know exactly who it is.

The wind blows again, shaking the attic walls. The window

flies open. A gust of freezing air pours inside. I stumble back, grab hold of my crutch before I fall. My cast lands sideways on the floor. The pain is brutal, sudden. A scream rips through me. Pulling myself up, I grab the edge of the window, lift my head to look outside.

His head snaps toward the open attic window.

I curse at my phone. If the screen didn't crack, I would've been able to check the time. I would've never forgotten our appointment today at eleven. Never. How could I allow myself to lose track of time? I move to the window, look down at him, motion for him to come inside. I close the window again.

A moment later, Duplain calls through the house. "Hello, Mrs. Blodgett? Are you up there? Door was open. I hope you don't mind I let myself in."

He sounds close. He must already be upstairs, I realize with a chill. "Up here," I shout. "In the attic. I'll be right down."

My mind races. I have to think, come up with a plan, do something. Because this is happening. This is happening right now, whether I'm prepared for it or not.

Duplain's boots stomp through the house, a ticking clock.

A bomb counting down.

I push myself off the floor. My weight shifts the beams, popping a long nail up through a floorboard. My breath catches. One more inch to the left and the nail would've punctured through my slipper.

The lights flicker, fade, like the house is taking a breath.

I trip on my first step, grab the crutch to steady myself. Pain shoots through my ankle, down my foot. The house moans as a tear ekes out of the corner of my eye, and somehow, it feels like the house is pleased.

The lights ignite again, brighter than before, lighting up darkened corners. I grit my teeth, hold back the pain, and weave my way through stacked boxes and bookshelves until I notice something, pause.

Duplain's voice booms from downstairs. "Mrs. Blodgett? Is today still a good time to talk about Ellory?"

"Be right there. I'm in the attic."

I turn back.

An old mattress hides in a dusty corner.

A mattress.

Next to it is an old soda bottle, the label peeled away. A constellation of opened candy wrappers litter the floor. In a corner are racks bursting with sun-washed clothing. On the floor are dusty mountains of stacked shoes.

Surrounding the mattress are walls of framed photographs. Each one is caked with dust, blurring the images. On the ground are shards of broken glass. Several pictures have fallen from the wall, shattered.

Was this what was causing the thuds I'd been hearing? Picture frames falling off the wall, landing on the wooden floor with enough force to break the glass, bend the frames?

When I'd first arrived, I'd commented how there were no pictures. Throughout the entire house, not a single picture of the kids, of Hugh or Gabe or Rebecca. Birdie told me her late husband had destroyed all of the family photos before he died.

But she'd lied. They were here. All of them. Enough to hang on every wall in this giant old house. An entire lifetime's worth is hidden here where no one can see. A constant reminder of a past life, locked away upstairs.

Unless you have a key.

I push myself off the floor, wobble to the wall of photos.

Swiping dust off the front of a picture frame, I stare at the face looking back. It's Birdie, younger than she is now. Pretty and radiant, she wears a tight black turtleneck, hair grazing her shoulders. Not a shock of white, but a soft, muted brown brushed with silver.

I swipe the dust off another. It's Birdie again, posing with a man at the beach. It's taken from a distance and they wear sunglasses, but still, I know it's her. She has no cane. She's smiling; they both are. I assume it's her husband—the man who'd later try to take her life before taking his own.

After wiping the dust off the rest of the frames, I step back, stare at the wall of pictures.

A girl smiles back at me.

Over and over again, pictures of the same girl. She looks so familiar. I know this face—I know *her* face.

She's exactly the same in these photos as I remember her.

"Mrs. Blodgett? The door's open. I'm assuming you're up there in the attic? Is now a good time to talk?" Duplain's voice, closer now, just below, right down the attic steps.

But I can hardly hear him. I can hardly hear anything at all. I'm in shock, head buzzing, room spinning.

Shock.

I could never forget her. Though time has dulled the edges, I know exactly who she is.

Her family had named her Paige.

But I knew her as Ellory.

30 MINUTES LEFT

"Is she dead?"

"I can't fucking believe this," Mars said.

Stepping away, Davey asked, "Shaw, what were you thinking?"

"I—I didn't know she'd fall. I didn't do anything. It all happened so fast…"

"This is all your fault. What's wrong with you?" Davey yelled back.

Paige felt someone's cold hands touch her neck. She couldn't move. She couldn't open her eyes. She wasn't even sure if she was still breathing. Maybe they were right. Maybe she was already dead.

Paige didn't know how much time had passed, but the world went silent. She wanted her baby. She wanted to name her Victoria, but she'd never gotten the chance to tell anyone, not even Jade.

Soon, she heard ruffling footsteps walking through fallen leaves. She tried to move, tried to open her eyes. But she couldn't. Her head spun. She saw stars. Blood had cooled on her skin and she felt wetness in her hair. Everywhere was numb.

"Who's going to be the one to do it?" Mars asked.

"Shaw has to do it," Davey insisted.

"What? Why me?"

"You were the one who fucking killed her, that's why," Davey snapped.

I'm not dead, Paige tried to speak. *I'm not...*

"Oh, my God...how could you? I can't believe this is happening..."

Jade.

Mars groaned. "Oh, shut up. Seriously, Jade, take that baby back to the car and wait for us there."

"*No*, you can't do this. She needs to go to a hospital—"

"Will all of you stop it?" Davey said.

"Seriously, let's just do this and get the hell out of here, okay?" Shaw said.

"Fine. Shaw—you have the honors."

"I saw a woodshed near the road..."

"...might be in there..."

"Go get it..."

Silence.

A thousand heartbeats.

Then a steady, angry sound. An unmistakable sound.

Paige tried to open her eyes. She tried to move her fingers, to start small, then work her way up to her hand, her arm. Then soon she could walk. Then she could run out of these cold, dark woods.

Help me. Please—Jade—Shaw—help me!

Paige was screaming inside her head. But no one could hear.

Her baby began to cry. Jade whispered to her, "It's okay, it's okay. Everything's going to be fine. You're going to be okay. Your mommy is going to wake up and everything's going to be okay."

"Jade," Davey began, his voice sounding close to her, so close she could reach out and touch him. "She's dead. I don't hear her breathing."

Paige felt his finger touch her nose as he held his hand close to her mouth to feel for air.

I'm breathing. I'm alive. Help me, please!

Why couldn't he hear her? Why couldn't he feel her breathing?

Why couldn't she move?

The unmistakable sound echoed again.

"It's going to be light out soon. Hurry up," Mars said.

Shaw sounded out of breath, exhausted. "I'm trying—I'm going as fast as I can. You want to do it?"

"No. *You're* the one who did it. *You* have to do it," Mars said coldly. "Clean up your mess."

Crunching footsteps. "Davey, give me your cell phone," Jade said.

"No. It's in the glove box, anyway. Why the hell would I give you my cell phone?"

"Because you don't want to do this."

Davey scoffed.

"Please, Davey. Just call the police. You can just tell them where she is. You can do it anonymously. They won't even know you were involved. *Any* of you."

Silence.

Paige's baby girl began to cry. Paige knew she should feel something, anything. Cold. The urge to feed her daughter. But she felt nothing. Nothing but darkness.

"Mars, I can't dig anymore," Shaw said. "The ground is frozen."

"Fine. Help me with her."

Someone grabbed Paige's ankles, pulled her across the forest floor. A hard kick to her back, and she tumbled into a shallow hole, her stomach flipping like she was on a roller coaster.

"Shaw—stop," Jade cried. "Shaw, *stop*. Please—don't do this. Just call the police. No one has to know what you did—"

"What I did? What *I* did?"

"Shaw—*enough*. Cover her up," Mars ordered.

A tickle on her stomach. She wanted to reach to scratch it, but she couldn't. Another tickle on her back. Cold dirt encompassed her. She could smell it. She'd never smelled anything so strongly before. It was noxious, smothering. The earth was eating her.

With a horrifying shock, she realized what Shaw was doing.

Her boyfriend, the father of her newborn baby, was burying her alive.

Stop! No, please help. Stop, I'm alive. Someone, please help me.

She screamed. She screamed and screamed for so long, but no one ever heard her.

Jade. Stop, please help me. Jade…please help. I'm here… I'm still here.

Paige tried to move. She wiggled her finger, her toes, her foot, her hands. She tried to open her eyes. She tried to blink.

"Wait—Shaw—stop," Jade said, her voice raspy, torn to shreds. "Stop, Shaw, *stop*. She's alive—I saw her foot moving. She's alive. *Shaw!*"

"Shut up. They're gonna hear you."

Mother— Mother, Paige fought to rasp out. But she couldn't speak. She couldn't get the words out.

Mother. Mother, help me, please. I need you… Please, I love you.

No one could hear her. Not Jade, not Shaw. Not her mother. And as the last of the dirt fell on her, crushing her beneath its heavy, pressing weight, all Paige could think of was her mother. The elated look on her face when she'd meet her granddaughter for the first time. The relief she'd feel when her daughter was finally home safe.

Paige took her final breaths beneath the earth behind her house, a house mere footsteps away, a house where her mother stood just inside the kitchen, pacing, praying that her only daughter would come home safe.

Paige tried to speak, tried to call out for her mother one last time.

But no one would ever hear her again.

34

My eyes focus on her school portrait. Ellory—*Paige*—stares back, her faded, dusty eyes looking into mine. She was a runaway when we met, all those years ago, when I held her baby girl in my arms in the cold, dark woods.

A baby girl I named Ellory.

I named her after her mother.

Ellory, she'd said. *Like the singer.*

I knew she was lying. And I don't blame her, even now. Because I did the same. To survive, I created a new identity, a new name, thinking if I changed my name, my mother would never find me. Just like she thought if she changed hers, her parents would never find her.

I looked at her, shook her hand, and smiled.

My voice echoes in my head, still fresh, even from all those years ago.

Hi, Ellory. I'm Jade.

Just looking at her picture releases a flood of memories, punching into my head, ambushing me. I slump to the attic floor, tears warm on my cold cheeks. My stomach knots. I wonder if she forgives me.

I held Paige's baby girl in my arms as I stood in the woods behind her house. Behind her parents' house.

Behind *this* house.

Only now it's eighteen years later. When I drove up to the mansion for the first time with Hugh, how could I have ever known it was the same house? The same woods? It was night, dark, when we were in the woods. I never even saw her house. I saw a driveway. I saw trees. I saw *her*...

How could I have ever known Birdie is Paige's mother? That Hugh and Gabe are her brothers?

The entire time I've been living inside this house, I've been living with Paige's family. Hugh said she'd disappeared, but that was all he—or anyone—had ever told me. I didn't even know what town we were in the night it happened.

How was I to ever know I'd come back?

Paige's baby in my arms kept crying. I didn't know what to do. I panicked. Davey and Shaw and Mars were arguing. They wouldn't listen to me—they wouldn't *listen*.

I held her baby. And beneath the pale moonlight that broke through the treetops, I saw Paige's toe twitch.

I kept yelling—*stop. She's alive. Stop.*

But they didn't hear me. They didn't *want* to hear.

I wanted to fight them, pull them away, tell them to get help, to help Paige, but I couldn't do anything. I was paralyzed, frozen, unable to do anything, even if I could. The baby kept crying. I couldn't leave Paige's baby. And I couldn't fight them, not three teenage boys, not by myself, not when I held a frightened newborn in my arms.

And so, I watched.

I stood there. And cried.

And watched.

Pushing myself off the attic floor, I crawl to a window, sobs splintering out of me. I look at the woods. I see them now in my memories. Three dark figures, backs pressed against the trees, faces in the shadows.

Three dark figures—

One.

Two.

Three.

Davey.

Mars.

Shaw.

We never broke into Ellory's home that night. The sun crept up too quickly and Shaw and Mars expended all their energy on breaking through the frozen earth to dig her tiny grave, so small Shaw had to curl her legs inward to fit her inside.

For the eighteen years since, I always wondered if I'd see them again. But I never did.

After Ellory—after Paige—was killed, they chased me through the woods. I ran. I took Paige's baby, and I ran. It was dark and cold and I hid in a thicket, praying the baby wouldn't cry. And she didn't. She stayed quiet for me, as if she knew what was happening; as if she knew we were in danger.

They didn't find us. I stayed awake all night listening for footsteps, and when the morning came, I escaped the woods, walked until I found a road. I then hitched a ride with a woman traveling to Hollow Falls.

I was grateful to be away. I'd never felt more relieved in my life. But Paige…

I wanted, so badly, to tell the police where Paige was buried. But how could I? I didn't know where I was. I didn't know the address or the name of the woods or any street signs or landmarks. I had no evidence. I didn't know anyone's real name.

I didn't even know Paige's real name.

And then the shock of knowing I was alone, knowing I was

only sixteen, knowing I now had a newborn to take care of, hit me all at once. But I never could've hoped for anything better.

It brought me to Jack.

After the woman I'd hitched a ride with dropped me off in town, I stayed inside a diner until the following day. It was open morning and night, twenty-four hours, for truckers and early breakfasts. I held Paige's baby close to me, tucked her little body into my heavy army coat, and fed her whole milk the waitresses offered to me for free.

But it wasn't enough for her. She cried. She cried so loud I was asked to move outside. Even then, even as my entire body shivered with cold and hunger, I wouldn't let the baby go. I kissed the baby's cheek. Prayed she wouldn't cry.

I'm here. I'll stay with you, little one, no matter what. I promise.

Already our fates were inexplicably tied together, tight as a knot in a rope.

Then a new shift began. A waitress coming in saw us sitting on the curb outside. She offered me a job. A place to stay. A warm, safe home, living with her—and her son, Jack.

They saved me. They saved *us*.

Me. Mrs. Blodgett. Jack.

And my newborn daughter, Ellory.

A family.

As the years passed, Jack and I fell in love, got married, moved down the street from his mom. And through it all, I always kept one eye searching for Mars, Davey, and Shaw. Jack did, too. While he never knew what they looked like, he knew everything that'd happened. He knew I'd run away, that my friend was killed, buried. Her infant had become the single best thing—and greatest challenge—of our lives.

And the years fell away, as years tend to do. And Ellory became a teenager. Mrs. Blodgett passed away. And Jack did, too.

Sometimes, I wondered if Shaw would return one day to silence me forever. I knew what he'd done. What he didn't do.

But I never saw him again. The only time I did see him was inside my own head. On those dark days when I'd let the walls collapse and invite him inside.

For years I'd let him torment me. I'd shut my eyes and see him digging my friend's grave. Her toe twitching. The frantic look in his eyes when he realized what he'd done.

And suddenly, the weight of understanding crushes me.

All this time, I've been inside Paige's house. If I'd only listened closer to the story it was trying to tell, maybe I would've realized where I was.

But I didn't listen. I didn't hear.

And Birdie believes her daughter disappeared. She's wrong. She's always been wrong. Paige has always been right here, her body buried for nearly two decades in her own backyard while Paige's real killer, Ellory's biological father—*Shaw*—goes free.

"Mrs. Blodgett?"

I look up.

Duplain hovers at the other end of the attic, staring. Taking a step forward, he emerges from the shadows. He stops, looks down at me, so close the toe of his boot taps the edge of the mattress I sit on.

"Mrs. Blodgett? I've been walking around the house trying to find you. I, uh, heard a scream, didn't know if you or someone else was hurt?"

I shake my head. "No one's hurt."

Duplain stands over me. He bends down, helps me up.

"I'm sorry, Mrs. Blodgett. I wrote in my calendar to meet with you here today at eleven. I can come back if this is a bad time."

"No," I say quietly. "Now's fine…"

Though I can't remove my eyes from the walls of photos, I see him fidgeting from the corner of my vision, shifting his weight back and forth on each foot.

"I used to know someone who lived here, a long time ago.

When I pulled up, I couldn't believe this was where you lived. It really took me down memory lane."

I turn my head, look at him for the first time. The bones in my neck grind.

"Memory lane?"

He studies me. "Yeah. I mean, no offense, but I remember this house. It gives me the creeps. Always did. There used to be a family who lived here. Terrible what happened to them… I heard after their daughter died the old man went crazy and shot his wife before shooting himself. I guess you're the new owner. Congratulations."

I shake my head. "I'm not the—"

"Wait," he says, cutting me off. I hold my breath, think of what he'll say. He studies me intensely, says, "You look familiar. We must've met before. Have you ever gone to eat at Muldoon's? That real expensive steak house down in Tarrytown?" he asks, steps back, surveys me with a hand held to his chin. "No, that's not it. I know you from before. *Way* before…"

He knows who I am. And I know exactly who *he* is. He's Private Investigator Shawn Duplain.

But his friends used to call him Shaw.

35

Shaw's eyes dart to Paige's photographs, his mouth falling open as his gaze sweeps over the wall. "Who are you? How'd you find my number?" he asks, taking a step back.

"I found you online. I need to find my daughter," I say. "What a coincidence you've been in this house before."

A muscle in his jaw clenches. "I've never been inside before," he whispers, and we both know it's a lie. "I don't know what you're insinuating."

"You don't remember?"

"Who are you?" Shaw asks. "Who are you, really?"

Dread once again pushes itself back into my brain. If I had to ever face Shaw again, this isn't the best place to do it. I shouldn't be in this musty old attic, alone, with no way to get help and no escape plan. We should've agreed to meet in a police station or somewhere with other people around so I could feel safe, where if he tried to hurt me again, others would be there to stop him.

Not here. Not alone, just me and him and my ankle that doesn't work. My phone that doesn't work. Not like this. Not at Paige's house. This was a life-and-death decision. And I failed miserably. But I didn't know. And the plan may not have worked if we met anywhere else.

With these thoughts, knowing this mistake may be my last, my heart beats louder. Thunderous. He could lunge at me right now. He could chase me, or worse—lock me away up here forever. He could kill me.

"I remember you." Shaw's tired eyes narrow in recognition. "You look just like that girl—Jade."

"Shaw—stay away from me. Don't come any closer."

"*I knew it.* You're her. You're Jade. You have the same face—that same panicked look."

I nod. "You're right, Shaw. I am panicked."

He gulps, stares at me, fighting to avoid glancing at the wall filled with photographs of Paige, the mother of his child, the daughter he killed, the friend he stole. A girl who never made it through high school. A girl with an entire life to live. All stolen from her because of him.

"Paige used a fake name, too," Shaw says. "But you know that. You're in her house, for Christ's sake. You know way more than you're letting on."

I stand from the mattress, grab my crutch to help steady myself. Shaw steps forward, fast, lurching. He brings his face close to mine—his breath smells stale, a sick person's breath, mucus and coffee. He hovers so close, only one more inch forward and he could kiss me.

I'm petrified. My lip starts to shake. He sees it, looks down, looks up, drags his eyes over me, and I'm naked, alone, exposed, feeling like he's looking into my mind, seeing everything. But still, I hold my breath, refuse to turn away. I have to be strong.

"God, this *cannot* be happening." Shaw unlocks himself from me, begins to pace back and forth. "Why'd you bring me here? Why am I in her house—Paige's house—looking at Paige's things?"

"You became a private investigator, Shaw—you tell me."

"Fuck you, Jade—Iris, whatever the hell your fucking name is."

I don't smile or laugh or change my expression. I remain still, calm. My phone grows hot in my palm as I clench it tight in my pocket. My heartbeat thrums in my ears.

"My name is Iris."

He scoffs, shakes his head. He unzips a black fleece jacket, red crawling up his neck, flushing his cheeks. His hands go jittery, and he shakes them out. A wedding band glistens on his finger. Someone actually married this man, this monster, and that fact somehow shocks me most of all. How can you not know he's a monster before you marry him?

"You want to play your little game, I'll play," he says. "We have the name Ellory," he says, glancing at me, unamused, still disbelieving she's a real person. "This house, Paige's house. I think there's no question, Jade. You want revenge. Revenge for something *I didn't do.*"

My eyes widen. No, his denial shocks me most of all.

"You can lie to yourself all you want, but we both know the truth."

"So what, then? You brought me here to punish me? Is that it? You want to punish me for what I did? But I never hurt *you,* Jade. I never touched you. I let you go. You know I did. Now you have to let *me* go." Shaw holds his hands up, turns, begins to walk back toward the attic staircase.

"Wait."

He stops. Turns.

"Don't you want to know who Ellory is?"

Shaw looks to the ceiling, contemplating. Even from a distance, still, I can see the anger ripple through him. He's torn. He doesn't want to turn back. He wants to leave.

But he can't.

He wants to know. He has to. It's ingrained in him, the knowing. He needs to solve his case. He won't be able to let it go.

"Fine." He sighs. "Who's Ellory? Tell me. Then I'm leaving, and you'll never see me again."

"You already know the answer. It's why you agreed to take on her missing-person case. Why you want so badly to find her. Admit there's something inside you that needs to know if it's really *her*."

His eyes fall, trace the floor in thought. He looks back at me, realization flooding his face. "My daughter?" His voice catches, and for the smallest of moments, my heart breaks before hardening again, solid as stone.

I look at him and nod.

She's still alive…and it overwhelms him. Lifting a hand, he scrubs it over his face, scratches his cheek. Then he shakes his head, looks down at his brown boots. "No, I'm not doing this. I'm not." He turns, stumbles, trips over the corner of the mattress, the mattress Paige undoubtedly was forced to sleep on when her father locked her up here nearly twenty years ago.

Shaw trips forward, and he outstretches his arms to catch himself. The fall happens too fast, too fast to brace himself, and his hands slap the wooden floorboards, catching all of his weight, popping up a loose board.

The bones in his wrists snap as the floorboard slams into his nose, punches into his forehead. In an instant, blood shoots from his skull, pours down his face.

I gasp, scramble back against the wall from the shock of red overtaking him, and he's shiny with blood, his lips parted, blood dripping down his face, into his open mouth, reddening his teeth.

I stand frozen in shock, grip my crutch so tight my arm shakes. Shaw rolls over on the floor, spitting blood into the air, a fountain, and it begins to pool around his head, a halo of red. I gasp, look down at him in horror, as he stares up at me, unblinking.

My breathing grows loud, unsteady, shaking, and I stare at

him, unmoving, try to understand what has just happened. One minute he was backing away from me, turning to leave, the next, he's immobile on the floor, his blood seeping into the wood, a puddle spreading around him, giving off a faint fog of heat as it hits the cold attic air.

He hasn't moved. Why hasn't he moved?

"Shaw?" I say and approach him where he lies on the floor, motionless. "Duplain?"

Blood melts from his head, thick and oozing. His left eye has ruptured, blood filling the cornea. I look at him again. It's then I see.

Earlier, a long construction nail almost punctured through my slipper...

That same nail has found a home—inside Shaw's temple, embedded deep in his skull.

I inch closer. His boots twitch. He stares at the ceiling, eyes yawned open in pain. I look down at him, stare into his eyes.

Heterochromia: as rare—and genetic—as Ellory's.

One, the color of a newborn fawn. The other, the color of the sky.

"Help me."

The sound bubbles through his lips, and I jump, surprised he's still alive. His throat bobs up and down as he cries, and he reaches an arm out, grabs hold of my cast. I cry out, stagger away from his grip. The blood pool expands across the floor.

I look at him again. A wheeze escapes his blood-slicked lips.

"Help me—help me, *please, Jade.*"

"You murdered my friend," I whisper as I watch him on the floor. "She deserved to live. You don't."

His limbs coil together, a dying spider. Tucking my crutch under my arm, I hop around him, careful not to step in any blood, and head toward the stairs.

"Wait."

I ignore his cries.

"Please—help me."

I drop my foot down to the next step, careful not to trip. I wonder if his blood will leak into the ceiling downstairs, make a stain. I hope not. It will become one more thing Hugh will need to fix and only keep us longer in this house.

I look back at Shaw. He rests at the other end of the attic, unmoving, eyes open and staring and dead. Carefully, I go back downstairs, locking the attic door behind me.

Pressing my back against the door, I exhale, shut my eyes. My heart is hammering. Shaw is dead in my fiancé's mother's attic. He's dead, bleeding, *oh, God, oh, God*. I locked him in there. I left him—is that the same as killing him? Did I kill him? I can't hear my own thoughts, can't hear anything above my pulse thundering in my ears.

Then I realize it's not my ears that are ringing. I pull my broken phone out of my back pocket, swipe the screen with a finger to answer the call. *Crap*. The screen is horribly cracked. I swipe again. The phone doesn't recognize my touch with the deep fissures in the glass. I keep swiping to answer until the call ends.

I couldn't read the number on the damaged screen. What if it was Ellory, needing my help? Or another one of her friends, like Leah, calling me, trying to get through. Maybe someone has seen her, heard from her…

I turn back to the door. I can't leave him in there alone—can I? Should I? Oh, God, I need to go help him. Even after all he's done, still, I can't move away from the door. My phone rings again. I swipe the glass, gently, fingertip barely grazing the screen.

The call connects. I raise the phone to my ear.

"Hello?"

Silence.

A strangled voice on the other end lets out a cry.

"Mom."

36

The air escapes my lungs with the sound of her voice. I've wanted to hear it for so long. It feels like it's been an eternity without her.

"Ellory? Oh, God, are you okay?"

"He's locked me in here. Help me, Mom."

My stomach twists.

"Ellory—hang up and call 911."

"I'm here. I'm in his house."

"Whose house?"

"His name is...Shaw Duplain."

The call goes dead.

"Ellory? Ellory? *No, no, no*—" I squeeze my phone tight, wish she'd come back. Everything is going wrong at once.

I look down at my feet, at the cast strapped around my foot, and I know I have no choice. I need to make it to the kitchen and call the police, tell them Duplain kidnapped my daughter, his daughter, took her right out from under me. Abandoning the attic door, and Shaw along with it, I slowly step into the hall and go down two flights of stairs, stair by stair, holding on to the banister as I hop on one foot.

By the time I reach the bottom, both of my knees are killing me. But I can't care or think about that now. I need to call the police, and to do that, I need a phone, and I need one now. I saw it there on the counter, one of those old black rotary phones.

As quickly as I can, I make my way through the hallways to the kitchen. A car sounds in the distance. In the dining room, I rush to the nearest window, slide open a drape, peer out to the driveway.

They're home.

Hugh, Camille, and Rebecca step out of the car. They circle around, walk to the rear passenger door. It swings open, and there he is. Gabe. He wears sunglasses and a heavy black overcoat that ends at his knees, and I wonder whose funeral he's attending.

A gush of warm air hits my cheeks, the house raising its internal temperature for his arrival. I pick up my pace, move faster toward the kitchen. Birdie only gave me one crutch, instead of two, and I use it to balance myself and redistribute weight off my broken foot. It helps, but only a little. I still haven't gotten the rhythm down, and my pace is slow. Some part of me can't help but think that may have been Birdie's intention all along.

The front door closes in the distance. I need to get out of here, need to get to my daughter, broken ankle or no broken ankle, I don't care. I need to get to her, to know she's okay. I need to call the police. Then I'll call Sloane, ask her to drive over as quickly as possible.

Until I can get out of here, I'm trapped with Paige's family—

A jolt hits me.

What if they knew all along?

What if Hugh knew…?

What if they know who I am? That I was there that night in the woods behind this house? That I was with Paige? That I watched her die. That I took her baby—the baby girl I named Ellory.

I always knew she wasn't mine to take.

In the back of my mind, through all of these years, I knew Ellory had a family out there, somewhere. Paige's family. Shaw's. People who had a better claim on her than me. A legal claim. But I didn't care. I loved her the moment I saw her. I wanted to protect her from the same life Paige escaped. And I wanted to protect her from Shaw.

But all of that's over. Ellory's eighteen. Thankfully, I'm past the point of legal battles and custody issues. Thankfully, because I'd rather die than have someone take my child from me.

But that doesn't erase the fact that my daughter is Birdie's granddaughter.

The question now is—what if Birdie knows?

What if *they* know?

But how would they? Even *I* didn't know where I was, whose house this was, who they were…so how would they know it was me?

It can't be a coincidence. Can it? Did Hugh know all this time? Is that why he brought me here? Why? Why would he want to marry the woman who was there the night his sister was murdered?

Unless he wanted revenge.

If they knew who I was, how I'd taken Paige's baby and raised her as my own, how I was there when Paige died in the woods—if Birdie ever knew…

She'd kill me.

Not only that, Rebecca told me after Paige disappeared, Birdie's husband committed suicide, shooting Birdie in the hip in attempted murder before turning the gun on himself. Would Birdie blame me for her husband's death? For her own near death? She's alive, yes, but at what price?

A thought hits me. Oh, God…she *must* know. She must've

known the exact moment she met Ellory for the first time. It must've felt like she was staring at Paige's ghost. I thought it was strange, how Birdie kept staring at Ellory that day. She couldn't take her eyes off her. Of course she couldn't.

Ellory looks exactly like Paige.

Footsteps pound down the hallway. The kitchen is just another twenty feet away. I can see the entrance down the main corridor. It's so close—

No...

It's then I realize something dreadful.

"Iris, where are you?" Hugh calls behind me. "Iris?"

Not only is Shaw's body up in the attic, his blood seeping down into the floor, down into the ceiling of the room below—but his car is still parked in the driveway. I step toward the window, peer out to see Hugh parked his car only twenty feet away from Shaw's.

How am I going to explain this? I can try to hide his body in the attic, but how do I explain his car? Worse, what do I do if Birdie confronts me about her only grandchild—Ellory?

I reach the kitchen. Last I remember, the phone was near the stove. My eyes scan the countertops, but I don't see it. I look again, quicker this time.

"Iris?" Hugh steps into the kitchen. I turn around, try to mask my fear and uncertainty. "Iris? Are you— Hey, there you are," he says when he sees me, and for a split second, I try to analyze his reaction. He seems happy, relieved to see me. It eases me, just for a moment. Maybe he doesn't know who I really am. Maybe he doesn't know Ellory is his...*niece.*

Oh, God, how can I look at him now? How can I ever ignore this fact?

Hugh steps inside, sees me leaning against the counter. A wide grin stretches across his face. He moves deeper into the room.

Tossing his coat and scarf on a chair, he walks toward me. Grabbing the back of my head, he pulls me in for a kiss, lingering until I tug away. Sucking in his bottom lip, he takes the taste of me off his skin, swallows me down inside.

"I can't wait to marry you," he whispers. "Wife."

My body goes rigid. I have to at least try to act normal. There is no dead private investigator in the attic. No, Hugh, your little sister isn't buried in your backyard. No, of course I didn't steal your murdered sister's baby...

"How's your ankle?"

"What?"

Keep it together, Iris.

"Your ankle. Is it feeling better?"

"Not really. But I've been, uh, walking a little more than I should," I explain. "Lots of stairs in this house."

He nods absently. "Whose car is that?"

"Nobody's," I say and summon a smile, bite my tongue, say nothing further, fearing if I open my mouth, the truth about Shaw will come pouring out.

To my surprise, Hugh laughs. He sits down on a stool, unbuttons the collar of his white shirt, loosens the neck before grabbing me, pulling me toward him. He glides down the collar of my sweater, softly kisses my neck.

Looking up at me, he whispers, "Well, it has to be *someone's* car."

"Right, it—it's Sloane's," I say, knowing no matter what, she'll always have my back and go along with it, just in case he speaks with her for one reason or another. "The house was her halfway point up to a ski cabin she rented for the weekend. She left it here and met up with the guy she's going with. They're taking his truck the rest of the way. You know, because of the... snow." I close my eyes, open them to see Hugh watching me.

He didn't buy that, not for a second, but still, he nods, says, "Yeah, it's supposed to snow a little tonight. I hope she has a nice time."

I exhale in relief.

"What town's she going to?"

I blink. Crap. "Um, I don't know, but I know it's pretty far up there."

He nods, returns my awkward grin. Dimples form in his cheeks. "Let me help you walk to the great room. Today is Mother's birthday, so we're going to open her presents before I go to work." Grabbing my crutch, he helps me tuck it under my armpit.

"That's right. You're going into the office today to help on a project." My muscles tense, knowing I'll soon be alone with Birdie, Rebecca, and Gabe. *"Wait,"* I nearly scream. "Hugh, wait." I stop walking, place a hand on his chest. "I need to borrow your phone. It's an emergency."

His eyebrows knit together. "What's wrong? Has something happened?"

I shake my head, then nod. "Yes—it's Ellory. She called me, but my screen is so smashed I can't dial the number. I need to call 911—it's an emergency."

He laughs. *Laughs.* All the blood drains from my face. Doesn't he at least want to ask *why* I need to call the police about Ellory? If I wanted to scream before, now I want to claw his eyes out.

"Hugh," I snap. "This isn't funny. I need to use your phone."

"I'm sorry," he says, and his face settles into concern. He looks down at me, rubs the sides of my arms. "I was laughing because I don't have my phone. I left it out in the car. Battery died. It's charging."

"What?" I say, and for some reason, I get the impression he's not being honest with me. My car is about ten years old, not new and electric like Hugh's, but wouldn't his phone stop charging once he turns the car off?

"Here," he says and grabs my hand, flinging my arm around his shoulders, lifting my feet off the floor. The sudden jolt of movement shoves the thoughts out of me. "I'll help you walk. Whatever's happened, Ellory's smart. She'll know to call the police. Later you can call them, okay? I promise. I bet they'll tell you she's fine."

"No, *stop*. Ellory is missing and you don't want me to call the—" I stop myself. Hugh clearly doesn't want the police contacted about Ellory. But what if the real reason is he doesn't want to involve the police because of *me*? Suddenly, I go lightheaded with fear.

They know.

They know about Paige and me and Shaw and that night in the woods. They know I was there. That I took Paige's baby. They know who I am. *Hugh* knows everything. And they want to keep me here, cut off from the police, from my daughter, my friends. They want to cut me off from outside help and support.

Coldness slithers through me. Is this what Hugh is doing now? I can't read him, can't put the pieces together, not now, not this fast.

Somehow, I have to get out of here. But if I can't, Hugh will be gone for the day. Maybe I'll have a chance to snatch Rebecca's phone, or even Gabe's, and call the police. No matter what, Hugh's right. Ellory *is* smart. She might already be out of Shaw's house, at the police station, waiting for me. Or she might not. She could still be waiting for me to save her.

I focus on seeing her again as we round the corner into the great room. Closing my eyes, I force myself to try to keep it together. There's a dead man in the attic. My daughter has been kidnapped. I'm trapped in a house with Hugh's family who may want to kill me.

Being alone and trapped here is the last thing I want. But maybe nothing else bad will happen while Hugh's away...

"Come on," Hugh says, tugging me inside the great room. "They're waiting for you."

37

In the great room, the fireplace roars, giant flames licking the blackened stones. Wood smoke and caramelized sugar mix in the air. Beneath the pleasant scents lingers something malodorous, something pungent and sharp. Pepper spray? Ammonia?

Birdie and Rebecca sit together on a love seat, shoulder to shoulder, both in matching gray—Rebecca in a soft turtleneck and loose pants, and Birdie in another ankle-length skirt with a delicate pattern of thorns.

And Gabe... I drag my eyes across the room to see him sitting in a wingback chair, his head tilted back, leg crossed over a knee. He doesn't turn his head to look at me, yet his hazel eyes flicker as they flash my way. Beside him on a little table is a plate of fresh cookies. Gabe rests a hand on the plate, claiming them.

Rebecca nods toward me. "Hey, Iris. How's the ankle?" A sympathetic expression crosses her face. I try to read her, try to see if I can somehow figure out how much she might know. "I bet it hurts because of the weather." She nods toward a tall window filled with storm clouds.

"It's okay. Thanks for asking," I say, hesitant, and bite my bottom lip with worry. *Phone... I need to get to a phone.* I wish I could scream it at the top of my lungs. I wish I could run out of here with healed bones, wish I could see Ellory right this moment.

I imagine myself bulldozing them out of the way as I hurl myself through the house and tear out of the driveway. Instead, I have no choice but to go along with Hugh's movements as he steers me to sit beside him. Directly across from me, Gabe sits calm and still, and I watch his expression, find I can't read him, either.

Hugh's grip is unusually strong around my arm as he pulls me down next to him, and I wonder if his view of me has subconsciously shifted inside his mind. If he knows I was involved with his sister's murder, does he still view me as his fiancée—or her killer?

Or his hostage?

Hugh takes my hand, uses the other to prod a long iron poker into the flames. I'm still mad at him. Not only is he now blocking me from calling the police, but he told Birdie things about me—deep, dark secrets about Jack and Ellory—things I barely wanted to share with him. And he told her. He also told her I'd found Ainsley's wallet in Gabe's bedroom. God knows what else he's shared. They all could know everything, for all I know. Not only about my past and that night and what really happened to Paige. But how I know about Gabe's confession, too.

Every one of them. Birdie. Gabe. Rebecca. Perhaps Kara and Camille, too. They can all know about everything. All I can do is wait until someone makes the first move. But who will it be?

And what will they do?

Three sets of eyes meet mine at the exact same moment. I feel like a deer in the woods, unknowing I was being hunted on all sides.

I bite my tongue, scrape my eyes across the room to glance

at Gabe. For someone who was just discharged from the hospital for a heart attack, he looks surprisingly well. His skin seems tanned, almost, as if he's been outside at a mountain retreat instead of lying in a hospital bed. The black shirt he wears has faint lines across the fabric—not lines, plaid, crisscrossed in evergreen and baby blue. With his greasy hair parted and a hardened scowl, he looks like a villainous professor.

"Did you do anything exciting while we were gone?" Rebecca asks, not hiding her gaze as she turns to stare at the black cast affixed to my foot.

I glance at her as I think of a reply. She leans forward, elbows on her knees, looking genuinely interested in what I've been up to. And so I tell the truth…at least, part of it. I leave out the part where Shaw fell onto a nail in the attic. How I watched him as he lay dying. How I locked the door shut behind me.

"I went outside and saw the neighbor's dog. She was out looking for him, so we spoke a little, but it was too cold to talk long," I say. "Her name's Evonne. Do you know her?" I ask, already knowing the answer. Evonne has been Birdie's neighbor for years. How else would she have known about Paige and Rebecca and the fire that'd taken her family?

As my mind races, I don't even realize the room has gone quiet.

"Her husband was *obsessed* with Paige," Birdie says, unbidden.

"Mother—" Hugh interjects. His blue eyes sharpen.

My palms begin to sweat. Hearing Paige's name makes me flinch in anticipation. I look around the room. No one has noticed. I keep my eyes locked on my hand still resting in Hugh's lap.

"Evonne's husband, Doug?" Rebecca asks, falling deep in thought. "Wow. Here I was, thinking we'd never mention *that* name again."

"You're right. So I'd rather not discuss it," Birdie says. "That woman—the entire thing makes me sick."

Hugh sighs, leans in to whisper in my ear. "Evonne's husband had developed feelings for Paige that he shouldn't have. He'd beg to give her piano lessons, then he'd come over and Birdie would find him taking pictures of her, things like that. He was a few years older than I am now, at the time. Paige was a kid, like sixteen."

"That's horrible," I say.

Hugh nods, peers at me sideways. "Just don't trust everything Evonne says. She has motives you don't understand. Promise me, okay?"

Rebecca releases a deep sigh. "Anyway, Iris, we're going later to grab an early dinner, if you want to come. We always go to Mother's favorite place on her birthday."

"Um, maybe," I say, scrambling for an excuse. "I have to see how my ankle's feeling. It's been hurting today."

"Be careful, Iris," Rebecca begins. "If you keep saying *no* when we invite you places, soon we're going to stop asking you altogether."

I'm counting on it.

Gabe laughs darkly and turns away, as if he can hear exactly what I'm thinking. Pushing his glasses up his nose, he leans forward, picks up a little gift bag near his feet.

"They didn't have much in the hospital gift shop, but I think you'll like this, Mother."

Rebecca takes it, passes it to Birdie. Her face glows in the firelight, storm clouds swirling overhead, draping the room with darkness. Gabe reaches to turn on a lamp, dropping part of his face into shadows.

Birdie opens the bag, pulls out a stained-glass sun-catcher painted with white calla lilies.

"Happy birthday," Gabe says, and my gaze dances around the room. Birdie hardly needs another trinket for a gift. Objects already clutter the room—stuffed birds, porcelain dolls, dried flowers dangling from strings. I feel claustrophobic, like the room is closing in on me. It doesn't help their eyes are watching my every move.

Do they know who I am? What I know? They'd kill me if they did. They wouldn't be inviting me out to birthday dinners and opening presents—would they? All I can do is try to pretend things are okay, to not draw attention to myself. I'll never be invisible, but I can try.

I just need to wait for an opportunity to call the police and Sloane.

Birdie stares at me over her cat-eye glasses. Gabe does the same, inspecting me like I'm livestock. I gulp.

Gabe clears his throat, releases his stranglehold stare. "So, Iris," he begins. A smug smile crosses his lips as he speaks my name. "I see you're still here. I thought you would've run away by now, after I heard what you really think about me and my family."

There goes my plan not to draw any attention.

"*Gabe,*" Hugh warns. "Don't."

My back stiffens. Rebecca drops a cookie on a plate, glares at me sideways. I don't reply. Instead, I turn away, stare into the fire. I narrow my eyes. In the soot at the bottom of the fireplace, a metal zipper is blackened by flames.

Ainsley's wallet had a zipper.

I grip the arm of the sofa tight. Even now, I can imagine Ainsley's wallet vividly in my mind—the zipper, the smooth red leather—as easily as if I were holding it in my hands.

"I still can't find Ainsley's wallet," I say, as if it's the last thing on my mind. "Have you seen it?"

Hugh looks at me. "Iris, stop."

"Maybe *you* didn't even see it," Gabe bites back. "Maybe you thought you did, but you didn't."

I turn back to Gabe. "Hugh said you were going to return Ainsley's wallet," I say, gripping Hugh's hand tight, fighting like hell to keep my voice even. If they only knew how fast my heart is racing.

Gabe grins. Uncrossing his leg, he sits forward, elbows on his knees. "I heard she passed away." His voice makes my stomach sick. "Seems I've missed my chance."

I grit my teeth, dart my eyes toward the doorway, try to figure out how I can steal Rebecca's phone or Gabe's. I'll call the police, tell them everything. Somehow picking up on my thoughts, Hugh tightens his fingers around mine, holding me back.

"Can I open what's left of my gifts now, please?" Birdie says, holding out a hand to Gabe.

Gabe turns to grab a long pair of scissors hidden behind the plate of cookies. My heart stops. He stands from the armchair, crosses the room, places them in Birdie's waiting palm. I exhale.

"And for the record," he says, moving to stand in front of me. The pungent scent returns. I realize it's a sickly hospital scent: disinfectant mixed with body odor. It's strong, affixed to his clothing like smoke. He moves so close I have to tilt my head back to see him. Hugh sits forward, places himself between me and his brother. "I had that heart attack because of you. You put me in the hospital, Iris. Thanks to you," he says, glancing over at Hugh, "I had to cash out my 401(k) to pay for all the medical bills. All $107,000 I had saved, gone." Gabe's eyes flash with heat, but he steps backward, falls into the armchair. "I'd ask you to repay me, but you're more broke than I am."

"I said I'd—" Hugh begins, but Gabe holds up a hand, stops him from speaking.

"I told you before I don't want your money. But Iris does."

I freeze. My mouth falls open. I feel everything right now. Anger, fear, frustration. My hands begin to shake. I take my hand out of Hugh's, tuck it between my thighs, try to hide it. Hugh glances at me, concerned.

I think back to the bank statement I found. But it wasn't a

bank statement at all. It was Gabe's 401(k) statement. God, I've been so wrong. How could I have been so wrong?

The entire room grows thick with awkward silence. An angry flush crawls up my cheeks. I can't stay here. I can't.

I stand up on one foot, and Hugh passes me my crutch, lets me rush out of the room without saying a word. I'm not waiting another minute. I make the long trek to the kitchen to look for the phone again. I need to call the police about Ellory, then call Sloane to come pick me up.

Their voices fade as I step into the kitchen.

Knowing where Ellory is and not being able to help her is unbearable, and I pinch back tears, wobble over to where I last remember seeing the phone. On the counter sits an expensive metal mixer, an espresso machine, and oversize wooden charcuterie boards. But no phone. Where is it? I saw it here only recently. I remember because it reminded me of one my mom used to have. It was in the corner by the stove. Birdie must use it while cooking.

I look again, scanning the endless granite countertops, searching for the phone, any phone. Nothing. Turning around, I check in cabinets, finding nothing, but in the wall is a plug, a small, distinct plug, one used for old phone jacks. It was here. I know it was.

"Iris?"

Hugh hovers in the archway.

"Hey—do you know where the kitchen phone went?"

He looks at me, confused. "The what?"

A knot grows in my throat. Why is he looking at me like that? "The phone in the kitchen. Birdie had it. It was black, one of those old rotary ones. I know you've seen it."

I look around the stovetop area again near the phone jack before turning back to Hugh. We're not alone anymore. Birdie steps inside, throws me a withering look. She believes I'm responsible for Gabe's heart attack. Does she also know about

Paige? I can't ask her outright. I wouldn't even know where to begin.

"You okay?" Hugh asks. "You sure it's okay if I go to the office?"

"Birdie," I say, and I can hear how frantic my voice sounds. "Where's the phone?"

She lets out a gentle laugh, no more than a breath. "What do you mean? There was never a phone here."

"Iris," Hugh begins, "you're sure I can leave?" He places his hand around my arm, guides me closer. His grip is tight. I pull away. When my heavy cast accidentally steps on his toes, he doesn't so much as wince.

"I'll be fine," I say uneasily, glancing back at Birdie.

Hugh nods, the muscles in his jaw flexing. Thankfully, he helps me walk back to the foyer on his way out. But the three flights of stairs to my bedroom is something I'll have to handle on my own.

He grins, leans over to kiss me. "It'll all be fine. Just give Gabe a little space. He needs time, that's all. Try to talk to Mother and Rebecca. They like you."

I raise a questioning eyebrow. He opens the front door. Dead leaves blow inside from off the porch, scrape across the threadbare rug. As Hugh shuts the door behind him, I let out a deep breath, preparing for the long journey upstairs to grab some things and go. I'll have to try to drive myself.

Reaching for my phone in my pocket, I click it on. Somehow the cracked spiderwebs across the screen are even worse than before, but I can see there are no missed calls. Ellory hasn't called back. I try again to swipe the phone open to make a call, but the screen fails to respond.

"I need you to get along with my family. You don't have to love them. I'm not asking you to. But at least try. For me. Please—like your life depended on it..."

Hugh's words from earlier float in my mind as I glance out

the front window. What did he mean? Why would he say that? After I'm out of here, I'll find evidence if it kills me. I'll learn what happened to Ainsley's wallet, the confession. Everything. Even if I have to confront Gabe myself. I'll learn the truth.

Heavy gray clouds settle over the house. The foyer falls into darkness. And then a knock at the door.

38

"Camille?"

"Hi, Iris."

Hair bleached the color of a haystack blows in the cold wind. She shivers, pinches her puffy coat shut. "Camille, this is going to sound strange, but can I please borrow your phone?"

She presses her lips together. "Nice to see you, too. Is Gabe here?" I step outside, close the door behind me. The clouds have grown dark overhead. Camille glances down at the cast strapped around my foot. "What happened? Are you okay?"

"Yeah, I'm okay. Please, Camille. It's important. It will only take a second."

She stares at me, shakes her head. "I left it here when I left. Sorry."

Crap. That's right. How could I forget?

"Right, I'm sorry. How are you?" I ask and think of where her phone could be hidden now. Hopefully, Gabe left it in his armoire. I'll have to check his room when I go upstairs. "I thought you went back to your mom's to get your things after you bailed Gabe out of jail."

"I did," Camille begins, adjusting her purse on her shoulder. "But I decided to stay with my mom a little longer…" She trails off, looks down at her boots. Her pants flutter a little at the hems, like flower petals. "Because I'm, um—I'm pregnant."

I stare at her, unsure what to say. "Congratulations, Camille. It's none of my business, but I thought you said you were afraid of him."

"I know," she shouts over the wind. "Last I talked to you, I told you I was leaving him."

I nod. *I also thought Gabe killed you, buried you in the backyard after you told him you wanted a divorce*, I think but don't say. "But then Gabe said you're staying together," I say instead.

Camille looks away, and for a second, I pick up on the feeling that she's hiding something. Something big. Something that keeps her tethered to Gabe, for some reason.

"There are some things you can't walk away from. I can't just *leave* him. I'm tied to him in more ways than one." Her voice sounds glum, lifeless, drowning in the wind.

I give a flicker of a smile. "I know what you mean. A baby does link you both together forever."

"Yeah," she says. "That, too. Which is why I'm here. I have to tell him. He has to hear it from me."

I nod, wrap my arms tight around myself. Fat snowflakes begin to fall like feathers from the sky. "Do you remember Ainsley, the woman you met at dinner that night?" Camille stares at me in concentration. "The night Hugh and I got engaged? Long brown hair, tiny. Was wearing a bright red dress?"

"Oh, yeah," Camille mumbles. "I remember her. Why?"

"Do you have any reason to think Gabe would…dislike her?"

Camille steps back, probably hoping she'll see someone through the windows who can pull her away. "No. I don't. Honestly, I'm not sure what you're suggesting."

"I'm just asking."

"Why? What happened? How is she?"

"She's dead."

Camille's brown eyes widen. "Oh, I'm sorry. But if you think my husband—"

"I'm not implying anything." I raise a hand. A white flag. "I'm only asking."

Snowflakes drift sideways onto the porch, curl beneath the roof. They land on Camille's coat sleeve, darken the fabric as they melt.

"How'd she die?"

I look down at my cast in thought. Anything I tell her, she'll tell Gabe and the others. It's taken me this long to learn with this family, once you tell one, you've told all. So for now, I decide to be vague.

"The police said she did it to herself. I was the one who found her."

Camille shifts uncomfortably. "You know, Gabe was with me the whole time that night. After dinner, we all came home together in the same car. Remember?"

Shivering, I nod. "Yes, and then we spoke outside in the garden and—" I stop. A thought hits me.

I never told Camille what night Ainsley had died. Why would she assume it was the night we all went out to dinner for our engagement?

Ignoring it, for now, I continue. "Before you left to go to your mom's, did Gabe leave the house that night?"

"No, Iris, Gabe did not sneak out to *murder* someone."

"Can I ask you about his name?"

The wind blows sharp, violently lashing her long hair across her face, getting caught in her sticky red lip gloss. "His name?"

"I'm just curious why Gabe's last name is Vieira when Hugh's last name is Smoll. I've never seen brothers with different surnames."

"You have some nerve." Slinging her purse around, she digs inside, pulls out a giant pink wallet. Holding up a driver's license, she says, "His last name is *my* last name." I study the ID she shoves in my face.

In the tiny picture, Camille's eyes are rimmed with lash extensions, and her cheeks are sculpted with bronzer. Her highlighted mahogany waves are dyed auburn, as fox red as Sloane's. She looks like a different person. But there, printed clear and bold, is her name: *Camille Isabel Vieira.*

She lowers her ID, slides it back into her wallet.

"After Gabe's father…" Camille begins unsteadily, clears her throat. "After he tried to kill Birdie, Gabe didn't want anything to do with him. When we got married, he saw it as a chance to start fresh. He took my last name. Some paperwork is probably still in his other name. Some is probably in mine. You've been married before. You know how difficult it is to change things. Gabe didn't want to carry on his father's legacy, not to his…child." She swallows back tears, rubs her stomach.

Suddenly, I don't feel cold anymore. Heat blooms across my face from embarrassment. Not able to bring myself to speak, I turn around, open the door, and limp back inside. Camille follows, disappears down the hallway toward the sound of her husband's voice.

Hoping everyone is distracted by her arrival, I go straight to Gabe's bedroom to find Camille's phone. But when I twist the doorknob, the door doesn't open. He's locked it.

Efforts thwarted, I go to my room down the hall to pack. Now that Camille's here, after the conversation I just had with her, there's no way in hell I'm waiting another second. With Hugh gone, I'll sneak out, get in my car, try to see if I can drive with a cast on. If I can't, I'll wait at the end of the driveway until someone takes pity on me and drives me into town. I don't care. I'll wait all day.

Reaching my bedroom, I shut the door behind me. As

quickly as I can, I wobble across the room, kneel on the floor, pull out a few clean shirts and a couple of pairs of leggings. I can always borrow clothes from Sloane.

My shoulders slump. I love Hugh. But I've alienated myself from the family, put myself in a corner I'm not sure I can claw out from. And I don't trust any of them anymore—not even Hugh. I wish things had turned out differently. Not just for us. But for Ellory. She had me and Jack, but I thought marrying Hugh would bring another chance at forming our own little family. A second one, a new one, built beside the first, not on top. A new chance to find happiness, to live our lives together, with love and peace and support. But that's all over now. Gone. Ended.

I tug a sweater out of the drawer when a slip of paper falls, slides beneath the dresser. I reach under, pull it out. It's a picture of Hugh. He's standing outside beside a beautiful woman with shiny black hair just like mine.

I examine the photo. In Hugh's arms, he holds a baby girl in a purple dress, a matching sideways bow wrapped around her little head. The woman's arm is raised, clasping the baby's hand in hers.

I go cold with horror. The woman is wearing my engagement ring.

39

I rip the ring off my finger, throw it across the room.

Hugh had a wife, I know—but a daughter? How little I knew the man I intended to marry. Not only has he given me another woman's engagement ring—but to never tell me, to never even hint that he had a child?

I never could've ignored Ellory's existence. Never could've kept her a secret. How could I? Even if Ellory didn't live with me, her name would still come up in conversation. I'd always say how much I miss her and love her and wish she could be with me. How can Hugh—a father—never even let it slip that he has a daughter?

I freeze. Hugh has a daughter—but where is she? He told me his wife was dead. So where is their child?

Tears stream down my cheeks. It's over. Hugh and I...we won't work, *can't* work. Not with all these secrets and lies and—

A knock sounds at the door.

For a second, I debate if I should open it. I can hide, pretend I'm not here. I could go in the bathroom, turn on the water, say I'm in the shower. My shoulders tense when the door cracks open before I can even stand from the floor. Rebecca pokes her head inside.

My back stiffens. Too late to hide now.

"Hey," she coos. "Can I come in?"

I swallow the lump in my throat and nod. "Do you have your phone on you?"

Rebecca shakes her head. "Sorry. Don't know where it is."

I narrow my eyes at her. Something tells me they're all in on it—but what is *it*? Why don't they want me to have a phone? Why do they want to keep me here? Is it because they know I found Gabe's confession? The only other thing I can think of is Paige and my connection to her. That has to be it. So why not confront me? Ask me?

Just come out and say it, I want to scream. Say it so I can tell you all the truth—that I had nothing to do with Paige's death. Then I can call the police and be with my daughter.

Rebecca sweeps her gaze around the room: the open drawers, the piles of clothes. "Going somewhere?" she asks, looming over me.

"No," I lie, "just looking for something." Her eyes darken. She steps closer. "But thanks for checking. I really should clean up now."

She doesn't take the hint. Instead, she moves closer, closer, until she's standing over me as I kneel on the floor. Crossing her arms, she studies the room. Then her eyes light up. "Did you lose this?" She bolts toward the bed. Bending down, she pinches something small in her fingertips, holds it out to me.

My engagement ring.

My heart beats wildly. Suddenly, I'm terrified.

"That's—exactly what I was looking for," I lie again.

I lock eyes with her as she crosses the room, grabs my wrist, pushes the ring back onto my finger. "There," she whispers, stepping all over my clothes on the floor. "That's better."

My belly writhes, feeling nauseous. Perfect—I've found the perfect out.

"I'm not feeling well." I press a hand against my lips like I'm about to vomit.

Rebecca offers to help me stand. I squirm away from her, hobble into the bathroom, lock the door. Turning on the faucet, I splash cold water on my face, hoping when I go back, she'll be gone.

After a few minutes, I shut off the water, hold my breath, open the door.

She's still standing there.

"So he told you?" She nods her chin toward the floor.

I follow her gaze toward the trampled piles of clothes, to the glossy photograph I left resting on top.

My neck feels stiff. I nod. It creaks, wooden.

"So you know who that is?"

"Um, yes. That's Hugh's first wife."

Rebecca's voice lowers as she speaks. "Yeah. Noelle."

Noelle.

"And their daughter, Willow."

I feel faint.

"Unbelievable what happened to them. Of course Hugh told you."

She's testing me. I nod again. It's all I can do. Because all I know, all Hugh has ever told me, is that his first wife died. I didn't even know her name. And I certainly didn't know they had a daughter named Willow.

"Are you sure?" Rebecca asks, tilting her head. "You look sick. If he didn't tell you, I wouldn't be surprised."

I sway in the doorway of the bathroom, clutch onto the sides to steady myself. Rebecca studies my movements. I can lie, but my movements always give me away.

"Oh, my God, Iris. You had no idea, did you? *Tsk.* See, Kara was right. She said Hugh wouldn't come clean. Good thing we didn't bet on it." She laughs to herself. The sound wrings out my insides. This is my life. It was *our* life… How can she laugh?

"Tell me," I say. "I need to know."

Rebecca picks up the picture. Sitting at the edge of the bed, she holds it up, stares at it lovingly. "If Hugh didn't say anything, I'm sure he has a reason—"

"Rebecca. Tell me."

She lets out a deep breath. "He's going to be pissed. But I like you, Iris. I think you're good for our family. You know what it's like. The struggle. The grind. And you're good for Hugh. No matter what they say, I think you're amazing. You can make him happy. Just like *she* made him happy…" Her words fall away.

I feel myself grow pale, feel myself fall away, too.

"You should know," Rebecca whispers to herself. "You're engaged. You're part of this family now." She steps closer. "Hugh's wife and his daughter were murdered."

40

"What?"

It sounds like a breath, barely a word. Rebecca keeps her dark eyes on me, watching as I stitch everything together in my head.

She laughs darkly. "You know, Iris. *Think*. It was a drunk driver about five years ago."

Drunk driver. About five years ago. My mind races a million miles an hour, and my head begins to pound like someone has clamped my skull in a steel vise. The only thing I can think of is what Sloane told me about Ainsley and her then-husband, now ex.

Sloane's voice bubbles up inside my head.

That DWI… It wasn't just one person. The accident killed an entire family.

It couldn't have been Ainsley. She and her husband had nothing to do with it. They didn't kill Hugh—because Hugh is still alive. Had Sloane heard Ainsley wrong? Or did Ainsley truly believe Hugh had died, too?

My head spins. I look at Rebecca. Silent and still, she watches me.

"Ainsley?" I whisper.

Rebecca's face flutters with recognition when I say her name. Slowly, she nods. "So Hugh *did* tell you," she mumbles, pointing at the picture. "He told you everything."

I nod stiffly, my head throbbing. "Yeah," I say numbly. Another lie, but I need to know what Rebecca thinks.

Ainsley had nothing to do with those people being killed. Sloane said Ainsley's husband had been driving that night, but forced Ainsley into asserting she'd been the one driving instead.

In my mind, I hear Sloane's voice: *He was the one who was driving. But he didn't want to take the fall for it. It would've ruined his career.*

Rebecca exhales. "Hugh was devastated. Ainsley's husband used his power to get her out of serving time. She should've been locked up for a decade. Can you believe it? No jail time for what she did. She killed a baby, Iris. Little Willow was only seven months old."

A tear falls down my cheek.

"And Hugh," Rebecca continues, shaking her head. "The doctors weren't sure he'd ever get out of his coma—"

"What?"

Rebecca's forehead wrinkles. "He was in a coma. He was in the car."

I stop breathing. Hugh was *in* the car? That must be how he got the painful-looking scar along his rib cage. I think of it as thoughts surge inside my head.

Ainsley...she was right. Hugh *was* in the car that day. According to Sloane, Ainsley believed the entire family had been killed. She went to her grave believing they'd all died...

No. I stop myself. Ainsley knew—that night, the night of our engagement party.

In the restaurant, Hugh turned and looked at Ainsley. And

when he did, all the blood drained from his face. It looked like he'd seen a ghost. His entire body stiffened, and when I followed his frozen stare, it led directly to her.

Was that the first time he'd seen her, the woman he believed killed his wife and daughter? Was that the first time Ainsley had seen Hugh after believing he was dead? That her husband had killed him, his wife…and his child?

I think back, think hard. All those times Hugh and I had dates in the café…had Ainsley *never* seen him? She worked part-time—surely at least one time she'd seen him. But she hadn't. She'd said as much that day she came over to our house to help with the move. Ainsley wanted to meet the man I was moving in with. Ellory was surprised they hadn't crossed paths.

You've never met Hugh?

I collapse in a chair in the corner, unable to balance on one foot any longer. All the energy has drained from my body.

"He…" Words die on my lips.

Rebecca looks at me. "Hugh never actually told you, did he?"

I shake my head.

She exhales, pinches her lips tight. "I'd rather not be the one to tell you, but Hugh was driving that night. They were on their way home from taking Willow to have her picture taken with Santa. Ainsley hit the passenger side—T-boned, the police called it. Hugh's coma was a small mercy, in the end. He was unconscious, so he never saw his wife and baby…" Rebecca's words fall away, and I can tell her heart is breaking, too.

Ainsley's husband had not only killed Hugh's wife, but he'd killed his infant daughter, too. And he could've killed Hugh.

But do I tell Rebecca this now? Do I clarify that it wasn't Ainsley who'd been driving? Ainsley had told Sloane that information in private. She'd made her promise to keep her secret. Now that Ainsley is gone, wouldn't she want the truth to come out?

No—I can't say a word. Ainsley's husband is still out there.

If I tell Rebecca, she'll tell Hugh, Gabe, Birdie—in a single day, a dozen people would know. What if it got back to him? What would he do to squash the truth about what he'd done?

I bite my lip. God, I wish Hugh were here. Even now, after everything that's happened. He understands the pain of loss better than anyone, even better than Sloane. And now I know why. Now I know why Hugh's always understood me. He lost his spouse to murder, too.

"Well, they're probably waiting for me," Rebecca says. "We're leaving soon for dinner for Mother's birthday. You're sure you don't want to come?"

"No, thanks." I glance around the room at the piles of clothes strewn across the floor. "I really should clean up."

Standing from the bed, Rebecca places the picture of Hugh, his wife, and their daughter gently on the mattress. "I won't say a word about how you're angry with Hugh and threw your engagement ring across the room. I promise."

"I—I'm not—"

"Iris," Rebecca says, cutting me off, "I understand. Your secret's safe with me."

I close the door behind her and collapse to the dusty floor. Pulling my phone out of my pocket, I stare at the broken screen, begging for Ellory or Sloane to call. Maybe, somehow, the screen will work again, and I can answer. But as the minutes pass, my hope shrinks, and the tears begin to fall.

41

After the family has left for dinner, I dry my tears and limp to the armoire. Remembering what hides inside, I open the doors. Hugh's gun box feels heavier than before. I toss it onto the bed.

If they know what happened to Paige, I can't be here—not without a gun. Hugh can't save me now, not if all this time he knew who I was. I won't die here. I need to see Ellory. I need to see her. Hold her.

I tap a password into the gun box. Hugh's birthday. It doesn't open. The number two lights up the screen. I know what it means. Two attempts left. My hands shake. I guess another password—my birthday—tap it in. The number one blinks across the small screen.

One more attempt and I'll be locked out for good.

My head spins. I push the gun box aside.

Deep breaths… Just like Jack and I had taught Ellory.

A man in the attic. Shaw, Ellory's biological father. Paige's killer. In, out.

Blood pooling across the floorboards. They'll find him. They'll know what I did.

One, two.

Staring at the locked gun box, I try to put myself inside Hugh's head. Not an easy thing to do, being that I never really knew him to begin with. Awareness of this fact hits me like a bullet.

I shake my head. Think. Think harder. The password isn't my birthday. It's not his. I think of a date, hold my breath as I tap it in, knowing I only have one more chance. It can be a million things—his daughter's birth date. His wedding anniversary. The day he lost them both.

The screen fades to black.

The gun box unlatches.

The day we met. That's his password. The thought makes my heart twist. I push my feelings aside, reach into the gun box. But there's no gun inside.

It's something much, much worse. I remove the piece of paper, carefully unfold it, already knowing what's written inside. A signed confession. Identical to the one I found in Gabe's bedroom, only this one is signed by Hugh.

I read the list of names. There's a difference between this confession and Gabe's. A new name has been added.

Ainsley's.

Hugh believes Ainsley served no jail time, all charges dismissed, for killing his family. He believes Ainsley went free. But what kind of punishment would Hugh want? Would a lifetime in prison be enough to compensate for his family's needless deaths? For putting Hugh into a coma?

No.

He'd want her dead.

But he's wrong. He's always been wrong.

Ainsley was innocent. Yet, still, she was murdered. I know she was. I was there. I saw her body. I saw the blood.

But did Hugh kill her? Or Gabe?

Or both…

Either way, they killed the wrong person. They killed someone innocent.

A cry escapes me. I drop the note back into the gun box.

The family will be home soon. Hugh will be home soon. He'll find me. They all will. They know who I am. That I was there. They know who my daughter is, how she's not really mine. They killed Ainsley. They'll kill me, too. If not for what I did eighteen years ago, then for what I know now.

I take the confession back out of the box, fold it up into a tight little square, and shove it into my bra. Locking the gun box, I push it back into the armoire, shut the doors. If they don't find out I know they killed Ainsley, maybe it's one less reason for them to want me dead.

Grabbing my crutch, I open the bedroom door, rush toward the staircase, down to the second floor. The door to the study is open. I step inside. Hugh said Birdie sometimes put discarded phones in her husband's old desk.

I creep to the desk, click on a lamp to light inside the drawers. I pull open each one, finding nothing but the yellowed articles and obituaries I saw before. I stop, seeing a familiar name. One from Hugh's list.

Taking the confession from my bra, I unfold it, lay it flat on top, compare the names from the articles saved inside the drawer. There's an article for two men whose names are listed on the confession—Johan Orvers and Dean H. Ipswich.

My eyes scan the print. They disappeared years ago after they were believed to be responsible for a rash of arsons across the state.

Beneath that article is the flyer for a local grief therapy session that I saw in the kitchen days ago. Beneath that is an old article about a man named Edward Renata—his name is also on the confession—a man who was arrested for the rape and murder of a woman the day before her twenty-first birthday. He was released after a mistrial and never seen again.

All these names, every article, all matching the names on the list. A list of names signed by Hugh. Was Hugh confessing to killing all of these people?

The door groans open.

I glance up, see a black silhouette in the doorway. Rebecca steps into the room, edges toward the desk. Her dark eyes flutter over the papers, over the old news articles spilling across the top.

Over Hugh's signed confession.

What is she doing here? She shouldn't be here, in this house, in this room. Did I not hear them return? Did they ever even leave?

Rebecca breaks her eyes away, scrapes them up to my face. Panic engulfs me. I gulp, keep my gaze on her, wait for her to run around the side of the desk and grab me, slam my head against the wall until my skull pops.

But she doesn't.

She stares, lingers. Frozen.

I don't say a word. I wait for her to speak, to say something, anything. Finally, she does.

"Gabe. Come quick."

Footsteps pound from downstairs, climb the staircase, closer. Rebecca stays frozen, staring at me, daring me to move.

Without breaking my gaze from her, my hand grips my crutch, and before I can think, I connect it with her face.

She flutters for a moment, stunned, before tipping sideways, body slamming to the floor. I hop to the doorway, see Gabe running upstairs to the third floor, probably thinking I'm in my bedroom. I grab my crutch, limp to the staircase, hope I can get downstairs before he realizes I'm gone.

I run down the stairs on one foot, my ankle burning. I can't think about the fiery pain shooting through my ankle, as sharp and blistering as the moment I felt the bones break.

I reach the first landing. One more section of stairs, and I'll be in the foyer. I'm so close, I can see the front door. One more section to go, and I can escape the ground floor, find car keys, and drive far, far away.

Footsteps behind me.

I push myself harder, grab the first thing I see, spin, smash the heavy object into Gabe's jaw. He grunts, falls back. My purse and car keys were left upstairs, but I see Rebecca's bag near the stairs, and I snatch it up, whip open the front door, slam it into his face. He cries out. I slam it again into his nose, forcing him back.

I grab my crutch, rush into the darkness. Gabe's voice follows behind me, echoing from inside the house.

"Iris."

I drop my crutch on the ground, fall into Rebecca's car, lock the doors, my hands jelly as I feel for the start button, press on it hard.

The front door explodes open.

I smash the car into gear. My ankle screams with pain as I slam my cast on the gas pedal, peel out of the driveway, engine loud over his screams. The wiper blades frenetically swish over the windshield, clear away the heavy snow.

"Iris—we need to talk!"

Darkness stretches ahead of me. Tears flood down my face, blur my vision.

Glancing in the rearview mirror, I see nothing, nothing but the darkness of the house, tall and looming behind me, blotting out the stars like a stain.

"Come back, Iris."

His voice has calmed now, dulled down like a dream. He's gone, I'm gone. I'm *gone*. I'm going to the police. I'll tell them everything—how Shaw is dead. How they've killed Ainsley and all the names on that confession—*crap*. The confession letter, signed by Hugh. I left it on the desk in the study.

I scream, grip the steering wheel tight in my fists. Stretching into Rebecca's purse, I fish around, try to find her phone. It's dark, too dark. I can't see. The snow falls heavy. I wipe my eyes dry and switch on the headlights, my heart pounding so hard it feels like it can explode through my rib cage. The headlights flood the road with bright light.

It's then I see it.

A person in the road.

I swerve. But I'm a pulse too late. Tires skid across the icy bridge. I force the wheel sideways. The person releases a bone-chilling scream and rolls onto the hood, slamming into the windshield. The sound of crushing glass. The windshield explodes in a spiderweb of cracks.

I jerk the wheel, try to right the car. But I can't. The tires slide on the ice. The world goes sideways. I slam on the brakes, but they don't work—I'm going faster, my cast failing to press the brake.

I've hit the gas.

I'm flying, fog floating around me, white and fluttering in the headlights.

Screeching metal. The whir of the angry engine. My body slams against the steering wheel. A searing pain thrashes against my head.

Everything goes quiet as I slip into the waiting, icy darkness.

42

I'm frozen—cold and wet and stinging.

I open my eyes. Darkness engulfs me. My entire body shivers. Snowflakes fall around me as I lie on the ground. I lick my lips, taste blood, hear the shoveling of snow. No, not snow. Dirt.

I wriggle, move sideways, move my arms. My hands are tied. The freezing air makes it hard to breathe. I'm outside, somewhere, alone. No, not alone. I tilt my head back. Someone hovers near me. *Gabe.* He stands close, his back to me. He grunts, cursing as he struggles to dig a hole in the winter-thick earth.

Birdie and Rebecca stand inside the house, watching, their shadows dark against the lead-paned glass. Light pools through the windows of the house. I hear the quiet stillness of the river, smell the murky water. I know exactly where I am.

I'm in the garden near the riverside cliffs, lying in the exact spot where Hugh proposed. My head pounds. Every muscle hurts. What happened? I was driving over the bridge. It was frozen, I must've hit ice, slipped, skidded off the edge, the car diving into the ravine.

No.

I didn't slip.

I swerved.

Someone stood in the middle of the bridge. But who was it? Rebecca? Birdie? Camille—oh, God, not Camille. Her baby. Her pregnancy. I couldn't have... I couldn't.

Did I *kill* her? Did I kill her baby? Gabe's baby?

One more reason for them to want me dead.

I want to scream. And so I do.

Gabe keeps digging, faster, harder. He removes his coat, tosses it in the snow. He stabs the sharp edge of the shovel into the ground, hitting rocks, lifting them, scooping them away. He's digging a hole. A grave.

For me.

This time it's not a dream.

He stops digging, turns to me. Reading my expression, he nods and gives a small smile. "It wasn't me you saw that night," Gabe says. "It was Hugh."

Panic hits me.

He nods, angles his head as he looks at me. "I detest when a perfectly good grave goes unused. That wasn't the original plan. But plans change. I find in life, sometimes it's best to stay fluid. *Fluidity* is the foundation of a good plan."

Gabe smiles and turns away, continues digging.

My breath grows frantic. I close my eyes and see Paige—I see her now like I saw her then, all those years ago, deep in the cold, dark woods. Her toe twitched. I held her baby girl as Shaw dug a hole for her. He grabbed her ankles, kicked her down.

In the trace of moonlight that bled through the bare trees, she looked at me. She didn't move, didn't speak. Shaw or Davey or Mars didn't see. But I did.

And I did nothing.

I wish I could go back in time, run to her grave rather than hide in the woods. I wish I'd knelt in the dirt and reached inside the earth, dug her out with my bare hands. But I didn't. I ran, I hid. I did it to save her baby, but still, what if I'd done something more? Could I have saved her? It eats away at me. It's been eating at me for eighteen years.

But everything will be okay now. My fate will soon match Paige's. From inside, Birdie and Rebecca will be the ones standing idly by, watching me be buried, as Shaw buried Paige. They'll watch my eyes flicker and my foot twitch, and maybe, just maybe, they'll feel a pang of sorrow. But still, they'll stand by and do nothing. As I did.

I close my eyes, accept my fate.

Then somehow, I see him. Faint at first, fuzzy around the edges. Soon his face is clear, as if he were lying next to me in the snow-dusted dirt.

Jack.

I keep my eyes shut, let the memory overtake me.

I ran to him. He was face down in the dirty snow.

The man who'd called, requested to test-drive Jack's truck, had shot him, stolen the truck, and left Jack on the side of the road. Like garbage. Like nothing. The moment I saw him, I exploded into tears, unable to stop, wishing I could stay calm so he could stay calm. But I couldn't. In our final moments together, I'd failed.

I moved his head, tilted it to me. It flopped over, the muscles in his neck weak. Slowly, he scraped his gaze up to my face. His hand clutched his side where the blood was coming from.

It looked black as it poured from him, a water jug tipped sideways. It chugged out, thick and oozing. His fingertips grew pale white. Then his hands, his cheeks. And then every part of him.

Pressing my forehead to his, I took all of him in my arms. His head lolled on my shoulder. He removed his blood-slicked hand from his side, let the blood flow into the snow. I felt his warm blood saturate my jeans, turn cold on my skin.

My hands shook as I pulled back, stared at him one final time. He smiled at me, a weak hint of a smile, and moved his lips to speak. But I was crying too hard, too loud, to ever hear his last words.

And then he stopped. Jack just turned off, shut down. I never understood when people said a soul left the body. I didn't understand it. What would it look like? How would you even know? But I'd seen it. It wasn't even that he'd stopped blinking or breathing. Or moving or speaking. But what created his life, what made him *him*, had gone.

Just a breath. A heartbeat. Then it was over.

I stared at him, thinking he'd come back. He never did.

I open my eyes to darkness. Jack is gone. For years, Jack has been gone. I never wanted to relive that memory. I never wanted to think about how it felt to watch his life slip away. The moment his head rested on my shoulder, I knew it was over. I knew my Jack was gone.

No one and nothing could've prepared me for telling Ellory her father was dead. To hear her screams. To feel her entire body wilt and every muscle inside her throb with heartache as I held her limp body in my arms. Nothing could ever prepare a person for that.

And because I know this, because I was there to tell her the worst news of her life, I can't die like this. I can't die here, in this garden, Gabe grabbing my ankles to drop me down into a cold, shallow grave.

Ellory can't go through that again.

And so, I decide to survive.

In that same heartbeat, light floods the garden. A figure runs toward me. Hugh's voice, low and gravelly. "Iris, Iris. What happened? Gabe—what did you do?"

I open my mouth, try to speak. *Hugh, Hugh.* But I can't.

"Take one step closer, Hugh, and I'll fucking kill her."

Hugh stops, stares at me. Gabe stands in front of me, his feet so close they nudge my stomach.

"Gabe, what are you doing?" Hugh glances down at me. His hands shake as he holds them out in front of him. "Gabe!" he shouts, his usual calm voice shriveled with panic.

"She found your confession, Hugh. It's over. Rebecca found out, and Iris punched her, then stole her car. She tried to leave but she hit— She ran the car off the road because she swerved to try to miss hitting someone."

"Who did she hit?" Hugh asks.

Gabe looks down at me, holds back a laugh. "Her friend Sloane. I guess she was coming over to see Iris. And she ran her over. I saw her lying there, probably either dead or nearly dead. Now we have *that* to deal with on top of everything else."

Dead?

My heart stops. *No, no, no. There has to be some mistake. Sloane can't be dead. She can't be.*

"What are you talking about?" Hugh shouts.

"Iris. She knows."

Oh, God, Sloane. Sloane had been standing in the road. She'd come to visit me, maybe to take me away from here. She always waited at the end of the driveway. Why didn't she tell me? Oh, God, what did I do?

Hugh gulps. Glancing at me, his eyes are sharp with fear. I watch closely, watch as everything clicks into place in his head. Tears well in my eyes. He bites his lip, turns away. He can't even look at me.

"Gabe," Hugh begins, "drop the knife and tell me why it looks like you were about to murder my fiancée. What the hell is going on?"

Knife?

"She knows everything. If you let her go, the first thing she'll do is run to the cops. Is that what you want?"

"No, she won't," Hugh says. "Gabe, let her go. Iris can hear the truth. It's fine. It will be okay. I trust her."

"I don't. And it only works if *all* of us trust her."

"I didn't trust Camille. Or Kara. You didn't, either, not at first. And you didn't try to kill them. So why Iris? Why can't you just leave her be?"

"I hate her."

Hugh shakes his head. "That doesn't matter. We're a family. There are rules. We *vote*. Where's Rebecca?" Hugh asks flatly, turning to see her standing next to Birdie inside the house, faces pressed against the window. "Maybe she can talk sense into that thick goddamn head of yours."

"She's inside with Birdie. They're fine."

Hugh pushes Gabe aside, falls to his knees. Gently, he cups my cold cheek as he speaks. "This is why I needed my family to like you. Goddammit, Iris. I needed them to like you."

"I don't know how she cut herself. Honest—I didn't do this to her," Gabe says.

"You know I always know when you're lying." Hugh grabs Gabe's knife from his hand, brings it close to my face. Light flickers off the steel, glinting like a spark. "Here," he says softly. He reaches around, slices through the tape Gabe used to bind my hands.

"She's banged up pretty bad," Gabe says.

Hugh's hand flutters across my face, feels my forehead, my skull, my shoulder. My skin crackles with pain. I yelp, a wounded animal. Hugh holds his hand up in the light streaming from his headlights. His fingers are glazed with my blood.

"Fuck, where's it coming from?" Hugh rushes to ask. "Iris? Where are you bleeding?" He shakes my shoulders. But I don't have an answer to give.

"Her ribs." Gabe kneels beside Hugh.

Hugh lifts my sweater, grimaces.

"She's going to pass out eventually," Gabe says. "Let's just end this."

"*You* did this," Hugh snarls at Gabe. "How could you? She's my fiancée."

I feel my stomach for blood, to try to feel for what Hugh is staring at. My fingers trace my body beneath my sweater, stopping where my skin is broken apart. There's a gash in my side, slick with blood. *God, Sloane—no, I need to find Sloane.*

I cry out. "Please, Hugh."

Gabe leans closer. "Rebecca told me she wanted you to know that she had a good *feeling* about you. Good *vibes*, she said. Ugh, please. I never knew what she—or my brother— ever saw in you."

Hugh exhales, drops his head in a hand. "You *didn't* have to hurt her." He looks down at me, eyes fixed with sadness, yet he does nothing to help me. My fiancé, the man I loved, does nothing but watch me squirm. He stares at me as he speaks. "I was hoping things would end differently."

Gabe barks out a laugh. "Not now. Not with her like this. It can't. There's only one thing we can do now."

Hugh nods slowly to himself. Tears slip down his cheeks. Quickly, he wipes them away. "I know. But I can't let her go. I *can't*."

Gabe shakes his head. "You already know my vote and Birdie's. Iris hurt Rebecca's head tonight, so yeah, probably a *no* from her, too. That's three against one. Us against you, Hugh. It's over. Let her go."

I blink the tears away, stare up at him. Against the white light from his headlights, he looks like a shadow. "I found the picture," I begin, throat closing. "Your wife. Your daughter. I know what happened. Please…think of my daughter. Think of Ellory."

Gabe rolls his eyes before turning away.

"Hugh," I begin again. "You know how it feels to lose someone you love. She already lost Jack. *Please... I know you love Ellory. I know you only want what's best for her. Do you think she's better off without her mom? You had a daughter. You'd do anything...*"

Gabe moves closer, peers down at me. "If Ellory ever comes back looking for you, we'll take care of her, too, I promise."

I roll over in pain, cry into the dirt. *Sloane... Ellory...* I need to stand, need to get my hands free.

Hugh stares at me, all compassion for me deadened. I watch as his mind clicks off, erasing all his love for me in a heartbeat. Yet, still, he stares down at me, as I lie on the cold ground, soft snowflakes falling around us. He watches me, as I feel myself dying, like dreams do, slowly and painfully, all at once.

"*Please*—I didn't know she was Paige."

"What did you say?"

"She said her name was Ellory. Please—I didn't know."

"What are you saying?" Hugh asks, moving closer. Gabe leans over behind Hugh to better hear.

"Your sister... I never hurt her. I tried to stop it."

Hugh unlocks his eyes from mine. Stiffly, he turns to Gabe as if he's made of wood. "I can't believe it." They look down at me, unblinking. "Birdie was *right*. All this time, she was right."

"Well, you know what to do," Gabe says. "Go get her. We're out of time."

43

Hugh returns moments later, reclaiming his spot on the ground beside me. But he didn't return alone. Behind me, shuffling. *Tap clonk tap.*

Birdie.

Her cane drums along the fieldstone pathway. Gabe clears his throat, stands next to Hugh. I'm surrounded.

They glare down at me as I lie helpless, bleeding in the snow. Three of them.

Just like then. Just like that night. Full circle.

"Iris," Hugh begins. "Tell us about Paige."

I part my lips, frozen together by the cold. "Blanket," I choke out. "Then Paige."

Hugh nods and Gabe rushes inside, returning with a wool blanket. He drops it in the dirt next to me, crosses his arms. Hugh reaches to unfold it, carefully drapes it over my body.

"Paige," Birdie says, voice firm. "Tell me what you know."

Tears cluster in my eyes. And I tell them everything. I explain how when I was sixteen, I ran away from home. I hitched a ride with a girl who called herself Ellory and her boyfriend, Shaw. How Shaw later picked up two of his friends along the way, brothers named Mars and Davey.

Birdie listens to every word, never letting a moment of emotion cloud her expression. And so, I talk. I talk about how Ellory was pregnant, how they planned to break into her house—*this* house. How I tried to stop it. How I tried to save her…and how I knew I couldn't. But I could save her daughter. A daughter I named Ellory.

And I confess how I found the attic. How I saw the photographs of Ellory—of Paige. I connected the dots. I could never forget her face. I see her face every day—in my daughter.

Slowly, Birdie's mask dissipates. She holds a hand to her mouth and sobs.

"I tried to find her," Birdie cries into her palm. "I couldn't find her. It killed me. And then that day—"

"Birdie," Hugh says, "don't."

She pauses, glances at him. "I had been searching for my daughter for eighteen years. And then—"

"*Stop,*" Hugh begs again.

Birdie ignores him, drags her eyes to mine. "Then I saw her. One day, Hugh took me along on his weekly drive down to watch the woman who'd killed his wife and daughter. What was her name?" Birdie asks, tapping her cane on the ground.

"Ainsley," Hugh answers.

"Yes, that's right," Birdie says with a nod. "You always wanted to watch her. I advised against it, but once you set your mind on something, that's it. Hugh got out of the car when he realized she wasn't working that day. But I was tired, so I stayed inside. Then I saw her. My daughter. She was right there as if no time had passed. When Hugh returned, I said if he ever owed me anything, he would approach you, talk to you, try to learn your names, learn anything about you he could. And he did."

"Iris—I didn't know it would go so far," Hugh says, avoiding my eyes. "When I met you that day in the café, I may have done it for Birdie. But I fell in love with you on my *own*."

"Don't," I choke out. "Don't speak."

"It just happened, Iris." Hugh stares down at me on the freezing ground, bleeding and shivering in the dirt. "I fell in love with you for *you*. I knew Birdie would love it if I brought you here—brought you *both* here."

"But you still had that job," Birdie says. "It's far too easy to get a poor woman fired these days. I take no pride in stealing employment away from a working mother. But you needed a little push." Birdie laughs before sighing. "If only your daughter didn't hate you, she wouldn't have run away so fast. I could've gotten to know her a little better."

I sob. *Sloane… Ellory…* I'm blinded by tears, as I've been blinded by Hugh. He never loved me, not really. Everything he'd ever done had been orchestrated to get us into this house. And Birdie got me fired from my job. Little did she know she didn't have to. I was about to lose our house anyway. But she couldn't have known that because I'd never told Hugh about the eviction.

My mind whirls, my heart breaking more and more with each painful thought.

"I was hoping one day I could return Paige's photographs to the walls. Then I'd no longer need to climb into the attic when I wanted to see my daughter."

"The attic?"

Hugh chimes in. "A historic house of this size can have multiple attic access points."

"You think we didn't notice you lurking around, trying to find the door to the attic?" Gabe says. "We knew it was a matter of time before you wormed your way up there."

Birdie cackles. "There's a second staircase in my bedroom closet. Hugh was kind enough to carry Paige's photos up for me so I could return to see her whenever I wanted. We couldn't keep them around the house for your arrival. Not with the clear similarity between Paige and Ellory. And when he told me how frightened you were, saying how you'd heard footsteps in the attic…you were hearing *me*."

Tears fill my eyes again when I imagine Hugh telling them *everything*, even my fear about someone hiding in the attic. I feel naked, my innermost fears exposed for all to see. Hugh never loved me. He can say he did. But he didn't. He never did. I really had been alone inside this house, all this time.

"So tell us now. Once and for all," Birdie says. "You claim you didn't harm Paige, yet you ended up with her baby." She circles me, cane tapping the stone. "And you know who killed her. So tell me—*who*."

I pull the blanket tight. I'm cold. So cold. "Shaw—Paige's boyfriend. Ellory's real father," I confess. The secret I've tried so hard to keep all of these years pours from me so easily. "He's in the attic. He's dead."

"You're lying," Gabe says.

"Go look." My teeth chatter.

Gabe, Hugh, and Birdie exchange glances with one another.

After a moment, Gabe says, "I'll go check."

He disappears inside the house. Hugh inhales a deep breath, sits beside me.

"Ainsley," he begins, blue eyes bloodshot. "She killed my wife. My daughter never saw her first birthday."

"Why didn't you tell me? You knew about Jack. You could've told me."

He shakes his head. "I couldn't. Not ever. If you found out your friend killed my family, it would've been over. Why do you think my path never crossed hers? I stayed away from her. I couldn't have her know we were dating. God, you'd have broken up with me, Iris, and Birdie would've— She would've lost her chance to know Ellory."

"I wish I could hate you," I whisper. "I want to hate you."

He takes my hand. I don't have the strength to pull away. The warmth from his skin stings at first. Then it's like nothing I've ever felt. Euphoria.

"Please forgive me, Iris."

"Don't bother," Birdie says, looking away. "You're wasting your breath."

Hugh ignores his mother and continues.

"The doctors told me later they weren't sure I'd ever wake from the coma. Do you know how many days I wished I was still there, in that hospital bed? How many days I wished *I* had been the one to—" Hugh stops himself, rubs a hand over his face. "But I survived," he says somberly. "I survived and Ainsley… She never spent a single day in prison, because the man who married her was a criminal defense attorney. So I'm asking you—what would *you* have done?"

"What?"

"You, of all people, would've done the same if you'd ever found the person who killed Jack. I know you would've. We can live with our choices, Iris. But we can't live knowing we did nothing."

He brushes his finger along my frozen cheek, gentle, loving. My heart thuds slower, blood thickened from the cold. If I hold my breath, I can no longer hear it beat inside my ears. Blood drips from me, growing cold as it freezes on my skin. I don't know how much time I have left.

"You killed Ainsley," I whisper. "Out of revenge?"

Hugh looks down at me and nods.

"Gabe did," he mumbles. "That night at the restaurant… you'd *invited* her. I—I froze. I didn't know what to do. I'd never been that close to her. It was overwhelming. I wanted to strangle her. But before we could even talk about it, Gabe stole her wallet. He had her address and broke in. Normally we never leave bodies behind, but Gabe had no choice. He was going to go back but was arrested for attempting to harm you instead. But I don't blame you."

Hugh knows I don't have much longer. It's why he's telling me these things, confessing to me these horrible things. He knows I'll soon be dead.

"That night," Hugh begins. "The night you claimed you saw Gabe outside digging… That grave was meant for your friend. But, like Gabe said, plans change. All we can do is adapt."

I stare up at him, unblinking. Fear has overtaken me to the point where I wonder if it will be the constant pulse of my life forever, however long forever might be. "Let me go," I try to say, but no sound comes out.

A door slams. Someone coughs. Gabe has returned from the attic. Wordlessly, he picks up the shovel, swings it over his shoulder like a baseball bat.

"Birdie, go inside. It's cold, and I have one more grave to dig."

She leaves, never looking back. Hugh hovers over me, somehow protective, a vulture guarding a carcass. Gabe begins to dig a second grave. The earth is frozen, and he struggles to break through.

I shiver and force myself to think of something—anything— else. How I will escape. If Sloane is okay. How I'll beg her forgiveness. What I'll do when I see Ellory again. I'll never let her go. We're tied together, she and I. Tight as a knot in a rope.

"What'd you find?" Hugh asks Gabe.

Gabe stops digging. "I never thought I'd say this, but there's a dead guy in the attic."

The snow falls heavier. Hugh's eyes flicker to me. "You weren't lying, then," he says in disbelief. "Iris, please forgive me. I never wanted this to happen. Not like this. I struggle every day wondering if I did the right thing. All of us do. We decided to do it years ago. It's why we each have a signed confession," he admits. "Me. Gabe. Birdie. Rebecca. And Kara and Camille, though their hands are still clean in this, for now."

I tilt my head, look up at him. My neck creaks like an old wooden doll.

"What?"

"We each have a signed confession. Whoever dies first takes the fall for all." Hugh stares at me, lips parted. "Years ago, after Paige disappeared, Birdie went to grief counseling. Soon, she met Rebecca, who'd lost her family. Years later, they met Gabe. He lost his sister. Another couple of years go by, and they meet me."

"No," I say. "This can't be real."

"I was grieving my wife and daughter for a year when I found them. They saved my life, made me realize that while justice doesn't always prevail, we have the power to set things right. An eye for an eye."

"I don't understand. Are you saying...you met each other at grief counseling?"

Hugh swallows hard as he stares at me, eyes plump with tears.

"Please, forgive me."

"You're not—*a family*?"

Hugh smiles ruefully. "Oh, we are. We're more than a family. But it's not DNA that binds us. We've each killed for one another. Like with Gabe's sister, raped and murdered. One day before her twenty-first birthday. The police caught who did it. But he was let go before the trial was even finished—on a technicality. He'd killed another young woman before we found him."

"Oh, God..."

"And Rebecca. Her family was killed in a fire. Arsonists targeted them. The police found them, too. They got five years in prison for killing her entire family."

For the first time, Hugh breaks his gaze with mine and looks up, toward the house. I follow his eyes to see Rebecca watching us from the window. He turns back to look at me again. "You tell me you wouldn't do the same thing—for Jack. I wanted to give that to you, to help you find his killer and get revenge. It wasn't supposed to end like this."

My heart slows. I can't speak, can't push a single word off my tongue.

Hugh takes my hand in his. The sudden flash of heat tingles the frozen blood in my fingertips. "We don't do it for pleasure, Iris. We do it because we have no choice. We all live with tremendous guilt. You have no idea. But we *deal* with it. We carry it with us. It was *always* the right thing to do. For them. For my *daughter*."

Snowflakes fall into my eyes. The world becomes cloudy, a wispy blur.

"We created our own family, careful not to be tied to those whose lives we'd taken. Rebecca killed for Birdie. I killed for Gabe. They're all right here, somewhere." His eyes trace the ground, sweep over the snow-covered garden.

"Gabe isn't—"

"My brother?" Hugh asks, looking over his shoulder to the man digging his fiancée's grave. My grave. He shakes his head. "No, not by blood."

"And Birdie."

"Isn't our mother, no. Come on, Iris. We don't look anything alike."

"And Paige isn't your sister."

Hugh furrows his dark brows, shakes his head. "She's Birdie's daughter, but not our sister."

As Hugh grips my hand tighter, I look at him and remember a lesson I learned long ago—people can be the scariest things on earth. And then, behind Hugh, something moves in the shadows.

44

Gabe continues to dig at the edge of the garden. He cries out, frustrated by something. I look over to see him hitting the dirt hard with the shovel, but that's not all I notice. Sloane crouches down behind the stone wall.

I burst into tears of joy. *I didn't kill her—she's okay. She's here, she's okay, it'll all be okay.*

Hugh mistakes my tears of happiness for tears of sadness. "Don't be upset. Please. I wanted to tell you. I did."

I have to keep Hugh's attention on me. Maybe I can get them both distracted, keep them looking my way so Sloane can somehow get me out of Hugh's grip. Still, he holds my hand, and I realize it's only to keep me close.

"Ainsley..." I trail off. "Ainsley wasn't driving."

I ready myself for my performance. No matter what, I have to keep his eyes on me. Hugh tilts his head, studies me. It's then I force a loud cough. And I don't stop. I cough and cough until my throat burns. Hugh can't get a word in. "What?" He shakes me. I don't stop. My head lolls sideways as the coughs grow louder. "What did you say?"

Hugh shouts my name in frustration. "Iris, my God, are you okay?"

I say nothing. My lungs are beginning to hurt and my throat is on fire, but it's working. Hugh's attention hasn't strayed away from me.

Behind him, Gabe hits the frozen dirt hard with the tip of the shovel. He climbs out of the grave, face going red.

Dropping the shovel, he gasps, "Hugh." Lifting a hand, he clutches his shoulder. "Help."

Hugh doesn't hear him right away, not above my loud, forceful coughs. Slowly, he tugs his eyes away from me, turns to Gabe.

"*Hugh*," Gabe chokes out, falls to his knees.

The color seeps out of Hugh's face, and he rushes to him, catches him before he collapses.

"Hang on. You're going to be okay," Hugh tells him. "You're having a heart attack. Breathe, just breathe. Come on—breathe. Look at me, brother."

Gabe's eyes roll back. He grits his teeth, saliva spitting out of his mouth as he gurgles in pain.

I stop my charade, look at the shovel Gabe dropped. Pushing myself up, I flip the wool blanket off me, feel my muscles crackle from the cold. I fight to stand, fight to bend my joints, stiff and rigid with cold.

Hugh clutches Gabe on the ground, shouts, *"Rebecca. Birdie. Get help."*

Rebecca sprints into the garden, rushes to Gabe's side. Filled with panic, she doesn't see me creep toward the shovel. She only notices me when I stand over them, shovel clenched in my bone-weary fists.

"Iris—"

The shovel connects with the side of Hugh's skull. He twists, falls backward, Gabe's body limp beside his. Rebecca screams, grabs my arm. I twist, and Sloane erupts from the shadows, takes the shovel from me, hits Rebecca in the back of the head.

Rebecca cries out in pain, confused, and whirls around, shocked to see Sloane behind her.

"Go, Iris, run!"

"I'm not leaving you!"

"*Go!*"

Sloane brings the shovel back, hitting Rebecca again, as I stagger away as fast as my frozen feet can move. Warm blood pulses out of my ribs like a freshly thawed stream.

Wounded. Limping. Exhausted.

I'm ideal prey.

I run, though in reality, only one foot is working. I wish I could forget my ankle is broken, forget there's a giant cast strapped around my foot. But I can't.

My mind is void of extraneous thoughts. Survival has taken over. Instinct. My muscles thaw as I hobble along the side of the house, my left leg taking the brunt of my body weight.

Stopping at an unlatched kitchen window, I peer inside. It's dark, and I try to lift myself to crawl inside. But I'm weak. Weak and unable to pull myself up through a window.

My only option is to go around to the front of the house, try the door. I need to call 911. There are several people here—someone has to have a phone somewhere. I could try to run through the woods toward the road, but it's too far. I'd never make it on uneven ground, not with my ankle, not this weak, this exhausted.

Slowly, I creak the front door open. The house is dark, darker than the pitch-black sky.

I'm in shock. I know I am. I'm fully aware. But thinking about it won't help me now. I stop walking, clutch onto a wall, steady my breathing. How could I have been so gullible? I trusted him. Loved him. All this time, what was I to him? A pawn? Just a woman his *fake* mother ordered him to introduce himself to? All because she saw Ellory.

My stomach twists. Something burning claws up the back of my throat.

Ainsley is dead. Shaw is dead. Dead—right in front of me. They're both dead. Countless others are dead, too. And I'm… I'll be dead if I don't find a phone. And so will Sloane. Birdie's inside the house, somewhere, along with Camille. Gabe is incapacitated in the garden and so are Hugh and Rebecca. For now.

Were they all in on it? Did they all know Hugh only invited us to move in with him because Birdie wanted to learn more about my daughter?

We're more than a family. But it's not DNA that binds us.

Of course they all knew. They all knew everything, right from the start. They're a group of murderers, not a real family. They're killers, killing people for some twisted version of justice against those who've harmed their loved ones. They've been doing it for years—and getting away with it.

Until now.

The house crackles, brittle with silence. I rush across the foyer, ankle burning with each step as I begin the long journey to the kitchen. Light seeps into the hall from the great room. Peering around a corner, I spot Camille's phone on a table.

Gabe must've returned it to her. I can't believe my luck. Creeping inside, I snatch it.

A groan.

Camille sleeps on a sofa, inches away, her hand draped across her belly. I hold my breath, click on her phone.

Locked. But it can be unlocked.

I step deeper into the room, hold the phone up to Camille's face.

It scans her features and unlocks.

Camille stirs, groans.

Hands shaking, I dial 911.

"911. What's your emergency?"

The operator's voice rattles the phone, the volume too high.

"Hello? What is your emergency?"

I hop backward out of the room, press the phone to my chest, try to muffle the voice. The operator keeps speaking, voice vibrating against my skin.

"Hello? 911—please state the reason for your call. Hello? Please state why you're calling."

I can't hang up. I need to keep the call going. Hopefully, they can find our location.

I look back at Camille.

She's staring up at me.

Her mouth yawns open. "Gabe! In here—in the great room."

My heart stops. I yelp, fall back against the wall.

Footsteps from down the blackened hallway.

Clonk tap.

"Hello? Please respond—what's your emergency?"

The footsteps edge closer. *Clonk tap, clonk tap.*

I hold my breath, grip the phone tight.

"Help—she's in here."

I rush away, the phone slipping through my shaking hand, landing on the floor.

The operator's voice echoes through the hall.

"Please stay on the line. I'm sending—"

Clonk tap.

The footsteps stop behind me.

I turn.

A figure plunges through the shadows.

Birdie's cane slices the air, slams into my throat. I gasp, lift my hands in defense.

She raises her cane again. I push her back, but she comes forward, anger contorting her features. Grabbing her shoulder, I pull my arm sideways, land a solid *thwack* in her face.

She yelps, stumbles back. Birdie's hands fly up, clutch her face.

"My *eye*."

I look at my hand. Fresh blood smears across my knuckles. Across my engagement ring.

I race back to the foyer to the front door to find Sloane when I hear someone.

"Iris? Where are you? Where are you, Iris?"

Camille.

I look toward her voice to see her standing across the other side of the foyer, the only thing between us a waterfall of snow. It cascades through the hole in the roof, the snowflakes glowing ethereally in the moonlight, twinkling like crystals.

She steps forward, heels clacking across the floorboards.

"Stay away from me," I say. "I don't want to hurt you, Camille. Think of your baby."

She laughs. "As if you care about Gabe's baby."

"I do," I say, inching toward the front door. "I do. I care. Especially since you'll be raising it on your own."

"What?"

I lick my lips. My fingers search the wall, desperate to find the doorknob. "He's in the garden," I say, clenching my teeth as a bolt of pain shoots through my foot. "Gabe—he's outside. He's hurt."

"Liar."

I shake my head. "I'm not." I stop, feeling something in the darkness. Not the doorknob, but one of Birdie's antiques. Lifting the marble sculpture in my palm, I hold it tight. "I don't want to hurt you, Camille. Just let me go."

Still, she walks forward, stepping around the soft spot on the floor where the snowflakes fall, melt into the Persian rug, leaving a giant black hole in the center.

Then she runs at me. I push her away, push her back, and hobble to the staircase. She grabs my leg, pulls me down. I scream, and still, she holds me tight, pulling me down with her.

"No, get off me!"

She clutches my cast, the Velcro unlatching. I shake her off, and before she can grab me again, I climb up the stairs on my knees. Camille stretches to reach me again, but she misses, falls back. I don't turn to look at her until I reach the second-floor landing. Looking through the banister, I can't see her.

I push myself up, limp down the hall into the study, lock the door behind me. Gasping, I cross the room, grab the silver letter opener I'd seen hidden in a drawer, clench it in my fist, slide beneath the desk.

The police are on their way. They can trace the GPS on Camille's phone—right? I catch my breath, try to calm myself before I hyperventilate. *Sloane will find me. She's here. She's okay. We'll both be okay. I'll be with her soon. I'll see Ellory soon.*

Breathe in and out. In. Out.

I remain in the darkness, knees curled to my chest, cobwebs tickling my cold skin as I hide under the desk. No one will find me here. I'll hide until the police come, until I hear them call through the house. My heart slows. My eyes shut.

The doorknob rattles.

My eyes snap open.

Three knocks.

"Iris?"

Dread engulfs me.

"Iris, I know you're in there." *Hugh.* Camille must've seen where I went, told him. Either that or he followed the trail of blood. He pauses, waits for sounds. "Iris…" He says my name calmly, too calmly for a man who's just been hit over the head with a shovel, for a man who's just watched his brother—*fake* brother—have a heart attack.

"Don't do this. Open the door."

I stay silent.

Shadows flutter along the floor as he paces the hall outside. A bang on the door. The room shakes.

"*Iris.*"

He tries the doorknob again. I press my back against the inside of the desk, clutch the letter opener tight, silver warming in my hands. Red and blue lights pulse on the wall opposite the windows. I gasp out in relief.

The door explodes open.

Before I can escape, Hugh grabs me, drags me out from under the desk, pins my arms to my sides. I slip one out of his grip, tearing my sweater. The police lights flicker in his eyes. The letter opener slips from my grasp, skitters across the floor.

"*Iris—stop—fighting me.*"

"No." I try to twist away. But I'm too tired—too broken. "Let go!"

"*No...*" he whispers, and he sounds fragile, breakably small. "I need you to forgive me."

In the shadows, I drag my eyes to his. My lips tremble. From terror. From not knowing what he'll do. His grip tightens around my arms. He shakes me. My head jolts backward.

"Iris—please—I'm sorry. *I'm sorry.*"

I gulp. He pulls me into him. My cheek pressed on his chest, his heartbeat pounds. He pets my hair down the back of my skull. I'm frozen. I can't move. My eyes stay wide-open, staring into the shadows of the room. Panicking, I scan the floor, search for the letter opener. But I find nothing. *Where is it? Where is it?*

The blue and red lights outside amplify, dance across the dark paneled walls.

"You have to know," Hugh whispers. His voice is weary, quaking. He releases my wrists, clamps his hands tight around my throat. "I didn't mean for any of this to happen."

Hugh's eyes darken with rage as he squeezes my neck. Air disappears. I stare back at him, try to wriggle from his grip. He drags me down to the floor and locks his legs around me, keeping my body entangled in him like a snake. The motion turns me sideways, and I stretch a leg out toward the wall, blindly hoping I catch hold of the letter opener where it fell in the shadows.

He squeezes harder. Pressure builds inside my head. With one hand, I claw at his eyes, rake my nails across his handsome face.

"Do you forgive me?" he asks as he stares down at me. "Do you, Iris?"

Hugh locks his eyes with mine as he strangles me, harder, tighter. The bones in my neck crack. The letter opener gleams in the shadows, a long slice of silver. The red and blue lights fade to black. My foot hits it. I thrust my arm out, grasp the handle. My vision blurs.

"Yes," I gasp. "I do."

I raise the letter opener and plunge it into his heart.

27 DAYS AFTER

FRIDAY, FEBRUARY 21

45

We've been watching the news all day. The entire country has. The microwave beeps, and I blindly tear open the bag, unable to look away from the TV. Today is Hugh's arraignment.

I carry over three bowls of butter popcorn, pass them to Ellory and Sloane. "Turn it up."

Sloane grabs the remote, raises the volume.

"*...while some continue working to identify the remains, others have begun...*"

FBI forensics teams have been excavating the bone garden behind Birdie's manor house. So far, they've found three skeletons and an unidentified femur bone. I told them in my interviews they'd find more.

My statement was confirmed when the medical examiner discovered Hugh's signed confession letter...the one I'd secretly tucked inside his pocket.

On it, they'd found the names of six people: the two arsonists who'd killed Rebecca's family; the man who'd murdered Gabe's sister; Ainsley; and Evonne's husband, Douglas Erboss.

Also included on the list was a name I'd added that final day in the study, perfectly replicated to match Hugh's boxy handwriting in thick black ink.

Shawn Duplain.

Hugh can deny murdering him, of course. But no one will believe him.

And so, they keep digging.

And with that digging, they keep finding.

And the country is still seized by the shock of the murder house and the family inside.

I also told the police about Paige. Where she was buried. I remembered she was near the edge of the tree line in the woods, but I told them Gabe had confessed to me the location of her body before he died. The forensics team was able to find her bones using ground-penetrating sonar. Thanks to them, Ellory's biological mother will finally have a proper burial with a white marble headstone.

The police discovered Gabe, dead in the garden from a heart attack. And Shaw…allegedly still alive when I'd locked him in the attic. During the autopsy, they found he didn't die from the nail puncturing his brain, but from an aneurysm when a blood vessel later ruptured. Doctors appear on popular daytime shows sometimes to debate whether or not he could've survived if the paramedics had arrived sooner.

Ellory shakes her head as she watches the news. I wrap an arm around her shoulders. It feels good to have her back. To have her home. My fears of losing Ellory forever, as I'd done to my mom when I'd run away, were unfounded. I can't describe the weight lifted from me, like I've shed an old skin.

The police told me only three things about Ellory's kidnapping:

1) Shaw had kidnapped her.

2) Shaw had held his daughter hostage in his basement.

3) Ellory was lucky to make it out alive.

I'll admit speaking with the police was difficult, but I managed to hide my smile. Still, I can't believe how lucky we were in the end. We'd survived.

Unlike so many before us, somehow, we'd survived. Maybe Sloane's right. Maybe karma is real. Or maybe it was something else. Maybe, finally, I got some luck. Whatever it was, it saved us.

After everything that's happened, we're happy and settled. And we've forgiven each other. Even though I'd accidentally hit Sloane with Rebecca's car, she suffered only a sprained wrist and some bruises. I'll never stop apologizing, but Sloane has long forgiven me, and that's what matters most.

Every morning when I go to work, I apologize to her. And I thank her. With my new job as lead barista at Hotté Latte, I'm not only honoring Ainsley's memory every day, but now I can pay our bills, though I no longer have a mortgage to pay...thanks to Ainsley.

Not even Sloane knew, but a stipulation in Ainsley's divorce was she had to name a beneficiary before the money was transferred. She'd named Ellory. No one was shocked more than my daughter—except me, when Ellory told me she'd bought back our old home.

"It only makes sense," she said, handing me the deed to keep safe. "It's right down the road from the college. And it's what Dad would've wanted."

I smile at the memory and gaze around our living room, realizing my memories are still here, just where I'd left them.

Sloane groans in the chair next to me. "Come *on*. Why do they keep showing him?"

"Because he's handsome," I say.

For the fiftieth time today, the news replays footage of Hugh being escorted into the courthouse for his arraignment. His blue eyes flit back and forth among the hordes of reporters and microphones shoved in his face.

"Karma sure is a bitch." Sloane shakes her head. "You shouldn't be watching this, Iris."

"No. But I want to."

His hands are cuffed in front of him and the white bandage over his heart extends up to his neck, peeking out from behind the collar of his orange prison uniform. The letter opener had missed his aorta by four millimeters.

"They might as well just skip the trial," Sloane says. "We all know he'll get life. Shit, Iris. You're lucky you never got married."

"I know…" I trail off. "Maybe I'm finally getting some good luck."

I turn back to the TV. I'd paused it just as the camera had flipped to Hugh heading into the courthouse. His blue eyes blanch in the camera flash, making them appear white. Black pupils hole-punch in the centers like chasms.

Ellory sighs next to me. "Let's hope he gets life, no parole. Birdie, too. The last thing we need is them knocking on our door in ten years."

"You're going to have to get a guard dog. A big one. Make sure it's nice on the inside, scary on the outside," Sloane says. "Like me."

I laugh, but secretly, I'm terrified. Hugh may go away for life, but Birdie, Rebecca, Camille, and Kara won't get much prison time, not after the police found Hugh's confession connecting him alone to all of the murders.

In time, hopefully, they'll forget about us.

But you never know what people are capable of.

29 DAYS AFTER

SUNDAY, FEBRUARY 23

46

Snow has fallen heavy and thick over the cemetery when Ellory, Sloane, and I visit Paige for the first time. Tombstones sprout out of the glittering snow like little mountains of stone. The sky overhead ruptures in swaths of faded purple and blue.

We trudge through the snow and find Paige Sinclair's final resting place. I lift the shovel I'd dragged over from the back of the car, begin clearing away the snow. Ellory stands beside Sloane, both wearing black coats with black scarves wrapped around their red, cold-bitten cheeks.

I stab the shovel into the snow, stand beside Ellory.

Together, we read her tombstone:

Paige "Ellory" Sinclair
1989–2007
Mother & Friend

"I wish I knew her," Ellory sniffles. "But we made our own family, didn't we?"

I can't tell if she's sniffling from the cold or from seeing the resting place of her biological mother for the first time. We had Paige's remains relocated here, so at least she can have a marked grave, no longer alone and forgotten in the cold, dark woods. We know her name, her full, true name, and the very thought brings tears to my eyes.

Finally, I feel free. My nightmares are gone. I'm sleeping well, feeling healthy, moving better. My ankle has healed. I'm the proud owner of fifteen stitches along the side of my rib cage. The scar won't be too bad. Not with the handmade salve Sloane made for me.

And I've let go of Hugh. Of our engagement. Of all of the promises that never were.

The fog has cleared—for many things.

Finally, I accept Jack's fate. I'll love him forever. He'll always be Ellory's dad. And as for his killer...one day, I'll find him. I know I will. And it's that belief, that *hope*, that brings me peace. Sometimes justice, like all good things, takes time.

Ellory finally knows the truth. She knows about Shaw. About Paige. How she got her name. She even knows about Jade. And she knows everything that happened that night, and every hour leading up to it.

Ellory knows it all.

She even knows how, three months ago, I saw Shaw again for the first time. I owe it to Sloane, really. She'd been on a dating app and wasn't having any luck with matches. Then she saw a man with eerily familiar eyes—the same eyes as Ellory.

One was blue. The other, brown.

Sloane showed me the man's profile that same night. There was no mistaking who it was. He looked exactly the same. I saw his face, and I thought: *Oh, God, he's close.*

I had to do something. I was tired of letting fear control my life. Every time I felt stress or anxiety, every time I looked at forests or trees, I'd see Shaw and Davey and Mars. Three dark figures in the cold, dark woods.

After seeing Shaw again on Sloane's dating app, I tried to ignore it. But it stirred up memories I'd been trying to suppress for years, and soon the nightmares and insomnia returned, and I wanted it to end. I wanted to be free.

And in a single heartbeat, the man who'd buried my friend alive was back in my life.

I told Sloane everything.

The next day, I told Ellory. I sat her down, confessed everything. I explained how Shaw was her biological father. How he'd killed her biological mother right in front of me. How I'd taken her, just a newborn, raised her as my own. How I'd named her after her mother. A part of me was unsure how Ellory would take it.

At first, she didn't handle it well. She was angry. Her face was red all the time from rage. She became so frustrated and upset she lashed out, stayed out late, drank too much, partied with the wrong boyfriend. But then she understood. She accepted it. Digested it.

And we faced the truth together. We acknowledged our history together.

We plotted together.

The kidnapping was Ellory's idea.

She wanted to make Shaw pay for what he'd done to her mother. I couldn't say no. I could never say no to Ellory. And so, I fell headfirst. I lived and breathed her idea. We both did. So did Sloane.

Ellory never even met Shaw. We made sure of that.

The night Ellory disappeared, she'd asked her friend Leah to pick her up at the end of Birdie's driveway, take her to hang out at the new nightclub. Sloane picked her up outside, while Ellory told her friend she was driving away with her father, establishing the first of a long trail of breadcrumbs.

Sloane drove Ellory to the café. Ellory said she didn't mind living in the back office temporarily. As long as Shaw was arrested and went to prison for kidnapping her in the end.

So I called him. After Ellory went missing, I dialed his number, begged him to help me find her. He was so enraptured with the idea of being a savior, he couldn't say no. And I knew when he heard the name *Ellory* he'd get caught in our snare. He couldn't resist after that.

Our plan was in motion.

Shaw, helping me find the not-missing Ellory.

Shaw, unknowingly being stage-managed by me and Sloane.

All the calling of Ellory's friends, the police, the crying, the desperate hope to find my missing daughter, and I knew she was safe. But it had to be done. There had to be a trail of evidence against him. Everyone had to believe the lie. And so I had to make myself live, each day, under the ever-present perspective that my daughter had disappeared. Every thought, every word—everything had to support our narrative.

Sloane kept Ellory fed with food from the café, and Ellory kept herself busy on Sloane's laptop, helping her with payroll and ordering and shift schedules. Sloane even paid Ellory for her work and got her registered to start college courses in the fall, too.

It's funny, in a way. In the end, Hugh and I really did want the same thing. Hugh, Gabe, Rebecca, and Birdie came together for revenge. To snuff out those who'd escaped justice. But all this time, unknowing, I'd been doing the exact same thing.

While we weren't planning on being evicted from our home or being forced to move in with Hugh and his *family*, we made our plan work. We adjusted. We sacrificed. The three of us sacrificed something every day. And every day we knew we were closer to making Shaw pay for what he'd done.

He wouldn't take the fall for Paige's murder. But he'd take the fall for kidnapping and holding his daughter prisoner.

We made sure of that. Together. The three of us.

A family.

As Shaw drove to Birdie's house that final day to meet with me, Sloane drove Ellory to his house. Ellory set up his basement perfectly, staged it to seem like she'd been held there for days.

To be fair, in the end, I didn't want Shaw to die. I only wanted him to be taken away in handcuffs, and for him to see I was *alive*. That he may have killed my friend, but *I* survived, and so did Ellory. I wanted to show him his life was a lie, and he was a killer. To never forget that I knew. That I was alive out there, and I knew.

No, I never intended for Shaw to die. The goal was for him to be put in handcuffs, not a coffin. Sometimes, things just work out better than planned.

Sloane pushes a tear out of her eye, kicks at the snow with her toe. "Time to go," she says, walking back to the car. "We have an early day at the café tomorrow, don't we, partner?"

"Be right there."

Ellory shivers beside me, curls her shoulder into my chest. I kiss the top of her head. She turns to look at me. The sun sets over the cemetery, shooting ribbons of lavender and gold across the stone-dotted snow.

"Paige loved you. And I know you would've loved her. She would've been the greatest mom."

A tear falls down Ellory's cheek. "I do love her," she whispers back. "Even though I never met her and never will. But I already have a great mom. And I owe *her* a thank-you." She looks at me. Sunlight catches in her beautiful eyes, and I feel proud that for once I know the secrets swimming inside.

"For what?"

"For not leaving me alone that night in the woods."

My eyes swell with tears. Tears of hope. Tears of love. The same tears that swelled in my eyes years ago when I was in those cold, dark woods.

"I'd do it all over again."

Ellory smiles. We turn away from her mother's tombstone and go back home.

We all keep secrets from each other. Inside every person is a well so deep no one else can reach the bottom. Ellory and I will have secrets we keep from one another in the future. But I don't mind.

Right now, I am free. I have no more secrets left to tell.

★ ★ ★ ★ ★

ACKNOWLEDGMENTS

I owe, first and foremost, a thank-you to my wonderful agent, Melissa Danaczko, who has been on this incredible journey with me from the start. Your wise insight and incredible talent have made every sentence I write better. Here's to another two books and beyond.

An enormous thank-you to the best editor I could ask for, Dina Davis, who saw something in my words and took a chance. This book was made stronger with your brilliant insight. It's a privilege to work with you and the entire MIRA/HarperCollins team. For every step of the way, thank you to everyone whose hard work brought this book into the world. I'm so grateful for you.

Thank you to the talented, generous authors who gave this book an early read and offered kind words, which I'll always treasure: Samantha Downing, Megan Collins, Nishita Parekh, Jenna Satterthwaite, Maia Chance, Lindsay Cameron, Allison Buccola, and, last but not least, Kimberly Belle. Check out their books—they're all fantastic!

To my readers—thank you. You're amazing and I love you. To book bloggers, especially Kerry @kurryreads, Linzie @suspenseisthrillingme, Bianca @book_notions, Magen @bonechillingbooks, Trey @readingwithtrey, Abby @crime-bythebook, Sherri @sherrireads, Danielle @coffee.break.book.reviews, and Alix @thebookishalix_, and many more—I'm so thankful for your support.

Also thank you to the crime fiction community: Kathleen Willett, Tessa Wegert, Ashley Winstead, Alexa Donne, and so many other brilliant authors. I see you and I appreciate you. Thank you for being book champions. It warms my heart to see authors lifting each other up instead of tearing each other down.

No matter how many books I'm lucky enough to write, I'll always be writing for my family (I promise I did not base the family in this book off you guys!), my mom; my brave sister, Stef; brother-in-law, Haythem; and their amazing kids, Mina, Sam, and Sofia; my brother, Brian; my fur baby, Henry; and Graham, the best little boy I could ever ask for. Also thank you to every family member and friend who has supported and encouraged me. Above all, thank you to my husband, Kyle. This book is being published only two days after our first date twenty-four years ago. That went fast. I'm so lucky to have you as my partner in crime.

Last, this book is for any family seeking justice for a loved one and for those who feel they have endless bad luck. Your time will come. Never give up.